Z ANE PRESENTS

The SEVEN DAYS

R. Kayeen Thomas

Dear Reader:

The Seven Days by R. Kayeen Thomas is the follow-up to the NAACP Image Award-nominated novel *Antebellum*. Once again, Thomas has woven an amazing story that stimulates the imagination, conversation, and controversy. It is an incredible tale that serves as a bridge between the times of slavery and the present, where many are still enslaved by their own mentality.

In *The Seven Days*, two men, brothers by blood but complete strangers by fate, discover that their bloodline is one that harbors many secrets, many powers, and many responsibilities. Thomas is a prolific writer who has a remarkable future ahead of him in the literary world. He is a deep thinker who takes the time to create the imagery, the dialogue, and the realness that keeps readers riveted with every word. An out-of-the-box creative mind is always refreshing in a world where books often seem to mirror each other. Thomas once again proves that he is anything but ordinary.

As always, thanks for supporting R. Kayeen Thomas and the authors that I publish under Strebor Books. We appreciate the love and we strive to bring you the best, most prolific authors who write outside of the traditional publishing box. You can contact me directly at zane@eroticanoir.com and find me on Twitter @planetzane and on Facebook at www.facebook.com/AuthorZane.

Blessings,

Zane

Zane
Publisher
Strebor Books
www.simonandschuster.com

ALSO BY R. KAYEEN THOMAS
Antebellum

ZANE PRESENTS

The SEVEN DAYS

R. Kayeen Thomas

SBI

STREBOR BOOKS

NEW YORK LONDON TORONTO SYDNEY

Strebor Books
P.O. Box 6505
Largo, MD 20792
http://www.streborbooks.com

ISBN 978-1-59309-427-0
ISBN 978-1-4516-5999-3 (ebook)
LCCN 2012951574

First Strebor Books trade paperback edition April 2013

Cover design: www.mariondesigns.com
Cover photograph: © Keith Saunders/Marion Designs

10 9 8 7 6 5 4 3 2 1

Manufactured in the United States of America

For information regarding special discounts for bulk purchases,
please contact Simon & Schuster Special Sales at 1-866-506-1949
or business@simonandschuster.com

The Simon & Schuster Speakers Bureau can bring authors to your live event.
For more information or to book an event, contact the Simon & Schuster Speakers
Bureau at 1-866-248-3049 or visit our website at www.simonspeakers.com.

For Dad

Acknowledgments

To God, who continues to endow me with the gifts of inspiration and creativity, I thank you endlessly. I thank my wife, Monee, and my daughter, Zion, for indulging me when I have imaginary conversations with my characters. To my mother and father, Marilyn and Weldon, and my brother, Daniel, thank you for showing me that family is more important than anything in the world. To Zane and Charmaine, thank you for continuing to believe in me, despite the tense corrections. To Strebor Books and Simon and Schuster, thank you for presenting my work to the world. To Bassirou Sarr, who came through in the clutch with the Wolof translations, thank you for your expertise. To Israel Metropolitan CME Church, and the CME Church as a whole, who continue to stand by me and my work, and embrace me as their son, thank you for your love. And to everyone who has or will pick up a book with my name on the cover, you all give my life meaning. Thank you all.

T he day was scorching, but Toby barely felt the sun. The rays bounced off of his broad shoulders and slid down his straight back. He strode through the slave quarters with more confidence than it was healthy to have, and gave those who had no reason to smile a chance to flash their teeth as he passed by.

Two months. That's how long it had taken him to finish. Sneaking into the woodshop at night when his wife and daughters were asleep, ignoring the burning and stinging in his hands and the dirt and cotton stuck beneath his fingernails, he had worked. He realized that he couldn't simply make one—either Cia would throw a fit or Leah would fall into a tantrum, completely convinced that their father loved one sibling more than the other. No, he had to make two. And they had to be perfect, because his daughters deserved no less.

Night after night, he had carved and sanded, making sure the wood was smoother than silk. Then he had taken the material that his mother snuck out of the big house, and sewed it together like he had seen Farah do so many times. He used thin pieces of yarn for the hair, and dyed them black before he glued them, so the girls would know they were beautiful. And he used black ink to make the smiling faces. The night that he finished, he sat the two figures on the table in the woodshop and stared at them.

Cia and Leah had recently turned fourteen, and he'd seen the overseers glaring at them in the fields. It was merely a matter of time before he'd have to die trying to protect them, and he wanted to make sure they had something to remember him by.

His daughters would scream and jump with happiness, and he, at least for a moment, would forget that they were slaves.

The day was scorching, but Toby barely felt the sun. He strode up to his twin daughters as they ran in the grass surrounding his cabin. Farah sat and smiled at them, enjoying their laughter and absence from the cotton field. Old Man Talbert had decided that the slaves were not to work in the fields on Sundays, as it went against the Ten Commandments. Toby didn't care about the Ten Commandments, but he loved his daughters. And so he had waited until Sunday to give them their gifts.

He didn't see Old Man Talbert and his son walking up from the distance. The elderly man's cane indented the ground as he made his way to the slave quarters, leaving remnants of his presence, while his son, months shy of twenty-five, strode proudly beside his father. Both could tell that it was Toby in front of them, even though they were quite a ways off. They could tell it was him from his stride. It had more confidence than it was healthy to have for a slave.

The old man turned around to the three young men following them. The Pritchett boys, Billy, Charles, and George, were the sons of an old lawyer and friend. The youngest of them was seventeen, and the oldest was the same age as his own son. Old Man Talbert's voice shook with age as he spoke to them and pointed to Toby.

"There he is right there. You stay close on me, now. These niggers can be unpredictable."

"Yes, sir," the three men responded excitedly.

Talbert turned back to his son and held his hand out. His son handed him the rifle he was carrying, and he tucked it under his arm.

"You'll be taking over this here plantation one day soon. You know that, right?"

"Yes, Father."

"Are you ready?"

"Yes."

"That young lady you're courting, you planning on marrying her?"

"Yes, sir."

"Good. That's the Lord's way…get married, start yourself a family, raise your children right. That's what I tried to do."

"You did, Father."

"Yeah, well…I'm getting old now. The Lord will be calling me home pretty soon."

"Don't say that…"

"It's the truth, isn't it? No use lying about it. Hell, I'm glad to go."

Young Talbert stayed quiet. Even in his mid-twenties, the thought of his father dying still made his bottom lip quiver.

"That's why I'm making sure to teach you all I know, son. That's why I wanted you to come out here today. You can't run the plantation effectively if you don't understand how to deal with the niggers."

Young Talbert turned indignantly to his father. "I know how to deal with the niggers, Father."

"No, you know how to lay down with the wenches."

With hot coals resting in his cheeks, Young Talbert fell quiet again.

"No use getting embarrassed, son. We've all been there. The Lord says a man falls seven times and rises back up." Old Man

Talbert leaned over close to his son and strained out a whisper. "What you think Pritchett sent them down here for? They ain't looking for a housekeeper."

Young Talbert glanced back at his three friends and grinned before looking back at his father.

"What I'm trying to show you, son, is that dealing with the niggers is no easy task. They animals, son. Walking, talking, breathing animals. They come from a place where Satan runs rampant, and if you don't tame them right, they'll bring the devil straight to your doorstep."

"Yes, sir."

"Now, Toby, right there, that's a prime example. He's got a feeling about him that he's as good as a white man. You can tell by the way he looks at you. That's nothing but the devil, son. You hear? That's the devil, and it's got to be stopped immediately. Otherwise, all the niggers will start thinking that way. And can you imagine what would happen if we had a field full of niggers who all thought they was as good as white men?"

"No, I can't imagine, Father."

"And you don't want to, neither. So, here's how you deal with uppity niggers."

Toby watched as his daughters threw their dolls in the air, laughing as they caught them and spun them around. Toby's mother, Elizabeth, had heard all the commotion and come around from her cabin. Even she was impressed with the craftsmanship of the dolls, and gave her son a hug as she watched her grand-babies laugh and giggle.

She was the first to see the five white men, and her gasp sucked all the oxygen out of the air.

For a moment, time stopped. Farah shot up from her seat and immediately jumped in front of her girls, who stood wide-eyed and frozen. Toby stood terrified, but with his fists balled and knees slightly bent, ready for anything.

Elizabeth knew there was only one reason why a slave master would venture into slave quarters on a rest day. A solitary tear ran down her cheek as her body began to shake, and she threw her hands up and fell to her knees. The force of her body hitting the ground forced out her scream.

"NAW!!! NAW, LORD!!! NAW, LORD!!!!! AHHHH-HHHH!!!!!!!!!"

Old Man Talbert nodded at the Pritchett sons as he leveled his rifle at Toby, daring him to move. The first of the sons rushed toward Leah, but Toby leapt into him, knocking him to the ground. He jumped on top of the attacker, preparing to pound the life out of him, but one of the other Pritchett brothers pulled Toby off and began to kick him. Toby jumped up, despite being kicked, and lunged at his second attacker, who tripped over a branch as he was attempting to run away. Toby grabbed his head and was about to smash it into the hard ground, but the butt of a rifle, swung like a baseball bat, connected with his temple and knocked him temporarily senseless. The explosions in his head began to die down in time for him to hear the gunshot, and through blurred vision he looked frantically at his wife, mother, and daughters.

It was not until he realized that they were okay that he began to feel the blood seeping from his leg.

"Kill him! You kill that nigger right now!"

Charles, having climbed up from the ground, pointed angrily at Toby as he looked at Young Talbert. "What are you waiting for? Kill him!"

The son looked at his father, then back at his friend. "Are you hurt?"

"What?"

"Are you hurt?"

"No, but…"

"Then I'm not going to kill him. He's worth a few thousand on the auction block easy, and him being broken is invaluable for keeping the rest of the niggers in line. You want revenge? Grab whichever wench you want and take it out in her. But he stays alive."

Old Man Talbert grabbed his son's shoulder as Toby ground his teeth in pain. "You really do know how to deal with the niggers, huh?"

"Yes, Father."

The old man patted his son on the shoulder proudly before turning to the Pritchett brothers. "You heard my son. Do as he says."

George, the oldest of the Pritchett boys, stepped forward and looked menacingly at Old Man Talbert. "My father will hear about this!"

"Money is money, son. Your father will understand. Now go on and grab you a wench."

The eldest brother tried to maintain his anger, but he realized Old Man Talbert was right. He took his menacing look and threw it over to Farah, who looked down at her husband as he growled in pain.

"Toby!!!"

"Shut up!" George stepped over Toby, kicking him intentionally, and walked straight up to Farah. Without warning, he punched her across the face, and Toby's eyes went wide as his wife collapsed.

"NO!!!"

Toby's cries caused his leg to catch fire. He couldn't move, but he kept trying. And each time he failed, his wails got louder.

The Pritchett boys laughed as they overpowered Toby's wife and daughters, striking them into submission. Elizabeth did her best to try and save her grandchildren, but a strong kick leveled her to the ground and left her struggling to breathe.

"When I'm through with you," the eldest brother sneered at Farah as he yanked her up from the ground, "you're gonna wish you never met that nigger." He pulled her bleeding face up so that she could look into his eyes. "I want you to think of him when I tear you apart."

That's when Toby felt it. It started in his belly, a feeling like someone was trying to strike a match in his gut. He barely noticed it as he watched his family being snatched away. He was too busy trying to push himself up off the ground, trying, to no avail, to will himself to get up and snatch the rifle from Talbert's son.

Then the match in his stomach ignited, and the explosion within him caused his entire body to jerk backward. The pain in his leg was gone, replaced by hellfire that began coursing through his veins, getting hotter with every heartbeat. He threw his hands to his head and began clawing at his face.

"AHHHH!!!! AAAAHHHHHH!!!!!"

Toby's screams were so guttural that his wife and daughter stopped fighting their kidnappers, and instead looked horrified at Toby, who now had veins popping out of his skin as he writhed around on the ground. Elizabeth, having partly recovered from her blow, crawled over to her son as his shrieks reached a fever pitch.

She tried to grab him, but her arms stopped short as her mouth fell open. And just like that, Toby's screaming stopped, and once again time seemed to stand still.

Slowly, Toby began to stand up from the ground. His leg still housed the rifle bullet, but it had no effect on him as he pushed himself up and stood straight in front of the white men. Young Talbert had his rifle trained, but he had a hard time holding it still. He noticed the same thing that Elizabeth saw while reaching for her son, and the same thing that froze the Pritchett boys where they stood.

Resting in Toby's eyes, where there were once a pair of hard, determined eyes, were now two smooth, jet-black stones.

"What the...?"

The youngest Pritchett brother couldn't finish his sentence. Before his last word could escape, Toby had leapt in front of him and smashed his fist down on the top of his head. The sound of cracking skull and pummeled brain matter echoed off the trees as the youngest brother shook in place where he stood, and then fell to the ground with a forearm indented in the top of his forehead. Immediately Toby turned to the middle brother, who let the daughter he was holding captive go.

"Shoot him!" Old Man Talbert yelled at his son, who let off two rounds. The first one missed. The second hit Toby in the shoulder. He smiled in response as he stepped toward his next victim.

By the time the middle brother could convince his legs to move, Toby was already in front of him, and he shoved his fist into the young man's torso. His fist went in so deep that when Toby opened his hand and turned it upward, he was able to grab firmly onto the bottom of the brother's ribcage. With moderate effort, Toby picked the boy up and slammed him onto his head. He still had a rib in his fist as he yanked it out of the brother's body, which stayed upright for a few seconds before it crumpled to the ground.

With his face set hard and cold, Toby turned to George. "I am Abioye, son of King Amaru, and heir to the throne of Telemut. You will die knowing my name."

Farah stared at the man that she thought was her husband. The accented voice that had emerged from his mouth did not belong to the man she married, and though her legs felt like they were strapped to boulders, she forced herself to take a step forward.

"Toby…?"

Her husband's face turned to her, and the dark stone eyes caused her to hyperventilate. "No…your husband is…"

Before Toby could finish, three bullets struck his body. Two of them pierced his body, causing him to stumble, but recover with another smile. The third stuck him in the side of the head, and he fell to the ground, unconscious.

Old Man Talbert forced himself to hobble over to the body. "I…I'll be damned if this nigger ain't still alive! No blood or anything!"

Old Man Talbert and his son stared at each other in disbelief as the eldest Pritchett brother, his fear now having subsided, began mourning over his younger siblings.

Seven days later, Toby hung by his wrists in a steel box. The encasing was tall enough that Toby's feet couldn't touch the ground, and large enough for the local sheriff to walk in and ensure that the slave wasn't dead. Judge Matthew Pritchett had gotten word about the death of his two sons, and sent the message that he wanted to be present to see Toby die for what he'd done. His trip would take six days, he'd notified the sheriff, and he fully expected for "that goddamned nigger" to be alive when he arrived.

By day three, the sheriff commissioned the local blacksmith, in the most immediate of terms, to build a steel box that could "trap the devil himself," and to have it ready by day's end.

The day Judge Pritchett arrived in town, there was already a mob ready for his command. The news of the murders had spread, though the fantastical parts were left out, and the townspeople were eager to see Toby meet the most gruesome end possible. There were only a few who lacked excitement—Old Man Talbert and his son, who had told the sheriff that they would be absent from the public lynching, George, the eldest Pritchett son, who had only spoken gibberish since the murder of his brothers, and the deputies who were assigned to watch over Toby during his time in jail. Ignoring the advice of the sheriff, one of them walked up to Judge Pritchett as he was tying up a noose in front of the drunk and rowdy mob.

"Judge! Judge! I...I think it's somethin' you need to know 'bout this here nigger! This ain't no ordinary nigger, Judge! It's somethin'...somethin' straight outta hell gotta hold of 'em!"

The judge spun around, half drunk himself. His fury caused his face to turn bright red. "You damn right somethin' outta hell got a hold of 'em! He killed my boys!"

"Sir...I...I think you should reconsider this, sir."

"What? You don't think we should kill this nigger for what he done?"

"No, sir...I mean, he 'serve to die for what he done but, Judge, you ain't seen what we seen the last couple days..."

The judge held up his hands to get the attention of the crowd, but that did nothing to pull them out of their drunken stupor. Eventually, Judge Pritchett pulled his gun out of his holster and fired three shots into the air.

Everyone's mouth shut as he put his pistol back on his hip and began talking. "Look here, fellas; we got ourselves a nigger lover!"

Immediately, the mob ignited again, and focused all of its attention on the terrified deputy, who began seeing his life flash before his eyes. Judge Pritchett's wrath snatched him from his highlight reel as the lawyer grabbed him by his shirt and yanked him forward.

"You listen to me, and you listen good! That animal killed two of my boys! I don't give a damn if that nigger made a pact with Satan himself, that black bastard is gonna die tonight! Now unless you boys know how to tie up a noose, or fancy gettin' hung, I suggest you step aside…"

The judge let the deputy go with a shove. Once released, he looked at his colleagues, who all seemed to know that the sky was about to fall, though no one would believe them. Understanding that there was no use in trying to talk sense into the mob, they all ran home, put their families in their cellars, and prayed until it was over.

Elizabeth, having heard of Judge Pritchett's arrival, snuck off the plantation amongst all the commotion. A few times she was seen, walking as fast as her aging legs could carry her, and would've likely gotten detained, but everyone knew she belonged to the Talberts and she had her papers with her. She was growing too old to be any trouble anyhow.

Forcing her muscles and bones to push forward, she had finally made it to the jailhouse, and the steel box out back where her son hung by his wrists, suspended in mid-air.

"Jesus!"

The stench inside let her know that they hadn't taken Toby down in days. His waste lay pooled under him.

"Mama…?" Toby spoke in a strained, barely audible voice. He did his best to pick his head up. "Mama…?"

"Yea, baby, I'se here. Right here."

"Mama…where's Farah?"

"She…she done ran away…her an' the girls. Ain't safe for 'em no mo', baby. Jus' ain't safe. They done good so far…ain't been brought back yet…"

"Mama…"

Elizabeth stepped closer to her son.

"Mama…I got somethin' 'side a me…can't control it…I keep tryin' fight it, Mama…but I can't…"

Toby's mother ignored the stench now, and walked close enough to her son that she could see the sweat dripping from his body. "I seen what you got in you, Toby. I seen it wid my own two eyes. Now dem white mens…dem white mens comin' a' kill you tonight. They gon' make you wished you was dead long befo' you die, too. Whatever it be that you got 'side you, no matter if it be from God or da devil…whatever it be that you got 'side you, you let it out this night! Don' you fight it none! You lets it out, an' youse take dem white folks straight ta hell wid you!"

The sound of the mob cut through the silence, and Toby knew they couldn't be far away. "Mama…you go…now! Go now!"

Elizabeth hesitated.

"I loves you, too, Mama…now go!"

Elizabeth backtracked until she had stepped out of the metal box, and disappeared into the woods as the mob came over the hill, arriving at the prison.

An hour later, Toby's mother would not have recognized him. His face had swollen to three times its normal size, and many of his bones lay cracked and smashed within his flesh. His right eye hung from its socket and bounced around on his cheek, and three of his fingers had been chopped off with an axe, and now choked him as they were stuffed into his mouth. Finally, four white men lifted his head and slid a noose around his neck. He could barely hear the laughter of the men around him, but the drunken camaraderie in the air, the brotherhood that inspired his mutilation, caused him to wish for death.

Once the rope was tight and secure around Toby's neck, three of the men stumbled over to the other side of the oak tree, and began hoisting Toby up. Every inch felt like a foot, and Toby began to know what it was like to suffocate. He groped and clawed at the air as his feet left the ground, and the entire weight of his body pulled down on his neck as his lungs fought to expand.

The three white men, satisfied that he was up high enough, tied the end of the rope to the tree next to them, and watched Toby's legs kick for the ground.

The lack of air was all he could see and feel. It was all he could comprehend. Though his remaining eye had gone wide with terror, he never saw the metal bucket that Judge Pritchett brought up to him. He never felt the liquid that was tossed all over his body. All he could feel was death, cold and heartless, creeping into his body.

And just when he thought it was all over, the fire inside of him and the liquid that rested on his skin ignited at the same time. Toby's body now lit up the night sky, and Judge Pritchett laughed, completely unaware of his fate. The fire was much too bright, much too intense, for the aristocrat to see black eyes and a smile on a burning slave.

With a tug, the slave reached up, grabbed a hold of the rope that he hung from, and yanked down on it. It snapped immediately, and Toby's body fell to the ground.

All the laughing stopped when the mob realized that Toby was standing up straight.

With a burning hand, Toby reached toward Judge Pritchett, who screamed and jumped backward into the mob, leaving two full buckets of flammable liquid behind. Quickly, Toby grabbed the two buckets and flung them into the mob.

As the propane landed on the drunken men, Toby sprinted into the crowd, igniting everyone he touched. Before long, everyone in the mob was afire, and the screams reached all the way into town, where the deputies hugged their families close.

Taking his time, Toby strolled through the crowd of burning men, taking each one out of his misery. He tore out hearts and ripped off limbs, smashed heads and crushed throats, and when he found his rage was still unsatisfied, he walked over to the tree that he had been hung on, ripped it out of the ground, and began beating the men into the hard earth.

Between the thunderous pounding coming from the woods, and the maniacal screams, the townspeople were convinced the times of Revelation had come. They prayed to be taken up to heaven with the Lord.

It wasn't long before the arms of Toby's body began to fail him. He was still aflame, but he refused to stop destroying his enemies. They would know his rage, and they would feel his wrath. And so he continued lifting the tree, and crashing it down, until his body, having burned too long, refused to function any longer.

Not having anything else with which to fuel them, the flames on his flesh began to die as Toby collapsed where he stood. With the uprooted tree lying on top of him, he used his last breath to laugh out loud, and he died.

PART ONE

"The country is all abuzz with the upcoming elections!" the female reporter spoke with emotional excitement. "In this historical time in American history, and no doubt world history, we are looking at the possible installation of the first African-American President of the United States!"

The newscast had been repeating every ten minutes or so, and Nathan had the scene memorized. The multicolored crowd jumped up and down in anticipation, while a large black bus pulled up and into the open park area, stopping far enough away from the cameras to give it an air of mysteriousness as it waited idly in the parking lot. The flashing of cameras provided a staccato beat for the masses.

"You can feel the electricity in the air! The Senator has just pulled up, and this crowd can barely contain itself! After his meteoric rise up through the political ranks, the Senator now is nothing short of a superstar! These people may as well be at a concert!"

Slowly, deliberately, the large door of the black bus swung open, and a walnut-colored man emerged, wearing a bright smile and waving at the people gathered. The noise level of the crowd doubled as it tried to push forward, but was held at bay by security guards.

"Here he is! Here he is, ladies and gentlemen, the man many hope to be the next President of the United States!"

The man walked forward and attempted to shake the hands that were groping at him. One younger-looking white lady held her baby out and over the barricade that had been set up.

Nathan grabbed the remote as the Senator grabbed the child and began to kiss it on the cheek. Shaking his head at the television screen, he held up the remote to change the channel, but realized that there would be nothing better on. He would much rather watch a black man on television being applauded than being arrested, but he'd seen so much of the latter that the former no longer made him smile. Defeated, he dropped the remote back into his lap and laid his head on the sofa.

His depression poured into the room like a high tide.

The television screen was the only source of light in the room. If the shades had not been drawn so closely together, he would not have been able to tell by the fresh light of the sun that a new day was beginning. Instead, he relied on the fact that he'd woken up at 6:30 a.m. every day since college.

He fit well within the dark mood of the room. The shadows from the pictures on the wall, the large table, and the plant by the window seemed to silently complement his pain. His disposition would scream to all who observed him that he was the loneliest man this side of the city line, despite the fact that there were two others in the house.

Standing, Nathan made his way over to the refrigerator. He was healthy-looking, with nice muscle tone, a lean build, and had salt-and-pepper hair and a moustache. People who saw him without a coat on tended to be surprised, and an attractive lady at the gym had once told him that his face added a decade onto his body. He walked tall and proud, despite his perpetually long face.

"A person may never meet you, may never say a word to you, but will automatically respect you because of the way you walk."

Nathan remembered his father, Thomas Freeman, speaking as he, a seven-year-old boy, sat on his father's lap beside a colored-only water fountain in rural South Carolina. Nathan had only recently learned to write 1960 on the headings of his school assignments without turning the six into a nine.

"No matter how you're feeling, never walk around like you're anything less than royalty. Besides, we got power in our blood…"

Now, even at fifty-five, Nathan had never forgotten. The sudden thought of his father struck a nerve in Nathan's chest.

A half-hour or so passed, with the solitary man sitting by himself in front of the television, trying to place himself in an alternate reality. The sounds emerging from the smaller bedroom brought him back from his daydreams, and Nathan wished he could fall into the floor.

The man that emerged from the smaller bedroom was tired. Like every trial and tribulation he was meant to endure in life had struck him the night before. Although he knew exactly where he was, he was lost. His face was sunken in and his eyes were the same color as the fresh rose petals that hopeless romantics threw onto their beds before making love. It was apparent, looking at his size and his height, he should have weighed much more than he actually did. His clothes were shabby and torn, and although there was a refurbished bathroom right next door to his room, his stench hollered that he hadn't showered in days.

For a while, Clarence tried to hide it from his parents, but two years ago it had proved useless. The constant rocking back and forth, the jitters and the incoherent stares couldn't be ignored. For two years, Nathan had watched his son fade away like the final scene of an overly dramatic movie. And for two years, Nathan had tried to maintain the hope of seeing his son with a light in his eyes and a smile on his face one more time.

That hope was gone now, though, and the remnants of it burned like salt on an open wound.

"Uh, Dad, you mind lettin' me hold onto a couple bucks?"

Nathan didn't even turn his head. He looked into the television screen, trying to ignore the stench and the reflection in the television screen.

"C'mon, Dad, I ain't gonna get messed up today, I promise. I'm gonna take the money, and go and get me a nice shirt, and find me a job. I jus' need a lil bit a money to eat with; that's all. I'm gonna go down and get me a burger, then I'm gonna go find that job. I jus' need a lil bit a money, Dad."

"Don't call me that."

"Huh? Call you what?"

"Dad. Don't call me Dad. My son is dead."

"Awww, c'mon, Dad. Don't be like that. I jus' need a few dollars…"

"MY SON IS DEAD! YOU HEAR ME? DEAD!"

Clarence stumbled back in surprise, feeling the kick in his father's words, and retaliated in kind. "It's a few dollars. Give me the goddamn money."

Nathan focused back on the television screen. Right before he managed to zone out again, both he and Clarence heard movement in the larger bedroom. The one he and his wife shared.

"Aw hell…" Nathan whispered to himself. And before he got up and attempted to stop the inevitable, his wife found her way to the doorway.

"What's going on out here? I heard someone shouting."

Clarence quickly put on his most innocent smile. "Mama, can I have a few dollars, to get somethin' to eat?"

Nathan could feel his wife's heart drop.

"What happened to the job you were supposed to be getting, sweetheart?"

"It ain't come through yet, Mama. But don't worry 'cause I got another one I applied for. I'm waitin' for the man to call me back. So I need a few dollars to get somethin' to eat and get me a nice shirt for when I start the job, Mama."

"Baby, why don't you take a shower? Then you could put on some nice clothes, and I could even go with you down to get a new shirt. How's that sound?"

"Naw, Mama, I can get everything myself. I just need a few dollars for it."

"Come on, baby, let your mama take you to the store. Maybe we could even go and see a movie, like we used to do. Remember when you were—"

"Naw, Mama, I don't remember. Now can I please get the money?"

The reminiscent smile on Sonya's face slowly disappeared, and she looked down at the floor. "How long are you going to keep doing this to yourself, baby? How long?"

"Mama, can I please get the goddamn money?"

Sonya slowly shook her head. "Alright, baby, bring me my purse. It's on the table by the door."

Clarence found his mother's purse and rummaged through it, taking every piece of money he could find. He tried to make up for this theft by lying to his mother, telling her sweet nothings that she would partially believe, throwing logic out of the window.

"Thanks, Mama. Thank you, thank you. And I really am about to go and get this job. Watch! Next time you see me, I'ma be a workin' man. And I'ma give you all this money back, I promise. I just needed a lil bit for today."

After he got what he needed, he quickly ran over to a coat lying in a heap by the door and threw it on. Then he opened the door and darted out, leaving it swaying behind him.

The disgust of Nathan and the sorrow of Sonya combined to create an air thick enough to choke on.

"Lord, bless our child," Sonya said out loud as she closed the front door, as if God had entered as Clarence was leaving.

"You're kidding, right?" Nathan turned his head and stared at her.

"Now, why would I be kidding about something like that, Nathan?"

"Assuming there is a God, why would He take the time to bless Clarence when you keep giving him money to shoot up with?"

"First off, Nathan Freeman, there is a God. You know there is. Now we may be on hard times right now, but don't you go giving up on the Lord. The Lord hasn't given up on you yet."

"Spoken like a true holy roller."

"Second, that boy has to eat. I will not have my baby starving on the streets."

"He belongs to the streets now, Sonya. At some point you'll have to admit it to yourself. He's not ours anymore."

"He belongs to the Lord, that's who he belongs to."

"Okay, look, Sonya. You begged me night and day to let him move back in with us and, eventually, I gave in. That was my fault. You begged me to help him out with clothes, with food, with everything, and I gave in. And my reason for doing it even went beyond you. I did it because, like you're doing now, I hung onto this little ray of hope that Clarence would one day throw his needle in the river and go get a job at the bank. But it's time to step into reality, sweetheart. Clarence is a crackhead. He won't go to rehab, he won't go get counseling, all he wants to do is sit in that crackhouse down the street and shoot up all damn day."

"Nathan!"

"It's the truth! And it's time you accept it. The only way that boy is going to turn around is if he realizes that he has nothing.

He has to realize on his own what he's done to himself. And you make it impossible for that to happen. I can't kick him out 'cause you'll cry around the clock until I go out and find him and tell him to come back in. I can't deny him any money because you give in and hand over your purse to him every time he asks. You are his crutch, Sonya. And as long as he has you, he'll remain a crackhead forever."

Sonya turned quiet and her eyes started to well. After she grabbed hold of her emotions, she shook her head, wiped her eyes, took a deep breath, and straightened her back, standing as tall as she possibly could. "I will not turn my back on my son."

"Well, then say goodbye to him now. It'll be easier than doing it when they find him overdosed in a gutter." Nathan got up and started to walk toward the door.

Sonya's eyes started to well again, and this time she let one tear fall from each eye. "It's like you don't even care," she said with a voice that stopped Nathan in the doorway.

He paused for a few seconds, then turned around and faced her. "I do care. I care more than you know."

He walked out the door and sat on the front porch. In an attempt to clear his head, he started watching the various cars go by, but ended up wishing he was in one of them.

Outside the air was crisp, and the sudden drop in temperature kept Nathan alert. He blew into his hands and then rubbed them together to keep them warm. He remembered that his father used to do the same thing during the winter. His father, Thomas Freeman, the man who would never let his chin drop lower than his Adam's apple.

Beginning to lose himself in his memories, Nathan continued to reflect about his father, and then about his childhood, all the way back to the one-room schoolhouse down South with no windowpanes...

By age seven, Nathan had learned just about everything they had to teach him at the colored schoolhouse, and spent most days helping the teachers with the older students.

Thomas Freeman realized that his son was gifted. Though he had never gone to school himself, he made it a point to associate regularly with people who had, and Nathan impressed him more than his friends ever could. So when he found out that the schools up North were actually doing what the court said, letting white kids and black kids go to school together, he identified where his son needed to be.

"I'm sellin' the land," he declared to his wife, Martha Freeman, and his son on Nathan's eighth birthday. It was a humid evening, and they were all gathered around the birthday cake that Martha had made earlier.

"We movin' up North. I hear a black man got a chance to be somethin' up North, and ain't no better gift I can give my son than the chance to be somethin'."

Martha and her son stared at each other with wide eyes. They had often talked at night, while Martha was preparing Nathan for bed, about what it would be like to go to the big city, telling make believe tales of dancing and stardom instead of bedtime stories. But they also understood how long their land had been in the Freeman family, how it had belonged to the Freemans even before slavery ended, and how promises were made from one generation to the next to keep it that way.

"We never had no genius in the family before," Thomas responded, reading his family's mind. He was made a father in his twenties, and took over the farmland after his poppa's body was found face down in Chestnut Creek, courtesy of the local Klan chapter. The patch over Billy Johnson's left eye was the gift Thomas' father left for his son. They shared the same penchant of never letting their eyes touch the ground, and putting their pride over their safety. Until he realized his son's potential, Thomas had accepted, and even anticipated, following in his father's footsteps.

"My father would understand," Thomas reassured himself and his family before directing his son to blow out his birthday candles.

Four months later, Nathan was an alien. He didn't talk like the other students, he didn't walk like the other students and, for the majority of the school year, he barely said a word. Neither he nor his parents had anticipated the level of depravity that it took to survive in the city, and they all began to yearn for the days of unobtrusive farm work. Those days were gone, however, and they all unearthed their ways to survive. Nathan's was only speaking while in the confines of their tiny, one-room apartment, where things made sense. Outside of that, he refused to open his mouth.

The white teachers and students began referring to him as "that slow little Negro boy," and the Negro students came to his aid more out of obligation than relevance. During a teacher conference that had taken months to get scheduled, Thomas and Martha Freeman stood dumbstruck while Mrs. Landey, Nathan's homeroom teacher, told them that their son was probably retarded.

"I'm sorry, Mr. and Mrs. Freeman, I'm sure this is hard for parents to hear, but I don't think your son belongs in this type of educational setting. There are exceptional schools designed to fit his specific academic needs."

"And what are his academic needs, Mrs. Landey?" Martha Freeman had grown hard during her time in the city, though she tried her best not to let her family know. "You said it yourself, he does all the work! His grades may not be perfect, but they're decent, right?"

"Yes, but...well, Mrs. Freeman, I have a class full of students, both Negro and white. I may not like it, but that's the way it is, and I have to deal with that. It's all I can do to stop my classroom from turning into a jungle, and the last thing I need is some mute little Negro boy twiddling his thumbs while I'm trying to teach…"

Thomas sat quiet, with his jaw set tight and his eyes narrowed. If the city had made Martha hard, it had turned Thomas Freeman into a creature. He'd realized very quickly that, in the city, pride could either get you murdered or make you infamous, and he hadn't traveled hundreds of miles away from the Klan to get taken out by crooked cops or overzealous hustlers. Though it wasn't his plan, he ended up making himself invaluable to Jimmy Jinx, the most infamous colored gangster in the city. His eyes would always focus on the blood on his hands whenever he tried to wash them, but he and his family were safe.

"You wait a goddamn—" Martha began, but Thomas put a hand on her shoulder while he stared at the teacher. She glanced at her husband, and then sat back in her seat, satisfied.

"When my son comes back to school, he'll be talking. He'll be talking enough for all the white boys you got, and then some. And believe me, he gon' have some stuff to say…" Thomas leaned forward into Mrs. Landey's face. "…but let me find out that he ain't bein' treated fair, or that you ain't giving him the grades he deserve, and we gon' meet outside this school building, you understand? Teacher or no teacher, I moved up here so my son could make somethin' of himself. He got a problem, and we gon' fix it. But if you get to be the problem, Mrs. Landey, then I'ma have to fix you. We understand each other?"

The tone of Thomas' voice stopped Mrs. Landey's voice from escaping. She nodded her head vigorously as she sat frozen in her seat. Thomas motioned to Martha, who gathered her things, cut her eyes at Mrs. Landey, and walked out with her husband behind her.

It was that night that Thomas Freeman sat his son down at the only table in their apartment, and shook his world.

"I'm gonna tell you a story 'bout one of the men in our family. If I'm countin' right, he's your great-great-great-great-grandfather. His name was Toby." His father spoke as if it was common knowledge. Nathan wanted to laugh, but his father's face showed seriousness that Nathan had never witnessed. Thomas took a sip of whiskey and reflected on the words that had been passed down through his family before he continued.

"They say all the men folk in our family get our pride from him. Toby was a slave, but he wasn't no ordinary one. They say his granddaddy was royalty over in Africa. Brought that royalty over from Africa wid 'em, and passed it on down his bloodline."

"What's royalty, Daddy?"

"It means he was a king back where he come from. That made him royalty. Made Toby royalty, and make us royalty, too."

"You mean we kings, Dad? Like, with crowns and everything?"

Thomas took another sip of whiskey. "Yeah, we kings, but this ain't our kingdom."

"I…I don't get it…"

"It's the reason your granddaddy got himself killed, and your great-granddaddy, and the one before that, too. Somethin' 'bout having king's blood in yo' veins that don't allow you to bow down, even to white folks. I'd probably be dead by now, too, if we hadn't moved up North. 'Stead I, well, I turnin' into something I don't really want to turn into, but I got to in order to survive. You understand?"

"Yes, Dad."

"Yo' grandmamma, she always used to tell me don't never get too angry. She say that royalty we got in us, it comes with somethin' else. Comes with a rage, a blood lust that we can't control sometimes. That's when she tell me the story of Toby."

"So what happened to Toby, Dad?"

"They say that royalty in his blood come with something he

ain't know was there. One day the white folks come and try and take away his wife and little girls, and whatever was inside him come out. They say he killed those white folks as easy as you breathin' right now, and even when they shot 'im in the head he still ain't die. Couple days later the mob tried to lynch him, and yo' great-great-great-great-granddaddy left every man in that mob wid a closed casket."

"He killed them?"

"They say *killin'* ain't the word for what he done to those folks." The father refilled his whiskey glass. "She told me that story when I was 'bout your age. She told me, and I ain't believe her… 'til I moved up here, and realized the things I was capable of. Now I ain't so sure she was making it up."

Thomas' voice trailed off as he reacted to the scenes that played back in his mind.

"Dad?"

Snapping out of his trance, Thomas turned back to his son.

"They say whatever Toby had in 'im, we got in us 'cause we from the same bloodline. The women in our family always used to tell me and my brothers never ever get too angry, or Toby might come for us, and we'll get the night eyes. At least that's what your grandmamma called it. Don't never get too angry, she always told me, cause if you do, Toby'll come for you. And if he get you, it ain't no comin' back. You destroy everything and every-one in your path, until finally you destroy yourself."

"Dad, I…I don't know what you're talking about…"

Thomas Freeman slammed his hand down on the table. Nathan nearly jumped from his seat.

"You don't have to know what I'm talking about! You got power in your blood that you ain't ready to understand yet! So I don't wanna hear about you being too scared to talk in school no more, you understand? You a king, goddammit! These people should be bowing at yo' feet, worshipping the ground you walk on! You go into school tomorrow, you open up your mouth, and you let 'em know that!"

"But, Dad, I can't..."

"I ain't askin' you, boy, I'm telling you! I'll be in the school with you tomorrow, and I'ma stay long as it takes until I hear you speakin'! Starting tomorrow, you make yourself known!"

Dropping his eyes, Nathan stared down at the table. "Yes, sir."

It wasn't long before he felt his father's index finger on his chin, raising his face back up. His eyes apologized for yelling, and Nathan forgave him.

"You never put your head down, and you never get too angry. You never lose control. Every man in my family lived by those rules, and you'll be no different. You drop your head, and you disrespect your blood. You get too angry, and Toby might come for you."

Nathan nodded his head at his father, and the room fell silent as both father and son contemplated the new information. Nathan began to stand up from his seat, feeling the heaviness of tomorrow's task weighing down on him, but after a few steps he stopped himself, paused, and made his way back to the table.

"Dad?"

"Yeah?"

"Can you tell me the story of Toby again?"

Thomas Freeman smiled, recalling and reciting the story that his grandmother had told him, and that her grandmother had told her. Nathan's stomach jumped with his father's intonations, and though he was too young to realize that this was the story he'd been waiting for, he was old enough to comprehend that something was different when he went to sleep that night.

The next morning, Nathan told his father that he didn't need to come with him to school anymore. It was the first time he had seen his father smile in months, and Nathan took that grin with him into the classroom and up to Ms. Landey's desk.

"Good morning, Ms. Landey."

"Oh my God! The mute speaks! Hey, everyone, look!"

The class stopped talking and Ms. Landey stood and motioned at Nathan. "The little black boy speaks! I guess you aren't retarded after all."

Nathan began to draw back into himself, lowering his head as laughter from the children began to fill the class. But he remembered his father, and he remembered Toby, and kept his head up.

"I'm not retarded, Ms. Landey. I just didn't want to talk. I'll be talking from now on, though, and I want you to know that I realize you haven't been grading my papers. You've been marking them with Cs and giving them right back to me, the same way you've been doing with all the other Negro kids. I've got every paper you've ever given me, and I've checked each one with Courtney's. We always get the same answers, but she always gets As, and I always get Cs. That's not fair, Ms. Landey."

The classroom was silent now. The black students began to nod to each other, while the white students stared at Ms. Landey, eager to hear her response.

The teacher's indignation picked her up from her seat and she scowled as she glared down her whistleblower. "How dare you accuse me of such a thing, you dirty little upstart!"

"I'm not trying to be disrespectful, Ms. Landey; I want things to be fair. So does my dad. He told me to tell you that he's willing to meet with you outside of school to discuss it."

Nathan didn't know he had reiterated a threat, but Ms. Landey's pale face let him know he had struck a nerve. Her fear of Thomas Freeman quickly won over her outrage. She pointed for Nathan to sit down at his seat, took a deep breath, and began with her morning lesson.

Nathan brought home straight As from that day forward.

"Why don't we go to breakfast?" Sonya peeked out the screen door at Nathan. "It's been a rough morning. We should get out of the house."

Nathan was jerked away from his memories, and hated his wife for a few moments before he turned and saw the sincerity in her eyes. "Why can't you cook?"

"I don't feel like cooking. We should go out. It might lift our spirits."

Without excitement, Nathan stood up slowly and made his way back inside the house. He put on a pair of pants and a shirt, and looked at his long face and salt-and-pepper hair in the mirror. He still loved his wife, although it had become harder and harder to show it. He hoped that instances like these reminded her that she still had whatever heart he may have had left.

Sonya waited by the door as Nathan grabbed his keys. They walked out, one after the other, and he locked the door. After getting in the car, Nathan started the ignition, and just before he put the car into drive, Sonya turned toward him.

"Thank you."

Nathan nodded slightly, shifted the gears of the car, and they drove off in silence.

Chapter Two

T he night sky was peaceful, as if God Himself had put everything to rest after the sun had set. The stars shined bright in their set places in the sky, as the wind hummed the nocturnal soundtrack that would continue to play until the slightest of light rays broke through, indicating the dawn of a new day. The air up here was thin, like a strand of thread, and for a while it sat undisturbed in the peaceful dark, until first a grumble, growing louder and louder, and then an object, pierced through it.

Only something manmade could disturb such serenity.

The plane continued to make its way through the dark clouds, going hundreds of miles an hour. The occupants in the cargo bay were mysterious figures, with equipment hiding their faces as if they are ashamed of their purpose. The two pilots, sitting in the cockpit, directed their attention constantly from one gauge to another to another, making sure that all elements of the flight and the plane were conducive to the mission.

The three men in the back sat still, clearing their minds of everything else except the task at hand. This was how they were trained; to ignore all else, and focus solely on the successful completion of the objective. Attached to their clothing was tactical weaponry, and these men had mastered the use of each one of them. They had trained for countless hours in every environment imaginable, enduring conditions that would have easily broken any lesser of men. But these three had survived, and had shown themselves worthy of the task set before them. Even their slow, steady breathing reflected the hours of training they had completed. They were weapons; human robots programmed over and over again with the same simple command—complete the objective.

When the global positioning system in the cockpit showed that the plane had reached its destination, one of the pilots rose from his seat and walked toward the back. He told the three men that it was time, but they'd anticipated it, and had already rechecked their equipment to ensure that everything was in order. As if on cue, all three of the men stood together. When the pilot remaining in the cockpit was given the word, he pressed the flashing, bright red button in front of him, and the back hatch to the plane opened, revealing a screaming night sky. The wind, displeased with being disturbed, charged through the compartment with incredible force. The three men withstood it. They had been trained to. After going through the necessary preparation procedures, each of the men mechanically walked to the edge of the hatch, and, one after the other, jumped from the plane.

Their stomachs rose into their throats as they fell rapidly toward the earth. They put their bodies in the right aerial position to slow their descent, and after reaching the correct altitude, they pulled strings attached to their clothing and deployed their parachutes. They were now low enough to get a good view of their target. The bunker was well lit, and although they were still airborne, with the night vision equipment they could make out security personnel on patrol around the building. They landed softly, expertly in the bush on the outskirts of the bunker, and it was only after removing the equipment that was no longer necessary that one could make out the differences between the three men. Two of them stood out, their skin tone contrasting with the darkness. The other blended in well.

They moved through the brush with stealth, weapons drawn, and faces tight. They walked low enough to avoid being seen by any of the security, but high enough to keep aware of their surroundings.

When they came into close proximity of the first guard, the first of the three signaled to the other two to stop and wait. Then he snuck up behind the guard, who had been daydreaming for the past hour, quickly covered his mouth with one hand, gripped the top of his head with the other, and snapped his neck. After laying the guard down silently on the ground, he signaled for the others to continue following him. They were now at the target building, and each of them covered a particular direction, so as to make sure that all of their sides were covered. They made their way up the stairs and along the makeshift balcony. This was the entrance route with the least resistance, as they had already determined, and the door on the far side of the walkway was where they planned to enter. Everything was going according to plan.

Just as they reached the ladder that marked the halfway point between the steps and the entrance, two guards unexpectedly emerged from the door.

Initially the guards had been laughing, lightening the mood of the night, but as soon as they saw the three men, they immediately opened fire. The trio of operatives took cover positions and fired back, dropping the two guards fast, but not fast enough. Their weapons were silenced, but the guards were not, and the shots fired were sure to draw more guards to their location.

They ran for the door, knowing they must complete the mission as quickly as possible. After entering the bunker, they made their way down the stone stairs and stopped at the corner. They could hear footsteps approaching, and again, as if by cue, they each peeked around the corner and shot the approaching guards. They then started making their way down the hallway, toward the metal door where the American scientist was being held, but before they could get there a dozen guards came from around an adjacent hallway and began to open fire. The elite soldiers each ducked around a corner, narrowly avoiding the bullets aimed at them. The guards, after they stopped firing, began screaming something in a foreign language. There were too many people talking for the soldiers to translate, and they could only make out words and phrases—"enemies," "kill them all," "move the scientist," "no escape." Two of the three men kept their backs against the wall and held on tightly to their guns, but the third one, the black man, threw his gun on the ground.

"Tango, what the hell are you doing?"

The soldier didn't answer. He took a deep breath and calmed himself, like he had done on the plane.

"X, you pick up your weapon, goddammit!"

Xavier didn't answer; he waited for the right moment. And when the army of guards was close enough, he came from around the corner and struck the first one in the throat, crushing his larynx. Then he started attacking the rest of them, rendering most of them dead with one blow. Xavier kicked one in the knee, popping it out of place, then punched one in the ribcage with his fist angled, puncturing the heart, then back-fisted one on the side of the head. For a reason foreign to Xavier, none of the guards were shooting at him. They were all trying to attack him, and he was killing them one after the other. He was not tired, he was not fatigued; he was doing as he had been trained. He side-kicked one of the guards in the nose, then turned around and grabbed another guard's arm, maneuvered around, and broke it. Then he popped out another one's elbow, turned around and broke his neck. More guards were coming out from everywhere now, but Xavier could have gone on fighting forever. He smiled, knowing he was perfect in his combat, and there was no way he could be beaten.

As he reached the peak of his pride, he realized something, and everything stopped in its tracks. His body stopped moving, the guards stopped attacking, and he stood there, as if time itself had stopped to pay homage to his revelation.

Xavier realized he didn't know who he was.

He understood what the mission was, he understood what he was supposed to do, but he didn't know anything about himself. His fellow soldier had called him X, so that must have been his name, but other than that—nothing. Horrified, he stood there and racked his brain, trying to figure out the questions thudding at his head. *Who am I? Where did I come from?* He dropped to his knees and struck his head against the floor, hoping to trigger some thought, some long lost memory, but nothing came.

Xavier looked up from the floor to find that each one of the guards surrounding him had an AK-47 in hand, and as he closed his eyes, they all fired into him at the same time.

Soaked in sweat, Xavier jerked awake.

As his eyes adjusted to being open, the first thing Xavier noticed was the sunlight racing in through the window. It illuminated the entire room, but the beautiful dresser that faced the curtains got most of its attention. The pictures on top were illuminated as well, and Xavier stared for a while at the images of himself smiling, embracing his family, in order to bring him back into reality.

The room smelled of pleasant scents that attached themselves to family life: potpourri, baby powder, perfume, and fresh laundry. The bed sheets, which had absorbed most of Xavier's sweat, were adorned with floral prints. The colors matched the carpet, which had been very well kept, and matched the paint on the walls. The entire scene was a freeze frame from a made-for-TV movie. There were two or three pictures on the wall, all depicting nature at its most complacent, and all matching the color scheme and décor of the room.

The children's toys strewn around the carpet were the only things out of place in the room. A little black Barbie doll lay facedown beside a toy truck in the middle of the room, and an open children's book sat beside the mirror, waiting to be resumed. The toys fit in the room, as if they had sprouted themselves up from the carpet.

Though the toys were strewn, left by the children and ignored by the mother the night before, they still seemed to fit. Everything in the room seemed to fit.

Everything except the Desert Eagle .50 handgun hidden under a stack of magazines in the small drawer on Xavier's side of the bed. It had never fit.

Xavier felt a hand caressing his arm, and turned to face the beautiful woman lying in the bed next to him. The concern on her face asked Xavier what was wrong before she opened her mouth. He shook his head and breathed deep, trying to forget about the dream that had awoken him so violently. She leaned forward and lightly kissed him on his cheek, and then on his arm, where her hand had been.

She spoke softly, "Was it another nightmare?"

"I don't know, Theresa. I don't know. Everything was fine, and then...and then it all went to hell."

"It was about your days in the military again?"

"Yeah."

Theresa sighed deeply.

"You keep having these dreams about what you used to do, baby. You don't like talking about the military, but maybe we should. I want to be able to help you."

"It's nothing."

Before Theresa could respond, there was a set of knocks at the bedroom door. Xavier smiled involuntarily. He looked at Theresa to make sure that she was okay with ending the conversation for the time being, and when she nodded her head, he yelled, "Come in!"

The two children burst into the room and ran around screaming with such joy in their voices that Xavier and Theresa couldn't help but to laugh. They picked up the children and played around with them on the bed, tickling them and rolling them around until everyone was tired. Then they all lay down, with Theresa holding their son, Xavier Jr., and Xavier holding their daughter, Felicia.

"Daddy." XJ looked over to him. "Can I get a tattoo?"

"What? No, you can't get a tattoo!"

"Why not, Daddy?"

"Well, first of all, you're too young. What would you look like going into kindergarten with a tattoo?"

"But you have tattoos!!!"

"Yes, that's because I'm an adult."

"But my friend Dante at school, his brother has a tattoo and he's not an adult."

"Well, that's Dante's family, not mine."

"And..." interjected Felicia, "if he can get a tattoo, then Mommy can buy me some makeup."

Theresa rolled her eyes. "I'm not buying you any makeup.

Who wears makeup in the second grade, Felicia? Where did this whole makeup thing come from, anyway?"

"Tasha's mom lets her wear makeup some days."

"Tasha's mom is a hoe."

Xavier immediately looked over at Theresa, who realized that she'd made a mistake.

"You know what's coming next." Xavier laughed, and Felicia was the first to inquire the inevitable.

"What's a hoe, Mommy?"

XJ followed up quickly. "Yeah, Daddy, what's a hoe?"

"Alright, it's time for you two to get ready for school." Xavier started pushing his daughter off the bed and toward the door. Theresa did the same thing to their son. "Go wash up and put your clothes on."

"But…"

"But nothing. Go wash up, put your clothes on, and get ready for school. I'll be in there to help you in a second."

The two children looked at each other in an attempt at solidarity. They inched forward, but very slowly, and looked back at their father to judge his reaction.

"I'm not going to say it again."

Solidarity broken, the two children quickly ran out of the room and into the bathroom.

"Thanks for the save!" Theresa laughed when the kids were out of earshot.

"Don't thank me. You still have to worry about little Tasha's mom calling you about that hoe comment. Felicia's going to tell her when she gets to school."

"Ugh, you're right." Theresa cursed herself as she started getting dressed. "I'll figure out some way to apologize later."

"Apologize for what? We all know she's a hoe. It's no secret."

"Still, apologizing is the right thing to do," Theresa said as she started to make her way out of the door. "I'm going to fix breakfast. Are you going to eat?"

"Yeah, I'll be down in a minute."

As Xavier heard his wife's footsteps echoing off the walls, he prepared to go and join his children, who were playing in the bathroom. He closed his eyes and yawned, but memories of his dream came to him, and he decided to keep them open.

Slowly, he got out of bed and stretched, noticing the aches he had at thirty-five that weren't there a decade ago. Turning around, he caught a glimpse of himself in the vanity mirror. His physique would rival a bodybuilder's. Every muscle on his body seems augmented, a gift he had taken away with him from the military. There was a time when he would have stopped to admire himself, but fatherhood had replaced his hubris. He nodded at his reflection and hurried to join his kids.

Fifteen minutes later, Xavier began to walk down the stairs. He could smell the eggs, bacon, pancakes, and potatoes cooking in the kitchen, and congratulated himself for marrying a woman that could cook. His children were already sitting at the table, eating their eggs and waiting for their pancakes to be served. They smiled at him as he walked into the room, and he began to think, as he so often did, that he didn't deserve what he had. He walked up and kissed Theresa.

"Ewwwww!" the children reacted as if a jar full of bugs had entered the kitchen.

Theresa laughed, then started to wash her hands.

"Come on, kids," she said. "I don't want to be late for work."

As the children started to eat faster, Xavier grumbled slightly under his breath, loud enough for Theresa to hear.

"What is it, baby?"

"I don't like you working. We can get by off of the interest from my account. And the military is still sending me checks. Why not stay home with the kids?"

"Because I don't want to," Theresa replied. "We're getting ready to have a black lady in the White House, and you want me to be a stay-at-home mom? I love my job, and I'm doing fine at being a mother and a working woman. You have a problem with that?"

"No. I don't understand why you would work if you don't have to."

"Well, I'll explain it later. Right now I have to drop off the kids and get to the office."

Theresa rushed the children away from the table and told them to get their bags and coats. Xavier walked up behind her, despite her rushing, and slid his hands around her waist.

"You know I like a take charge kind of woman, right?"

Theresa turned around and smiled. "Well, then, you'll love me tonight. I've been reading up on some stuff in that book we got for our anniversary."

"Really…? And you can't take the day off to show me?"

"No, I can't. You'll have to wait."

Xavier turned around, playfully disappointed, but Theresa grabbed his shoulders and made him face her again. When he looked at her face, it was set and serious, and she stared deeply into his eyes.

"I love you, Xavier."

"I love you, too."

She stared into his eyes for one more second, then relaxed her demeanor and blushed.

The children rushed downstairs with their things and yelled to their mother that they were ready to go. Theresa threw on her coat, kissed Xavier goodbye, and made her way toward the door.

"Bye, Daddy!" the children called out as Theresa opened the door.

"I'll see you all later."

The door closed, and after a while Xavier heard the car starting, then pulling out from the driveway, and the family was gone.

Xavier sat down and finished his breakfast, taking in the silence. He didn't especially enjoy it. It reminded him of times past, where silence and darkness were his primary weapons. His house did a good job of overpowering those reminders, though. He could look up at the refrigerator and see pictures drawn by his children, of birds and ninjas and pink flowers. He could taste the syrup that his wife used to write "I love you" on the pancakes. He could see his daughter's tiny shoes on the floor, with a picture of Snow White on the sides and the bottoms.

His wife was only half right. There was a part of his past that he missed, and a part of his past that he didn't. Without trying, his mind traveled back to the unpleasant, when he was only a few years older than his own children, and when life didn't seem like it was worth the time.

Anger management issues.

That's what the teachers would always state as the root of Xavier's problems. "He's a good student, and very smart. He just can't control himself once he gets angry."

Xavier's fourth-grade teacher, Ms. Lucille, fresh out of college and eager to put her elementary education degree to work, took the questioning a step further.

"Is there a father in the home, Ms. Turner? Or a male family member that could help with disciplinary issues?"

Tammy Turner wasn't great about controlling her anger, either.

At least not when someone mentioned Xavier's father. She delivered such a litany of curse words that the young white teacher was convinced there must have been two of her.

Tammy Turner gave birth to Xavier in May of 1973, assisted by two nurses and a doctor who would not shut up about Watergate. Tammy couldn't have cared less about the President's issues. She was having a baby by a man whom she was madly in love with, though his absence proved that her adoration was un-requited. It didn't matter, though. She was having his baby, his son. He couldn't leave her now, no matter what he said. No matter how much he claimed he was going back to his wife. No matter how much he said being with Tammy was a mistake. He couldn't leave her now. She held her baby close after the delivery, singing lullabies and waiting for a man who would never show up.

She had met her love thirteen months prior, in the cool of the afternoon, at the pond where she went to hide her shame. Her legs and arms were still adjusting to the strength that the pole demanded, and she was sitting down, massaging her calf muscle as he walked by. They both took note of each other. His face was mean, even abusive, but his eyes were soft and apologetic, like he was tremendously sorry for things he hadn't done yet.

Tammy had seen him before. In the month that she had been working at the club, he'd been there on three different occasions. Well-dressed and sinister, he never walked through the doors with any less than four men, and was usually the only one who managed to keep his cool around the abundance of shaved vaginas. He was older, closer to fifty than forty, and had enough class to wait and stab a disrespectful drunk in the alley out back instead of in the middle of her routine. He tipped well but refused lap dances, opting instead to shake his head at his ogling companions, and when he announced that he was ready to leave, they all settled their tabs and followed him out as quickly as they had come.

Here, by the pond, though, he was alone, and Tammy summoned up the courage to call out to him as he walked past. He was guarded at first, instinctually standoffish, but she knew enough born assholes to know that his rudeness wasn't genuine; more of a learned characteristic. When she didn't take offense, his shields began to drop.

Tammy understood what is was to become someone you hated in order to survive, but she was young enough to believe she could still live out her dreams. He was old enough to predict her future, old enough to tell her that her dreams would never come true, but instead he caught a crush on her ignorance, and she fell in love with his lies. The first time they made love, he never removed his wedding ring, and she never asked him to.

Just over a year later, the sound of her phone crashing to the floor stirred her newborn son, as she realized the three numbers she had for her lover were never his, and his associates continued to inform her that he wasn't available. One of them, a skinny, goofy looking man with horse teeth, would come to her home in the next few days with two large manila envelopes containing fifty thousand dollars each, and a note saying to never contact him again.

Tammy stared at that letter for three days, only feeding Xavier when she could no longer stand his cries. On the fourth day, she took her baby down to the foster care agency and spent the day filling out paperwork. She left the agency by herself, with her baby son's blanket in hand, and went straight to her friend Stacy's apartment, where a line of heroin was waiting for her virgin nostrils.

Years later, when Xavier was old enough to both ask and understand, she would tell him that she blinked, and one year, and one hundred thousand dollars had disappeared.

Xavier got up and put his plate in the sink, then went back over to the table, got his children's plates, and put them in the sink as well. Running the hot water, he put the dish liquid into the large bowl, filled it up, and began washing the dishes. The steam filled the air, and he closed his eyes and imagined that it cleaned his soul as he breathed it in.

After he was done, he walked back upstairs to the bedroom and looked in the mirror. He was very muscular, a perk that came along with all of his military training. Everything from his biceps to his abs was perfectly defined, and he took off his shirt to make sure that everything was as it should be. Then he changed clothes. He put on a pair of old sweatpants, a sleeveless T-shirt, and a pair of tennis shoes. His family had never seen him in this apparel. He only wore it during the hours that he had the house to himself. Standing in front of the mirror once more, he prepared to indulge in a part of his past life. The only part that he felt had some purpose in it.

He went down into the basement and walked through the short hallway. The door he approached was always locked whenever there were others in the house. His children were afraid to knock on it, because they thought the same monster that hid under their beds at night lived in that room during the day. Theresa knew what was behind it, but only had an idea as to what it meant to her husband. Even with that, she didn't bother it for fear that it may have held a part of him that she was not yet ready to encounter.

Xavier unlocked the door and stepped into the room. It was much bigger than the rest of the rooms in the basement. In fact, it was the largest room in the house. In the middle was a huge mat with an elaborate oriental design on it. Surrounding the mat were various types of exercise equipment, from a bench press to a treadmill and a punching bag. On the wall, hung up very neatly in a large wooden display case, were all sorts of martial arts weapons. On the opposite wall, in an identical case, were various types of firearms. There were no windows, and the door that Xavier had entered through was the only one in and out. The room smelled of incense and sweat, and the large mirror at the far corner of the room reflected a man hesitant to enter into his own domain. He had been taught that a man's greatest enemy was himself, and this room was where they went to war.

Xavier conducted the ritual of bowing as he stepped into the door, then slowly made his way toward the mat. Before walking on it, however, he lit incense and placed it in the holder. Carefully he stepped onto the firm surface, and once he was in the middle, knelt down on both knees, sat back on his feet, and let his mind wander. He was looking for peace, and where most times his mind would rest on an image of a waterfall or an ice-capped mountain range, today it went back to his mother. And his father.

After her second overdose, it was Stacy who forced Tammy to go into a rehab program. Tammy had no family in the area, and had declared Stacy her power of attorney after her first brush with death. Weary of wondering whether or not she had a dead woman waiting for her in her apartment, and contrite over how much of Tammy's money she had stolen and spent on herself, Stacy called the clinic one day on her lunch break. By quitting time, two police officers, an attendant, and a psychiatrist from the center were waiting for Stacy outside of her complex.

"Do you all normally send this many people to get a patient?"

"You did the right thing." The psychiatrist, Dr. Carter, put her hand on Stacy's shoulder while ignoring her question. Stacy watched in horror as the two officers strapped Tammy down to a gurney and wheeled her out of the unit, screaming.

"You probably saved her life," the doctor continued.

"She...she has a son," Stacy stammered through her tears. "She has a son named Xavier. He's in the foster care system. She jumps awake every night, thinking she's hearing him cry. Maybe...maybe you can use that...to motivate her or something..."

The psychiatrist thanked her, and gave her one last pat on the shoulder before she jumped into the plain white van. Tammy's muffled screams faded as the van pulled down the street.

She wouldn't remember her first month in the clinic. Whenever she tried to think about it, all she could come up with were flashes of multicolored agony.

The staff had thirty days to hold her without consent. After that, she was free to go, or stay as long as she liked. Tammy felt like she was posed in a sprinter's stance at the end of the month, until Dr. Carter came in to say goodbye. Curious about Stacy's story, she had done some research and found the whereabouts of Tammy's son. She handed Tammy a wallet-sized photo of a little boy who seemed acutely aware that he had lost something, and promised Tammy that if she gave the program some more time, she could help her get Xavier back.

Tammy spent the rest of the day crying in her room. She stayed at the clinic for another three months, and the day she left, she walked straight back to the foster care office again.

It was too late, though.

Xavier's eyes had already changed. What were once bright, mesmerizing pupils were now clouded over and gray. Tammy knew there was something different about her son. She knew, but felt she had no right to question. She had abandoned him, left him to be raised by the state. Whatever demons her son had now were hers alone to deal with.

The years passed, and Xavier grew increasingly more violent. Tammy was never in any danger, though. He wouldn't so much as raise his voice toward his mother, knowing somewhere deep down inside he was terrified of being left in a cold room with unwanted children again. But when he picked up a chair and hit a student across the head during a fourth-grade spelling bee, Tammy realized the problem was beyond her control. In desperation, she took Xavier to see Dr. Carter on a dreary Sunday afternoon. The psychiatrist spent two hours talking with the little boy while rainclouds peeked in through the window. She emerged from the office with much of the blood having drained from her face.

"He's angry," she told Tammy outside of her office, while Xavier sat on the floor and played with a bucket of Legos. "He's a regular, ten-year-old boy in every other way, but he turns into a grown man when he loses his temper."

As the years grew on, Xavier got worse, and Tammy realized that a straight-laced life wasn't worth its weight in salt. Managers didn't care if your troubled son needed you at home, and no one paying decent money wanted to hire a former stripper. Two jobs and seven days a week was what it took to keep a roof over her and Xavier's heads, and pay her son's get-out-of-jail money. She lost count of the number of times she had come home exhausted, listened to her messages, and trudged back out to the local precinct.

She wouldn't let her son stay in jail. Not even after all his outfits consisted of gang colors, and blood sometimes stained the clothes in the laundry. She wouldn't abandon him again. She owed him that much. She did, and so did his father.

It took her a while to track him down. According to all accounts, he'd become a changed man and moved back down South, taking the money he'd earned from his unscrupulous activities and buying his family's land back.

In 1991, Xavier heard his father's name mentioned for the first time. He was eighteen and, as the counselors at the juvenile detention facility informed him, too old for the kiddie jail anymore. Terrified that her son would be shot or end up in prison, Tammy took off from work early on the last day of school, took out a piece of paper she'd kept hidden in her underwear drawer for the last two years, and dialed the number on it. Xavier was already at home, blasting his new Ice Cube cassette through the headphones of his Walkman. He never even heard his mother come in, but her yells and screams forced him to cut down his music, and creep out of his room and down the hall. He could hear a man's voice, raspy and definitive, coming through the speakerphone.

"I'm sorry, Tammy. I can't."

"What the hell do you mean, you can't? He's your goddamn son, Thomas! Your flesh and blood!"

"No, I have a son, Tammy! I have a son, and he's nothing like this boy you're describing to me! I gave you a hundred thousand dollars, Tammy! A hundred thousand dollars! Do you know how hard it was to get that kind of cash in 1973? You know how many favors I had to call in? How many people got hurt?"

"Listen, you bastard, I don't give a damn about that money!"

"Well, you should, sweetheart! You really should! You ever ask yourself why I gave you so much money? Why I would bust my ass to scrape that kind of money together? I realized that I wouldn't be no kind of father to that kid, Tammy! I realized it when you first told me you were pregnant! Even when they told me you had the baby, I didn't feel a thing. They might as well have told me you bought a fish—"

"You sonofa…!"

"—but I owed you, Tammy. I owed you because you were gonna be having a baby without no father. So I spent all those months you were pregnant getting that money together. All those dreams you used to tell me about, about going back to school and getting a degree and becoming some hot shot businesswoman, that's what that money was for! You could have started a brand-new life! You could have taken that boy, moved wherever you wanted, and started over completely! But what did you do, Tammy? Go on, say it! Let me hear it!"

"Go to hell!"

"What, you thought I wouldn't know? You thought I wouldn't find out? You thought my people wouldn't come back and tell me how strung out you were? And how much of my money that slut Stacy was taking from you?"

"You shut up! Stacy saved my life!"

"Oh, you mean by getting you in that rehab program? You ever wondered why those folks came out to Stacy's place to get you? Why you didn't have to fill out the paperwork and wait for a space to open like everyone else? She made the call, but I made that happen, baby! Meanwhile, to this day, Stacy has fifty thousand dollars stashed away in a safety deposit box downtown some-where! I wonder where she got that kind of money from?"

Exhausted, Tammy reached out and braced herself on a seat in the kitchen before she sat down. The conversation was draining the little energy she had.

"I don't want to do this with you, Thomas. He needs a father. Xavier needs a father."

"No, he doesn't! Xavier needed a mother who could take a

hundred thousand dollars and figure out something better to do than sniff it!"

The words kicked Tammy in the gut. It took her a full minute to recover.

"He's gonna die, Thomas. Hell, I'm surprised he's lasted this long. You can't live the way he lives and not pay for it. And if he dies…well, I know you don't give a damn about me, but I'll die along with him. He's my life. I can't live without him."

"What do you want from me, Tammy?"

"I want you to be his father! Come back here to meet him! Talk to him! Show him how to be a man! I can't show him that. I tried, God knows I tried, but I can't."

"I'm damn near seventy years old, Tammy. What do you want me to do? Play catch with the kid in the park? Coach his Little League team? He's eighteen years old and I'm an old man, Tammy…"

"He's still your son!"

"No, my son, the son that my wife and I raised, he's got his Ph.D. He's off in Africa wrapping up research about our family bloodline. I poured everything I had into my boy, and he did me proud! You…you were a mistake. And I tried to make it right, Tammy. I swear I did. But it didn't work."

"So that's it, huh? You just gonna sit around while your own flesh and blood gets killed in the streets?"

"Look, you want my advice? Tell him to go to the military. Tell him to enlist."

"Screw you…"

"I'm serious! What you're asking me to do, I'm telling you I can't. I won't. But I've seen plenty of knuckleheads come back from the Army shaped up and flying right. They don't make any promises, but it might be worth a try. Hell, the boy probably done already killed a few people. He may as well do it legally!"

"You don't know Xavier. He won't join nobody's army."

"Then you convince him! Tell him what you told me, that he'll be dead before he knows it if he stays around there. And if everything else fails, tell him…" Thomas took a deep breath. When he spoke again, his voice shook ever so slightly. "…tell him his father says it's a good idea."

Xavier waited for some time after his mother had finished her conversation to come from around the corner. Tammy had sensed he was nearby, but her tears prevented her from calling out to him. Silently, he walked up and sat down beside his mother at the kitchen table.

"That was my father on the phone?" Tammy nodded her head. "What's his name?"

"His name is Thomas. Thomas Freeman."

Xavier let the unknown name sink into his chest. "Why don't I have his last name?"

"What use is it giving you the last name of someone you never met?"

Later on that evening, while his mother was working the night shift, Xavier went back to the phone in the kitchen. He stared at it for almost ten minutes, and then picked it up and hit redial.

The voice sounded more real coming through the receiver than through the speakerphone. He could hear the hard breathing now, and the sandpaper in the throat.

"Can I talk to Thomas Freeman?"

"Yeah, this is Thomas Freeman. Who's this?"

"This is Xavier Turner. I wanted to let you know that I heard you and my mom's conversation earlier today, and I'm going to see an Army recruiter in the morning."

The silence afterward seemed to expand, like a balloon that

would never pop. Ultimately, it was Thomas who overcame the awkwardness. "That's...that's great. Look, son, I..."

"It's okay. I understand. You've got your own life. Just wanted to call and let you know."

That would be the last time Xavier would ever talk to his father. The conversation would dart around him, buzzing in his ears, for as long as he drew breath.

Xavier finished meditating and stood up on the mat. Still remembering his past, he breathed in deeply and exhaled, so that his emotions would not get in the way of his being productive. After a couple of seconds, he took a fighting stance on the mat, prepared himself, and began his training.

Chapter Three

I t was the morning rush, and the diner that Nathan and Sonya had gone to was overcrowded. Shouts back and forth from the cooks to the wait staff stunned Nathan as he walked past the kitchen, and he found himself relieved to take his seat.

The restaurant was loud, but the noise was welcome. Nathan glanced around the establishment, noticing those who seemed especially cheerful. They didn't realize it, but they mocked him as he stared. He considered forcing a smile, in an effort to pretend, before he shook his head and wished he wasn't there. Sighing, he turned and looked out of the window.

The young family he eyed seemed to float out of their old, rusty Cadillac. The man had cornrows in his hair, moving with an assurance that only came from city living. The woman glowed as her micro braids swayed back and forth. She had on a T-shirt and stretch jeans, and moved as if the mythical deities themselves carried her on their shoulders. She grabbed their daughter out of the back seat, and the little princess laughed as her father twirled her around in the air, making her barrettes applaud. When she landed from her flight, the little girl sang about the chocolate chip pancakes she was getting ready to eat. The innocence in her giggles made the sun shine brighter, and Nathan discovered the smile he had been searching for.

"Are you ready to order?" The waitress brought Nathan back to reality, and he instinctively hardened his face again.

"Yes," Sonya replied. "You want some coffee, right?" She looked at Nathan.

"Yeah."

"Okay, first, we'll have two coffees," Sonya began. Then she went on to place her order. Nathan hadn't looked at the menu, but he already knew what he wanted.

"And you?" The waitress looks at Nathan.

"I'll have the chocolate chip pancakes."

Sonya looked at him strange for a few seconds, then shrugged her shoulders and handed the waitress her menu, who promptly returned with a pot of coffee. "Just holler if ya'll want a refill, okay?"

"That's fine." Sonya sipped her coffee. "Thank you."

The waitress left the table and Sonya took advantage of the broken silence. "So what made you want to get chocolate chip pancakes? You trying to have the doctor put you back on the blood pressure medication again?"

"I don't know. I guess I felt in the mood for them."

"You could have fooled me."

Nathan took a sip of his coffee, then added some milk and sugar and stirred it around.

"I promise, Nathan, sometimes I feel like I will never fully understand you."

Nathan sipped his coffee again, then played with the mug handle.

"Another royalty check came in from the book today." Sonya looked down at the table. She was touching a sore spot, but her desperation for conversation had given her no choice. "It's still doing well."

Nathan froze, with his finger still on the mug handle. Slowly, everything around him turned a shade of bright red. He took a deep breath, and fought the urge to shove the table over and start screaming. Clenching and unclenching his fist, he lifted his head slowly, he stared his wife in the eyes, and suppressed his voice down to that of a menacing whisper. "I told you never to talk about that with me again."

"I thought you'd want to—"

"I don't."

Sonya took a deep breath herself, knowing she'd done something she shouldn't have, but wanting to continue talking anyway.

"Nathan, when the Lord gives you a gift, He means for you to share it. Share it with as many people as you can. I don't know why that's such a problem, honey. Not only are you very, very intelligent; you've written an amazing book that many people have read and loved. Why can't you be happy about it?"

Nathan didn't say anything. He sipped his coffee and tried to fade into the noise once again.

"I remember," Sonya started to reminisce. "I remember when Clarence was younger. When he used to lie on the couch and pretend to read *The Seven Days* so he could impress you. He used to lie there, sometimes for hours, trying to be like you. You remember that, Nathan?"

Nathan felt like someone was taking small razors and making little incisions all over his body. "For the love of God, Sonya, please stop. Stop talking about this."

Sonya's sudden anger surprised even her, as she slammed her hands in her lap and narrowed her eyes at her husband. "I will not stop! I will not stop talking about this!"

Nathan looked at Sonya like she had lost her mind.

"I have a brilliant husband, who has written a bestselling book! People have talked about it on the television; they've written about it in newspapers, in magazines! People teach classes on it at colleges and universities! And my husband wants to pretend like the book doesn't exist! Like he never sat down in front of the computer and wrote such a masterpiece! And why not? Because a few bums on the street don't know about it! Because—"

"SHUT UP!"

Nathan's yelling echoed off of the walls, and the restaurant fell silent as everyone stared at the feuding couple. Noticing the attention he had drawn, Nathan tried to compose himself as, one by one, fellow diners returned to their conversations.

Once he assumed he was no longer the center of attention, Nathan allowed his controlled anger to return. He leaned forward and addressed his wife through clenched teeth. "I put everything into that book! I worked on it night and day for almost four years! Every word in that book has a piece of my soul wrapped around it. You think I like ignoring it? You think I like having to pretend like it was never written?"

Sonya, still shocked from Nathan's outburst, gathered herself enough to reply. "So why do you do it?"

"Because it failed! *The Seven Days* failed! You know who talks about my book? Rich white people who swear that it will make them more cultured! And rich black people who want nothing more than to sit in a room with those same white people and debate for hours on end, so they can feel smarter when they leave the room! Middle and upper class bastards who are content quoting my book at their tea parties! That's who reads my book! Not the guys on the corner hustling, not the single mothers, not the prison inmates, none of them know anything about my book! They couldn't care less whether it sold one copy or a million! They don't give a damn!"

As Sonya stared at her husband, she saw the anger begin to melt away, and the remorse begin to form.

"I wanted to reach them." Nathan shook his head. "All that

research…all that information…I mean, how many times did I travel back and forth to Senegal? How many people did I talk to? How many stories and myths did I hear and record? I don't know…maybe I should have found some rapper and turned all the chapters into lyrics or something. Maybe I should have written a series of magazine articles…I don't know, Sonya…"

Sonya reached her hand across the table and placed it on top of Nathan's. "Why quit, though, Nathan? Why do you have to quit? Why can't you write something else and make sure that people hear it? And why can't you be happy with the success of your first book? You can use your influence from this book to reach whomever you want."

"I can't do it again." Nathan removed his hand from under Sonya's and picked up his coffee cup with it. "I can't do it again. How many times can you tell people that you've got royalty in your blood? How many ways can you retell the story? My fire is gone, Sonya. Between the book and Clarence, I don't have anything left in me. I…I feel like I'm dying."

Sonya opened her mouth to speak again, but the waitress showed up with the food and placed her meal in front of her. She did the same with Nathan, then refilled his coffee cup and looked down at both of them. "You all need anything else?"

Neither one of them said a word, and finally Nathan shook his head. The waitress shrugged and walked away.

The chocolate chip pancakes on Nathan's plate seemed to mock him now as they lay there. He considered sending them back, then remembered why he had ordered them in the first place, and began to cut off a small piece. As he put his fork in his mouth, he looked out of the window again, and wished his father were there to comfort him.

By the time Nathan had finished high school, in 1971, Thomas Freeman had moved he and Martha out from the one-room apartment. They now lived in a multi-level house on a street known for its affirmative action success stories. Black lawyers and doctors, politicians and scholars all walked briskly with their heads down to the ground whenever Thomas Freeman emerged from his dwelling. His reputation had reached his neighbors long before his Cadillac found its way into the driveway.

"I want my son around smart black folks! Folks that ain't got to do what I got to do to survive!"

Nathan's father had been insistent, but it was unnecessary. There was no one to oppose him. The hardened voice that demanded respect from fellow criminals had long since gone unquestioned in the Freeman household. Those who knew anything at all about the family knew that this was not on account of fear, for Martha Freeman had garnered a reputation of her own when the circumstances called for it. Both she and her husband were fervent about shielding their son from the non-pleasantries of his daddy's career. Instead, it was blind trust that kept Thomas Freeman's words etched in stone. On more than a few occasions he had demonstrated to his associates that his only loyalty was to his family, and he would not hesitate to sacrifice his life, their lives, or money belonging to either, to ensure that his wife and son's best interests were looked after.

It wasn't long before Thomas' associates realized that keeping his family safe was in their best interest as well.

In 1967, with the Black Panther Party becoming the new heroes of the streets, and Nathan starting his first year of high school, the growing son decided to see if his father was ready to let him go.

"No." It rolled off of his father's tongue effortlessly, as if it required no thought, only natural instinct.

"But, Dad, they're opening up a chapter a few blocks away! You've got to let me join!"

Thomas paused for a moment. The fact that his son was pushing the issue was not lost on him. The patriarch couldn't remember it happening in recent history.

"We moved up here so you could get a good education, not so you could run around with some hotheaded niggas and get yourself killed."

"They aren't hotheaded niggas, Dad! They're our comrades! They're brothers who are tired of The Man running all over them!"

"You sound exactly like one of those idiots! One of 'em has been trying to recruit you?"

"No, but I've been listening to what they're saying and they make sense! They make a lot of sense! The police being an army to control people of color in this country, the ghetto being set up for black people to kill each other. It all makes sense, Dad!"

"Okay, the kids talk a good game, I'll give 'em that. But when black folks make too many waves in this country, they get killed. Period. You saw what happened to that red-headed Muslim nigga, right?"

"You mean Malcolm X?"

"Yeah, him. They shot him right in front of his woman and kids! And got other Muslim niggas to do it, too! And you think these Black Panthers gonna last long? Hell, I give 'em a year, two max. In the meantime, you'll be in school, usin' that brain of yours to get you into somebody's college somewhere. I'll be damned if you end up shot 'cause of some black power nonsense."

"Dad, you're not even listening to me…"

"I said NO!"

Nathan was stunned. His father had never yelled at him before, and tears came to his eyes as he debated whether or not to walk away.

Thomas' face wouldn't show it, but he stunned himself as well. His son was following the news and reading the papers when other adolescents were outside playing ball. Nathan was well aware of what was going in the world, and he feared the day he would decide to become a part of it.

"Look, son, I'm…"

"Dad, I know what you do."

Thomas turned and looked at Nathan, whose glossy eyes had dried over and were now set hard and tight.

"What are you talking about?"

"I know what you do. I'm not stupid. You and Mom try to hide it, but I know. Most of the junkies in this city get high off your drugs. The money that you used to buy this house, and our cars, and Mom's clothes, you got all of it illegally. You kill people if they get in your way, or don't pay you your money, or make you mad on the wrong day. And most of those people, if not all of those people, are black. I know what you do, Dad. I'm not stupid."

This time it was Thomas' eyes that glossed over as he turned away from his son. He took five or six deep, deliberate breaths, but his voice was still shaky when he spoke again. "I realize you're not stupid, son. You came out of your mother's belly smarter than I'll ever be. I was stupid for thinkin' I could hide it from you."

"I'm not mad at you. I remember the apartment we lived in when we first moved up here. I remember how broke we were. You did what you had to do. But you always say that you don't want me to live your life. You always say you want me to be better than you. And that's what I'm trying to do, Dad. The Panthers, they don't have all the answers, but at least they're trying. They're trying to make things better. And I wanna try to as well."

Thomas turned and looked at his son again. The sight of his father crying made Nathan's knees buckle, and he sat down in the seat beside him, trying to maintain his composure. Thomas' voice cracked and scraped as he spoke.

"Do you know what I would do if anything happened to you, Nathan? Do you know how many people in this city would die? I can't lose you, son. If they kill you, they have to kill me, too."

"I won't get into anything dangerous. I won't even wear the berets. I won't use any guns; I won't yell at any cops. All I want to do is help them. Maybe write some articles and help with information; that's it. If it gets too hot—"

"I'll pull you out! And if that happens, it's no questions asked. I tell you to leave, you leave! You got it?"

"Yes, sir."

Thomas wiped his eyes and shook his head as he reached out and poured a glass of whiskey. "Damn, boy. I ain't got enough on my plate without being worried about you every second of the day?"

"You wouldn't be my father if you weren't worried about me."

"Naw, I guess I wouldn't."

Three nights later, Thomas' Cadillac pulled up in front of a small, storefront property in between the local delicatessen and pawnshop.

"This used to be Moe's old place," Thomas remarked as the driver opened up his door to let him and Nathan out. "They must be renting the spot since he died."

The sun had long since set, and the space was the only one on the block with the lights still on. Steel chains and closed signs decorated all the other establishments. Two young, black men, with black berets and leather jackets, stood inside the empty space, unpacking boxes and talking. Thomas recognized one of them from the local pool hall. The guys called him Dash because he ran track in high school. Thomas had no business with him, which meant he kept himself clean. Comforted, the father walked with his son up the stairs and in the door.

"Hey, man, who the hell are you?"

The other man looked about Dash's age, but was taller and had a darker complexion. He stared at Thomas with cold eyes. Dash had picked up a box and was moving it to the shelf in the back of the room. By the time he could set it down to see what the commotion was about, his companion had moved the right side of his jacket to the side to flash the pistol handle sticking out from his trousers at Thomas, who grinned menacingly as the whites of his eyes began to gray.

"This here is the new headquarters for the Black Panther Party for Self-Defense! Identify yourself, goddammit!"

When Dash saw who his colleague was talking to, all the color ran out of his face. He leapt across the room to place himself in between the two men. "Mr. Freeman! Mr. Freeman, he just got here, sir! Maurice…he just got here! Just three days ago! He don't…he don't know who you are! He don't know, sir!"

Thomas lowered his head and spoke in a tone that sounded like a low growl. For Nathan, fear came involuntarily. "Well, then maybe you should tell him."

Understanding the importance of his task, Dash nodded vigorously at Thomas, and then turned very slowly to face Maurice. "Look, Maurice…go in the back, okay? I'll explain everything in a minute…go in the back…"

"Hell no! This is our spot now, and we gotta protect it! We can't just let—"

"MAURICE, GODDAMMIT, GET IN THE BACK OF THE ROOM! RIGHT NOW!"

The wide eyes and frantic yelling let Maurice know he had stumbled onto something he may not have been ready for, and he slowly retreated to the rear, keeping his eyes on Thomas the whole time. Thomas' grin faded as Dash approached him slowly.

"Mr. Freeman...Mr. Freeman, I'm so sorry...that will never happen again, I swear..."

"My son is here with me, Dash. If he had pulled that gun out from his pants..."

"I know, I know, sir, and I thank God that he didn't! This was all just one big misunderstanding! He got here a few days ago from Oakland, sir...he don't know how things work around here yet..."

Dash fidgeted around with his hands and shuffled his feet as Thomas and Maurice continued to stare at each other from a distance. Finally, Dash took a sheepish step forward and leaned in to Thomas as close as he was willing to risk. "Mr...Mr. Freeman, please don't kill him..."

The request shook Thomas out of his hateful stare. He looked down at his son, and then back up at Dash with his face slightly softer. "I'm not gonna kill him."

Dash breathed a heavy sigh of relief as he wiped his forehead with palm. "You...you want to sit down, Mr. Freeman?"

"Sure. Why not?"

Dash quickly went over and grabbed three folding chairs that were leaning against the wall. He set Thomas' and Nathan's up first, and waited for them to sit before folding his down as well. Still a bit nervous, he kept on the balls of his feet as he sat, unsure of whether or not he'd need to jump back up and save his own life.

"So…umm…what brings you down…down here to see us, Mr. Freeman?"

"You know my son, don't you, Dash?"

"Yeah, Lil' Nathan. Everybody knows Lil' Nathan."

Nathan cocked his head curiously to the side. "They do?"

Thomas looked at his son, and Nathan decided to keep quiet for a while.

"My son found out somehow about your new, um, office here, and he's decided he wants to join."

"Join who? Us? The Panthers?"

"No, he wants to join the circus, Dash. Why the hell else would I be here?"

Dash took a moment to make sure the sarcasm wasn't dangerous, and then looked over at Nathan. "I don't know, sir. I mean, I'm sure he's a great kid, but he looks kinda young. The Panthers ain't no place for little kids."

"Yeah, I know. I heard stories about some of the hell ya'll niggas causin' out West. If it was my choice, he'd be home readin' a dictionary right now. But he's growin' up, and I gotta start to let him make his own decisions."

"I understand that, Mr. Freeman…but, maybe this isn't the right organization to experiment with the boy's independence. I mean, we goin' head to head against cops, sir…"

"You damn straight!" Maurice eavesdropped from the back of the room, and shouted his agreement with Dash.

Thomas looked at the newcomer, and then at Dash, who was back on the balls of his feet again. "You better tell him to shut up."

Dash quickly turned back to his partner. "Maurice…"

"Yeah, I got it, man."

Reluctantly, the Panther fell back against the wall again, and Dash turned back to Thomas. "Like I was saying, Mr. Freeman, we goin' up against cops…"

"But that's not all you're doing."

Nathan's comment caught them both unaware, but Dash's curiosity got the best of him. "What you mean, lil' man?"

"Your ten-point program. You're not just going up against cops—you're trying to get jobs and houses for black people. You're trying to get black people to not have to be drafted in the military, and to get the schools to teach the truth about American History, and to get black people released from prison, right? Isn't that what you guys are trying to do?"

Dash looked back at Maurice, who was inching his way forward from the back wall. When Thomas noticed him, he took the pistol out from his pants and placed it on the stack of boxes beside him.

"The little brother's been doing some research, huh?"

"Look…" Thomas leaned forward, ignoring Maurice and focusing on Dash. "This boy right here is smarter than the three of us combined. He can't do anything but help your lil group here. If it gets too hot, I'll be the first to come and pull him out. But in the meantime, I want you to give him a shot. He won't be holding no guns, he won't be wearing no funny black hats. You keep him behind the scenes, working on the little fliers and papers. I promise you, in a month you won't be able to operate without him."

Dash looked back at Maurice again, who was now close enough to look like he was part of the conversation. They nodded at each other before Dash turned back around.

"Our first meeting won't be for another two weeks, Mr. Freeman. We need some time to fix this place up…"

"I can help!" Nathan jumped up from his chair with excitement. "It's only two of you right now, and you'll need all the help you can get. I can come after school tomorrow!"

Dash smiled, impressed with the boy's enthusiasm. "Aight, lil man. Come through tomorrow and we'll put you to work."

Nathan grinned at his father, who couldn't help but smile back.

"Your mother is gonna kill me, boy. Go on out and wait in the car. I'll be right there."

Nathan ran out the door, leaving the three men eyeing each other silently in the space. Dash rose up to the balls of his feet again.

After about thirty seconds, Thomas broke the silence. His voice was heavy and strained as he spoke. "Dash, that's my son. That's my only son."

"I'll take personal responsibility for him, Mr. Freeman. Like you said, if things get too hot, he's out."

Thomas nodded contently, and then stood up and stretched. Nonchalantly, he strolled over to Maurice. "What did you say your name was again?"

"Name's Mauri—"

Before he could finish, Thomas had pulled out a small, short bladed knife and shoved it through his cheek. He used his free hand to muffle Maurice's screams so Nathan wouldn't hear them.

Dash was shocked, but not surprised. He stumbled out of the chair he sat in and scolded himself for not anticipating the turn of events.

"Shut up! Shut up!" Thomas hissed in Maurice's face as his muffled screams tried to grow louder. His victim wasn't listening, so Thomas yanked the blade down another two inches. "Shut up, or I'll slice your whole goddamn cheek in half!"

Maurice couldn't see through the blinding pain, but he could hear fine. He did his best to quiet down.

"Anybody else had flashed a gun at me, I'd pull their nuts out through their throat. Consider yourself lucky, boy. You'll go to the hospital and get bandaged up, and in a few weeks you'll be good as new with a scar to brag to the ladies about. My son is the only reason you still alive right now. But make no mistake about it, panther or no panther, you ever speak to me like that again, and you'll eat a bullet. You understand?"

Maurice nodded his head as best he could, and Thomas yanked the blade out of his cheek. He collapsed to the floor with both hands over the new wound.

"Dash, go on and get him to the hospital. Keep a cloth on his cheek and put pressure on it so he don't lose too much blood. I'll see ya'll tomorrow when I come and pick up my son."

Thus began a year and a half of memories that Nathan would never forget. He would've been content with just the conversations that he, Dash, and Maurice would have while setting the new head-quarters up, but word spread fast about the new revolutionaries in town. The local media had been reporting about the gun-toting vigilantes in California, and quickly discovered the new hometown office. Pictures of Dash and Maurice, in their black jackets and berets, began appearing on watch lists around the city, and their infamy made them heroes of the streets before they could officially begin operations.

None of that mattered, though. Even with their newfound fame, the police had still devised a plan to prevent them from ever opening. It had been decided in a smoke-filled room that a Black Panther presence was not wanted in the city, and that the problem should be taken care of. It wasn't until one especially attentive detective noticed that in almost all of the surveillance photos, there was an adolescent boy following the two men around. In most of the pictures his image was cut off, as if he was staying just far enough behind the two men to miss having his image captured. There was only one clear image of the boy's face, however, and the detective brought them to Captain O'Leary, who had planned to ignore the images until a stone in his gut forced him to ask for one.

O'Leary took a long look at the picture, and shook his head as he reached in his bottom drawer and pulled out a bottle of Pepto-Bismol. Taking a swig, he sat it down by the telephone before picking up the receiver and dialing a number he made sure the detective didn't see.

"Yeah, this is O'Leary. We gotta call it off. I'll call you back with details." Hanging up the phone, he looked back up at his confused detective. "I should promote you, son. You know who that kid is?"

"No idea, Cap. Should I?"

"That there is Nathan Freeman. That's Thomas Freeman's little boy."

"The Thomas Freeman?"

"Yep. And you probably just prevented this city from goin' straight to hell. Takin' out two loudmouthed niggers is one thing. Going to war with Thomas Freeman is somethin' altogether different. Hell, he's got some of the guys in this office on payroll! We've gotta rethink this. Operation is off until further notice."

Three weeks later, the headquarters opened to a line of black upstarts going out the door and around the corner, and little thirteen-year-old Nathan Freeman officially had his own reputation. Every pamphlet that was written was either done entirely by Nathan or edited and approved by him. Dash and Maurice gave him all of their speeches to look over before they delivered them, and every once in a while, when the police got too close to comfort, Thomas Freeman, who did in fact have people in the department on payroll, would drop a tip to his son at the table before bed.

The Panthers became untouchable, the police department

became frantic, and Thomas Freeman grew a head of gray hair. He contemplated making his son leave the organization more than he remembered to brush his teeth, but he also watched as his son became an icon. He didn't have to ask his men to watch over Nathan anymore. Instead, there was an army of Panthers that went with Nathan everywhere, and would gladly take a bullet for the teenager.

Nathan had become more powerful than Thomas ever could, and Thomas often considered the irony. He even had to let some of the men who worked for him go, as the Panthers had convinced so many addicts to get clean that business had taken a small hit. Thomas didn't care, though. Seeing his son help lead an army was worth going broke over, and he had more white clients than black ones anyway.

For nineteen months, Thomas idolized his son as Nathan helped to lead a movement. Which is why, on one frigid spring evening, the proud father stood outside of the Panther headquarters for a half-hour, dreading what he had to do. There was a meeting going on inside, of the top officials in the organization, and his son was in there with them. Throwing his fifth cigarette butt to the ground, Thomas slammed his hand on the top of the Cadillac, scaring the driver waiting for him behind the wheel. Shaking his head, he walked up the steps and into the building.

The meeting went silent. There were ten men in the room, three of whom Thomas didn't recognize, although they were wearing the Panther uniform. They began to reach for their guns, but Maurice quickly held his hand out, signaling them to stay cool. The fear in his eyes and scar on his cheek convinced them to obey.

Nathan took one look at his father and jumped up, dropping the pad and paper that sat in his lap. "Dad...what's wrong?"

"I'm pulling you out." Nathan began to protest, but the look on his father's face made him stay quiet. Thomas turned and looked at the other members in the room. "Ya'll may not know this, but I been yo' guardian angel and—"

"We...we know, Mr. Freeman," Dash cut him off, making sure to sound respectful in the process. "Nathan never had to tell us how he always knew the pigs were setting us up. We never wanted him to. But we always knew, sir."

"Good. Then listen to me now, and listen good. I got a guy on the force, white guy, owes me his right and left legs. I seen this guy three times in the past week, and each time he tell me the same story. I ain't wanna believe him. Then today, he comes to find me, and tells me it's going down soon. Real soon. He says he's never seen anything like it. I looked in that white boy's eyes, and I came straight here. I gotta take my boy home."

All the men in the room looked around at each other, afraid to ask the inevitable.

"Wh...what is it, Mr. Freeman?" Dash swallowed hard. "What did he tell you?"

"They got orders passed down from Washington. They takin' you boys out. No questions, no arrests, no courts...they got the green light from D.C., where they don't give a damn about you or me. Here, Oakland, and everywhere else they got the Panthers set up. The United States government jus' put a target on ya'll backs. They ain't stoppin' 'til all ya'll dead."

Nathan shook his head in disbelief. "No...no, they can't. They can't do that! What about due process? What about our rights? What about...?"

"They don't give a damn about yo' rights, son! Don't you see? Niggas like me can live forever, for all they care! But ya'll...ya'll disturbin' the natural order of things! White folks is on top, and black folks is at the bottom! It's the way it's always been! Da hell did ya'll think...you was gonna start tellin' black folks to fight back against whitey and they was just gonna stand there and let you niggas do it?"

Nathan stared at his father in disbelief. "Dad..."

"No, you let me talk now, son! I ain't got your brain, and I ain't gon' never have your brains. But what I do got is some common sense. I been livin' here on this Earth longer than each an' every one a' ya'll. And I'ma tell you somethin' that ain't none a' ya'll figured out yet. White folks is some evil bastards. They as evil as they ever gon' come in this world. And here you is thinkin' that jus' cause a few of 'em callin' themselves friends of black folks, and spittin' all this civil rights talk, that they really on yo' side? All King did was sing gospel songs and get beat upside the head, and they shot him off a goddamn balcony! And you think you can run 'round here with guns cursin' at the police and they just gon' pat you on da back and tell you to keep on fightin'? White folks ain't never gon' give this country up! Never! If you knew that... if you really knew that, then you wouldn't be surprised at all from what I jus' told you. But you young, and you stupid, and you got hope in somethin' that ain't there. You hopin' for somethin' that don't exist."

Dash fought back tears as he stood up from his seat. "What if we don't believe that, Mr. Freeman?"

Thomas Freeman looked at Dash, and then around to each of the other men sitting in the room. Sadly, he grabbed his son around the shoulders. "You boys is better men than I'll ever be. I want ya'll to know that. But facts is facts, and they gon' kill you."

"Then help us, Mr. Freeman!" Maurice jumped up from his seat as well. The feeling of dread was palpable in the room. "Help us!"

Thomas shook his head. Remorse was etched into his face. "I'm selfish, son. I'm sorry. I love my boy more than life itself. I love my boy more than I love your people. If I help ya'll, he stays in danger, and I can't let that happen."

As Thomas led his son out of the door, he stopped and turned back to the group of men sitting in the room. Forced to come to terms with their own mortality, they all sat quiet and afraid to move. "My advice to you boys is to run. Close up shop, split up, get out the city. I can make sure ya'll get wherever you gotta go, easy."

The young men looked around at each other, but they already knew their answers. Dash cleared his throat as he spoke through his own emotions. "That's not how the Panthers do things, Mr. Freeman. That's not what we're about."

Thomas dropped his head slightly. "I know."

Nathan couldn't help it anymore. He had spent almost two years with a group of men, and weak emotions weren't welcome. Looking at his friends sitting in that room, with death sentences looming over their heads, was enough to remind him of something that he and every other Panther member had long since forgotten. It was enough to remind him that he was still only fourteen years old.

He leaped out from under his father's hands, straight toward Dash. But Thomas Freeman knew his son too well. He quickly sprang forward with him and wrapped his forearm under his belly, stopping him in midair.

"NO!!! NO!!! DASH!!! MAURICE!!! I WANNA DIE A PANTHER!!! I WANNA DIE WITH YOU!!! DON'T LET HIM DO THIS!!! I'M A PANTHER!!! I'M A PANTHER!!! DASH!!! MAURICE!!! PLEASE!!!"

Nathan fought against his father's grasp, swinging and clawing to get back to the rest of the Panthers, but his fourteen-year-old body wasn't up to the task. His father held him off the ground with one arm as he began making his way out the door.

Dash and Maurice both turned their heads away. They knew, as did Nathan, that tears weren't welcome, and so they shed them silently, with faces tight and stiff with pain.

Nathan fought with the insanity of a child being taken from his home. He fought blindly, and screamed until his words were an incoherent mixture of tortuous sounds. When he and Thomas finally made it into the car, Nathan smashed his fist so hard against the window in the back of the Cadillac that it shattered before Thomas could pull him back. Nathan couldn't feel the blood coming from his fist. He couldn't feel his eyes changing either, the whites going from a light gray to dark brown. And he was fighting too hard to feel the match in his gut trying to ignite and give Toby life again. He could only feel his father wrapping him up in his arms. Thomas squeezing him, almost suffocating him, robbing him of air to let him know how much he loved him, and his son's eyes began to lighten as his suit jacket muffled Nathan's cries, and the match within him was smothered.

Within a month, all the Panthers were dead. Dash was shot in a police raid as he tried to run out of his back door, and Maurice took out six officers in a shootout before his body was riddled with over one hundred bullets. One of the only distinguishing marks left on his body was the scar on his cheek.

Nathan didn't speak to his father for months, and the silence ate at Thomas Freeman like termites on rotten wood.

Nathan had become a legend. The black students at his high school made a basketball jersey with Panther on the front and his name on the back, and petitioned the school board until the Superintendent conceded to it being hung up in the school gymnasium, despite him never having played a sport. He didn't talk very much after the massacre of the Panthers, but he rarely went anywhere without a group of people following him.

Thomas Freeman continued doing business, but it wasn't the same. The drug fiends now gave him looks of shame from the alleys they had collapsed in. And his son was killing him. Nathan would nod his thank-yous and appreciation, maintaining the respectfulness that was always his nature, but the only time Thomas ever heard Nathan's voice was when he overheard him speaking to someone else. The silence began to drain the life out of Thomas' body.

Nathan spent two years in a wilderness. Instead of trees, there were flashes of a time when he and his friends laughed and joked and debated and argued, and he couldn't find his way out. It wasn't until he had almost graduated, until distinguished-looking men, both black and white, whom he did not know, began coming to his house with college paraphernalia, that he realized there was a whole other world that he had yet to enter.

It hit him flush on the cheek during a trip that his parents convinced him to take. One of the sophisticated men who'd visited his home offered to take him to campus for a weekend, and Thomas volunteered him before he could refuse.

Two hours. That was all that stood between the world he knew, and an alternate universe, complete with books big enough to have to be carried one at a time, and people smart enough to understand them. A universe full of professors and scholars, debates and arguments and opinions. A world that he never knew existed.

And suddenly, Nathan understood why his father had pulled

him out of the Panthers. He understood why he would risk the hate of his own flesh and blood to make sure that he stayed alive. Thomas Freeman knew this world existed, and knew that he could never be a part of it. But his son was made for it. Tailored out of his mother's womb. And the hate of his son was a small price to pay to ensure he ended up where he belonged.

Nathan arrived home late on a Sunday night, knowing he couldn't live in his memories anymore. He waited until his parents were in a deep sleep, and snuck out to the cemetery. He wept over Dash's grave, with only the stray cats and a homeless man to hear him, and he said goodbye to the Panthers for the last time. Then he went home and fell asleep.

When he awoke in the morning, he had forgiven his father.

On commencement day, black folks with no children came out to watch Nathan Freeman walk across the stage. As valedictorian, he was given fifteen minutes to make his own speech. He only needed five. By the end, the entire auditorium was in tears as he walked off of the stage and into the arms of Thomas Freeman.

"I forgive you, Dad. I love you."

And Thomas knew he could die happy.

"You thinking about your dad?"

Sonya's intuition yanked Nathan back into the present, and it took him a few seconds before he could respond.

"Uh...yeah. How...how did you know?"

"Because that's where you go when things get hard. You go to your dad."

The remainder of their meal was eaten in silence, with Sonya humming gospel tunes and Nathan looking around the restaurant, searching for something he couldn't name. When they were both done, the waitress brought them their check, and Nathan reached into his pocket for his wallet. Sonya looked at him for a moment, trying to remember the man that she had married.

"I'm sorry," she said. "I should have never brought the book up."

"No, I'm sorry. I shouldn't have raised my voice."

Nathan placed the money on the table and stood to put on his coat.

"I have choir rehearsal this evening." Sonya continued to sit. "I'd like it if you could take me. You haven't been to church in so long, and everyone would be happy to see you."

Nathan looked at her. She was still sitting at the table, looking up at him with her eyes wide. He realized that she was searching for something that might not be there anymore, but he couldn't stop her. He didn't want to.

"Alright," he replied nonchalantly. He could see her smiling through the corner of his eye. "Just call me when you're on the way home, so I can get ready. Do I have to stay for...?" He stopped his sentence short, not wanting to ruin the warm feeling between them, despite how artificial it was. "I'll stay for the whole thing," he continued. "Just call before you get home."

Walking out into the parking lot, Nathan spotted a group of young men standing on the sidewalk. Two of them had on hoodies, and the rest had on jackets with different designs on them. One had the image of a smoking gun on the front. Nathan stopped, with Sonya right behind him, and stared at them. He told Sonya to follow him, and walked up to the group. When they noticed him coming the air tensed up, and since none of the guys in the group knew what to expect, they prepared themselves for anything. Nathan reached the group, and the group silently threatened him.

"What's going on?" Nathan looked around at all of them.

"Nothin'," the one with the gun on his jacket finally responded.

"I was wonderin' if I could ask you all a question?"

"What, you need directions or somethin'?"

"No, nothing like that. I was wondering if you all ever heard of a book?"

"A book?" The group relaxed, and the men began to chuckle. "You came ova here to ask us 'bout a book?"

"Yeah, a book. It's called *The Seven Days*. You ever heard of it?"

One of the men in hoodies broke out laughing, and the others followed. After a while, they calmed down, and the man with the gun on his jacket looked at Nathan.

"Naw, dogg." The men in the group continued to smile at each other. "You came to da wrong group a' niggas for dat."

Nathan nodded his head slowly, and turned and walked away.

He and Sonya got to the car and climbed in, with the laughter from the group in the background. Nathan stuck the key in the ignition, but before he started the car he turned and looked Sonya in the eye.

"Do you understand now? Do you see what I'm talking about?"

"Nathan, none of those guys have touched a book in years, baby. They probably can't read."

Nathan placed his forehead on the steering wheel and closed his eyes. "I wish it were that simple for me, baby. I really do."

Sadly, Nathan backed out of parking space and pulled off.

Chapter Four

It was late afternoon. Xavier could tell by the size and angle of the tree shadows that were cast on the ground.

He dropped to the floor and did four sets of one-handed pushups, more out of habit than anything else. Before the show came back on, he glanced up at the clock and realized what time it was. His family would be home sooner than he thought, and he wanted to be completely relaxed and focused on them when they got back. After contemplating for a second, he turned off the television and prepared to go outside for a run. Quickly he changed into a jogging suit and a pair of sneakers. He picked up his iPod, but put it back down again. He wanted to make sure his head was clear, and the music he had in there wouldn't help. Once he felt set, he opened the door and stepped out into his perfect neighborhood, running out to the street.

"Watch out, you black bastard!"

Xavier swiftly turned around, muscles tense and ready, before he saw the car that had pulled up beside him, and relaxed. The solid white Crown Victoria screamed law enforcement to anyone with expertise, and the slightly overweight Latino man in the driver's seat pointed a menacing finger out the window.

"Don't you have a drive-by you need to go pull?"

"I was waiting for your cousin. She told me to tell you she gets in tonight on the bottom of a paddleboat. Meet her at midnight with some Taco Bell."

Both men stared at each other, and then burst into laughter as the man in the car offered his hand through the window. "That was cold, man. I like Taco Bell."

Xavier shook his friend's hand. "What you up to, Chance?"

"Duty calls, man. A detective's work is never done. You?"

"Just clearing my head."

"How's the family?"

"Everybody's great. You guys should come by."

"How about Thursday night?"

"Sounds good."

"Alright, then. I gotta run, man. Some idiot in the city decided to rob a jewelry store and shoot the owner."

Xavier laughed and shook his head. "You should really take your job more seriously."

"Believe me, bro, the only way you survive this job is by *not* taking it too seriously. By the way, you ever think about what I said? With your skills, man, I could get you a nice gig."

"You know I can't."

Chance sighed and shook his head in return. "Well, if you ever reconsider, you know where to find me."

"Thanks, man."

As Chance drove off, Xavier saw Mrs. Mayfair from a distance. Her full head of white hair swayed slightly as the wind blew, and formed a beautiful contrast as she tended to her rose garden. Looking up, she saw a dark-skinned man coming down the road, and Xavier could see her face start to form into an ugly, piercing stare. He continued to walk toward her, however, and when she recognized that it was Xavier, she quickly changed her face into a warm smile and called out hello. Xavier smiled back and waved.

It took Xavier a while to realize that his hands were moving. Even after waving to Mrs. Mayfair, and running another few blocks, they fell back into the rhythmic motions of blocks and strikes that had become second nature. He laughed at himself, and then decided to stop fighting his urges. Stopping where he was, he imagined four different attackers with varying heights, builds, and fighting styles, and began executing moves as if they were all there. When he was done, his four imaginary attackers were dead, and he broke into a light sweat. Contented somewhere deep down, he took a step back and relaxed, breathing deeply, and unknowingly hit his head on a low-hanging tree branch.

Instantly he heard Sensei Diop in his head. "Never lose sight of your surroundings."

Though he was alone, Xavier was embarrassed by his mistake. He threw a strong round kick at the branch in retaliation, and it snapped off handily and fell to the ground. Remembering his teacher, Xavier took a seat beside the broken branch, and wished his sensei were there to correct him personally.

It was the beginning of spring, March of 1991, when Xavier walked into the local train station with his knuckles still sore from the previous night. He was stepping into a different world, but he wasn't sensible enough to be nervous yet. Instead he wondered when he'd be able to kill someone legally for the first time.

"Train to the Army barracks will arrive in forty-five minutes!" a heavyset lady thundered through the intercom, but none of the recruits were listening. The guy across from Xavier, a clean-cut white male a few years older, kept a look in his eyes that made it clear a slight breeze would send him back home.

Xavier could smell the fear of many of the men in the room. It was a familiar odor, and he smiled as it welcomed him into the waiting area. It smelled like the air in the ghetto right before someone got shot, when it was too quiet for death not to be around the corner. It smelled like inevitability, Xavier realized, as he looked around the room and concluded that most of these somber-looking white boys wouldn't be alive by this time next year.

Maybe his father was right after all; maybe this wasn't such a bad idea.

There were a group of guys in baggy clothes, mostly black and Latino, standing and making noise at the television in the far corner. The slang and curse words told Xavier they were familiar company, and he dropped his duffel bag and made his way toward the group. There was no doubt that they understood the morbidity of their enlisting as well, but the idea of an early death had been pondered long before the Army came knocking.

"Yo, what the hell ya'll lookin' at over here?"

The closest person to him was a stocky Latino guy in an Adidas jumpsuit. He looked over at Xavier, took a second to size him up, and then pointed at the television.

"You see that black guy on da ground right there? That's Rodney King. You see them white guys standing 'round him? Those is da cops beating the hell out of Rodney King. Any questions?"

Xavier looked up at the television. The image was blurred a bit, but he could make out a black guy on the ground getting kicked and stomped. "Damn!"

"Yeah, they been showin' this all day."

"Ain't nothin' new, though. Cops beat the hell outta me once; broke my hand an' everything."

The Latino guy sucked his teeth as he looked back. "That ain't nothin'! I had a cop take my head an' smash it up against the sidewalk! I was laid up for a month! Still…it's different when they got it on tape like this. The whole damn country seein' it!"

"Yeah, I guess you right."

The two men watched silently as the images of Rodney King's beating continued to flash on the screen.

"So…you ready to die for your country, homie?" the guy asked Xavier.

"Hell no! I'm ready to kill some folks and get paid for it, though!"

Xavier's comment had caught the young Latino off guard, and he struggled to figure out how to respond. Finally, he turned around and held out his hand. "They call me Chance."

Xavier stared at him long enough that he should've dropped his hand and went back about his business, but he didn't. He kept his hand out, and kept staring until Xavier grabbed it. "I'm X."

Satisfied with his new introduction, Xavier tried to pull his hand away, but Chance wouldn't let it go. He looked up and saw that Chance was staring at him intensely. His gaze dug so deep that Xavier had to turn his head away. Uncomfortable, Xavier tried snatching his hand away, but to no avail. Instinctively, he balled up his other fist and began to cock it back.

"X, I ain't no killer."

Xavier stopped his fist from moving. He didn't lower it, as he was still prepared to dislocate something, but Chance's words sparked enough curiosity to make him pause.

"What the hell you talkin' about?"

"I mean, I done a lot of things, and I seen a lot of stuff, but I ain't no killer. My pops ain't no killer either, but he fought in 'Nam. He knows me well enough to know that I'm like him. He tells me first thing I need to do, soon as I step foot on the base, is make friends with a killer. With somebody that got it in they blood. He says that's my best chance of gettin' out this Army alive."

Xavier put his fist down. He now spotted the fear in Chance's eyes. The fear that would disappear once he blinked, replaced by lighthearted humor and crude jokes. He recognized the trait from the people he had grown up with, the ability to hide terror with laughter. To convince everyone you weren't scared. Some of his closest friends had mastered it. Xavier had never needed to.

"So you think I'm a killer?"

"There's somethin' dark in your eyes. I saw it when I shook hands with you. Even if you ain't no killer, I'd much rather be yo' friend than enemy. Feel me?"

It was Xavier's turn to size Chance up, noticing the rival gang colors on his clothing. "You bang?"

"Up until this morning."

"How you know we ain't enemies?"

"We getting ready to go to war, homie. Does it really matter?"

Xavier had to laugh at the irony. "Aight, look, don't worry. I got you. You with me from here on out."

Chance nodded vigorously. "Cool."

Only then did he let Xavier's hand go.

Months later, after they had officially become soldiers, the train station would become a distant memory, and they would both recount it with the same nostalgic pitch in their voices. Their lives changed forever that day, and they began a course that ended with them trusting each other with their lives.

It wasn't until after basic training that Chance and Xavier would learn that they were assigned to the same unit, and ended up deploying together on their first tour of duty. It was there in Kuwait, where the blood mixed with sand and left reminders of murdered friends on your boot, that Chance learned he had been right about Xavier. He wasn't crazy, like some of the other guys in their unit. He didn't scream in the middle of the night, or laugh hysterically when they came under attack. But he was a killer, down to the marrow in his bones.

Chance first noticed it while they were in basic training. He saw the grace with which Xavier could assemble and disassemble a rifle, the quiet joy on his face when he hit a target dead center, and the elegance in his knife strikes as he simulated disemboweling another human being. But Chance chose to ignore it, convincing himself that there was no way his best friend could be that good at something so evil. After being deployed, however, Chance was forced to accept the truth; killing was an art form for Xavier. He delivered headshots to enemy soldiers with a passion that others would use to paint a portrait. He created masterpieces out of dead bodies, and symphonies with his dagger.

The blood of enemies that Xavier had spilt in battle was currency in the military. Upon returning home, he was awarded medals for bravery and outstanding service, promoted to private first-class, and was recommended for Special Forces training.

Chance knew, though he had grown to love Xavier, that he couldn't stay with him. He had never grown accustomed to the numbness a rifle left in your palms after emptying a clip. He would do his next tour of duty without his protector by his side, and would sprint out of the Army's door before the ink could dry nicely on his discharge papers.

Special Forces training may as well have been heaven. Xavier had no idea there were so many ways to kill a man, but learning them made his heart flutter. On Monday of the third week, he was lined up in formation, anticipating the day's events, when he first saw Diop. The man seemed to float on his toes as he walked, as if the laws of gravity refused to challenge his will. The smoothness with which Xavier loaded a gun or unsheathed his blade, Sensei Diop had when he turned his head or shifted his weight. Every one of his movements was poetry.

Captain Talage introduced the stout African as a martial arts specialist, commissioned by the Army to teach advanced hand-to-hand combat to Special Forces units. After a few more introductory words, the captain left, leaving the sensei standing in front of them, and Xavier and the rest of the students stood silent for what seemed like forever before the stocky African spoke.

"None of you will master what I teach. You will not come close. Most of the time you spend with me will be futile, as you will forget as quickly as you learn, paying me the ultimate disrespect. But a man must eat to survive, and as such, I am here. If there are any here who believe I could learn more from you, than you from me, please step forward now."

Xavier couldn't help it. His admiration had turned to annoyance, though he'd grown disciplined enough not to show it. This man wasn't in the Army. He hadn't seen the things Xavier and the rest of his cohorts had seen. Yet he had the balls to stand there and declare what he and his comrades could and couldn't do. Graceful or not, somebody needed to teach this guy a lesson.

With his face set and his chin up, Xavier stepped out from the line. The sensei took note, hiding his surprise, and walked up to Xavier slowly.

"What's your name, soldier?"

"Turner, sir!"

"Your whole name."

"Xavier Turner, sir!"

"Well, Xavier Turner, what is it that you think you can teach me?"

"Respect, sir!"

None of the other students spoke, but Xavier could hear their mouths drop open. The African smiled. "Really?"

"Yes, sir!"

"Would you like to try?"

Xavier fought to stop the grin from crossing his face. "Yes, sir!"

"Very well."

Xavier walked forward and stood in front of the instructor, whose smile faded as he looked back at his upstart of a student.

"Nothing you see, henceforth, ever took place. There will be no retaliation or consequence for anything that transpires, and it shall not be mentioned outside of anyone in this group. Is that understood?"

"Yes, sir!" the trainees responded in unison, and kept their formation, with the exception of their eyes, which stayed glued on the two men moving around in front of them.

Xavier took a quick jab with his right hand. The sensei didn't move. He bounced around a little bit more, warming himself up, and took another jab. Again, the African didn't move.

This isn't so bad, Xavier thought to himself, smiling again, as he threw another jab.

This time, the African did move, and before he could pull his jab back, Xavier's right hand was broken.

Xavier resisted the urge to scream as he stumbled back, with a small piece of bone protruding out near his middle knuckle. He looked up at Diop, who was standing there, emotionless, and his anger began to build. Fueled by the pain, he charged at the instructor, who dodged him easily, grabbed his broken hand, and threw him. He landed hard on his left arm, and the cracking sound caused the fellow trainees to break formation ever so slightly as they cringed.

When Xavier finally made his way back to his feet, his right hand was mangled, and his left arm hung limp at his side. But his eyes had grown two shades darker, and his teeth grinded together as he growled at Diop.

"I will kill you," the instructor said, again, without emotion.

Xavier charged at him, headfirst, ignoring the searing pain that came from both of his arms. When he got close enough, he threw a wild kick at the sensei, who easily caught it, swept his other leg out from under him, and popped his knee out of joint.

The scream came involuntarily as Xavier's leg hit the ground. One of the trainees turned and vomited as Diop walked over to Xavier and leaned down to face him. Before he could speak, Xavier's right hand shot up and grabbed the lapel to the instructor's shirt. The bone coming out of his hand scraped against Diop's face. The awe on his face was evident.

"Why do you continue fighting when it is clear you cannot win?"

Xavier, whose eyes were now a charcoal gray, struggled to keep a grip on Diop's collar as he pulled himself an inch off of the ground. "Go to hell!"

Diop stared at Xavier, pondering deeply, before he grabbed his hand off of his lapel, twisted it until Xavier's arm was exposed, and dislocated his shoulder.

Xavier writhed on the ground for the better part of a minute, forbidding himself to scream again, before he passed out.

When the captain returned, he found the trainees in the same formation that he'd left them, with their faces chalk white, Sensei Diop sitting with his legs crossed on the dirt, deep in thought, and what looked to be a dead trainee on the ground. "Jesus Christ, what the hell happened here?"

"Nothing, sir!" all of the trainees responded in unison.

"Excuse me?"

"Nothing, sir!"

The captain eyed the trainees, and then looked over at Diop. "Is he dead?"

"No."

"Is he going to die?"

"No."

"Torrez! Brown! Get him up and to the goddamn medic! The rest of you got five miles for playing stupid!"

"Yes, sir!"

"Move!"

Two of the soldiers began to gently lift Xavier, as the rest began running in formation down the road. Before the captain could leave, Diop stood back up. "Captain!"

"Yeah?"

Diop pointed to Xavier. "I want him with me."

The captain looked at Xavier, whose head hung limp as the two men got him off of the ground. "That boy's broke in more pieces than a jigsaw puzzle! What the hell do you want with him?"

"I want to train him."

"Okay, so train him! Train him and every other man in this camp! That's what you're here for, ain't it?"

Diop walked up to the Captain, who tried to keep his composure. "I want him with me. Let me train him, or find another instructor."

The captain looked from Diop to the unconscious Xavier, and then back to Diop. He lowered his voice as he leaned forward. "This ain't no gay stuff, is it?"

Diop clenched his fist. "I don't know. Ask me once again, and we shall see."

Captain Talage heard the slight change in Diop's voice, which was enough to make him think twice about restating his question.

"Okay, fine. Take him. From what I can see, it's gonna be about six months before he'll be any good to anybody anyways."

"I'll worry about that."

Talage nodded and ran off after the unit, while Diop followed Torrez and Brown as they carried Xavier to the infirmary.

Two days later, a groggy Xavier woke up in a hospital room within the nearby Army medical center. He tried to pull himself up, only to find that both of his arms and one of his legs were in some type of restraints. It would take the sedative to wear off a bit more for him to realize that his restraints were casts.

Moaning, he shook his head back and forth, trying to make some sense out of what was going on.

"Try and rest."

The African accent caused Xavier's eyelids to shoot open.

"What...what...?"

"Again, try and rest. You're under a heavy sedative. There will not be much that makes sense right now."

Xavier wanted to react, but the few words he'd managed to utter had drained all of his energy. His eyes rolled as he slowly let his head fall back against the pillow. He was asleep before he realized he'd been awake.

The next day wouldn't be so peaceful. Under a lower dose of the sedative, Xavier awoke and proceeded to call for the attendants to let him out of his casts. Diop sat quietly as the nurses explained to him that his right hand and shoulder, his left arm, and his right knee were all broken, and he would likely be in his casts for the next two to three months.

When they left, Xavier glared at the African, who sat in the same spot that he had the day before. "What the hell are you doing here?"

Diop paused, and then leaned forward in his chair as he spoke. "Did you know that your eyes grow darker as you get angrier? That doesn't happen to many people."

"Damn that! What the hell are you doing here?"

Diop breathed deeply as he paused, as if trying to meditate. His calmness had no effect on Xavier.

"I said, what the hell are you doing here, man?"

"I'm going to train you."

Xavier began laughing, but stopped as the pain began radiating from his arms. "You're outta your mind."

"Maybe. But your eyes grew dark. Very dark. I saw them."

"So what? My eyes got dark when I got mad, so what? They've been doing that since I was a kid! I still don't know why the hell you're here!"

"I told you, I'm going to train you."

"Train me to do what?"

Diop sat back in his seat and let the question linger in the air. It took Xavier a while to realize he wouldn't be getting an answer to his question, and by then he had begun to grow tired.

"You broke both my arms and my leg, you prick."

"Do you know another way to get a warrior to listen?" The words sat on Xavier's chest as Diop leaned forward once again. "Warriors do not listen. They react. They fight. That is what makes them warriors. Many only take heed when they realize their defeat. Few fight despite its inevitability."

Diop stood up and walked over to Xavier's bedside. "You fought, even when you knew you were beaten. Even when you knew death was imminent. You fought."

"So what?"

Diop looked down into Xavier's tired eyes. "I will not force you to be my student. That is not how it works. But you are a warrior, and warriors hate to be beaten. I can make it so that you will never be beaten again. That is my offer to you. Think about it. I will see you tomorrow."

Diop turned and walked out the door, and Xavier fell asleep

with those words in his ears. They would bounce around his dreams that night, causing him to toss and turn, wake and fall back to sleep. And in the morning, as the sunlight forced its way through the dingy window and Diop's silhouette came gliding back into the room, they would linger still, tugging at him, forcing him to accept his new mentor's offer.

"How do you plan to train me if I'm stuck in a goddamn bed for the next three months?"

Diop sat back down in the seat beside the bed, opening a bag he'd brought with him. "This time will be the most important part. This is the time when we align your mind with your spirit. First, we must identify where your anger comes from. Anger is the enemy of the warrior."

"Whatever. I got nothing else to do. What you wanna know?"

Diop reached into his opened bag, rummaged around, and emerged with a book that he placed on the table. Xavier could turn his head enough to make out the title and furrow his brow. "What the hell is *The Seven Days*?"

The African stared at the book for a moment, and looked back at Xavier. Excitement jumped in his eyes. "Tell me about your father."

It took Xavier the full three months to heal from his broken bones, but by then he had completely lost track of the time. He stepped out of the doors to the infirmary and soaked in sunlight with a new appreciation. Diop had spent the better part of Xavier's healing by his bedside, molding and shaping his perceptions, strengthening his mind, and dulling his emotions. Only physically was Xavier the same person. In every other way, he was someone else.

"I feel lost," he told Diop as they were walking away from the medical building. "I feel like I'm stepping into a new world."

"The world has not changed, Xavier."

"I know, I know. But I feel like it has. What do I do?"

"Continue your training."

In the months that Xavier had been in the medical center, the Special Forces instructors realized how effective Diop's instruction had become. Hand-to hand combat and weaponry effectiveness had increased noticeably during training exercises, and the first of Diop's students, who had since completed training and gone active, had come back reporting that their units had requested instruction in the same tactics and techniques. So when Diop approached Captain Talage with a request that most would have found ridiculous, he decided to ask General Morris, who was over Operations, before he laughed in Diop's face.

"You do whatever you want, Captain, but I'll tell you this…if every class of graduates that come from your facility are the same quality as the last one, then you may have a promotion coming down the line. If that African is the reason your folks have the hand-to-hand skills that they possess, I'd keep him on board and keep him happy."

Before Xavier could inquire about where they were going, the jeep that had picked them up pulled in front of a shabby warehouse at the edge of the facility. Xavier followed Diop out and up to the entrance, and walked inside after his teacher to find that the warehouse hadn't been abandoned at all. The floors were shiny, wooden and cold. There were weights in the corner, punching bags hanging from the ceiling, and weapons of every kind, from katana swords to semi-automatic pistols, placed along the walls.

"What is this?" Xavier looked around the space in awe.

"This is where we will live. From here forward, you will eat, sleep, and breathe combat. Not because you're angry, but because it will be a way of life."

"How can I make fighting my way of life and not be angry?"

"I will teach you. But you must trust me. Anything I ask you to do is for a reason, and those who trust do not question. Do you understand?"

"Yeah, I understand."

For the next six months, Xavier followed a tortuous routine. He spent entire days learning and perfecting techniques—right and left punches, knees, and elbows, and right and left front kicks, round kicks, side kicks, and back kicks. Any in-between time was spent doing pushups, sit-ups, squats, and crunches, and after regaining his wind, Diop sent him back into the striking repetitions. After six months had passed, Diop began teaching Xavier ground techniques—takedowns and throws, chokes, arm locks and leg locks, and he drilled those along with the standing techniques for the following six months.

It wasn't until a full year had passed that Diop began inviting others to train with his student. He had handpicked soldiers from different bases who were known for their hand-to-hand combat skills, many of whom were considered masters in their respective martial art, and requested their participation.

"You know the basics," Diop told Xavier as he stood in front of a well-built soldier who was clearly ready for a fight. "Now you must learn how to use them."

Xavier didn't know who he was fighting, only that he was getting pummeled repeatedly. After a particularly bad beating, he began to feel the fire start to rise within his stomach again. He jumped up from the floor as his eyes began to darken, and immediately Diop jumped in front of him.

"Let your anger go, Xavier! It will not help you in this situation. Use what you know, not what you feel!"

It took what felt like forever to Xavier, but he began to learn about the importance of timing, of not only knowing how to strike, but knowing when to strike, when to duck, when to dodge, and when to block. He began to realize that each strike had its own personality, its own way of being, and he began reading both the attack and the attacker.

Another year had gone by before Xavier realized he wasn't losing anymore, but by then it didn't matter. By then, each fight was a poem, a symphony of movements that had to be conducted exactly the right way. The fight was the work of art; victory was the frame.

"It's time for you to begin learning weapons," Diop declared as another martial arts specialist limped out of the warehouse.

Xavier looked around at all the instruments on the wall. "Which one?"

Diop smiled. "Any one. All of them. Weapons are nothing but an extension of yourself. A frying pan can be as effective as a gun, if you've learned to master yourself. Master yourself, and weapons come naturally."

"All that's fine, but I'll start with the guns. I'm not trying to take a knife into a gunfight, you know?"

Diop shook his head and laughed. "I've seen a man with a knife win a gunfight."

"Yeah, right."

"The problem with soldiers is that they believe guns are essential for victory. They are not. Train with a gun like you train with a sword, and you'll understand."

After another two years, and rumors that went from seeing Xavier knock a man out without hardly moving, to seeing him glide from tree to tree like the old Kung Fu movies, Talage had had enough of Diop's one-man training program going on at the edge of the camp. Having been promoted to major in the years that Xavier had been under Diop, he'd been hesitant to bother the teacher and student. But even General Morris, who had become a major fan of Diop's work with the Special Forces, became skeptical about why Private Turner was allowed to train with Diop for as long as his eldest daughter had been enrolled in her college.

Finally, an opportunity came to put Xavier to the test. It was 1997, and his CIA contact came to visit on a warm, uneventful day, and invited the general to a game of golf. While on the course, heading into the back nine, the wiry agent expressed his need for a man to use for a specific operation. When the agent described the type of person he needed, the general almost jumped out of his seat. He'd met Turner on two different occasions in the last four years, and realized he'd be perfect.

"I've got just the guy you're looking for. Give me a chance to make sure he's as sharp as I've been told he is, and I'll send him straight to you."

General Morris immediately organized a training op for the long-term student in order to see if the four years of Diop's training and government money were worth it. If Xavier passed, he'd be promoted, and recruited for the operation. If he failed, he'd have to undergo Special Forces training again, and the Army would take back the facility it had loaned to Diop. The general sent Major Talage with the news, and although he framed the training op as optional, both Diop and Xavier understood it was mandatory.

Xavier never opened his eyes, just took in a deep breath and exhaled as he spoke. "Sure."

"Alright. The general wants to do it on Friday at nineteen hundred hours. Be at the Pit on time."

"Yes, sir."

Talage wasted no time making his way out of the door.

Diop nodded, and no more was spoken about the impromptu training until Friday at eighteen fifty hours, when they both began making their way to the designated location.

General Morris had one of his specialists to design an examination, and he flew in personally to witness the outcome. It consisted of three parts—close quarter combat was the first; reconnaissance, surveillance, and neutralization was the second; and extraction was the last. Each test took place within the same two-mile radius outside of the training facility, and each consisted of ten highly trained operatives who were told to bring their target back alive, but to treat the situation as a live operation and to consider their target armed and dangerous.

The exam lasted a total of eight hours, and in the end, Xavier was the only participant who left the area on his feet.

"I want four-year training programs set up at our other two training facilities starting immediately!" General Morris declared after witnessing the results. "Diop, you're gonna build me an army!"

"I'm afraid I cannot do that, General."

Xavier and Major Talage both whipped their heads around at the same time, and the general, not used to be being denied, lowered his head and deepened his voice. "Excuse me?"

"I said I cannot do that, General. Training Xavier was my personal choice, and I appreciate the opportunity to do so. But I cannot do the same with anymore of your soldiers. I will continue the same instruction regimen, provided that Private Turner remains stationed at this facility. Otherwise, I will submit my letter of resignation immediately."

Major Talage sprang forward with outrage on his lips. "Now wait a goddamn minute…!"

But the general held his hand out, and the major quieted down as quickly as his shouting began.

General Morris looked from Diop to Xavier, and then back to Diop. "Explain this to me."

"What I taught to Xavier is more than mere combat, General. It is not only a series of techniques, it is a way of living, a way of being. I have poured everything into him, because he is my student, and I am his teacher. I choose not to do that again."

The general stayed quiet as the soundtrack of the forest played around them. Then, unexpectedly, he turned to Diop. "You'll keep training our boys like you've been doing?"

"Yes, sir."

Quickly, he turned back to Xavier. "You still interested in the operation?"

"I don't know anything about it, sir."

"I know that. Are you still interested?"

"Yes, sir."

The general reached into his pocket and pulled out a fresh cigar. "Well, we're contracting you, Diop, which means you got me by the balls here. And we can't afford to lose you. And Christ knows I sent some of the best men we got in there after your boy, and he made it look like a walk in Times Square. So I guess I got no choice." Turning to Xavier, he held out his hand. "Congratulations, son. Welcome to the Agency."

Major Talage couldn't hide his shock. "What? What agency? You mean the CIA?"

"Did you see what he just did, Talage? I think he deserves it."

"I…I've applied for the Agency three times, sir…"

"You wanna fight him for it?"

Talage glanced at Xavier, and dropped his head.

"Alright, it's settled then. Talage, Diop, take a walk for a few minutes. I need to speak with Turner alone."

"Yes, sir!" Talage answered with feigned excitement, while Diop looked back and forth from the general to Xavier. Finally, he began walking toward the warehouse.

When the African was out of earshot, General Morris lit his cigar and turned to Xavier. "This conversation never happened, Turner."

"I understand, sir."

The general puffed on his cigar and watched the smoke dance around in the night sky. "You ever heard of the War on Drugs, son?"

"No, sir."

"Well, it's a mess, I'll tell you that much. Agency's trying to correct some of its mistakes. They were, ah, a bit overzealous with their narcotics operations here in the States."

"Yes, sir."

"Anyway, the agency's trying to right some of its wrongs. They unleashed a monster they couldn't control, especially in the ghettos. That's where you come in. You grew up in the inner city, right?"

"Yes, sir."

"How was it?"

Xavier paused, and found himself at a loss for words. He hadn't thought about where he'd grown up at all in the last few years. He'd blocked it out, along with everything else that tapped into his anger, while training with Diop.

"Never mind." The General chewed the end of his cigar, then puffed on it once again. "Must've been horrible. I can't imagine."

"Yes, sir."

"I'll give it to you straight, Turner. The agency needs someone who can get into ghettos. Someone who knows what it's like to grow up there, and can blend in."

"Why, sir?"

"Like I said, they unleashed a monster they can't control. There are major drug players on the street now that aren't giving their share back to the government, and Uncle Sam can't have that. These thugs are trying to get smart, Turner. We've got to be smarter."

"Yes, sir."

"I don't have all the details. You'll get those tomorrow when you meet your handlers. What I do know is that you'll go into different ghettos with a cover, you'll blend in and fit in, and when the agency gives you the name of a target, you'll take them out. Pretty straightforward, right?"

"Yes, sir."

"Good. Your plane will leave in twenty-six hours. You'll meet your handlers in Langley. Be at the airfield with your things. Don't tell anyone what you're doing or where you're going. If you do, you put them at risk. That includes Diop."

"Yes, sir."

"I'm serious, Turner. The agency doesn't play. They'll just as soon kill you as shake hands with you. Don't tell anyone anything. You understand?"

"Yes, sir, I understand."

"Good. You're dismissed. Good luck."

"Thank you, sir."

Xavier got ready to turn around when the General called out. "Oh, and Turner...!"

Xavier snapped back around to face the superior. "Yes, sir?"

"Make me look good, son."

"Yes, sir."

The sun was beginning to peek through the night sky as Xavier made his way back inside the warehouse. Diop was sitting up, waiting for him, and cut on the lights inside the space as Xavier walked past him.

"Your rib is broken."

Xavier stopped his stride. "How did you know?"

"You're moving different. You mask the pain well, but your rhythm is off."

The student stood still and unmoving, with his back still toward his teacher. Diop shook his head. "I would ask what you're new assignment will be, but you can't tell me."

"No, I can't."

The silence in the room was pregnant. Diop already knew what was coming, but inquired anyway. "You have questions for me, Xavier. What is it?"

Slowly, Xavier turned around to face his mentor. His face was full of emotions he couldn't explain. "Why me, Diop? All the people in this camp, all the people in this army, and you chose to train me? Why?"

Diop nodded expectantly, and invited Xavier to sit on the floor with him as he contemplated his next words. No one else would've noticed the slight grimace on Xavier's face as he lowered himself to the ground with his legs crossed, but Diop was acutely aware. He waited for his student's pain to subside before he began.

"I am from a place on the west coast of Africa, a province named Telemut. That is my home. The tribe of Telemut was once a mighty nation, ruled by wise kings and protected by powerful warriors. When I was very young, I was told that my blood was royal blood; that it traced all the way back to King Amaru, the very last prince my people had before the white men arrived."

"So…you're from an ancient line of warriors?"

"No, it's more than that. It was also said that I shared the blood of Prince Abioye, his son. The last to receive the *doole*—the powers of the ancestors."

"Okay, I'm a little confused."

"There is a legend, that in the royal blood of Telemut lies the *doole*. It is a power that comes from the spirits of those with royal blood who have died before you."

Xavier wrinkled his brow as he shook his head. "You're losing me, Diop."

Exasperated, the African jumped up to his feet and began pacing around the floor. The action was so out-of-character that Xavier almost jumped to his feet as well, thinking there must have been something wrong. When he noticed the seriousness on Diop's face, however, he settled back down on the floor and decided not to speak again for a while.

"I was told that I had a responsibility! That I had to become a great warrior! That I had to master my mind, body, and spirit. If the *doole* chose me, and I wasn't strong enough, it would consume me…but if I was strong enough to control it, then I would amass great power, unspeakable power, and be able to make my people into a great nation once again! So I left Telemut, and I traveled the world, finding warriors on every continent, learning from them, training with them, meditating with them, knowing one day that the *doole* would choose me, and preparing to return my people to greatness…"

"What happened?"

"I returned home after fifteen years, convinced I had learned all that I needed to know. There was a test, a ritual to see if the *doole* had chosen you. It hadn't been done for centuries, but it had been passed down, and the elders of the village knew it. I was tested, and I did not pass."

Xavier could hear the sadness in Diop's voice, and he let the silence convey his apologies.

"Before I was to be tested, I met an American who had been traveling back and forth to Telemut quite a bit. My grandmother spoke of him when I returned, and I encountered him a few days later. His name was Nathan Freeman. He was studying the *doole* for his Ph.D., except he didn't call it that. He called it *The Seven Days*."

"Like the book you have?"

"Yes."

"Why? Why did he call it that?"

"He'd been doing research for quite some time, though he hadn't gotten very far. He didn't speak Wolof and the translators he hired could barely speak English. The most information he was able to get was something about a seven-day process, so he named it *The Seven Days*."

"How did he even know about the *doole*?"

Diop pointed at Xavier as if he'd just solved a case. "That was my question as well! He said that his father had told him about it…that someone in his ancestry named Toby had had it. He believed he was of the royal bloodline as well."

"That doesn't make sense. He wasn't from Telemut."

"So I became very suspicious, and began to follow him. Eventually he invited me to accompany him, as I spoke English much better than anyone he'd hired. I obliged, thinking I could learn something to expose his lies and rid the village of his presence. But the more we learned, the more his theories began to make sense."

"What theories?"

Diop sat back down, facing an intrigued Xavier, before he continued.

"We were able to fill in many holes about the legend, but it took years. We traced people across different villages; found books that most people never knew existed. Finally we got enough information for Nathan to begin to draw some conclusions. The *doole*, we found out, does not come from all the spirits in the bloodline. It only comes from the spirits of those who died in some sort of rage. And so the power of *doole* was limited to the number of spirits fueling it. And when one receives the *doole*, they also take on the personality of the last recipient. So, if Nathan was right, then the next person to receive the *doole* will be taken over by Toby, because he is the last known recipient."

"Taken over? You mean, like, possessed?"

"Yes. In this country, you call it possession."

Xavier closed his eyes and shook his head. "I'm confused again. This sounds like an Aesop Fable. What does all this have to do with why you trained me?"

"Try and understand me, Xavier. Please. I'm telling you this for a reason."

"Okay…"

"We found that Prince Abioye died on a slave ship, one of the first to ever attempt bringing slaves back to the colonies. The legend says he destroyed the ship on his seventh day with the *doole*, which is when it takes full control. But he had siblings on that ship, and all of the slaves did not die. There was another ship that came right behind it, and picked most of them up as cargo. So the bloodline did not die. Instead it came to America. Those with the royal bloodline were among the first of the slaves in this country."

"I don't know anything about any slaves, Diop."

"But Nathan did. He was an expert. According to him, hundreds of thousands of slaves died in a rage in this country. Died being lynched, being shot, castrated, whipped, and the list goes on. His ancestor, Toby, was the only slave to ever get the *doole*, but Nathan believed that there are countless more spirits from the bloodline that died in a rage during slavery than in any time before."

"So if anyone gets the *doole*, they'll be...what?"

"I don't know. But the potential for power is extraordinary. Nathan estimated that, with the breeding of the slaves and the large numbers of children born, there could have been thousands of people with the royal bloodline born during slavery. And that does not include those born afterwards. There's no way to know how many of them died in a rage, but Nathan was convinced it was more than half. People of our bloodline are not known for their passivity."

"You still haven't told me what this has to do with me?"

Diop stared at Xavier. "I was told that I was part of the bloodline after I got angry one day as a boy. I was fighting with another boy in the village, and the elders said they watched as my eyes began to blacken, and they had to knock me unconscious to keep me from killing him. That the black eyes were the sign of the *doole*. It was said that when Abioye received it, his eyes turned to black stones in his head, and when Toby received it, his eyes became black as well."

"So you trained me because my eyes get dark when I get mad?"

Diop smiled, trying to ignore the sarcasm in his student's voice. "Do you remember when I started training you? In the infirmary? Do you remember when I asked about your father?"

"I told you I didn't have one."

"But you do, Xavier. You do have a father. His name—"

"...is Thomas Freeman." Xavier cut his teacher off, feeling the anger begin to burn in his chest. "I know his name, and that was none of your goddamn...!" Xavier stopped, feeling the familiar anger of his childhood, and closed his eyes. He began taking in breaths and attempting to control his anger. When his pulse had died down a bit, he looked back at Diop. "You had no right to go spying on me."

"I'm sorry for going behind your back, but I had to know."

"Know what?"

"Nathan used to tell me about his father when we traveled. He was dying of cancer back in the States, and Nathan spent a fortune calling him every day. His name was Thomas Freeman."

"What are you saying?"

"I'm saying I believe Nathan Freeman is your brother. If that is true, then you are of the royal bloodline, just like him, and just like me. And I saw your eyes myself, that day out on the field. I've never seen anything like it. It was exactly like the elders described. That's why I trained you, Xavier. I believe you have something that I could never have, and I believe I'm the only one who can prepare you for when it comes."

The space grew silent as both men contemplated the information. Diop, relieved from the burden of his long-kept secret, sat anxious to hear Xavier's response. Secretly, he prayed for his pupil to accept the burden, as he had, and dedicate his life to preparing for the inevitable.

"So...you think I'm going to get superpowers from a dead slave?"

Diop's unanswered prayer caused his shoulders to drop. He shook his head and sighed sadly. "You don't believe me."

"Diop, I love you. You're the only father I've ever known. You changed my life. And if this myth is what got you to train me, then I'm grateful for the legend. But you can't expect me to believe it. I mean, it's a great story, but come on..."

Diop stood slowly and began pacing around the space once again. This time his steps were slow and deliberate, and Xavier could see the pain on his face, though he had no idea how to remedy it. He couldn't believe a crazy story simply because it came from Diop.

Just as he was getting ready to stand and get some ice for his ribcage, something that Diop said echoed back in his mind and knocked him back to the floor. "Wait, I have a brother?"

Diop stopped, but kept his back turned to his student. "I only checked the names. I did not check the family histories. It could be a coincidence...but for the record, yes. I think you and Nathan have the same father."

"How...how do I get in touch with him?"

Diop walked over to the corner and crouched down to grab his sack of belongings. "I haven't seen Nathan in years. After he got married and had his son, he began visiting less and less. And when his father finally died, he stopped coming altogether. But he did send me this. It took him years to finally put all the information together."

Diop walked back over to Xavier and handed him the same book he had seen four years ago in the infirmary.

"This? He wrote this?"

"Yes. He took his dissertation on *The Seven Days* and published it."

Xavier gripped the book firmly in his hands. "*The Seven Days*, huh?"

Diop watched as his student examined the book. He watched Xavier flip through the pages and look sternly at the author's photo on the back cover. Finally, he reached out and swiftly took the book back.

"Why did you...?"

"Time has a way of working things out. You're getting ready to embark on some very dangerous work starting tomorrow. You lose focus, and you will die, that I promise you. Forget this conversation. Bury it in your mind. When the time is right, it will come back, and I will do everything I can to help you. But for now, sit down, meditate, and force your mind to forget. Do this, and you will save your own life."

"And what about *The Seven Days*?"

"You don't believe in *The Seven Days*."

"But you do."

"Yes. And if fate should have it that you come to believe as well, then I will not be far behind. But it is easy to forget something that you do not believe. For that reason, I am grateful for your skepticism."

Xavier's life changed so drastically in the next twenty-four hours that the conversation with Diop easily became an afterthought. The idea of *The Seven Days* and Nathan Freeman got lost amongst fake aliases, counter-insurgency tactics and planned assassinations. And when he finally got enough leave to fly back to the training ground to see his teacher, he found that Diop had canceled his contract with the military and left the training camp.

"Bastard didn't even leave a forwarding address," Major Talage spoke as he unlocked the abandoned warehouse and let Xavier in. "Disappeared in the middle of the night."

The tears in Xavier's eyes surprised him as he walked around the warehouse, reminiscing about the only father he had ever known.

Xavier returned to his house, drained from reliving the past. He started to sit down and rest, but glanced at the clock and realized his family would be home any minute. Quickly, he went around the first floor, checking for out-of-place pillows or casual lumps in the rug. He'd become a perfectionist since leaving the agency, throwing all the energy he used to put into covert ops into being the consummate family man. Satisfied, he began to make his way upstairs to continue his inspection, but was held in place by the sounds of tires in the driveway.

It was these times, when Xavier had the privilege of anticipating his children burst through the door, when he was sure he had made the right choice. He stood in the hallway like he always did, braced for his children's impact, and not thinking about the fact that he had never locked his door since moving into the neighborhood.

Felicia blasted through the door first, followed by XJ, and they both ran into their father as if there was a goal line behind him. He withstood their force with ease, and picked them both up, spinning them around. By the time he put them down, Theresa had entered. She stood in the doorway, watching her children squeal, and waited until Xavier had put them down to approach him. He kissed her as if she had been gone for months. Once he pulled away from Theresa, he picked his children up again and carried them into the living room.

A few hours later, the smell of pork chops and mashed potatoes lingered in the air from dinnertime past. Xavier made his way to the sink to wash the dishes, but Theresa shooed him away.

"Go play with the kids." She picked up the dish detergent and opened the top. "That takes energy that I don't have."

Xavier kissed her on the cheek, and walked back over to his children, who were both sitting in front of the television set. They jumped up when they saw their father, pouncing on him once again, and by the time they got tired Xavier had broken a sweat.

"See? I told you." Theresa laughed from the sink.

Felicia and XJ crashed back down to the couch, breathing hard and smiling, before XJ reached for the television remote.

"Daddy, can I change the channel?"

"Sure."

The proud father watched in amazement as his son flipped effortlessly through the television channels, and then turned back to look at his wife.

"When I was little all I knew about the television was that I wasn't supposed to touch it. This boy knows how to get to more channels than I do!"

"Shoot, you should see him with my cell phone…"

Xavier tried to respond, starting to say something about making the kids read more books, but was distracted by the sounds of joy coming from his children. He turned back around and saw excitement on their faces as they jumped up, reenergized, and began dancing crazily in front of the television. He laughed for a moment, but his smile evaporated as he took a look at the screen.

It was a music video, with a young, tall, black man, riddled with tattoos and adorned with all sorts of jewelry, mouthing rap lyrics with an incredibly expensive sports car in the background. The rims on the car looked like they belonged on an eighteen-wheeler.

The beat and baseline to the song were both catchy, but Xavier didn't hear them. Instead he saw, when the song came to its hook, a voluptuous young black woman with pink satin lingerie, incredibly tall high-heels and a red lollipop, opening the door and stepping out of the automobile. She swayed her head so that her long hair fell to her right shoulder, and walked up to the grinning artist, making sure to accentuate the rocking of her hips as she moved. After getting close enough to kiss him, she turned and began grinding on the man, and making faces that suggested her immense enjoyment. The rapper looked down at the woman's derriere, then looked at the camera and grinned widely.

Xavier was disgusted. He looked back at his children, who were no longer sitting on the couch, but dancing in the middle of the floor, and seemed to have the song memorized. They mouthed every word like a favorite bedtime story.

Xavier snatched the remote off of the couch and flipped the television off. He withstood the urge to kick through the screen.

"Daddyyyyy?! What are you doing? That's my favorite song!"

A disappointed Felicia pouted while throwing herself to the floor.

"The hell it is! How do you even know that song?"

"We heard it on the radio!"

Xavier's head spun around as he looked at his wife in annoyance. "Theresa?"

"It's a nice song, Xavier! I didn't know the video was that bad, but the song is pretty good."

"So…what? You want our children growing up being pimps and hoes, is that it?"

Theresa giggled, and Xavier realized she wasn't taking him seriously. "X, no one who grows up in this neighborhood is going to become anybody's pimp or hoe."

Xavier could feel the argument coming. All of his years of training with Diop, of meditations and relaxation exercises, and none of it had prepared him for arguments with his wife. He opened his mouth, knowing his voice was getting ready to emerge louder than necessary, when his son cut him off.

"Daddy, how come you only let us watch the vanilla people on TV?"

The man of the house could feel his wife's smugness as he stumbled over his words. "The…umm…the what people?"

"The vanilla people, Daddy. How come we can only watch the vanilla people?"

"Who in the world are the vanilla people?"

"The people always on TV. At school we call them the vanilla people."

"So what do you call the people that aren't vanilla?"

"I don't know. I just know the vanilla people."

"Well, you should stop calling them that. It could make someone upset."

Young XJ thought for a moment, then shrugged his shoulders as he asked his next question. "Daddy, I'm the only one in class with vanilla people by my house. Nobody else has vanilla people by their houses."

"Well, you should consider yourself lucky. All that means is that you live in a better place than the rest of your classmates."

Theresa got up and walked over to the couch. She smacked Xavier on the head just hard enough to let him know that she was unhappy with what he'd said. Just as she was about to speak, Felicia looked up at her father.

"So does that mean that the vanilla people are better than everybody else?"

Xavier began to stumble over his words, and hoped that Theresa would change the subject, but their children continued looking at their father, eagerly awaiting a response. Xavier turned and looked at Theresa for help, and she shook her head.

"No, Felicia, that doesn't mean that the vanilla people are better than everyone else. It doesn't mean that at all."

"So what does it mean then, Mommy?"

"We'll talk about it later, okay? Right now your daddy is gonna take you upstairs and give you your bath."

Xavier stood up and motioned to the children. "Alright, let's go. Time to get clean."

"But Daddy…"

"No buts; let's go upstairs."

The children stood up and began to walk upstairs, with Xavier right behind them. Theresa looked at them from the couch, then leaned over and picked up the television remote. Just as she was about to turn it on, she heard her son and husband from up the stairs.

"But Daddy, the vanilla people…"

"Enough about the vanilla people, okay?"

She shook her head again, and turned the television back on. After flipping through channels herself, she settled on the station playing the rap videos, and listened to the music while the splashing of her children filled the background.

Xavier became better at his job than even General Morris expected. He had to remember how he used to talk and walk and act while still living in the ghetto, but the mannerisms came back quick. Most times he would portray a drunk or a crackhead, because no one expected anything of him when he did. He was left alone, and spent days sitting in urine-stenched corners of alleys, until he was given his target. Days later, he would provide the shock of a lifetime to a drug kingpin, whose delusions of power were so swollen that they'd turned down the propositions of the white men in black suits with government badges who'd come to visit them.

But the job came with a price. City after city, assassination after assassination, Xavier came to hate the environments in which he always found himself. The days before he received his target, while he was lying in wait and being invisible, he would hear loud music blasting, telling guys his age to kill each other, and then hear the moans and cries echo through the night when they did what they were told. Forced to associate with the other drunkards and drug fiends in the city, he would hear the tales of the damned, and become convinced that if there was a hell, it existed everywhere he was assigned. He grew to despise these worlds, despise the curses and the needles, the alcohol vomit and the condom wrappers. Though he found purpose in his work, in taking the lives of bad men, he wouldn't be able to continue much longer.

Then, while on assignment on the east coast, Xavier met Theresa Baker.

Marcus "Cain" Cunningham, the middle-aged, scarred-faced cartel runner who'd refused the men in black, had become his target. Xavier got his profile on a winter day, and started his surveillance by watching Cain pull a truck up to the curb in front of the local rec center. When the kingpin opened the back of the truck, a young woman in her twenties, with dark caramel skin and long thin braids, stood there smiling, and a mountain of winter coats towered behind her.

Mothers cried out to the sky in gratitude as their children swiped coats out of the air. Many of them took off the jackets they had on, which were largely inadequate, and threw on their new coats on the spot. The covert agent didn't know which one he was most affected by—the beautiful woman throwing winter wear out into the crowd, or the grins of children who would no longer freeze on the way to school. Either way, he was moved deeply.

Moved, but still determined. No matter how warm his heart, he still had a mission to complete.

That night, for the first time since he had begun working with the agency, Xavier changed his cover. He went into his apartment and took off his rags, showered, shaved, and changed into a nice pair of jeans, shoes, and an expensive button-down shirt. He walked around pretending to be lost and asking about different nightclubs. Eventually, he found himself in a place on the west side of town after overhearing that Cain was there. Fighting his way through the crowd, he made it to the back, where he flashed enough cash to be let into the VIP section and sat a few feet away from six other people, including Marcus and Theresa. Theresa, the woman from the back of the truck, was the only female. His presence caught both her and her boss' attention.

"I never seen you around here before."

The VIP lounge must have been soundproof, Xavier thought. He could feel the heavy bass vibrations from the music playing in the club area, but the room was silent except for the laughter of the people inside.

I could kill him in here, Xavier thought.

"Hey!"

Xavier snapped out of his daydream to find that most of people sitting with Cain were now staring at him. It wasn't very often someone ignored Cain, and his irritation was obvious.

"You hear me talkin' to you?"

"Yeah, yeah, my bad, homie. I was just daydreamin'."

"Whatever. Get the hell outta here, man. Go daydream somewhere else."

Xavier quickly glanced at the two men who had slid their hands down to their pistols. "Ay, ay yo…wait…look, what ya'll drinkin', man?"

"Cristal."

"Cristal? The hell is that?"

"You ain't up on this yet, homie. Just me and Jay-Z. Now get outta here before you get hurt."

"Look, let me buy you a bottle, aight? Let me apologize. I ain't mean any disrespect."

Cain laughed as he looked around at his entourage. Everyone except Theresa was laughing along with him.

"Bottles is four hundred a pop."

Xavier thought for a minute. "Aight, well, in that case…" Xavier reached into his pocket and flagged down the waitress at the same time. "Sweetie, can you get all my friends over here a bottle of, what is it, Cristal? A bottle of Cristal to take home, please?"

"You want to order six bottles of Cristal, sir?"

"No, seven. I wanna try it out myself, too."

The waitress started to laugh as well, but stopped when she looked back at Xavier's face.

"Umm…that'll be twenty-eight hundred dollars, sir."

Xavier casually put six five-hundred-dollar bills on the table.

"Keep the change, baby girl."

As the waitress left with a pep in her step, Cain leaned forward and looked straight at the stranger two tables down. "Who are you, man?"

"I'm a friend."

"What kinda friend?"

"Whatever kind you need."

"I don't need no extra friends."

"Yeah, that's what I hear. Marcus doesn't need any extra friends."

The waitress came back carrying three bottles of the expensive champagne, and a man in a pinstriped suit followed her with four others. After sitting each of the bottles down, the waitress bashfully pointed to Xavier, and the dapper man walked over to face him.

"Sir, my name is Antonio Lace. I own the club. I wanted to come and personally thank you for business. Anything else you need, you can ask for me personally. Mr. Cain will tell you, my VIP customers are always happy."

Cain cut off the club owner. "Tony…"

"Yes, sir?"

"Can you make sure everyone gets home safely? I have some business to discuss with…what'd you say your name was?"

"I didn't. You can call me Black."

"I have business to discuss with Mr. Black here."

"Uh…yes, sir…"

One of the men sitting with Cain had both too much fat and too much muscle. He tried to jump up from his seat, but ended up slowly rising. "Hell naw! I ain't leavin' you, Mr. Cain! Who the hell is this bastard, anyway? Give me the word and I'll blow his goddamn head off!"

Cain looked over at his friend and protector. "Tiny, calm down and go home. All of ya'll, go home. I'll get with ya'll in the mornin'. Theresa, hold up a second."

Hesitantly, everyone who'd come with Marcus grabbed their champagne bottles and shuffled out of the door as Marcus whispered into Theresa's ear. When he was finished, Theresa looked frantically from one man to the next. Finally, Marcus nodded at her, and she rushed out of the room.

Once they'd all left, Marcus turned back to the stranger. "The white boys sent you, didn't they? The white boys from the government?"

"Yeah."

Marcus shook his head and laughed to himself. "Crackers done got smart, man. Hell, you look just like my cousin."

Xavier didn't answer.

"You here to kill me?"

"Yeah."

Marcus nodded his head, and pulled a blunt out of his side pocket. "They ain't got no smoke detectors in the VIP lounge.

You can smoke whatever you want in here. Never thought I'd be so grateful for that…"

"Why did you send everyone away?"

"What was the point in keepin' them here? They'd all have gotten killed anyway. And even if Tiny lucked up and got you, they'd send another one."

"Why were you handing out coats today at the rec center? Most of the kids got parents addicted to your drugs. It doesn't make any sense."

Marcus took a long drag on his blunt, and then coughed as he exhaled. He spoke with a strained voice. "You know why I gave myself the nickname Cain?"

"'Cause you sell cocaine?"

Marcus laughed and coughed at the same time. "That's what most people think. Truth is, I saw this preacher on TV one day talkin' bout Cain and Abel. Looked the story up myself and found out it was true…Cain killed his brother for no reason. He got mad 'cause he didn't have what he thought he should have. And I thought, man, that's me. I never had what I thought I should have, so I'm killin' my brothers. So, I told everybody after that to call me Cain."

Xavier was struck silent.

"I do stuff like that, hand out coats in the winter, backpacks for school, turkeys for Thanksgiving, hams for Christmas…I guess I'm tryin' to make up for the wrong I've done."

Xavier shook the confusion out of his head. "You don't make any sense."

"And what about you? You here to kill me 'cause I won't pay them white boys, right? Who the hell you think supply me? I never been to Columbia, cuz! I never seen a coca leaf in my life! How the hell you think it gets to me?"

"I don't know…it's not for me to know…"

"Yeah, 'cause you an errand boy, right? Hell, I got one too. They tell you to kill a nigga and you kill a nigga…don't matter that you a nigga yourself."

Xavier sprang up and pulled the handgun from under his shirt. Walking over, he kicked the table over in front of Marcus and aimed the gun at his forehead.

Marcus took another long draw on his blunt, then let his head fall back and rest on the couch behind him. "You think I ain't know I had to pay a price for what I do? I always knew this was comin'. This weed helps, though…wheeeew…"

Xavier kicked himself as he realized he forgot the silencer. He grew uncomfortable with his sloppiness as he grabbed the metal piece from his back pocket and attached it to his pistol.

"I saw Theresa lookin' at you when you first walked in."

"That doesn't matter."

"If it didn't matter, you wouldn't a' said nothin'".

Xavier fell silent again, and Marcus started laughing.

"All she does is balance the books. She don't do nothin' illegal. She in her junior year at the university, too. Ya'll should do the damn thang."

"Shut up."

Marcus chuckled a few seconds more, and then sat up, placing his elbows on his knees and his forehead against the silencer. "Seriously, go holla at her. Ya'll both tryin' a' do some good in the world, you just don't know how to do it."

Xavier wasn't aware of the drop under his eye when he pulled the trigger. Marcus' head dropped where he sat, but his body didn't move. An hour later, the waitress would think he was praying before stepping into his blood.

Xavier tried to compose himself, but couldn't take his eyes off of the corpse as he walked out of the VIP lounge and shut the door behind him. He turned around to come face to face with Theresa, who looked as if she'd seen a ghost.

"Is he dead?"

Pained, Xavier nodded his head. "Yes."

"Take me with you."

Xavier stared at her, trying to convince himself not to do it, and knowing it wouldn't work. Finally, he grabbed her hand and they walked out of the club and into the cold night air.

Theresa would never know the details of what Xavier had done before he met her. All she knew was that he was in the military, nothing more and nothing less. The circumstances that led to their meeting in the club would be a mystery that she wouldn't mind letting go unsolved. For the rest of that night, she did as she had been instructed, emptying Marcus' safe and dividing the money up evenly between his five lieutenants, leaving them with the only message Marcus had given:

"Tell 'em all to get out of here!" Marcus had whispered in her ear. "Take the money and go! Any of 'em try and keep dealing, I'll climb up from hell and drag 'em back down, I swear! You tell I said that! Understand?"

Xavier knew, looking at Theresa as she wept over her friend that night, that he was finished. He left Theresa in the hotel room the next morning with a note that he'd be back in a couple of hours, and took the first plane he could get into Washington. General Morris' new office was in Arlington, and he was waiting in front of his office door by the time he arrived.

"I'm done, sir."

"Turner…what an unexpected surprise. Come on in so we can talk."

"There's nothing to talk about, sir. I'm done. I'm out."

General Morris looked at Xavier long and hard. "It's not quite that easy, soldier."

"It is for me. I'm retired, General. Starting today."

"And what if I say you can't retire?"

"I'm trying to do this the right way, sir. I'm trying to leave out the front door."

"There is no front door with the agency, son."

Xavier stepped forward, closing the distance between himself and the General. "You're my only connection with the agency. You got me in, you can get me out."

"I can't."

"Listen to me. If I go off reservation, I will kill everyone they send after me."

"You're a little optimistic."

"You've seen me in action, sir. You tell me."

The general looked at Xavier, and then pulled out another cigar. "Dammit…"

"It won't be long before they try and cover everything up. And we both know how thorough they are about cleaning up their messes."

"What do you want me to do, Turner?"

"Call them. Tell them I came to see you. I had a breakdown, I'm psychotic…tell them whatever you have to. But get them to retire me. I want out."

"It'll be a mess…"

"No, it won't. Maybe for someone else, but not for you. You're over Joint Operations. If you say I'm retired, then I'm retired."

General Morris walked over and took a seat behind his desk. "What do you want? You want more money? A different detail? What?"

"I want out, sir. Can you make that happen, or do I have to do it myself?"

It was early evening when Xavier made it to the hotel, and Theresa was sitting still in the room.

"I thought maybe you would've left," Xavier said as he let the door close behind him.

"It's a nice hotel. I decided to stay. Where did you go?"

"I quit my job."

"Oh. So what do we do now?"

Xavier sat on the foot of the bed, facing the most beautiful woman he'd ever seen. "I say we introduce ourselves. My name is Xavier."

"I'm Theresa."

"It's nice to meet you."

"You too. So…now that we're acquainted, can I get a ride? I'm late for class."

Another couple of hours later and the children were lying in bed. Their deep sleep allowed them to ignore the sounds of pleasure echoing off of the walls from their parents' room. The loud moans, sighs, and screams bounced from wall to wall and made their way throughout the entire house.

Xavier knew his wife well. He forced himself into her from behind, and the torque of his hips made his wife gasp with every stroke. At the right moment, when he felt her body tense up, he came out of her, stood her up straight, and maneuvered in front of her. Hoisting her in the air, he could feel her arms wrap around his neck as he lowered her onto himself, and then lowered them both onto the bed and rammed into her from the bottom.

His timing was perfect, and her orgasm caused her body to convulse.

By the time her climax was over, Xavier and Theresa were on the floor beside their dresser, soaked in sweat and breathing heavily.

Xavier looked up at Theresa's face, satisfied at the climax that he knew she would experience after being on top. Theresa felt another eruption coming, and kept her eyes shut tight while she snuggled around her lover. It was all he could do to grab hold of Theresa's waist and push himself in deep one last time before they reached their peak together. Theresa gave one last moan, and then collapsed into Xavier's arms, and they lay there, holding each other, until the magnificence of lovemaking faded, and reality once again shaped itself around them.

Xavier grabbed them both a towel, and then they made their way back up to the bed, where they lay exhausted. When he gathered enough energy, Xavier moved closer to Theresa and wrapped his arms around her. She moaned slightly with satisfaction, and pressed herself closer to her husband. Relaxed and comfortable, they both lay there on the bed in a content silence.

Slowly, though, Theresa's brow began to wrinkle, and she turned around slowly so that she could look Xavier in the eyes. "I didn't like the conversation you had with the kids tonight."

Xavier closed his eyes and took a deep breath. "Theresa, I don't want to talk about this. We had some great sex, and I don't want to ruin it. Every time we talk about this, it turns into an argument. Either you get mad or I get mad. It's the only thing we ever argue about, for Christ's sake!"

"And why do you think that is?"

"Because we don't think the same when it comes to certain people."

"Certain people? We're talking about people that look like you and me, baby!"

"Maybe, but we're not the same as they are."

Theresa rolled her eyes. "Xavier, you're going to make our kids hate themselves."

"What do you mean? I don't know what you're talking about."

"Self-hatred! They need to grow up being proud of their culture!"

"Culture, huh? I guess that's why you have to take the kids to that school in the city instead of the one right down the street."

"Look, I don't want my kids being confused, okay? Now I'm no militant black power junkie, but our kids need to be around other kids that look like them. They need to be comfortable in their own community."

"Why can't the community we live in be their community?"

"Because that's not the type of community that I'm talking about. And you know it."

"These kids that look like them, the ones they meet in that school in the city, are the same ones telling them about all these music videos and half-naked women on television."

"Xavier, what is wrong with you? You grew up in the ghetto! I mean, yeah, I know it can be pretty bad, but it can be beautiful, too. Don't you remember?"

"No. I don't remember anything beautiful about it. I remember not having any discipline, any control, any guidance. I remember walking around with no pride in myself. I'm ashamed of my past. That's why I try and forget it."

"So you really don't care about black people one way or the other, huh?"

"No, I don't. I care about human beings, baby. I don't have time to concern myself with race."

Theresa remained silent for a long while, and Xavier didn't know if she was struck silent by what he had said or if she was just thinking about it.

Finally, Theresa rose from the bed and turned out the lights in the room. Before she closed her eyes, she decided to have the last say. "Xavier?"

"Yes?"

"Our children think that all white people are good, and everyone else is bad. I don't care what you say, you can't convince me that somewhere deep inside, you don't have a problem with that."

Xavier paused for what was supposed to be a moment, thinking about what his wife had told him. Eventually he lost track of time trying to rationalize different ideas in his head, and by the time he was ready to respond to his wife's statement, Theresa's soft snoring had already begun floating through the air. Unwilling to wake his wife for further discussion, he sat back, closed his eyes, and allowed her snoring to lull him to sleep.

Chapter Five

The streetlights shined their way through the bedroom window as Nathan lay beside his wife on the bed. She was underneath the covers, dressed in her nightgown, her hair wrapped to stay in place during the night. He had on his undershirt and a pair of plain boxers, and lay on top of the covers. His hands were laced behind his head, and he stared straight up, using the random paint designs on the ceiling to help him think about everything, and nothing, at the same time. Then, for no reason in particular, he turned and looked at the back of his wife's head. He could tell by her breathing that she wasn't fully asleep yet, and thought back to the last time they had had sex.

Their routine was one that they both had grown comfortable with. The last time Sonya had tried to initiate some kind of sexual encounter, it was so awkward and uncomfortable that it reminded her of losing her virginity. She felt more like a chore that needed to be completed than a wife making love to her husband. So Sonya waited, waited until the pain Nathan felt was so deep that it begged for some form of release. It was then that Nathan took his deepest despairs and concentrated them into each thrust into his wife. Sonya took this as her only opportunity to truly connect with and comfort her husband. It took her a while to get used to it, and the first couple of times she cried after Nathan fell asleep, mostly out of confusion. She had grown, despite herself, to enjoy it, recognizing that a man had to be in love to confide in his woman, even if it was with his penis. Every Sunday after they had sex, she said an extra prayer of thanks at the altar.

The side that Sonya laid on caused her back to face him, and the covers seemed to accentuate her shape. Without warning, she felt a slight touch on her side. Most times she would dismiss it as an accident, but this touch was different. Purposeful. She instantly awakened without opening her eyes. Not wanting to get excited for no reason, Sonya moved ever so slightly out from under his touch, praying that he pursued her. Nathan grabbed her softly but firmly around her waist with both hands, and pulled his wife back to him.

The air began to warm, along with Sonya's body temperature, and as she opened her eyes she started to feel kisses on the back of her neck. They started soft but quickly became firm, rough, like he was searching for some type of treasure hidden within his wife. Sonya started to moan slightly, and Nathan extended the area of his kisses to her shoulders, then her back. Sonya's breathing became short and quick, and when she felt him fully erect against her, she turned around and faced him. It took only a split second to examine his face, to make her absolutely sure that she wasn't dreaming, and she kissed him eagerly.

And then they both heard the front door open, and slam shut.

Nathan and Sonya stopped kissing. Nathan concentrated on the sounds coming from the living room, hoping that it was some strange man that had broken into the house, but knowing the truth so deeply that it hurt more than usual. A loud crash in the living room pulled Nathan out of bed and he started to put his clothes on.

"Nathan..." Sonya started, but Nathan looked at her for a few seconds, and turned around and finished getting dressed.

By the time Nathan entered the living room, it had been turned into a warzone. The lamp in the corner had been turned over and was lying on the floor. The cushions to the sofa were strewn all over the carpet, and there was glass from a vase lying in pieces near the door. Nathan saw Clarence in the corner of the room, pulling the drawers out from a cabinet, searching through them, and then throwing them against the wall. Most of them had broken from the impact, and were lying in a pile of wooden pieces under a family portrait. When Clarence was done searching through the cabinet, he looked up and saw his father. His eyes were bloodshot red, and they darted back and forth in his head like a pinball. His body was shaking, his hair was filthy, and he reeked of the worst form of degradation. Nathan did not move, and Clarence, with a crooked smile on his face, worked his way toward his father.

"Dad…"

"No," Nathan answered without hesitation.

"But Dad, I…."

"No."

Clarence's mouth turned from a crooked smile into a hate-filled scowl instantly. He started to yell something, then seemed to come to a realization, and his mouth went back into the crooked smile again.

"Well…uhh…I can't talk to Mom?"

"No."

"Where is she?"

"Don't worry about it."

"I just wanna talk to Mom!"

"No."

Clarence's face began to change again. "Who da hell is you to tell me I can't talk to my mother?"

"It doesn't matter. You need to leave, and you need to leave now. I'm tired of this."

"To hell with you, then." Clarence glared at his father, then glanced over Nathan's shoulder and started to yell. "Ma! Ma! I need to talk to you!"

"Get out."

Clarence ignored his father and continued yelling.

"Ma! Ma! Please, Mama, please! I need to talk to you!"

"I told you to get the hell out!"

"Make me!"

"Get the hell out of my house or I'm calling the cops."

"I don't give a damn!"

Nathan began to move toward the phone, but he heard shuffling behind him. When he turned around, he saw Sonya standing in the doorway.

"Mama, Mama, I jus' need some mo' cash, just for tonight."

Sonya, in her robe, stepped into the living room. "Lord, Jesus, please help my child…"

"Mama, just for tonight, Mama."

"Baby, I can't even pretend like I don't know what you need it for anymore."

Nathan calmly stepped to the side, and let them talk.

"Mama, look, I'll do whatever you want, okay? You want me to go to church with you, I'll go. You wanna take me out somewhere, I'll go. Just let me get this from you tonight, Mama, and I'll do whatever you want. I swear it."

Sonya dropped her head. "Baby…"

"Mama, I'm dyin, Mama! I'm dyin'! Please!"

Sonya grabbed at her chest, as if she could feel her heart cracking. Clarence dropped to his knees, and begged at her feet.

"Please, Mama…"

Slowly, Sonya moved back into the bedroom, and began looking for her pocketbook.

"Mama, thank you; thank you so much. I promise, Mama, whatever you want…"

Sonya stayed in the bedroom for a couple of minutes, moving things around and searching. Nathan stood calmly to the side, not moving or saying anything. After a while, Sonya emerged from the bedroom.

His face was convoluted with too many emotions at once. "You couldn't find it, could you?" Both Clarence and Sonya looked directly at Nathan. "I hid it."

Sonya's eyes couldn't hide her disbelief. "You what?"

"I hid it. I've been hiding your pocketbook every night since the last time he came by begging for money. I'm sorry; I had no other choice."

Sonya was speechless, and as she tried to sort through the different thoughts in her head, Clarence ran up and grabbed Nathan by the shirt.

"GIVE IT TO HER!"

"No."

Clarence swung wildly, hitting him on the cheek. Nathan staggered back, then shook off the blow and stood up tall again.

"GIVE HER THE GODDAMN POCKETBOOK!"

"No."

Whatever was left intact in the living room, Clarence started destroying with the violence and anger of a madman. Sonya was screaming for him to stop, but his screaming drowned her out.

"I DON'T HAVE TIME FOR THIS! GIVE HER THE GODDAMN POCKETBOOK!"

"No."

Without warning, Clarence pulled a gun out from the back of

his jeans. Sonya saw the firearm and collapsed to the floor, mumbling incoherently to the Lord. Nathan's breath caught in his throat, but he didn't move. Clarence walked straight up to him, and pointed the barrel at his forehead. His words sounded like pure hate.

"I'm not gonna say it again, goddammit. Give her the pocket-book."

Nathan hesitated. For a while they both stood there, father and son. As Nathan's life flashed before his eyes, he choked, realizing that Clarence was in many of the freeze frames.

Sonya's incomprehensible utterances were like background music, and for several seconds that's all any of them heard. Finally, Nathan found the strength to release his voice from his throat.

"You know...something always told me it would come to this. Something always told me, but I didn't want to listen. I would have gladly killed you, strangled you as soon as you came from your mother's womb, if I knew it would keep you from killing yourself. Killing yourself like this. If it's time for me to go, here, tonight, then I'm ready. Just like you're ready to shoot your own father so you can put that trash in your arms. Shoot your own father so you can continue to live in hell. Well, then, go ahead and shoot me. Do what you want. But my money is my wife's money, and her money is mine, and I'll be damned if you walk out of my front door tonight with any of it. I'll die first."

Nathan gazed directly into Clarence's eyes. His impending death rattled his sanity, and he pressed his forehead against the gun barrel. "I'll die first! You hear me? I'll die first!"

Clarence's muscles tightened and loosened, a symptom of the war that was going on within him. His eyes twitched, and his head pounded, and finally he screamed out. He screamed loud enough to bring Sonya out of her mumbling state and look up at him to see what was happening. He screamed loud enough to finally have the reality of what was happening hit his father, whose hands began to shake and whose breathing became short immediately after his son's deafening show of agony. He screamed loud enough to finally, for the first time since he remembered, make a split second decision with his heart before the narcotics took over again. He lowered the hand with the gun in it and ran around the apartment like a madman, releasing inhuman cries. Then he ran out of the front door, leaving it wide open, with a soft breeze coming through that caused the flowers on the floor to sway.

Nathan took a second to try and breathe, then fell over and leaned with his back against the wall. His face contorted into dozens of different emotions, one by one. His legs, which had been weak ever since hearing his son's scream, slowly lost whatever strength they had in them, and he slid down into a sitting position on the floor. With the back of his head against the wall, Nathan sat with his hands covering his face, and his mouth opened in a cry that would never emerge.

The windows were open. The streets looked blurry, like some painter's version of New York at night, and the seats had comforted far too many people to ever be clean again. Clarence glanced around, confused at where he was. Confused about everything. He knew only one thing for certain; that he needed to get some money as quickly as possible. His head was about to explode, his skin was on fire, and his chest was collapsing. He knew what he needed to cure himself, and he needed money to get it.

It took Clarence a while to realize that he was on a bus. He didn't remember how he got there, or how long he had been there. He was the only passenger, though, and if he were in his right mind, he would have been able to conclude that he had been on there for a while.

Suddenly feeling hot, Clarence turned his face toward the window and saw a large neighborhood filled with big, expensive houses. Before he realized it, he had pulled the stop signal on the bus. When it came to a halt, he attempted to walk down the steps and stumbled out into the night. His vision was blurry, with different colors flashing randomly in the corners of his eyes, each one representing a different type of agony. Staggering down the street, he walked as if he was following an imaginary line drawn by a toddler. The air was cool and comfortable, but to Clarence it stung like a thousand pinches. He started to look at the houses, seeing ones with cars in the driveway or lights on inside as potential targets, but not being able to decide on one. Then everything started to spin around him, and he stopped, trying his best to straighten out his world. Leaning against a tree, he vomited up whatever it was that he had eaten earlier in the day. And he stood there, eyes closed, leaning against the tree, with vomit drenching his shirt and stinging his nose. For a while he was somewhere else, anywhere else. Anybody else. Then the sound of a car engine woke him from whatever delusion he was in, and his eyes followed it to the driveway two doors down. Without thinking, he started to walk toward it.

The car pulled into the driveway and stopped, the lights turned off, and the engine was stopped. Clarence could see movement inside the car before anyone got out, and knew that there was more than one person in it, which meant more money. He felt for the gun in the back of his pants. The car doors finally opened, and an attractive woman emerged from the driver's seat. She walked to the back door and opened it up, and two children, a boy and a girl, got out excitedly and ran around the car twice before their mother instructed them to stand still. The girl reached back inside the car to get her dolls while the mother fumbled around in her pocketbook. It was the little boy who saw Clarence first, and his head tilted in curiosity. Clarence saw this face, and it reminded him of himself. Back when he was young, when he could read the things his father would write and try as hard as he could to comprehend them. Clarence saw the little boy, and the innocence that he could never have again. And, for a split second, he felt the love from his father that he had destroyed earlier that night. The love that he had traded in for a substance that he thought he loved more.

He realized that he hated himself, but he hated the little boy even more.

Clarence pulled out the gun from the back of his pants, and aimed it at the child. The boy, too naive to be scared, tapped his sister on the shoulder and told her to look. The mother was still searching for something in her pocketbook, and as the daughter looked Clarence over, she asked the same question she asked everyone she wanted to make friends with.

"Mister, you wanna come in and play?"

Clarence first aimed the gun at the girl, pulled the trigger, then aimed at the boy and did the same.

The mother didn't scream. She didn't shout out and yell for help. She didn't even look at Clarence. She spotted her children lying on the ground, blood everywhere, and her whole body started to shake. She convulsed so hard that she could barely move, but when she did she walked up to her children and told them to wake up so they could go into the house for their baths. She started crying uncontrollably, but she didn't sob. She didn't wail. She gently shook her children and told them to wake up. Clarence realized that he should have been feeling something that he wasn't, but he didn't dwell on it. Instead, he saw the pocketbook strapped around the mother's arm as she shook her children.

He rushed up to her and grabbed the pocketbook, but the strap was still around her arm, and it wouldn't break. He yelled at her to give him the pocketbook, but she didn't hear him. She caressed her children and kept asking them to wake up. By this time she was covered in blood, and Clarence grabbed her at a distance and punched her in the face. She fell to the ground, then crawled back over to her children and continued to beg them to stand up. Clarence once again reached for the pocketbook, but couldn't get it from around her arm. And suddenly, the mother looked up at Clarence.

"I...I...I think my children are hurt. I think they're hurt. I...I think they need help."

Clarence's mind was gone. All he could focus on was the pocketbook. He pointed the gun at the mother, sitting on the ground between her children. "All I wanted was the pocketbook! All I wanted was the pocketbook! Then none of this would have happened! If you'd just let Mom give me the goddamn pocketbook, none of this would have happened! None of it!"

The mother looked up, covered in blood, and saw the gun barrel aimed at her face. With the last stroke of sanity left in her, she screamed out the only name she could think of. Not because she believed he could save her, or save their children, but because she always knew if she had to say any last words, his name would be a part of it.

"XAVIER!!!!!"

Clarence pulled the trigger, and Theresa's head was forced back against the rear wheel of the car. Her eyes were open, but she didn't move.

Clarence grabbed the pocketbook and slid it off of her limp arm. Then he ran as fast as he could back up the road, toward the bus stop.

Chapter Six

Nothing moved inside the house. Everything was quiet and still, as if time knew it couldn't go back, but refused to go forward. From the outside, the house looked as if it had been used for a horror movie. Everything about it was dark, from the door that couldn't be seen because the porch light was off, to the window on the top left that used to show two little children playing before bed. There were still marks on the ground in the driveway where the police mapped out the crime scene, trying to figure out exactly what had happened. It was a job to them, something they did every day to put food on their families' plates. Xavier understood this, but he didn't care. He sat in his house now with the lights off, spending half of his time talking and playing with a family that no longer existed, and the other half begging time to rewind itself.

Xavier could only grasp onto reality for so long before his mind reverted back to fantasy to keep from losing itself, but when he did take hold he found himself without meaning. He thought of everything that he had planned out for his family. He thought of the property that he and his wife owned that was increasing in value steadily, he thought of the trust funds he had already set up for his son and daughter, and it became harder and harder to breathe knowing that his family wasn't. He realized that he was living out his life for them. He was living for his family. And of all the planning he had done, he had never anticipated this. He never thought he could lose them. Not all of them. Not all at once.

For the past three days Xavier hadn't done anything. He hadn't slept, except for the times when he fantasized that his wife was beside him. All the other times he had tried, he had seen three bodies lying in his driveway with the white sheets, stained with blood, laid over them. He had woken up screaming, drenched in sweat, just like when he used to have his military dreams. But these were real, and he knew they were real, and it tore him apart. He hadn't trained. He would not have eaten, but Theresa's sisters had been stopping by, trying to comfort him and get all of Theresa's affairs in order. Concerned that he would starve, they brought him food, and he ate to appease them.

He was at the grocery store when it happened. Theresa had decided to take the children into the city with her to visit one of their aunts. He had watched her car pull off from the driveway, then walked downstairs to the basement and did some light training. When he finished, he came back upstairs and saw that the sun was going down. He looked in the refrigerator, saw that it was almost empty, and knew his wife would want to go shopping when she got back. So, he decided to go shopping instead, and be finished by the time they got back.

Excited at the thought of surprising his wife, Xavier changed clothes and made his way to the supermarket. He spent more time than he intended because he wanted to make sure he hadn't forgotten anything. He didn't want Theresa to have to come back out of the house. Once he was done getting food, he made his way over to the school supplies section and picked up two boxes of crayons, one for each of his children, and two new coloring books.

He could see the flashing lights on the police cars from four blocks away. Like everyone else, he was surprised initially that the police were in his neighborhood, then figured that one of the elderly people may have had an accident. As he turned onto his block and saw the huge group of police cars in front of his house, he immediately stopped his car and sprinted the rest of the way home. When he got there, he was stopped by an officer, who told him that this was a crime scene and he couldn't be as close as he was. He told the officer that this was his house, that he and his family lived there, and the officer directed him to a captain. After telling him who Xavier was, the first officer whispered something in the captain's ear, then looked back at Xavier and walked away to find Detective Chance, who had given explicit orders to notify him if the husband returned.

Before the captain had a chance to speak, Xavier looked over his shoulder and saw three figures lying on the ground. Although each of them was covered, two were smaller figures, like children, one was larger, and each of them was covered with blood.

Xavier went deaf. He couldn't hear anything the captain was saying. He saw the officer moving his lips, but there were no words coming out.

"What are you saying? What are you saying? Just tell me where my family is! Tell me what happened?"

The officer seemed to speak in a foreign language, some gibberish that Xavier had never heard before. Xavier was feeling himself getting more and more upset, but Mrs. Mayfair, who had been watching, stepped in between him and the captain. She kept her head down, but Xavier could tell she had tears running down her face. She grabbed both of Xavier's hands in hers, and shook them vigorously. Then she looked up at him, and her face looked as though she had seen a ghost. She opened her mouth slowly, hesitantly, and forced herself to say what she had to.

"She cried out for you, Xavier. Right before the end, she cried out for you. It was as if God Himself came out of her mouth."

The doorbell rang and Xavier jumped up from the couch. He had been somewhere in between sleep and delirium for hours. He made his way over to the door, and looked out through the peephole. Chance was standing on the other side of the door. His wife, May, stood behind him, with her face drained of color. Xavier called out to Theresa that Chance and May were at the door, then realized what he'd just done, and shook his head. He told himself to try and hold it together, for at least as long as there were guests in the house. Then he slowly opened the door.

May quickly walked up to Xavier, but began to cry before she could get any words out. She reached up and hugged him tightly, repeating over and over again how sorry she was. Xavier thanked her, and when she finally let him go, he looked over at Chance, who walked over and grabbed his hand, then patted him on the back.

"How you feeling?"

Xavier shook his head and moved out of the way so that Chance could come in. May sobbed at the dinner table, and Chance went over to console her while Xavier made his way back over to the couch. Once he got her to stop weeping, Chance walked over to the couch and took a seat beside Xavier, who had his eyes closed.

"So how you doin'?"

"Not good, man."

The two friends paused, knowing there weren't many words to fit the situation. Xavier let his head fall back on the couch.

"I...I don't know what to do."

Chance shook his head. "And I don't know what to tell you... just...I'm sorry..."

Xavier didn't answer, just leaned back against the couch. Chance felt like he should say something else, but he was afraid to speak the wrong words, so he stayed silent.

"I want to kill him."

"Kill who?"

Xavier turned and looked at his friend.

"Come on, bro, don't talk like that. You don't even know who it is yet."

"But you will. It's your case, right? That's why you were here last night."

"Yeah, it's my case. I didn't tell them I knew you.

Xavier sat up and stared at the blank television screen. "I want to kill him."

"Look, I want this bastard to hang, too. That's why I took this case. But this isn't some op out in the jungle somewhere! You can't go all vigilante on me. You have to let me do my job, X."

"You can do your job. Just let me kill him."

Chance put his hands on his head. "You're serious, aren't you?"

Xavier didn't answer.

"So then what? Let's say you do find the guy who did this, and you get him. What then? What do you do after that?"

Xavier lifted up his head and looked Chance directly in the eyes. "I couldn't save my family."

"That wasn't your fault, bro. You didn't know..."

"It doesn't matter, Chance. I couldn't save my family."

They sat there, looking each other in the eyes, until Xavier lifted his head toward the ceiling and covered his face with his hands. He let out an exasperated breath.

"You know…sometimes I can't even tell what's real and what's not anymore. I'll lie in my bed and talk to my wife for hours, about the house, about the kids, about everything, and look over and see that she's not there. And then I'll think that she's working late or something. It's like a part of me knows what's really going on, but part of me doesn't. As soon as you leave, I'll probably run upstairs and get ready for my wife and kids coming home. I know what's happening, but then I don't. I don't have a clue."

Chance took a deep breath. "If there's anything I can do…"

"I already told you what you can do."

"What if I can't?"

Xavier looked over at his friend once again. "How many times did I save your life in Kuwait?"

Chance fell silent, knowing he couldn't run from his obligation. He spoke low enough to ensure his wife couldn't hear. "Look, I'm not making any promises, okay?"

"I'm not asking for a promise, Chance. Just info. If you figure out who…if you find him…"

"Yeah, yeah, I got it."

"Thank you."

Chance looked over Xavier's shoulder at his wife, who began sobbing again. "Alright, man, we're gonna go. May is still really shaken up about this whole thing, and you probably need some time to yourself."

"Yeah, thanks for stopping by…"

Chance waited for Xavier to stand, to walk them to the door, but Xavier sat there with his eyes closed. Chance decided not to say anything else, and he walked over, took his wife by the hand, and began to lead her toward the door. As they opened it, Xavier called out from the couch.

"Theresa! Theresa, Chance and May are leaving; come down and say goodbye!"

May started to say something, but Chance stopped her. She covered her mouth with her hands, and before she became inconsolable, Chance led her outside the door and closed it.

The church had been decorated nicely for the funeral. There were beautiful bouquets of flowers set up all around the sanctuary, and ribbons tied to each pew. The three open caskets that sat in the front were ordered nicely, with the largest being in the middle and the two smaller ones being on either side of it. The stained glass windows shone a tint of red and yellow onto them and decorated the caskets with light. Theresa's sisters, dressed in all black, took the time to greet all of the people who arrived.

Xavier sat in the back, away from everyone. If he weren't so busy trying to figure out if this was real or not, he would have taken the time to compliment the sisters on how well they had done with the organizing. They had decided, right after the accident happened, that Xavier had not been in the right state of mind to deal with it, and Xavier agreed. So he gave the sisters the money they needed and left it up to them. Now, while they greeted people, Xavier sat in the back, with a program in his lap. He had been staring at the front of it, off and on, for the past hour and a half. It was a picture of Theresa and the children at the table of a restaurant they all went to regularly. Xavier remembered when he'd taken the picture, insisting that it was the last shot left in the camera and he wanted it to be only them in it. All of them are smiling, dressed in summer clothes, and with plates in front of them. Their son managed to put up bunny ears behind his daughter's head before Xavier noticed. It all seemed like it had happened yesterday, mere hours ago. How could he be here now? What exactly was going on?

A crowd of people began making their way over to the confused husband. Theresa's oldest sister had made the mistake of pointing Xavier out in the back of the sanctuary, and all those who wondered where he was now rushed to give their condolences. Chance, who arrived in time to see sympathetic mob forming, sprang into action. He forced his way through the crowd, grabbed Xavier and took him out of the sanctuary, downstairs, and out of the front doors before the first of the people could reach him. As soon as they got out, Chance lit up a cigarette.

"I thought you may have wanted some fresh air."

"Yeah, thanks."

They didn't speak anymore. Chance took his time smoking his cigarette, and Xavier stared into the skyline. When he saw the butt of the cigarette hit the ground by his feet, he looked back up at his friend. They both would have loved nothing better than to leave and find a bar somewhere, but Chance knew what had to be done.

"You ready?"

Xavier walked over to him, and they silently crept back inside and up the stairs to the sanctuary.

The church was full of people now, but the back pews were still unoccupied, and Xavier and Chance made their way back over to the seats where Xavier sat before. They sat down in silence, Chance having nothing to say, and Xavier not being coherent enough to speak.

The musician began to play music at the organ, and suddenly Xavier became convinced that he was needed at home. Frantic, he stood and grabbed his coat.

"What are you doing?" Chance refused to move out of the way.

Xavier stopped, then looked around for a second, and turned back to Chance with a confused look on his face. "Chance, whose funeral is this?"

Chance began to say something, then closed his mouth and shook his head. Resolved, he pushed himself up from the pew and grabbed onto Xavier's shoulders.

"What are you doing?"

"I'm taking you down front. You need to see this, man. It's for your own good."

Chance and Xavier began to walk down the middle aisle. Unaware of what was happening, Xavier figured he would get it over with so he could hurry and get back to his family. But as he got further and further down the aisle, his knees began to get weak. He started trying to push back, to go back up the aisle, but Chance stood right behind him. Every time he tried to retreat, Chance pushed him forward, until finally, the father was close enough to see his daughter lying peacefully in her casket.

Xavier ran up to Felicia and commanded her to get up. He began to shake her a bit, and called to his daughter in a stern voice to stop playing around and get out of the casket. He turned around to the people in the audience, embarrassed that his daughter would do something so disrespectful. He apologized profusely for his children's misbehavior as he went over to the casket on the far left, where his son lay, and called for him to wake up as well. This time Xavier's voice began to soften and crack. He shook XJ, saying that it was time to go home, and began to look around, asking for people close by to him to help him wake his children up.

While he was looking for help, his eyes came to rest on his wife, and he froze.

The church was motionless. Everyone was stuck, watching a father come to terms with the death of his family. Even the musicians stopped playing, and the silence was deafening as Xavier approached his wife's casket, and everyone's heart began to jump. He spoke quietly at first, and only Chance was close enough to hear the murmuring of the list of things they had to do today, the pleading, ever so quietly, for Theresa to wake up. There was no sternness in his voice now, only an unbearable agony.

He tried to touch her, to shake her, but he couldn't. His hand hovered over her for minutes, getting closer and closer before he snatched it back each time. Finally, he threw both hands onto her shoulders and started yelling. When shaking her didn't work, he began to shake the casket, yanking on it so hard that it began to rock back and forth.

The crowd became frantic as Xavier continued trying to rouse his wife. Chance ran up and grabbed his friend, yelling for him to stop, but Xavier threw him off and continued to shake the casket, trying to awaken his wife. Chance fell to the floor behind Xavier and continued shouting for him to stop. The sanctuary was chaos now, and husbands began leading their inconsolable wives out of the room. Xavier became maniacal, and on one pull of the casket he stepped back and tripped over Chance's leg. He held onto the casket as he fell, and Chance rolled out of the way before Xavier and the casket came crashing down to the floor.

Xavier couldn't hear the people screaming around him. He couldn't see the women that had fainted being carried out, and the men rushing to the bathroom. He couldn't see Theresa's sisters, semi-conscious and mumbling, being transported to the ambulances that were making their way to the church. And he couldn't see Chance, lying there on the floor as he stared at Xavier in bewildered awe, not knowing what exactly to say or do.

He couldn't see them, but he could feel the fire in his stomach.

It was slight at first, nagging, even annoying, but then it exploded into an inferno that caused Xavier to scream out in pain.

Everyone around him thought he was responding to his wife's dead body on the floor, but in reality he didn't see it. His agony caused his eyes to water, and made everything around him a blur. The inferno within Xavier's blood began to spread, slowly setting his body aflame inch by inch. His shrieks echoed off the church walls, and the hair on everyone's skin began to stand tall.

The power began to flood his muscles alongside the agony, and his muscles tensed as his teeth grinded. Even the men stood horrified as they looked at the tortured father, his face contorted into a sick painting. No one was close enough to see his eyes, however. No one witnessed them as they began to change from white to black, from soft flesh to hard dark stone. Xavier felt it, though. He felt it, and he cried out all the more.

The ecstasy of rage began, and the comfort of insanity engulfed him. There were no thoughts for Xavier now. There was only pain and instinct.

But instinct told him to fight. Though he felt like he was dying, he still heard Diop's voice in his head. *"You must never give up! Ever! You must fight till the death! You must fight like the warrior you are!"*

Xavier began to push back against the pain. He fell over onto his side and made his way onto his hands and knees, taking control of his body again. Whatever was happening felt like it was trying to destroy him, but he wouldn't let it. Not until after he said goodbye.

Still writhing, he propelled himself forward, and looked down into the face of his dead wife.

And as quickly as it came, the fire in Xavier's bones vanished. Instinctively, he grabbed Theresa up under her arms and fell back against the seat of the front pew. His wife, all dressed up, lay in his arms, with her head limp against his left shoulder. He caressed her hair, and cried like a man who was mourning his soul.

Chapter Seven

Nathan wasn't sure where he was going. His legs carried him, and his body was mobile, but he was not conscious of anything around him. He bumped into and brushed against more than a few people, and the angry glares went unnoticed as he passed on.

He'd been walking for hours, focused on the same thought. The same event. The same gun barrel that had been aimed at his face, held by the hand of his own son. It had been a week, and he hadn't heard from Clarence, and didn't know if or when he expected to again. He didn't know if he'd smash a bottle over his son's head the next time he saw him, or run up and try and hug the life out of him. He didn't know if he'd ever speak to his offspring again, if he'd even respond affirmatively if someone asked him if he had any children. But he still loved his son, and that was what hurt him the most.

Overwhelmed with an emotion too extreme to identify, Nathan turned at the next street and began to walk back to his house.

Opening the door, Nathan walked inside to find Sonya sitting across from a man in a cheap suit at the dinner table. The man turned to see Nathan as he walked in, and Nathan, completely unconcerned about the both of them, put his coat in the closet and made his way across to the bedroom. Sonya opened her mouth, but the man spoke out first.

"How are you today, Mr. Freeman?"

Nathan stopped and turned to look at the man who sat at his table.

"I was telling your wife here how much I enjoyed your book. I was at one of your earlier book signings, when it first came out."

Nathan looked up at the ceiling for a moment, then turned and continued making his way into the bedroom.

Sonya shifted nervously in her seat as she called out to her husband. "Nathan, this—"

"I'll be in the bedroom."

"I'm a detective, Mr. Freeman." The man spoke out again and Nathan froze in front of the television. "My name is Detective Martinez, but everyone calls me Chance. I came to ask you all a couple of questions about your son, Clarence."

Nathan stopped and looked at Sonya, and realized that her face has been pale since he stepped into the house. Expecting the worst, Nathan took in a huge breath and walked slowly over to the table. He pulled up a seat and sat down beside his wife.

Chance paused for a moment, and began his acting routine, reciting the neutral lines that he had rehearsed in the car, and trying to block the memory of two children sitting on his best friend's lap.

"I don't know if you all have heard," began Chance, "but there was a pretty brutal triple homicide recently. Black family in the suburbs. A husband lost his wife and his kids."

"So my son isn't dead?" Sonya asked with wide eyes.

"No, ma'am, you're son is not dead. Not that we know of, at least."

Sonya grabbed onto Nathan's hand and closed her eyes in relief.

Nathan patted his wife's hand and exhaled himself, then looked back at the detective. "So what does this have to do with Clarence?"

"Clarence is a prime suspect in the case."

Sonya's eyes shot open as she looked back at the detective. "Are you saying my son killed that family?"

"It's more than likely that he did, ma'am."

Nathan sat up in his seat. "What makes you think Clarence did it?"

"We have an eyewitness who saw the entire thing from her window."

"Is she white?"

"Yes, she is. She's a little old, but she's given us a description that matches your son's."

"Eyewitnesses make mistakes all the time, detective. Your witness, an old white lady, saw a black person in her suburban neighborhood. She probably gave a pretty accurate description of me, too."

The detective nodded. "I understand where you're coming from, Mr. Freeman. Unfortunately, that's not all we have. There was a pretty clear fingerprint on the car. We ran the print and it came up a match to your son. He's been arrested on drug charges in the past, so he was in the system. Also, part of that print was in the victim's blood, so it rules out any coincidences."

"In whose blood?"

"The mother's blood, sir. It seems as though he accidentally touched the car while taking her pocketbook off of her arm. This was after he shot her."

"So...so you're absolutely sure it was him?"

"Honestly, Mr. Freeman, I am. The print gives him away."

Sonya stood up and walked over to the window. She leaned against it weakly, and spoke with a strained voice. "My son killed those people...killed a mother and her children. How old were they?"

"I don't know if that will help any, Mrs. Freeman."

"Please, just tell me."

The detective glanced at Nathan, who stared at the table, then looked back at Sonya. "The boy was kindergarten age. The daughter was in second grade."

Nathan shut his eyes. Sonya reacted as if someone had punched her in the stomach.

"I don't know if this helps any, but it doesn't seem like it was premeditated at all. This almost seems like a crime of passion, like something or someone set your son off and, in retaliation, he killed this mother and her children."

Everything was quiet for a few seconds, then a thought flashed through Sonya's mind. She walked back over to the detective. "When did this happen?"

"Excuse me, ma'am?"

"When did my son do this?"

"The incident occurred a week ago. The witness says it happened around eleven-fifteen p.m."

Sonya turned slowly toward Nathan, and stared at him with a look that he'd never seen before.

"What is it, Sonya?"

"It happened the same night he was here. He was retaliating to you!"

Chance quickly pulled a small notepad out of his shirt pocket. "Would you mind elaborating a bit, Mrs. Freeman?"

"My son…my son has a drug problem. I've been praying and praying, and I was always sure that Christ would see him through it. I always believed that, eventually, things would be okay. And sometimes he would come in and ask for money, and say that he needed it for clothes or food or something…"

"I understand, Mrs. Freeman. You love your son and you wanted to help him. I understand completely. Now, there's no rush, but whenever you're ready to tell me what happened on the night of the incident, it would really help me to figure out why your son did this."

"That night Nathan and I were lying in bed and my son came into the house. He was acting crazy, knocking things over and yelling and screaming and…well, he needed money. And my husband wouldn't give it to him. I mean, my husband never gives him money, but this time he hid my pocketbook so I couldn't give him any either. Clarence, he became enraged and pulled out a gun. And he pointed it at my husband's head. Lord Jesus, I was so scared I couldn't control myself."

"Why didn't you all call the police?"

"We couldn't try while he was in the house with the gun; it would have just provoked him. Finally, he…he ran out."

The detective turned and looked at Nathan. "Your son had a gun pointed at you?"

"Right in the middle of my face."

"And you still wouldn't give him any money?"

"I'm not as optimistic as my wife. I knew what he was gonna do with the money."

Sonya walked up and stood over Nathan as he sat. He looked up at her and she glared back down with fire in her eyes. "This is your fault. You killed our son."

"What are you talking about, Sonya?"

"All he wanted was the pocketbook. All you had to do was give him the pocketbook."

"He was going to get high with that money, Sonya! I'm sorry, but I couldn't…not anymore!"

"Yes, you could've! Now our son is as good as dead, and it's your fault! You killed our son!"

Sonya hit Nathan, open handed, across the face. Shocked, Nathan looked up at her, and she hit him again. Before long she found herself swinging both hands at her husband, striking him uncontrollably. Nathan put both of his hands up over his face and tried to move, but Sonya followed him, hitting him harder and harder, until the detective finally placed himself between the husband and wife.

When the chaos ended, Sonya stood on one side of the room with her chest heaving, and Nathan stood on the other, nursing his face. As he fingered the scratch above his eye, Sonya spoke out again.

"You did it, you bastard! You killed our son! You killed our son, that mother, and those two children! You couldn't love our son when he needed love the most!"

Nathan stood rigid after hearing his wife's words. Seconds of silence passed, then, without warning, he lunged back out toward his wife. The detective easily placed himself in front of Nathan, but fought to keep him from getting past.

Once Nathan exhausted himself, he stretched out his arm to its full length and pointed directly at Sonya. "You go to hell, Sonya! I loved my son more than anything else in this world! I loved him enough to almost die to keep him from killing himself! And I'll be goddamned if I let you or anybody else blame me for this! He did this! Not me!"

Sonya's face softened a bit, as she stared at her husband, then ran into the bedroom and slammed the door.

Her sobs could be heard throughout the house as Chance tried to compose himself. "I should probably be heading out, Mr. Freeman."

Nathan nodded his head, and watched the detective begin to pick up his things before he paused and threw his hands up. "Wow,

I apologize, Mr. Freeman. I forgot to ask you something. Do you have any idea where Clarence might be?"

"I'm sorry, detective. I haven't seen my son since he pointed a pistol at my forehead."

"Alright, then." Chance reached into his pocket. "If he contacts you, or you find out anything, please give me a call."

The card that the detective handed Nathan was dirty and a bit moist, but Nathan didn't notice. He placed the card into his wallet, and began to lead the detective toward the door.

Once the detective was outside, Nathan called out to the departing officer. "Detective?"

Chance spun around. "Yeah?"

"I'm sorry about what happened inside. You didn't have to come by here and tell us about Clarence. I just wanted to thank you."

Chance pulled up the collar on his coat. "Sir, believe me, I wish this had never happened."

Chance turned around quickly, hoping Nathan missed the tremor in his voice, and walked down the steps to his car.

Chapter Eight

There were no more glimpses of insanity for Xavier. His mind now knew full well what the reality was, and it provided him with no more temporary lapses into his previous life. It provided him with no more solace, no more protection from the truth. Xavier didn't hear voices calling out to him anymore. He no longer went to put his children to bed, nor did he discuss with his wife how work was. He knew now, without a doubt, without any glorious denial, that his family was dead. Shot in cold blood right in front of his house. Some nights he dropped to his knees, on the same floor that he used to play with his children on, and prayed to a God he wasn't sure existed. He prayed for his insanity to return, to be lost forever in the fantasy that he once lived. He prayed, but he knew it would never happen.

People had talked about the funeral for days, and would continue to talk as long as the sight of Xavier with his dead wife in his arms kept them awake at night.

"Those screams did not come from a sane person," one of the pallbearers told Theresa's sisters at the hospital. "Get Xavier checked out."

Xavier lay in his bed upstairs, covered with the sheets and staring up at the ceiling. "I couldn't save my family..."

The words echoed through his head. He needed no reminder

to know what he must do. Life as he knew it had ended, and he had no desire to start over again. Death had never frightened him, even before he had joined the military, and it didn't now. All he could ask for now was peace, and he only knew one way to obtain it. So he stared up at the ceiling, remembering everything he had learned from Diop, so he could honor his family in the way they deserved to be.

He remembered the combat tactics, the killing methods, the invisibility maneuvers, and the escape options. He reminded himself of how it felt to take a man's life, and prepared himself to do it one last time.

A knock came at the door, and Xavier stirred from his bed, moving heavily through the room. He put on a robe and glanced at himself in the mirror. The person he saw staring back was one that he hadn't seen in years. It was the Xavier that he swore his family would never come to know. But his family was gone now…

It was excruciating making his way to the door, and the house stabbed memories into his consciousness with every step he took. The memories colored every inch of every room with a dark gray aura that not even the lights could get rid of. Finally, Xavier closed his eyes, and made his way to the front door in his own darkness.

There was no one outside. Xavier looked through the keyhole and examined the front yard, but all he saw was grass. More curious than confused, Xavier threw open his front door, and saw a manila envelope taped to it, right under the peep hole.

For the first time in weeks, Xavier smiled. "You sneaky bastard; I knew you'd come through."

Xavier took the envelope and rushed back inside the house.

Everything stopped as he methodically tore the package open. It contained two items, a typewritten note and a picture. Xavier had never seen the young man in the picture, but he knew who it was. His mug shot was in color, so even though his eyes were only half open, Xavier could tell that they were bloodshot red. His hair and clothes were unkempt and his face was desolate. He looked like one of the reasons Xavier had raised his family in the suburbs and forbade his children from watching music videos.

Xavier stared at the picture for so long that he lost track of the time, and after the man's face was burned into his mind forever, he picked up the note and read it.

"Clarence Freeman. Druggie from the city. 21st and Grove. Fourth floor, unit 409. "

Xavier swallowed the gratitude he felt for his friend. There would be time to express that later. For now, he walked out to the garage, grabbed the lighter fluid, and doused both the picture and the note. Coming back in, he walked straight to the fireplace, threw the two items and the manila envelope inside, and dropped a match on top.

When there was nothing left but ash, he put the embers out and marched upstairs to prepare for the night.

The moonlight poured over the city like molasses. For the residents of Grove Street, the urban vampires who lived in the shadows during the day, this was when life began. Blood cold as ice from narcotics injections, they howled drunkenly, both at the moon and at prostitutes strolling by, finding pleasure in neither.

The apartment building on the corner of 21st and Grove looked like it could use an adrenaline shot. Even the spray paint had faded and was barely recognizable. The bricks that the building was supposed to be made of dropped randomly from different parts of the walls like light raindrops on a spring afternoon. The building should have long been condemned, but the money that was made daily within its crumbling walls was more than enough to pay off the state building inspector.

Even if someone Xavier knew were to see him here, they wouldn't recognize him. He fit into the neighborhood like a missing piece to a jigsaw puzzle. His clothes were ragged and torn, his eyelids fluttered in his head, and he walked with the sway of a man who didn't belong to himself. Even the homeless people outside nodded to him as he passed, figuring that he was in a worse position than they were.

Stepping into the building, the smell of urine and feces immediately hit Xavier's nose, and although he showed no signs of it he fought hard to keep from vomiting as he purposely tripped over people sprawled out in the hallway. He moved slowly, like every step was a chore that was forced on him, and mumbled incoherent apologies as he stepped on people who couldn't feel it.

It took Xavier forever to climb the flights of stairs, and when he made it to the fourth floor, he feigned exhaustion.

Finally, he reached apartment 409.

Turning the doorknob slowly, Xavier gently pushed on the door. It was unlocked from the inside, and directly in front of him sat Clarence Freeman, high and incoherent, with his legs out on the bathroom floor. His head was tilted to the side, and there was a steady stream of saliva that flowed from the left side of his mouth.

Everything inside Xavier wanted to run up to Clarence and beat him to death, to stomp the life out of him, then somehow bring him back to life and do it all over again. But his training had long since won out over his urges. Deliberately, he took off the makeup and disguises. He wanted his family's murderer to see him face to face.

Slowly and quietly, he closed the door and put his plan into effect. He took the latex gloves that he had brought with him out of his pocket, and put them on his hands. Then he walked into the kitchen and searched for the sharpest knife in the drawers. After he was sure he had found it, he made his way into the bathroom, making sure not to touch or brush up against anything.

Clarence continued to sit on the bathroom floor, oblivious to anything that was going on around him. At one point, his eyes looked up at Xavier as he failed to make himself speak. Standing over Clarence, the assassin reached down and put the handle of the knife into Clarence's palm. Then he gently grabbed the top of his head, and pulled it back so that his eyes looked up at Xavier's.

"I want you to know why you're going to die. My name is Xavier Turner. You murdered my wife and children."

He grabbed the back of Clarence's hand, and closed Clarence's fist around the knife handle. Making sure to imitate Clarence's natural movements, Xavier reached Clarence's hand across to the far side of his neck, placed the knife blade against it, and with one swift motion cut Clarence's throat.

Xavier narrowly avoided the blood spraying from Clarence's neck as he leapt out of the bathroom. He turned around to see Clarence with his head against the floor as he made gurgling noises from his throat. It lasted for about thirty seconds, then stopped, and although Clarence's eyes stayed open, Xavier saw the light start to fade from his pupils. He began to back up without turning around, and the last thing Clarence saw before he died was a man whose face looked a lot like a familiar little boy, covering his head with an old worn blanket and leaving the apartment, shutting the door quietly behind him.

C hance sat in front of the Freeman house, gripping the steering wheel until his knuckles turned white and his palms began to moisten and slide.

He knew what would happen as soon as he knocked at Xavier's door. Maybe that's why he'd run away, ducking out from under the porch before his friend could see him. He wanted to convince himself that he wouldn't be complicit in the murder of his own suspect. He wanted to believe he hadn't just sent a young drug addict to hell with two pieces of paper and a manila envelope. But he had. And if he had to, he would do it again. Print the same picture, type the same note. When a man took out a crew of enemy soldiers by himself in order to prevent you from being captured, and then asked for a favor, no matter how many years had passed, you put your personal feelings aside. But that didn't stop Chance from sweating, gripping the steering wheel of his unmarked car, wondering how he was going to face Nathan and Sonya Freeman and tell them that their son was dead.

Nathan had been sitting in front of the television for the last two hours, but hadn't paid it any attention. Sonya spoke as little to him as possible. At first it concerned Nathan, not knowing when his wife would stop being angry with him. Then he realized, eventually, his wife would need him as much as he would need her. Clarence was now a murderer, and once he was caught, every-one in the country would want to see him die. That was what he and his wife had to look forward to. The American public, a group of people who weren't there when his son was born, who never saw him ride a bike or heard him sing a song on the way to school, sentencing him to death. They had to anticipate visiting their son in jail, and living with the knowledge that Clarence would be living out the rest of his life behind bars. Nathan realized this, and realized that the only way he and his wife would survive was with each other. It was up to them to remind each other that their son, their Clarence, was a smart boy. He was a bright boy, with everything in the world to live for, who threw it all away one day when somebody, somewhere offered him a pipe as an answer to his problems.

A knock came at the front door, and Nathan shook away his thoughts and stood up. The fumbling around in the bedroom stopped. Nathan knew that, for the sake of trying to ignore him, Sonya wouldn't come out of the bedroom. She'd wait and listen.

Nathan clicked off the television, walked over to the door, and opened it to find Detective Chance standing on the other side.

Here it is, Nathan thought to himself.

He took in a deep breath, and let the detective in as he called out to his wife. As he led Chance once again to the table in the dining room, he wanted to tell the detective that he already knew what he was going to say. He could almost envision the words coming out of his mouth—

"Clarence was apprehended. We found him a drug house on the other side of town, and he's now in police custody at the precinct. The state will probably go for the death penalty, and they have a good chance of

winning, so you should prepare yourselves for the possibility of your son being on death row..."

Sonya didn't speak to the detective when she arrived at the table, just nodded her head. Much to Nathan's surprise, as he turned around to get her a chair, Sonya grabbed his hand and squeezed it tightly. They both sat at the same end of the table, with the detective facing them. Nathan expected the detective to start talking immediately, to be as forthcoming and blunt as he was before, but instead he hesitated. Moments of silence started to fill the air as the detective seemed to avoid both Nathan's and Sonya's eyes.

Sonya looked at Nathan confused, and Nathan volunteered the first words. "So, I'm assuming you've found my son?"

The detective hesitated again, but only for a moment, realizing that there was no escaping what had to be said. He looked up at Nathan, and nodded his head. When he spoke, his voice was low and apologetic. "Yes, sir, we found him."

Nathan, determined to stay strong, nodded his head matter-of-factly. "Has he been charged?"

"No."

"Is he at the precinct?"

"No."

Nathan looked at the detective, confused. "Where is he then?"

"Mr. Freeman, we found Clarence in an apartment building on the east side of town this morning. His throat had been slit with a kitchen knife, and since there was no evidence that anyone else had been in there, the incident has been ruled a suicide."

Nathan opened his mouth, but no words came out. "I'm...I'm sorry, Mr. Freeman. Your son is dead."

Sonya grabbed her hair and screamed, splitting the air and startling everyone. Nathan looked over and grabbed Sonya as she fell out of her seat and to the floor. Barely able to walk himself, he led Sonya from the table back into the bedroom, where she collapsed on the bed. When Nathan realized nothing he said would help his wife, he came back out to the living room.

"I apologize, Mr. Freeman. I...I just thought I should be the one to tell you..."

Without any warning, two tears came down Nathan's face, one from each eye, and he felt himself about to collapse as well. He quickly sat down. Chance offered to call in the paramedics, but Nathan waved his hand, no. He took a moment to try and stop his chest from feeling like it was going to cave in.

"What...what happened?"

"We received a tip this morning that Clarence was in an apartment building on the corner of Twenty-First and Grove. I went with the police squad personally to check it out. We walked in, and he was sitting right in front of us in a pool of blood. No signs of forced entry, of a struggle, a fight, or anything. We walked in and he was gone."

Nathan covered his face with both of his hands and, for the first time since he could remember, he wept like an abandoned child.

At first Chance didn't move, accepting this as his punishment for the debt that he had to pay. When it got heavy enough, though, the detective quietly made his way to the chair and picked up his coat, preparing to leave. Nathan noticed the detective moving, and tried to straighten himself up a bit. He wiped his eyes with the back of his hands and cleared his throat.

"I'm sorry, detective, I...I just..."

"Please, Mr. Freeman, you don't have to apologize for anything."

Nathan stood up, grabbed a tissue, and blew his nose. "I...I thought you all would catch him. I thought he'd be in jail."

"Again, I'm sorry, Mr. Freeman. I wish I could have brought better news."

Nathan shook the detective's hand firmly. "No...no...I thank you for coming and telling us. I'm glad it was you, detective."

Chance felt the guilt stab through his ribcage. Nodding at the mourning father, he turned and trotted down the walkway, trying to keep from shedding a tear himself.

Chapter Ten

T
he man that looked back at Xavier was not the one he had come to know. An unkempt, menacing beard lay tossed about on his face. The same eyes that used to light up his son and daughter's afternoons were now a dull gray, and heavy eyelids, weighed down with blended scotch whiskey, struggled to keep them visible. The skin on his face had become pale, the will to live dissipating from it like evaporating sweat. There were ridges in places where there were none before, and the extra hair on his head longed to meet a pair of clippers. The only remnant of the former man was Xavier's physique, which wasn't as willing as his appearance to echo his mood.

"You look like a homeless bodybuilder," Chance declared after his arrival. It was the first laugh Xavier had had in days.

Now, as he stared at himself in the bathroom mirror, Xavier could hear Chance grunt and slam his shot glass back down on the table. His subsequent coughs were muffled by the sound of unusually loud intercourse that came from the room next door. The girl was faking it, Xavier knew. She'd take her money when they were done and return in forty-five minutes with a different man. It had been like that for the past four hours. Chance tried to get used to it.

"Jesus, did you have to pick the only motel in the city with a prostitute special? I feel like I just inhaled the AIDS virus!"

Xavier chuckled as he swayed in front of the mirror, then shook the cobwebs out of his head. "I told you, it's a special occasion."

Partially mumbling and stumbling slightly, he made his way out of the bathroom and back to the small table in the middle of the dingy room. Chance sat in a raggedy chair with his back to the television.

"Glad you could make it out to celebrate." Xavier motioned to a bottle of liquor on the table.

"Whatever. You know there are ways I can stop you, right?"

"And you know they'd never work." Xavier sat down on the bed and poured himself another shot of Johnny Walker Blue Label. "To the hooker next door. May she find true love."

He saluted the noisy wall, then put the small glass to his lips and threw the liquor back into his throat.

"So this is how it's going down, huh?" Chance watched as Xavier began to pour another shot. "You buy the most expensive alcohol known to man and invite me here to spectate? You expect me to sit here and watch?"

"No, I'll wait till you leave. Wouldn't do that to you."

"What if I refuse to leave?"

"Then you'll spectate, I guess."

"X, this is stupid, man. Let me get you someone to talk to. You can go first thing in the morning."

"I don't need to talk to anyone."

"Yeah you do! You're sittin' here talkin' about—"

"Look!" Xavier interrupted Chance as he put his full shot glass back down on the table. "I didn't call you over here for a counseling session. I didn't call you to talk me out of anything."

"So what'd you call me for?"

Xavier paused, staring down at the tattered carpet under their feet. "You're the closest thing I've got to family now. You helped me do what I needed to do. That counts for something."

"So now what?"

"Now I fall on my sword."

"You don't have a sword."

Xavier pointed clumsily over to the 9mm pistol that rested on the pillow of the bed. "Oh…but I do—"

"Come on, X! You said I was like family, right? You said I helped you before?"

"Yeah."

"Then let me help you again!"

Xavier shook his head. "I don't need help this time. My decision's been made."

"Your decision sucks, man."

Xavier's eyes are partially closed, but he smiled anyway. "You're a good friend, Chance. We should've hung out more after I got out."

Chance shook his head as he pondered, then threw his hands up. He reached down and pulled his police radio from off of his belt clip. "I can't. I can't do this, man. I can't stand here and not do anything. I'm sorry."

Chance pressed the button on the walkie-talkie, but before he could speak, Xavier leapt over the table and smoothly kicked it out of his hand. The communicator landed with a thud on the bed. The sheets muffled the voices that tried to escape.

Chance looked at his hand as if he'd seen a magic trick. By the time he looked back up, Xavier's shot glass had returned to his hand.

"I know why you want to stop me," Xavier started, "I get it. But I'm askin' you as friend to let me do what I gotta do."

Chance glanced over at the walkie-talkie, then back at his desperate companion. Sighing, he sat down and reached for the bottle of scotch. "You're crazy," he commented as he poured himself a shot alongside his friend. "So, what do we toast this time?"

"To family." Xavier rose his glass as he grew somber. "I was a good husband. I was a good father. I'm glad I didn't waste the time I had."

Chance paused for a moment, then raised his glass as well.

They both drowned their glasses to the tune of muffled crime reports and fabricated ecstasy.

Ten minutes later, with the alcohol bottle nearly empty, the two men rolled with laughter as they exchanged old military jokes. Chance's walkie-talkie had been going off incessantly due to a shootout in progress, and though they couldn't hear what had been said, it was enough to cut Xavier's laughter short.

"Can you cut that thing off? It doesn't shut up!"

"That depends. You gonna do your dragon lotus mongoose kick again?"

Xavier leaned over with laughter, with Chance following suit. When he composed himself, he waved his hand at Chance. "No…naw…I'm not gonna kick…I mean, do another kick again. No, I'm not gonna kick you!"

With both men still in stitches, Chance stood up. Steadying himself, he walked over and picked the walkie-talkie up from off the bed.

"This thing runs my life, you know that?" He gestures with the radio to Xavier, who dismisses it.

"Just turn the stupid thing off! I can't hear the prostitute!"

Chance put his finger on one of the knobs at the top of the device as the female voice came through once again. "Unit 16, make a run through of 5625 Timber Lane. Make sure all reporters and picketers are clear."

"Unit 16, roger."

Chance's smile almost disappeared. "Poor bastard," he whispered to himself as he cut the walkie-talkie off.

"You know the address or something?" Xavier, glad to be able to talk without being interrupted, reached out for the bottle once again.

"Yeah, that's Nathan Freeman's address."

"Oh. Well, I don't know the poor bastard, but I can drink to him anyway."

"Actually, you do know him."

Xavier's curiosity was an afterthought to his scotch. "Really, how?" he asked as his shot glass filled again.

"He's Clarence Freeman's father."

It took a moment for the name to ring the appropriate bell, but when it did, the liquor stopped pouring and the laughter stopped.

"Clarence…Clarence Freeman?"

"Yeah."

Xavier stood up from the rickety table. "Why are they calling cops to his house?"

"Xavier, look, don't do this to yourself, okay?"

Xavier pretended not to hear him. "Why are they calling cops to his house, Chance?"

Exasperated and drunk, Chance sat down sloppily and laid the walkie-talkie on the table. "He hasn't been the best since his son died."

Xavier put his palm up to his forehead as he began to pace his side of the room, and the humor faded from his voice. The prostitute started up again, but he didn't care.

"I killed his son."

"Jesus…" Chance threw his arms up. "…this is why I told you to let this go! You killed the man who murdered your family…"

"He…he was somebody's son…"

"They're all somebody's son! Every murderer, every rapist, every serial killer, they're all somebody's son, man! Hell, I had to stand there in his living room and tell him his son got his throat slit! Had to tell him and his wife! She damn near had a heart attack, X! And after all of that, you know what helps me sleep at night? That the bastard who killed your wife and two babies is in hell where he belongs!"

Xavier continued pacing the room as his anguish became more and more obvious.

Chance tried to break through again. "Look, they're always somebody's son, man. There's always two sides to every story. You know that. You took out enough people while you were in to realize you can't sit around and think about 'em. You'll drive yourself crazy."

Finally, Xavier stopped and looked up. "You ever lost a son, Chance?"

Disarmed, Chance shook his head.

The two men stared at each other until one was forced to drop his eyes. Xavier made his way back to his seat and stared at his liquor bottle until an idea forced his eyes to go wide again. "What if HE did it?"

"What if who did it? What are you talking about?"

"The father. Nathan Freeman. What if he did it?"

Chance looked around the room, confused and slightly annoyed. "Did what, Xavier? Nathan Freeman didn't do anything."

Xavier paused for a moment, and then nodded his head approvingly. "I killed his son…it would only be right…"

Chance started to throw his hands up again. "Man, what are you…" He stopped himself mid-sentence as he thought about what his friend had said, and his hands fell back to the table. "You aren't talking about what I think you're talking about, are you?"

"Probably."

"No, naw, you can't be. You can't be because that would be ridiculous."

"You never know. It may help him…get some kind of closure."

"You're talking about letting him kill you!"

"I'm talking about letting him do what I was going to do anyway. No matter who pulls the trigger, it's the same outcome, right?"

"I won't…have any part of this." Chance tried to stand up and stumbled forward, catching himself on the table. After he got himself up straight, he pointed to Xavier. "You wanna put a gun in your own mouth, you go ahead. Nobody's stopping you. But if he shoots you, with or without your consent, it's murder."

Xavier heard his friend and ignored him. "He deserves revenge, just like I did. He's got every right."

Chance began making his way to the door. Xavier's rationalizations turned his friend's stomach as he prepared to leave.

"Chance!" Xavier looked up at him once again. Gratitude forced itself through the liquor. "Thanks again. For everything."

Chance turned around and steadied himself on the wall before he tried to speak. "Look, Xavier, leave Nathan Freeman out of this. He's got enough to deal with already. I'm telling you, this will only hurt him. There's no happy ending this way. Don't do this."

Xavier sat back in his seat, pondering his friend's words. "I'll let him make his own decision."

Chance turned the doorknob and stumbled out into the motel hallway.

It was a miracle Nathan was still on the road.

His headlights screamed at others on the highway to get out of the path. He terrified mothers and children as his car came out from the darkness and thundered past, shaking the chassis of larger sedans and trucks. Nathan barely saw them. Each one was just a set of red brake lights that flashed in the dark and taunted him. Taking him back to a few hours ago, when he was supposed to be giving a lecture on his book. Instead his knuckles turned bone white as he yanked from one side to the next on the steering wheel, abusing the dotted lines as they tried to separate the lanes. His tires tried to protest, but they competed with Nathan's own cries, and they didn't stand a chance.

A simple lecture. That's how his publicist had put it. That's how the head of the sociology department phrased his language over the e-mail. A simple lecture about Nathan's book. Nathan was secretly pleased to accept the invitation. He'd hoped it would resuscitate him, because other than his quickening heartbeat, he was sure he was dead.

Clarence had been memorialized at a scantily attended funeral that had more reporters than mourners. Nathan quickly realized that people didn't line up to pay their respects to a man who murdered a family. Most who came were there to support Sonya, who hadn't spoken a word to her husband except to express her opinion on a casket and burial arrangements. She blamed him for Clarence's death, and Nathan didn't have the strength to convince her otherwise. Their house had become a black hole, an abyss that was nearly impossible to claw your way out of after you'd fallen into it. Even after the funeral, Sonya had people to throw her a rope periodically. Most days, Nathan simply drowned.

Finally, one day, the phone rang.

Nathan was being asked to speak at Toolig University. The sociology department had requested him and were paying double the honorarium. Donnie Davis, Nathan's publicist, phoned him with an excitement that seemed foreign to the author.

"It's a great opportunity to try and jump start your rounds on the speaking circuit again," Donnie said. "It's risky, but it might be worth it."

Had Nathan's common sense been intact, he would have seen a set-up immediately. His son's face was all over the news, many times with his and Sonya's names attached to it, and Toolig University was known for its high racial tension. Even Donnie felt bad, knowing as he was confirming Nathan's speaking engagement that his client was probably not ready for what was to come.

"They want to rip him apart," the publicist told his wife. "Nobody pays twice the honorarium for a speaker unless they plan to make him work for it."

But Nathan insisted he was ready. Anything to get him out of the dark void of his home.

They clapped for him when he first entered, like his audiences used to do when his book was first released. A few of the black students even stood up, although half of them were from another campus, and even then they were few and far between. The auditorium was filled to capacity, and it was mostly blonde hair and blue eyes that greeted him at the podium. Nathan could feel the anticipation when he entered, and not long after he began one of the three lectures he'd long since memorized, he began to hear whispers. Signs that his topic was interesting, but not what the audience had come to hear about. It took ten minutes for a white male with a boyish face who looked to be about Clarence's age, to stand from his seat and raise his hand, demanding attention in the middle of Nathan's words.

"Uh…yes…you there…you have a question?"

"Yes sir, Dr. Freeman, umm, I was wondering if you could address how we, as students, are supposed to take your lecture in the context of your son?"

"Excuse me?"

"Well, sir, I was just wondering—"

"My son has nothing to do with this lecture."

"Yes, sir."

Nathan looked down at the podium, composing himself. By the time he looked up, another student had risen from his seat with his hand raised as well.

"If you'll wait until the end of the lecture, I can address all questions then."

"Just really quickly, Dr. Freeman. How can you lecture on what *The Seven Days* means for African-American pride and redemption when your son murdered a black family and then killed himself in a crackhouse? Doesn't your son really negate everything that you're talking about?"

An incensed black woman, seated in the front row, popped up and turned to face the speaker. "Shut up, Jim! This is Dr. Nathan Freeman! He deserves to be able to talk without hearing your racist crap!"

"Wait a minute, Keisha. Jim has a point." Another young man in an Abercrombie shirt stood up. "All this talk about great African spirits while your son commits triple homicides to score some crack? It doesn't seem to add up."

The auditorium was ablaze now. Students jumped up two and three at a time and shouted responses to one another, and campus security guards began to file down the aisles. Nathan struggled to finish his sentence while the room began to spin. Words that he'd recited countless times became stuck, jumbled in the space between his tongue and his lips. He felt his chest begin to tighten as an older white man rushed up to the stage and grabbed a spare microphone.

"Settle down! This is no way to represent Toolig University!

Settle down and take your seats right now, or so help me, I'll have everyone in this room subject to disciplinary action!"

The dean's words were loud enough to be heard throughout the auditorium, and the anger that provoked them couldn't be ignored. Slowly, the students began to sit down and compose themselves.

It was too late, though. Nathan had begun gripping the podium hard enough to make his hands sore. There was no use looking back out into the crowd. Everyone's face had begun to morph into Clarence's, and the rage that tightened his chest told him he wouldn't be able to stay on the stage much longer.

"My son…" Nathan began to choke out. "My son…was a good kid…and you bastards…you spoiled, privileged bastards…have no right…"

"Your son murdered a mother and two children!" Jim stood back up, fueled by the nearly avoided chaos. "There's nothing good about that! Jesus, your son is a serial killer! Don't you have any regrets? Aren't you sorry at all?"

"I'm sorry he didn't kill you!"

The sound cut off in the room as if someone had pressed a mute button. Open mouths and wide eyes stared back up at Nathan, who still saw his son's face plastered on a room full of students. Even Jim's words got caught in his throat before he cleared it, and sneered up at the speaker.

"Sorry, Doc, I think your son only gets his rocks off killing the homies."

Nathan began to lunge out from the podium, but the Dean grabbed a hold of his arm.

The auditorium ignited once again, but the escalation was so quick that no words from the dean would have diffused the situation.

Jim and three of his companions found themselves screaming at a group of black and Latino students, who had come to confront him after his comments. They formed the epicenter of what was sure to turn into a riot, and the campus security guards were running around frantic. The dean signaled to three of the guards, who ran up to the podium.

"Dr. Freeman, the guards will escort you outside and back to your vehicle!" the dean yelled over the pandemonium of the crowd. "I don't think this environment is safe for any of us anymore!"

Nathan considered jumping into the fray as the administrator turned to one of the guards.

"Get Dr. Freeman out of here! When he's outside and safe, call the local police! I don't think we're going to be able to handle this one on our own!"

"Yes, sir!" The guard used his body to shield Nathan, and the two other guards followed suit. Walking through the crowd was like being part of a football practice, but they finally made it to the front doors and out to the parking lot. Nathan's anger deflected the soreness in his joints.

"That goddamn kid! I could kill that goddamn kid!"

"Dr. Freeman, you better head on out." One of the guards, a middle aged man with salt and pepper hair and walnut skin, turned to Nathan. He had the name Walter etched into his nametag. "This ain't the first time some craziness has happened at this school, and it can get pretty bad. Seems like you don't need no more trouble. Hope you don't mind me saying."

Nathan realized that Walter was right, but if he left he'd have nowhere to put his anger. He'd have to sit and boil inside his car, praying he got to where he was going before the pressure blew his doors off the hinges.

Conflicted, Nathan stood in the middle of the parking lot, looking back and forth between his car and the double doors that led back into the auditorium. Before he could make a decision, the double doors exploded open, and a sea of enraged college students came rolling out. The flying fists made it hard to distinguish who was who, but after Nathan sorted through the crowd and laid eyes on his target, he burst forward himself. Jim saw him and smiled.

"Dr. Freeman!"

Walter rushed up and grabbed Nathan's wrist. He tried to pull free, but the guard's grip was too strong. The more he struggled, the more Nathan's vision began to go from blurry to a clear and bright red. Finally, he swung around with all his might and threw a punch that was so hard Nathan struggled to regain his balance after he missed. Walter ducked, then stood back up straight. He kept Nathan's wrist in his hand.

"I told 'em not to bring you here, Doc. I lost a son myself few years back. I told 'em it was too soon, but they ain't listen. Now the police is on they way here. They get here and find you rumblin' with a rich white kid, and your problems is just gonna get worse! I ain't tryin' to fight you, Doc. But the cops is comin'. You want me to let you go, I'll let you go. But jail ain't what you need, and it ain't where we need you."

The sincerity in Walter's eyes cut through Nathan's rage, and he stopped pulling forward just as sirens could be heard approaching in the distance.

"Which car is yours, Doc?"

Nathan pointed to his car, and Walter grabbed his shoulders and rushed him to the driver's side door.

"You get on outta here!"

Nathan started his car and sped out of the parking lot. He

reached the campus entrance just in time to see four squad cars speed onto the campus.

It wasn't long before Nathan realized that Walter's words were only a Band-Aid. Replaying the scene from the auditorium in his mind had diluted the security guards words, and the rage came back with alarming strength. Nathan considered turning around and going back to the university, but by this time the reports were all over the radio and the police were arresting students. His opportunity to unleash his rage had gone.

Nathan went back to his hotel room, but couldn't sit still. The television mocked him, laughed at him as he tried to figure out a way to grab a hold of himself. Eventually, he threw the remote at the screen, shattering it, and then screamed aloud. The insanity of his cry pleased him, and he picked up the broken television and hurled it across the space. The sound of crashing glass and plastic continued to ignite him, and he picked up a lamp and smashed it against the wall, pulled down the dresser and watched it crash onto the floor, and grabbed the coffee maker and hurled it out the window. The rage was soothing, comforting even, and as he was headed to the mirror on the wall, he began to feel a fire in his stomach.

He also realized, at the same time, that he still had a wife at home.

Sonya. How could he have forgotten? How could he be so selfish? She had lost a son, too, and he was getting ready to take away her husband as well.

"Sonya..."

He called her name aloud, and the match in his stomach was smothered.

Nathan had to get to his wife. He wasn't supposed to be home for another day and a half, but he didn't care. She was his saving grace. He needed her now, or he would lose his mind, he was sure.

Nathan picked up the suitcase that he never bothered to unpack, and ran out the door. Four hotel attendants were coming out of the elevator, no doubt responding to the multiple reports of screaming and property destruction coming from other guests on the floor, so Nathan used the stairs. He walked by the front desk, ignored the greeting from the concierge, and jumped into his car.

Now in his car, forty-five minutes away from his salvation, he drove as if he believed his destination may be gone when he got there.

Swerving and skidding, Nathan kept his rage at bay by imagining the conversation between himself and his wife when he arrived at home. If any of her church friends were there, he would politely ask them to leave. And then he would sit his wife down on the sofa, in the living room, and apologize. He would apologize as many times as it took for Sonya to stop hating him. Nathan's eyes dampened as he imagined the scene. He would collapse onto her lap, weeping, releasing all the hurt and pain that he had felt since hearing about his son's death. And it might take a while, but Sonya would comfort him. She would because she'd have to. She'd weep alongside him, no doubt. They'd cry into each other's arms, wailing to a God that only one of them had shown any interest in. And then they'd start healing together.

Maybe he'd start another book. Not immediately, but when things started to go back to normal. Sonya had always asked about another book. He'd ask her about it after church one Sunday. It could take years to finish, but he'd do it. And he'd dedicate it to his wife.

The highway sign beckoned to him. His wife was waiting. He blew past the rest of the cars on the road, cutting off an SUV to take his exit and skidding around the curve.

Now that he was back in the city, the streetlights provided an unwelcome delay. He ran through each of them, playing Russian roulette with the city traffic. After two near misses with a sedan and an eighteen-wheeler, Nathan finally pulled up in front of his house, turned off his lights and shut the car off.

Exhaling, Nathan began walking across the street.

There were no reporters. They had been spending less and less time in front of the house after the funeral, and on the morning Nathan left for the university, he hadn't seen one at all. The porch light shone down over the door as it illuminated the space and welcomed Nathan home. Sonya hadn't bothered turning the porch light on in the nights before Nathan left, and Nathan figured the dark, depressing image of their front door was fitting. Now, however, it shone bright, as if Sonya were waiting for him. As if she'd heard his thoughts from the road, and waited patiently behind the door to piece their marriage back together. Eagerly, he slid his key into the lock and pushed his door open.

All of the lights were off in the house, with the exception of the kitchen and the bedroom. Nathan could hear sounds coming from the television in front of their bed.

She must be watching a movie, he thought.

Lying in bed, watching a movie, waiting for her husband to return. Sonya was such a good wife, and Nathan stopped for a moment and marveled at how much he didn't deserve her.

The noise from the television interrupted his thoughts. The volume was louder than it needed to be, but the sound was exceptionally clear. Maybe she'd bought a new television? If she did, Nathan thought, then God knows she deserved it. The steamy film she had on would be perfect for his entrance, and Nathan wondered if it would be too straightforward to take her as soon as he walked through the door. He began to feel a tingling in his midsection as he bit his lip and walked forward.

It wasn't until he reached the doorknob and peeked in the room that he realized the television wasn't on at all.

Nathan was confused. His eyes were taking in information that his brain couldn't process. He swooned, trying to keep his balance, and tried to shake the numbness out of his head. It refused to leave. Instead, it began slowly making its way down the rest of his body, so that eventually he couldn't move or speak.

She sat upright, her bare back facing him as it rose up and down like an aggravated ocean. She didn't see him. She didn't know he was there. If he could have made a noise, she wouldn't have heard it over her own yelps. She threw her head back and released three short, high-pitched cries. Nathan knew that was how she climaxed. It had been years since he'd heard it, but he remembered it like a favorite tune. He reached out and gripped the wall as she let her head roll from side to side, clearing a line of sight to the man lying on his back underneath her. The man who had been in such a hurry, that he hadn't taken his clergy shirt off. He lay with his head on Nathan's pillow, breathing harder than he did after the few sermons Nathan had heard him preach. His eyes were shut tight in an effort to take in all he could of his adulteress. He didn't see Nathan either.

Nathan fell backward, stumbling out from the room and back into the living room couch. He flailed his arms around, trying to grab something that wasn't there. The moaning from the bedroom stopped as both participants looked up to see that the door they had shut was now open, and panic replaced the ecstasy that had been in their voices. Sonya made it to the doorway in time to see Nathan fall headlong out of the front door and down the porch steps. She hesitated, not knowing what to do, as her pastor walked up behind her.

She turned around, shaking. "It…it was Nathan…"

"Do you have a back door?"

"No, it's broken."

Out on the front yard, Nathan pushed himself up from his fall. He fell forward and caught himself as reality began to sink in. His wife was sleeping with someone else. His salvation was gone.

The rage came back quick, and strong. He had had enough hurt and torment to last a lifetime, and so without trying to, he bypassed them. Bypassed the pain, the torture, the devastation of knowing that everything in his life that he loved was gone. He bypassed them all, and went straight to the rage.

Nathan could barely feel it when it first started. The fire in his stomach seemed secondary to his teeth grinding, and when he began pounding on the hard soil, welcoming the sting of the dirt as it flew into his eyes, he was able to ignore the fire altogether. But when it exploded, it threw him from his knees onto his back, and he gripped his stomach as if someone were trying to slice it open. His screams echoed through the trees. His blood was on fire.

I'm...dying... Nathan thought to himself as he writhed on the ground, embers coursing through his veins. But this was different. There was euphoria that penetrated his senses along with the pain that seared them. The ecstasy of insanity beckoned to him as he rolled around on the dirt, coughing up blood from the shock of so much pain. And his eyes. He felt his eyes harden, felt them begin to solidify into something ungodly.

He kept screaming, but he had a choice. Something was trying to take him. Fighting to get inside of him, offering to replace his pain with something sweeter. Something was offering him salvation. And he had no reason to turn it down.

Nathan threw his head back and shrieked, and with what he assumed was his last breath, gave himself away to the unknown.

And everything fell silent.

PART TWO

T he air of the early morning sent chills through the house. The trees moaned quietly outside the living room windows, impatient for the sun to rise and shower them over. Every house on the block, except one, was absent of light, with occupants who frolicked in their dreams until daybreak, when they would long for the comfort of their imaginations once again. They rested, cocooned by their mattresses and blankets, and enjoyed a peace that they wouldn't remember when they woke.

The creatures of the night should have been out, giving their final calls before they retired to their cracks and crevices, but they'd scampered and slithered away from 5625. They had felt the vibrations in the ground when the man had returned home. The screaming from the voice in his head. Though the night was dead in its silence, what they had felt come out of that house was enough to cause their early retreat, and refusal to return.

The husband and wife in the living room didn't notice the animal's departure. Instead, they stood frozen, where they have been since the pitch black of the night still loomed around them, staring at each other's silhouettes in the darkness.

An hour ago, Sonya had heard her husband burst through the door. His steps were heavy and his breathing hard, and she believed him to be drunk until she sped out of the room where her infidelity had taken place. There she encountered a stranger. A man that she knew was not her spouse.

She took in what she could of his image as her fear slowly turned to terror.

She couldn't make out specifics. Her panic nailed her to the floor, where she could only glance at the light switch before darting her eyes back at the man in the living room. But she knew that her husband's weight didn't hang from his shoulders like this man's did. She knew her husband didn't shift from one leg to the other, like he was always looking for a reason to run. She knew her husband never clenched his fist and stood ready for battle, like this man did repeatedly. And the slow, carnal groan that emerged from this man's throat, like a predator stalking its next meal, anticipating the kill to come, made her blood run cold. Her husband didn't have that kind of ferocity in him. This stranger did.

But what gave it away most were his eyes, his jet black, in-human pupils, which glared through the darkness. For a while, they were the only thing Sonya could see, and they horrified her so deeply that she never even felt the urine run down her leg and up the fabric of her nightgown.

And then, without warning, the glow faded, flickered, and disappeared. And what was left standing in the living room was Nathan Freeman.

Now, as the sun started to pierce through the windowpane, Sonya could see her husband more clearly, and threw both of her hands over her mouth in order to prevent herself from yelling. Nathan didn't notice. The confusion on his face was only matched by elation, and the two emotions fought to share the same space. He looked around slowly, and began to feel disconnected with a space that he'd seen every day for the last decade. He couldn't remember how he had gotten into his house, how he had ended up standing where he stood in the living room, but that didn't seem to matter much right then. What mattered was the fury, the fiery turbulence he felt coursing through his veins with every slow pound of his heart. What mattered was the new rage that tightened his muscles, that made him strike himself in the face repeatedly to release enough to allow him to think straight. What mattered was the voice of the third person in the room, whom he ran around in the bluish gray light of dawn, throwing over furniture to find. It wasn't long before he realized, as he stared at his pale and petrified spouse, that there was no third person in the room. The voice that he was hearing was coming from inside of his head.

That's when the laughing started.

It began as a light chuckle, a polite formality after hearing a bad joke. But then it sped up. The slow cackle became rapid, and Nathan placed his head in his hands as his shoulders bounced up and down. His cackle went from alto to tenor as his fingers gripped and clawed at the outline of his face, and just when Sonya was convinced she could not take any more, that she'd die where she stood out of horror, Nathan exploded in front of her with his eyes so wide that they seemed to burst from their sockets, and launched into a bellowing fit so loud that Sonya covered her ears as she screamed in his husband's face.

The wave of audible insanity continued, until Sonya's tonsils could no longer take the strain of her constant screeching, and gave out with a choke and gurgling of bloody mucus. Nathan looked at the liquid that Sonya spat onto the floor, and then looked up at Sonya, who had gathered enough feeling in her legs to start taking tiny, uncertain steps back into the bedroom.

Laughing, Nathan lunged forward again, grabbing Sonya around the waist, and held her tightly as he started to dance around the living room. Her bare feet were off of the ground as Nathan danced the waltz, counting to three in time before every step. Sonya beat on him with her fists, pounding his chest trying to make him stop, but he only danced faster. Her screams were soundless, but she attempted them anyway, contorting her face and emptying her lungs as she shrieked into the silent air.

Finally, he let his wife go, and she stumbled backward as she looked down at her nightgown. Her hands shook violently as she began to hyperventilate, taking short, rabbit like breaths while she wheezed, and Nathan looked at her, confused. Her nightgown, which was bright white just a second ago, was now stained a crimson red.

Nathan looked down at his clothes, and realized that he was covered in blood.

His shirt was so drenched with it that the front and back stuck to his skin. He tried to peel it off, but the sucking sound that the fabric made as it pulled apart from his flesh almost made him vomit. Crying out, he ran over to the large vanity mirror that lay on the living room wall and cringed. The thick liquid came as far up as his neck, and as far down as his knees. Splashed on him like tie-dye, it lay concentrated at some points, and transparent at others, allowing the original blue tint of his shirt and brown of his khakis to peek through. There were tiny drops sprinkled across his face, as well as under his fingernails, where they remained trapped until the tiny pieces of human flesh were removed.

The sun was up now, and the rays fell on Sonya as she continued to shake uncontrollably in the corner, and nearly burned the skin off of her forearm as she tried to scrub away the blood with her palm. Nathan, suddenly remorseful at seeing his wife so unstable, tried to approach her, but she quickly jumped to her feet. On the brink of having her sanity torn, she begged Nathan with her broken voice to please stay away from her, but her resistance only caused the voice in his head to yell louder. She watched the storm pour into his face, and when he jerked forward, she leapt higher than she thought possible, and knocked the television over as she landed.

The screen cracked and the television flashed on as it hit the ground, providing background noise for the chaos. It was Nathan who first made the connection, and crept over to the disabled screen, watching a white man with a microphone and a shattered face as he relayed the breaking news.

"...*the media has already dubbed these the Rousch killings, and the police are beside themselves trying to figure out what happened. Here's what we have so far...the three lawyers from Goldberg and Finch who were representing Stacey Rousch in her rape case were brutally murdered here in Washington Park last night. Sources tell us that considering the speed and the nature of the attack, it is assumed that they were slain by anywhere between eight and ten men who were likely under the influence of some sort of mind-altering drug. The crime scene, from what we have heard, can only be described as barbaric...*"

The pictures of the victims flashed across the screen, and the voice in Nathan's head quieted in satisfaction. Three young white lawyers, all in their thirties, smiled in a picture taken in a popular bar uptown. The two young men were cocky. Nathan could tell by how they sat, with their shoulders upright, grinning slyly as if they knew they were poised to take over the world. Their suits were tailored and their ties were silk, and everything about them made it clear that they had no intention of ever being poor. The young lady, blonde haired and blue eyed, was hiding nervousness behind her smile. Her demeanor showed that she was capable for the task set in front her, but her eyes showed an exception, a moral hang-up that would have to be buried. She'd worked too hard to get into the firm to let something like doubt stand in her way.

"...the picture on your screen was taken just two days before the start of the trial. Ladies and gentlemen, this has proven to be a stunning development in an already controversial situation. For those who don't know, Goldberg and Finch were brought on to represent Stacey Rousch, daughter of well known venture capitalist Don Rousch, after she accused Jamal Jenkins, an African-American student, of raping her while at Toolig University, where they were both enrolled..."

The laughter started again. It echoed off the walls, filling every room in the house, while Sonya sat crouched in the corner, covering her ears and mouthing the chorus to "Jesus Loves Me."

Nathan had no memory of the events of last night. Even as his laughter burst forward, he scrolled through the memories in his brain, trying to conjure the images of the three people on the television screen. Trying to dig up sounds, smells, anything that would help him piece his puzzle together. There was nothing there.

But of one thing he was sure: he had murdered those lawyers. It was their blood splattered on his clothing.

He felt it as soon as he heard the news report. The satisfaction, like the last second of an orgasm, vibrated through his body and shook him to his core, setting off endorphins that would dwarf any narcotic. Though the faces weren't familiar, Nathan could feel their deaths in the palm of his hand. He could feel the remnants of their last breaths on his fingertips, and smiled as he put his hand to his face and inhaled the scent of their demise.

There were no eight to ten men. There was only him, and the voice in his head.

Nathan tilted his head as the report continued.

"Just yesterday, a jury found Jamal Jenkins guilty of rape, causing a firestorm among the African-American and civil rights communities. The coincidence of these murders happening on the same day as that decision cannot be ignored, and the police have transferred Mr. Jenkins from his jail cell to the Zone 3 Precinct for questioning. Early speculation has him directly involved as retaliation for the trial..."

Nathan's laughter stopped abruptly. He watched on the screen as live footage showed a young black male in handcuffs being led through a crowd of reporters and into the precinct about a mile down the road. The carnivorous growl emerged from his throat again, and Sonya rocked even faster as she began to dig her nails into her scalp. And then he screamed, and his rage shook the house as he charged at the fallen television and began pounding it mercilessly. Sparks burst from the demolished screen as his fists slammed down, one after the other, until it finally went blank, and pieces of the glass were stabbed into his knuckles.

With weights on his chest, Nathan stood, holding his bleeding fists at his side, and looked out at the sunny day painted outside of his living room window.

The voice in his head told him what he had to do, but he was already prepared. He walked over to Sonya, who no longer had the energy or the willpower to run, and reached down to lift up her head. The glass in his finger pierced her deeply under the chin, and she wept in agony as he lovingly touched his lips to hers. Then he walked out of the door.

The world felt different, felt dark despite the morning sun. And pain seemed to float through the air like particles of dust. It was everywhere. It was in the eyes of the young child, being yelled at by his mother to hurry the hell up so she could make it to work on time. It was in the breath of the gray-haired man half-awake on the corner, with two empty bottles standing tall by his overworn boot. It tumbled out of the cracked windows of the public bus that passed, filled to the brim with people mocked by the world around them. Teased by things they could not have. The pain began to prick Nathan as he walked. The glass in his hands protruded with sharp edges, but he only grimaced when he passed the liquor store. And the voice in his head grew silent in its confusion.

The world hurt now. It kept a nagging, incessant ache, and Nathan couldn't figure out why.

But he would have time to worry about that later. He was reminded of this, as the very people whose pain sear his skin gasped as he walked by. He'd been bombarded so heavily with the distress around him that he'd almost forgotten where he was going. He remembered, now, as the pedestrians on the street cleared his path and stared as he passed. As the onlookers pointed and covered their mouths, petrified of the blood-soaked man taking steps down the sidewalk. Nathan put his aching to the back of his mind as he continued toward his destination, looking straight ahead as people dropped their morning routines and froze. He burned himself into the mind of strangers, and the voice in his head pushed him onward.

By the time he reached the precinct, there was a small crowd that followed him, though their fright caused them to stay some distance back. There were only a handful of officers outside, and they scampered around in a panic. None of them noticed the strange man as he approached the double doors of the building.

It was not until Nathan walked through that he realized the entire building was in an uproar. He pushed open the doors of the building and, finding himself in a madhouse, paused to grin and soak in the chaos.

An army of officers dashed, tripped, and ran over each other as the gravity of the situation continued to drape itself over the building. Three affluent white citizens were murdered in cold blood, mangled to the point of being unrecognizable. The public was in a panic, knowing the killers were still at large. The mayor had personally visited the Zone 3 precinct, the only all white precinct in the city, within the last hour. Relying on their reputation, he had given this captain, and these officers, the charge of bringing the band of murderers to justice. Everyone within the four walls knew what was at stake, and blood pressures spiked as the law enforcement officials went into overdrive. Papers erupted into the air, curse words flew across the room like bullets, and nappy headed suspects, loudly insisting their innocence, were shoved, manhandled, and thrown into interrogation rooms.

No one saw the crimson-stained man as he walked through the metal detectors. Everyone wearing a uniform had a task, and was sharply focused on it. But Nathan saw Jamal Jenkins. He saw him as he pushed across the room, hands cuffed behind his back, staring emotionless at the floor. He looked like a young man who had had the life ripped out of him. He went where he was shoved, and stayed where he was placed, and when he glanced up and saw Nathan, and saw the man covered in the lifeblood of his victims, he didn't flinch. He took note, and dropped his head once again, begging for death any way he could get it.

That's when it first ignited. The match inside of Nathan's stomach. It wasn't a gradual, progressive burning anymore, but an instant inferno. An incinerator within his muscles and bones.

Nathan doubled over, clutching his gut as if he was trying to rip it out, and then all at once, he jumped up, threw his head back, and screamed.

Even the officers who couldn't see him were scared witless by the sound that echoed off of the precinct walls. They dropped everything and gaped at the man at the front of the building as his face became deformed with pain, shaking and tightening with every octave as his shrieks intensified. And when the cries reached their peak, the light fixture above Nathan's head exploded, baptizing him with glass and sparks.

And then there was silence. Deep, deep silence. And all was still. And Nathan was gone.

The stranger deliberately looked up at the officers, and all the color drained from their faces. The suspects, still handcuffed, trusted their instincts and scooted themselves into the nearest corner. They tried not to shake as they beheld the man with the hate pressed on his face.

It was Jamal, shocked out of his hopelessness, who finally uttered the words that everyone was thinking. "What the hell is wrong with his eyes?"

Quickly, almost masterfully, the stranger reached behind him, grabbing the metal detector that Nathan had walked through just a few minutes ago. With a hard, swift jerk, he yanked it up from being bolted to the ground, and hurled it into the sea of police officers.

Those who stood closest to the stranger were deprived of their chance to scream. The hard metal structure was thrown with so much force that only the wall at the other end of the room was able to stop its momentum, and the people smashed between it and the concrete were stuck with blank expressions, oblivious to the knowledge of their death.

After that, the stranger painted the walls. Blood spatter from torn limbs and crushed organs turned an off-white space into a reddened ballroom, decorated with the entrails of its employees. The chorus of tortured outcries harmonized into a symphony that the stranger moved to as he artfully detached one person after another. Some had the opportunity, before their demise fell upon them, to pull their firearms and release a round, but it made no difference. The stranger fell upon them anyways, annoyed at the disturbance, and took extra care to make sure they felt every inch of their death as it came.

When Captain Rice saw the stranger run through the bullets, he dropped his gun to his side as he stumbled frantically over the bodies of his coworkers. Tripping, he threw his hands up as he fell, and accidently fired a shot that struck the dark figure directly in his temple. Jamal Jenkins watched in awe as the stranger collapsed to the floor, and the captain ran hollering out into the open air outside.

The sirens from the Zone 2 police cruisers, which were the closest, split the air as the backup officers began arriving in droves. Chance was the first from his zone to arrive on the scene, and after seeing the blank stares and incoherent mumbling of some of his surviving friends, he ran inside without backup to see what had happened.

Commander Nash arrived a short while later, but the recounts of the on-site personnel were so unbelievable that he left them all in the hands of the paramedics, opting to give himself and his precinct the opportunity to figure out what had happened. He was shouting orders to form a perimeter around the building when Chance emerged from the double doors.

The commander began to scream at his detective from afar, stringing together curse words and hurling them at Chance as punishment for not following protocol, but Chance couldn't hear him. He took three steps out of the doors and keeled over, vomiting violently, until all that came out was spit and breath laced with stomach acid. He looked at the commander as he tried to stand, and his superior rushed over to him as he stumbled and fell on the precinct steps.

When it was all over, more than half of the police officers of the Zone 3 precinct lay in pieces. The rest had managed to escape amongst the pandemonium, and psych evaluations would bring an early end to most of their careers.

The suspects were gone as well. Somewhere in the time of the massacre, in the midst of all the bloodshed, the stranger managed to set them all free.

When Commander Nash finally entered the building, he found himself in the middle of a slaughterhouse. The body of a seemingly ordinary black man was in the middle of the room, covered in fresh blood and lying unconscious on the floor. His head rested in the lap of Jamal Jenkins, who cradled it with his unshackled hands, begging him to get back up.

Three hours later, the Governor would vehemently demand answers that no one had, all while calmly refusing to comment on rumors of a mass murder to the press. Cameras clicked and flashed in front of him as he assured the public that he would give them more information as soon as he had it. Satisfied with his lies, he rushed upstairs to his office and phoned Commander Nash, cursing until his face turned blue. Nash informed him that they had a suspect, and the mayor demanded that he not leave the bastard's side until he was either dead or in jail. The Commander, bombarded by the media and officers thirsty for revenge, told the mayor that he would put his best man on it, and then hung up and called Chance.

Moments later, Chance sat in the hallway of the emergency room, watching doctors and nurses declare death on one person after another, and bloody cop uniforms float around on rolling gurneys. He had gone into the hospital room himself and hand-cuffed the unconscious man to the stretcher he was laid on. After, he went outside the room to breathe, but he couldn't get the scene out of his head. It stayed there like a headache, pounding on his brain. The faces of the dead in the police station popped up from the floor, surrounded by body parts that were never meant to be seen.

And in the middle of it all was Nathan Freeman.

Chance had lost track of the time when one of the emergency room doctors walked up and shook him from his trance. Looking at his chart with his eyebrow wrinkled, the young physician told Chance of his confusion. His chart stated that the suspect had been shot in the head, but there was no evidence of a gunshot wound. Pulling out an X-ray sheet and holding it up to light, the doctor pointed to the spot where they believed Nathan to have been shot, and commented quite assuredly that there was, in fact, no evidence of any head trauma at all.

Chance looked from the doctor, to the x-ray, and back, as he tried to stop the emergency room from spinning. Not knowing what else to do, he burst back into the room where Nathan Freeman's body was laying, ready to wake him and demand answers. But all he found was an empty hospital bed with handcuffs linked to each side, and a breeze from an open window.

Jamal Jenkins sat in the back of the police cruiser. The familiar feeling of handcuffs had returned to his wrists as he allowed his head to fall back, ignoring the black and brown officers in the front who yelled at him for answers about the precinct murders.

Their threats were idle. Meaningless. His life was already over. It had ended just over twenty-four hours ago, when a jury declared him guilty of a crime he did not commit. When they stared at him with cold eyes and declared him a college-educated rapist. A drain on the society that he'd swore to his grandmother he'd be successful in.

He hadn't given up hope, all the way up until the last day. Even when his grandmother told him that despite the fundraising they had done, they couldn't make bail and pay the legal fees at the same time. Even with the eleven months that he spent in the cold, damp cell, looking at the world from behind the long, silver poles, reaching his hand out sometimes just to feel the air on the other side. Even when his attorney told him that it didn't look good, he kept the fight going inside of him. This was America, after all. Where justice reigned. Where a man was judged by the content of his character. They had to find him innocent.

But they didn't. And Jamal's life was over.

"Watch out!!!"

The patrolman in the passenger seat shouted as he pointed excitedly to his left, but it was already too late. Before the driver could react, a man, moving impossibly fast, lowered his shoulder and smashed into the front side of the moving police cruiser. The hood bent and twisted as if it had hit another mass of speeding metal, and the cruiser began spinning across the lanes of the road. When he stopped, the driver, who could barely speak, looked over at his partner, who leaned unconscious against the window of his door. He moaned softly, but didn't open his eyes.

And then he saw the stranger.

Climbing up from the asphalt, the dark figure looked through the windshield at the driver, his jet black eyes causing the patrolman to fall silent before he stumbled over to the rear passenger side door.

The driver tried to call out, but he could barely hear his own voice as the stranger ripped the door from the cruiser chassis and threw it to the side. Reaching in, he grabbed the stunned prisoner, yanked his handcuffs apart, lifted the young man up, and disappeared down the street.

The blinds were shut tightly, like weeping eyes, blocking the fresh sunrays from entering into the large bedroom. Nature's morning soundtrack was muffled by the silence of the space; intense, desolate silence. The remnants of a family were here, like footsteps of persons long gone. The silhouette of a soft football, tossed at one time between a grinning father and son, fell haplessly against the wall. Flowers that were once cared for now lay dead in their vase on the dresser, with dead petals cursing the four walls as they free-fell to the soft carpet. The light scent of perfume still rose from an unoccupied pillow, but only went so far before it dissipates into the stale air. And the shell of a man sat calmly on his wife's side of the bed, surrounded by the mountain of stuffed animals that he and Theresa had purchased for their children over the years. Mixed into the stack were trinkets, forget-me-nots passed back and forth between his wife and himself, symbols of a once abundant love.

Xavier sat on his bed, fully clothed, drowning in what was left of his family.

The item closest to him was a soft, gray elephant. It had kept Felicia company just a few years ago, during the nights in her crib when her parents wouldn't come to comfort her, trying to get her to fall asleep on her own. Felicia's tears had stained every inch of it, and later, when they were sure she was asleep, Xavier and Theresa would sneak into her room and kiss their daughter softly, tucking the elephant even closer to her chest.

There were no more tears to cry. There were no more apologies to make. Xavier sat calmly in the same spot he had been in for hours, agonizing, trying to soak in every last memory. Every last nostalgic feeling. And when he was satisfied, the Desert Eagle .50 from his side dresser sat, fully loaded, just an arm's length away.

The Nathan Freeman idea was selfish. It took Chance to make him realize. Even if he convinced Freeman to take his life in retribution, Chance gave his word that he would arrest the father, and he would likely spend the rest of his life in jail. No, Xavier decided, save the man's life by letting him believe his son's death was a suicide. Allow him to get over his grief and move on with his life. Handle things on your own. Die with honor, like Diop taught you. Accept your fate.

Xavier began moving the stuffed animals and trinkets to the side, one by one, with the meticulousness of a bomb maker. Each one had a sea of memories that he had allowed himself to relive for the past twenty-four hours. Surprise purchases from the toy store. Christmas gift accompaniments. Valentine's Day purchases. The film reel had run through his head enough, and there were no more instances to conjure up. No more forgotten moments that an obscure toy or long lost piece of jewelry triggered. He had had his fill of all he had lost. And now it was time.

Once all of the items were stacked beside him, forming a memorial to the people he loved, he picked up his Desert Eagle and began to clean it with his shirt. The shiny metal purred as Xavier went over every inch, taking care not to miss any spots. When he finished, he looked down at the glowing steel, satisfied at seeing his reflection on the side of the barrel, and then stuck the front end of the gun into his mouth.

Offhandedly, he thought to himself how bitter steel was on the taste buds as he placed his thumb on the trigger.

And then his cell phone rang.

The coincidence was too much, and Xavier released a muffled laugh as his lips wrapped themselves around the gun barrel. Whoever it was had an uncanny sense of timing. Their call, however, was inconsequential. Xavier couldn't imagine taking his last breath while the annoying wail of a cell phone ringer pulsated in the background. So he removed his thumb from the trigger of the weapon, still keeping it tucked between his teeth, and waited patiently for the phone to stop ringing.

When it finally ceased, he took a deep, long sigh of relief, and placed his thumb back on the trigger, smiling as best he could.

His thumb twitched, and the phone rang out again.

Yelling out in frustration, Xavier took the gun out of his mouth tossed it onto the bed in front of him. Leaping, he made it across the room in a single bound, and picked up his cell before looking at the screen.

"Who the hell is this?"

"X…it's Chance."

Xavier calmed a bit as the instinct to throw the phone out the window dissipated. "Chance, this is kind of a bad time…"

"Look, I need your help, bro! I don't know what the hell is going on, but I'm not equipped for this! I'm not trained for this, and I'm scared out of my mind, and all I see is people's intestines lying on the floor when I close my eyes, bro! I can't do this! I can't do this, and I don't know anybody else here who can do this, and I don't know what kind of person gets shot in the head and breaks out of some goddamn handcuffs, and I don't…"

Even over the phone, Xavier sensed Chance's elevated heart rate and erratic breathing. He glanced over at the memorial on his bed, and decided that if he could help his friend out one last time before it was over, it was worth the delay.

"Chance, what the hell, man? Are you okay?"

"No! No, I'm not okay!"

Xavier hadn't heard his friend sound this horrified since their first tour together in the Gulf. He stood up straight now, paying attention to every word. "Chance, are you hurt?"

"No...no, I don't think so..."

"Then what's going on?"

Chance didn't realize he was wheezing. "It's Mr. Freeman... Nathan Freeman."

Xavier froze. "Nathan Freeman? As in the Nathan Freeman you told me about? Clarence Freeman's father?"

"Yeah..."

"What happened? God...he didn't...he didn't kill himself, did he?"

"No, naw, no...no, he's fine."

Xavier's muscles relaxed a bit. "Then what happened?"

"I don't know, man...he's...he's on some kind of rampage..."

"Rampage?"

"Yes, rampage!"

Xavier stayed quiet for a moment, then spoke again, trying to hide his anger. "Chance, I really was in the middle of something. This isn't funny."

Chance jumped up from the chair he was sitting in and held his phone in front of his mouth, shouting.

"Isn't funny? You think I'm joking? He took out half a goddamn precinct!"

"So what? You mean he's killing people?"

"No, I mean he's detaching people like goddamn Legos! Taking them apart like a goddamn science experiment, X...he's massacring people!"

Xavier pulled his cell phone away from his ear and stared at it, trying to figure out what was happening. He heard Chance still shouting unintelligibly as he put the phone back up. "This doesn't make any sense, Chance. I thought you said he was a middle-aged Ph.D.?"

"He is a middle-aged Ph.D.!"

"Middle-aged Ph.D.'s don't go on killing rampages."

"You're not listening, X! The bastard snapped! Had some sort of psychotic break or something! He's killed thirty people in just over twenty-four hours!"

The two men stood quietly on the phone, trading exhales, before Xavier shook his head and Chance spoke up again.

"Look, X, you can take it however you want it, but right now I need your help!"

"My help to do what? Take him out?"

"Hell yeah, take him out! The city is in a panic, bro! People aren't coming out of their homes until this guy is caught or killed!"

Xavier hissed angrily into the phone. "I'm the one that killed his son, Chance! I'm the reason he snapped! You want me to help you kill a monster that I created?"

"Yes!"

"No! No, I won't do it. Clarence Freeman killed my family, and for that he deserved to die. I've got my retribution, Chance. I'm done. Goodbye."

Xavier prepared to hang up the phone, but his friend hollered from the other end.

"Wait! X, wait!!!"

Xavier paused, looking back over at the memorial on his bed, and put the phone back to his ear. "What is it, Chance?"

"Look, just…just turn on the television, okay? Just look at the news!"

Xavier pondered hanging up the phone once again, but instead gave in to his friend. It grieved him to walk out of what was supposed to be his tomb, but he left and walked downstairs anyway. The dirty fingerprints and crayon markings on the wall made him wish that he hadn't.

He was almost in tears as he walked into the living room and found the remote.

The report was on almost every channel. Even the ones that weren't local had picked it up. Images of police officers covered in blood, being rolled on stretchers or rushed away in ambulances, ran across the screen, as each news reporter made claims of a group of psychopaths that attacked a police precinct. Eventually, the live footage of the reporter faded, replaced by wallet-sized photos of all those killed.

Xavier squinted his eyes, making sure he was seeing the screen right. "They're all white?"

"The victims? Yeah. I don't think it's random either. All this started after that Jamal Jenkins verdict came down two days ago."

"So you think Nathan Freeman is a part of this group that's killing people?"

"There is no group, bro."

Xavier paused as he listened to the news report. "That's impossible. Thirty people in a day? Half a police precinct? They're saying it's eight to ten people…"

"Yeah, I know what they're saying, X! How do you explain to the public that a fifty-five-year-old black man did all of this?"

"Forget the public, Chance. How do you explain it to me? You guys got guns, right?"

"All accounts say that shots were fired at the suspect, but had no effect until he was shot in the head."

"You got him in the head? Then why isn't this over?"

"X...X, I was at the hospital with the guy myself. I handcuffed his hands and feet to the bed. Next thing I knew, he was gone."

"After being shot in the head?"

"X, I'm telling you...I don't know what's going on, but I've never seen anything like it. None of us have. I need your help, man."

Xavier stared at the television, focused on the disquieted faces. The survivors of the attack all looked as if they'd seen ghosts, and their fear-stricken faces jumped out from the screen. The camera scrolled over to a family, a mother and a child, who had just been informed that their loved one was killed in the attack. The pain in their eyes made Xavier's knees buckle, and he quickly turned the television off before lowering himself to the ground.

"Chance..."

Xavier's voice sounded like it did at the funeral, before he walked down the aisle and pulled his wife's body out of her casket.

"Yeah...yeah I'm here, man...you okay?"

"Just give me a second."

Xavier dropped the phone to his side before bringing his knees up to his chest. He sat there, in a fetal position, rocking back and forth, until he regained enough of his composure to stop shaking.

Slowly, he picked the phone back up. "You there...?"

"I'm here, man. What happened?"

"Here's the deal. I'll help you find him, but I won't kill him..."

"What if he tries to kill you?"

"...and in return, if we bring him in alive, you leave me with him."

Chance's relief was cut short. "What?"

"You put us both in a room, together, for as long as it takes."

"As long as what takes?"

"Those are my terms, Chance. Take it or leave it."

"X, every cop in the city is out for this guy's blood! Just because you won't kill him doesn't mean someone else won't. And even if we do bring him in alive, X, this thing has gone up to the state level! The Governor is involved and the National Guard is on alert if it gets any worse. Getting you two in the room together will be next to impossible."

"Then you get me on site. Give me your word, Chance! If we catch him, you'll get me on site wherever he's being held. I can take it from there."

Chance threw up his hands. He knew the danger of what his friend was asking, but also knew he had no choice.

"Alright! Alright...you help me catch him, and I'll get you on site. You have my word."

"Good."

"Now get dressed. I'm coming to get you."

In another life, Jamal would have been horrified.

The house he was in refused to illuminate, despite the sun crashing into its windows. His first inclination was that he'd found himself in a funeral home, as the entire dwelling reeked of death, and the dark aura did constant battle with the fresh linen and pillow that had been placed on the carpet for him. Gingerly, he made his way to his knees, and realized that he was in a living room. There was a television in the corner that had been smashed into oblivion, and even in the gray dreariness of the space, Jamal could make out drops of blood sprinkled around the carpet and walls.

Immediately, he remembered the events of the past day, and became hyper as he swiveled his head and looked around the dark room for his savior.

Instead, he came face to face with Sonya, who caused him to scream out loud. She was in the same clothes as she was when her husband left the day before, and her blood left abstract artwork on her nightgown. Her eyes retreated into her face, which was pale and dry from lack of sleep, and the blood vessels that had burst in her pupils made her glare look like a curse.

She sat close enough to Jamal for him to feel her breath on his cheek. She stared at him, almost without blinking, as she had for the past five hours.

Jamal began to creep backward as Sonya's gaze remained unbroken. She smiled at him endearingly, but didn't move as he inched himself further and further away. Before long he was approaching the corner of the room, and thought through the fear in his head as he decided he would use the wall to help him stand, and then find a way out.

The arm that his hand fell upon put a wrench in his plans.

Screaming out again, he turned to see the man who had rescued him. He was slumped against the wall in a hostile slumber. His eyes were closed, his breathing was quick, and he jerked every now and again, as if someone were trying to drag him.

At a loss for what to do, Jamal reached out and tried to shake the man awake.

"NO!!!" Sonya screeched from across the room like a banshee, and Jamal froze.

She wasn't smiling anymore. It took Jamal to look back across the room to realize she was just as scared as he was.

Something was wrong with her voice. He could tell by the way she cried out. She croaked and gurgled, like someone had tried to slit her throat, but only got half of the way through.

Jamal finally made his way to his feet, as Sonya stared wide-eyed at her husband.

"Ma'am...who are you? Where am I?"

Sonya continued to stare at Nathan as she rushed over and grabbed Jamal's arm. Once in her grasp, she pulled him away, back to the other side of the room, as Nathan continued to jerk around in his sleep. Once she felt they were a safe distance away, she looked at the young man longingly, and then wrapped him up in an embrace as she began weeping.

"He brought you back to me..."

Nathan continued twitching in his sleep as the voice in his head grew tumultuous, frustrated at having to retreat back inside the cocoon of Nathan's mind. There was nothing like the feeling of being flesh and blood again. Of making a fist and having your fingertips rub against the skin on your palm, or grinding your teeth and feeling the enamel connect, scratching despite the saliva. It was euphoric, and equaled only by the feeling of his enemies' blood on his skin. Being out of his time was a small price to pay for the reckoning he had planned.

He knew, felt, as soon as he emerged from Nathan's pain, that his lust would not be satiated by anything less than bloodshed. He felt the pain of his brethren with his first breath, and spent much of his inception becoming acclimated with the constant agony. The strongest of it led him to the lawyers in the park, where he found his only relief. Where he medicated his pain with murder. But now...now the spirits of his kinfolk poured into him; the memories of those who had lived their lives in constant fear, who had experienced the horrors only talked about in history books, and deaths so gruesome that it had caused their souls unrest. Those memories began to pound him. Eat at him like termites on rotten wood. And he felt his strength, his thirst, and his rage, grow with every passing moment. He was desperate to be loosed upon the world again. To quench his parchment, his ever growing gluttony, with the blood of the enslavers.

But he had to wait. It was not yet his time. And as his frustration grew into frenzy, he could think of only one consolation.

Angrily, he shouted out within the mind of his host, and jerked Nathan awake.

Nathan shrieked as his eyes shot open, and he scrambled up from the floor as if he was on fire. Both Sonya and Jamal jumped violently as Sonya let the boy go, and then placed herself in front of him, blocking him from Nathan. Nathan spun around, chasing a tail that he didn't have, before he stopped on a dime and began walking rapidly around the room.

"We the people…!"

He stopped where he was, paused, and then laughed hysterically. Jamal's blood began to run cold, and Sonya stepped back, trying to move him out of the room.

When Nathan was finished cackling, he continued pacing. He was aware of the people in the room, but ignored them as he spoke.

"We the people! No…we the slaves! We the slaves!"

Nathan jumped up and down, clapping, celebrating his choice of words.

"We the slaves of the United States, in order to form a more perfect union, establish justice, ensure domestic tranquility, provide for the common defense, promote the general welfare, and secure the blessings of liberty to ourselves and our posterity…"

He froze again, this time closer to the window, where the light was slightly better. He looked at Sonya and Jamal, and then down at his clothes.

"This…this is fresh. This is fresh blood. It's not the same blood. It's different blood. It's fresh blood."

He stared at Sonya with a hand over his mouth, like a child trying to hide a giggle. When he could contain it no longer, he lifted his hand up in the air and began praise dancing as he sang out of key.

"There is power...power...wondrous working power...in the blood...of the Lamb!"

Nathan danced over to Sonya, who held her breath as he stopped in front of her. He looked directly behind her to Jamal as the smile dropped from his face.

"Who are you?"

"I'm...I'm Jamal Jenkins, sir."

"I remember you. I remember you from the police station. I remember you...and then I don't remember anything else. What's so special about you?"

"Nothing, sir."

"So why can't I remember anything after you?"

"I don't know, sir."

"What happened at the police station?"

"You killed everyone, sir."

Nathan stopped with his mouth open, and his eyes blinked several times. "What?"

"Well...almost everyone, sir. Some people escaped, but...well, I was there. I was there and you pretty much murdered everyone you touched."

Nathan looked around the room, confused, before he looked back at Jamal. "Who are you?"

"I'm Jamal Jenkins, sir."

"How did you get here?"

"You brought me here, sir."

"Ah...that's a beautiful mask, isn't it?"

He moved Sonya gently out of the way. She tried to resist, but he seemed stronger now than before. He slid her to the side without a second thought.

Nathan walked up to Jamal and examined his face up close.

"Yes...yes, it's beautiful. Handcrafted by Dunbar himself. The intricacy is flawless. The design...immaculate. Now tell me, who are you?"

Uncomfortable with Nathan being so close, but afraid to move, Jamal drew his face back ever so slightly as he responded. "I'm Jamal Jenkins, sir."

Nathan's face went from calm to menacing in the blink of an eye, and he shot out his hand and grabbed Jamal by the throat, lifting him off of the ground. Sonya began beating on him as Jamal's choking filled the air, but Nathan barely felt her attacks as he growled at the young man.

"TAKE OFF THE MASK!"

Near delirious, Sonya ran into the kitchen and grabbed a knife, then ran back into the living room and lunged headlong into her husband with the blade outstretched. It went deeply into his side, with only the handle protruding, and slowly Nathan put Jamal down on the floor and turned to his wife.

"Honey, would you please sit down?"

Sonya prepared to stand her ground, but lost her constitution when she saw her husband pull the blade out of his side and toss it away.

"You're going to kill him!" she cried out in her wet, sandpaper voice, and Nathan touched her gently on the cheek as she lowered herself down to the couch.

Deliberately, he turned back to Jamal, who was still coughing on the ground. "Why are you here?"

"You...brought me...here... sir..."

"WHY ARE YOU HERE?"

"You...brought me here...sir!"

Nathan rushed over and grabbed Jamal by his shoulders, flipping him over onto his back. He lifted his foot off of the ground and placed it directly over Jamal's head. Terrified, Jamal raised his hands over his face as he began to dissolve.

"What the hell do you want from me?!"

His tears made his voice strained as Nathan slammed his foot down beside Jamal's head. The impact was like thunder, and Nathan had to pull his foot up and out of the cracked wood and concrete. He raised his foot again as both Sonya and Jamal screamed out in fear.

"WHY ARE YOU HERE?"

"BECAUSE YOU SET ME FREE!" Nathan stopped, and lowered his foot as Jamal turned back over and wept into the carpet. "I did everything right! I did everything they told me to!"

Nathan sat down Indian-style on the carpet and waited for Jamal to compose himself. Sonya ran over to help, but the young man pushed her away. There was anger where there was once fear, and Nathan nodded his approval.

"That's all they ever told me!" Jamal swung his arm violently as he yelled. "That's all they ever said to me! Jamal, be different! Jamal, be different! These niggas round here ain't got nothin' for you! You'll end up shot dead or locked up!"

Nathan listened intently as Jamal released. His voice was still angry, but he had calmed down, and looked dead at his challenger as he continued.

"Grandmama tapped out her social security sendin' me to that private school. Said it was worth every penny. She had to watch Mama get strung out, then watch Jordan get locked up. By the time I was old enough to walk, she had me 'round white people all the time. Tennis classes uptown and violin lessons in the 'burbs. And then she sent me to Bridgemont Prep, and everybody said I was gonna make it. I was gonna do somethin', be somethin'. I wasn't gonna be like the rest of these niggas out here."

Even Sonya found herself enthralled, and stared at Jamal as he spoke. Nathan refused to blink as Jamal broke his gaze and looked around the room, disturbed at his recollections.

"I...I studied white people like it was assigned in school. The way they walked. The way they talked. The way they acted. I came back to the projects every day and pretended I wasn't there. Turned on the TV and found a sitcom with some happy-go-lucky blonde, and I lost myself. And everybody told me I was gonna make it. Everybody told me I was gonna be somethin'. Make it out the projects and do somethin' with my life. I was everybody's hope. Everybody was countin' on me. I wasn't gonna be like these other niggas out here. I was gonna make everyone proud..."

Nathan shed a tear from where he sat.

"When I got into Toolig, the whole block threw me a party! I made it! I was different! I wasn't like the other niggas out there, and they knew it. So they came to tell me. To apologize for beating me up. To ask for me to remember 'em when I made it big. Remember the hood. Remember where I came from. And then I got on the campus..."

Nathan barely got his words out through his weeping.

"And...and what...what happened?"

"Everything changed."

"What do you mean?"

"Everything changed! EVERYTHING CHANGED!"

Jamal stood up, grabbed the small coffee table that sat beside him, and hurled it across the room, hollering at it as it crashed against the wall. Then he collapsed back down to the carpet.

"I...I wasn't white. I didn't know it, but everyone else did. I didn't understand. I'd been at Bridgemont since I was eight years old...I learned everything...I didn't understand..."

Pausing, Jamal climbed up to his feet and took Nathan's place as he began pacing along the carpet. Nathan's pupils followed his every move.

"Stacey didn't really like me, but I made myself believe she did. She was beautiful, and her dad was super rich, and I thought if I could get her to fall in love with me, then things might go back to the way they were. Things might go back to normal."

Shaking his head, Jamal continued. "The other guys…the white guys…they hated it. Everybody wanted Stacey Rousch. But she had never been with a black guy…so I was at the top of the list. Her dad came to visit once, to the school, and she told him I was one of the janitors. That's how she introduced me. When he left, she came back to my room, and I never said anything. I just wanted things to go back to normal…"

The house fell quiet as Jamal stood in place, silently sobbing. His pain begun to eat at Nathan, who ground his teeth as he sat still and dutifully withstood the agony.

"She got pregnant." Both Nathan and Sonya's head swiveled over to meet Jamal's gaze. "She got pregnant, and she freaked out. It was an accident, but she freaked out. She told her dad, and the next thing I know…the next thing I know…I'm just like all the other niggas out there…"

Jamal turned and sprinted back to where Nathan sat. He stopped in front of Nathan, wanting to strike him, but instead bellowed out words like a madman.

"Two days ago, I died! I sat there and watched a jury take my life apart piece by piece! Every day in jail, I waited to be set free! Waited for one of those bastards from Toolig to tell them I didn't rape Stacey! They couldn't find me guilty! I did everything I was supposed to do! I was different! I was gonna do somethin' with my life! Ten months I waited, while my grandmama almost had a heart attack trying to raise money for my trial! Ten months

I kept waiting for them to see that I was white! And two days ago…"

"…they let you know that you were just another nigger."

There were no more tears on Nathan's face now. It was hard, cold as rock in winter, even as the voice in head pounded inside of him to get free.

He stared into Jamal's furious visage and picked it apart. "What is it that you would like to do, son?"

Jamal's eyes narrowed as he snarled, balling up his fists and rising up on his toes like a giant. "I want them all to pay."

The evening sun came through the back windshield as Chance turned right onto Timber Lane. Xavier sighed as the vehicle pulled in front of Nathan Freeman's home.

"Explain to me again why no one has been here to arrest this guy?"

"I told you, most of the officers couldn't make a positive ID. They said the guy who attacked them had something wrong with his eyes; like they were damaged or something. The only photo we have of Nathan Freeman has him smiling on stage and looking perfectly normal. Our guys aren't making the connection."

"What about you? You made the connection, right?"

"I don't know, man. It's shaky. He wasn't even at the hospital long enough to be logged in. All they have on record is a John Doe."

"But you saw him. You laid eyes on him. It was Nathan Freeman, right?"

"Yeah…I think. I told you, I don't know what's going on, bro."

Xavier grew frantic. He stayed acutely aware of what he had put on hold to help his friend. "Chance! Either it was him, or it wasn't!"

"Alright, yeah! Yeah, it was him! Jesus!"

They sat in the plain white car and quietly observed the neighborhood.

"You said Freeman has money, right?"

"Yeah. Wrote a famous book a few years back. Lotta college kids have to read it. I called his publishers during the investigation. He's still getting a fat royalty check every few months."

"Then why does he still live in the city? First thing I did when Theresa got pregnant…"

Xavier stopped, recognizing the words he'd spoken, and felt his despair grow even deeper. Chance took a look at his face and decided to break the silence.

"They say he likes being around black people. His book was about some kind of royal African bloodline that was supposed to be in a bunch of slaves and passed down to black people. Crazy stuff, but people bought it."

Xavier barely heard his friend. All of a sudden, nothing else mattered. He wanted to go home.

He turned to Chance with his face somber and defeated. The world had shifted now, and this had been a bad idea. He'd be no use to anyone. All he wanted was to get back to his house and follow through with his original plan.

He began to demand to his friend, in the strongest of terms, to take him back to where he lived, but Chance spoke before Xavier's words could come out.

"The book was called *The Seven Days*."

The words jerked a dying man back to life.

Xavier stared at Chance as if he'd resurrected a ghost. All at once the memory of Diop's revelation raced back to him. The understanding of why Nathan Freeman's name sounded so familiar struck him hard enough to make him jump, and he put his head in his hands, trying to figure everything out.

He climbed out of the unmarked car, looking around, but searching for nothing. The world wanted to start spinning around him, tossing him about in a confusion that would threaten to overtake him. But there was new purpose now. One that made his heartbeat thump in his chest.

If Diop was right, this thing would probably kill him. Something with that much scorn did not know how to die easily. But neither did Xavier. If he perished, he would perish fighting, and that was more than he could ask for.

He took in a deep breath and held it, like his teacher had taught him. Like he used to on missions that went awry, with enemy bullets chipping off concrete beside his head. He held it, and held it some more, and when he finally exhaled, his mind was clear.

Xavier blinked twice, then began walking briskly toward the door of the Freeman house.

"X, what the hell are you doing?"

Chance was barely out of his car before Xavier reached the front steps.

"Mr. Freeman! Mr. Nathan Freeman!"

Chance drew his gun, ready for battle, as the door cracked open. Xavier couldn't see the woman peeking through the small space, but he could hear her voice clearly. It sounded like glass breaking.

"Leave and the gates of hell shall not prevail against you..."

Xavier stared forward, both confused and frightened at the greeting. "I'm sorry, ma'am?"

"Leave. He'll come back soon."

"You mean Nathan Freeman? He's not here? Where is he?"

"He doesn't understand; vengeance is mine saith the Lord. He doesn't understand..."

"Ma'am, where? Where did he go?"

Sonya shook her head on the other side of the door. "Mamas

are gonna weep on that interstate, soon as they find out those big books and can't save their babies. God bless their souls…"

Pained with sadness, Sonya slammed the door before Xavier could ask another question, and Chance ran up behind him.

"What the hell was that about, bro?"

Xavier spun to face his friend. The frenzy in his eyes made Chance pay attention. "Is there a school on the interstate around here?"

"The interstate? No, not around here. Go far enough up twenty-four and you run into Toolig, but that's too—"

"Nathan Freeman is going North to Toolig University. Those kids are in trouble…"

Chance looked at Xavier hard, trying to find a reason to disbelieve the look on his face. When he couldn't, he picked up his walkie-talkie. "This is Martinez for Commander Nash. Over."

"This is Nash. Over."

"Commander, I have reason to believe that the suspect from the precinct murders is on the move on Interstate 24. Requesting backup. Over."

"How do you know where he is?"

"It's a long story, sir, but the info is valid."

"It damn well better be! Outside of five miles, we don't have any authority! Where are you going?"

"Toolig University, sir."

"What the hell?"

"Sir, it sounds crazy, but my lead is solid. I wouldn't ask if it wasn't. Awaiting your orders, sir."

The silence on the radio made Xavier begin to think of contingency plans.

"Martinez!"

"Yes, sir."

"This is the only break we've had on this bastard all day. I'm sending two tactical teams after you. I'll make some calls to try and cut out any interference, but after you pass Toolig, you're on your own."

"Yes, sir."

"Martinez!"

"Sir?"

"I spent three hours going over the tape from yesterday's attack. Still don't believe it. You keep yourself safe, understand?"

"Yes, sir."

Chance and Xavier sprinted to the car, and Chance floored the gas and swerved to the other side of the street as he flipped his sirens on. The two men sped down the block toward the highway entrance.

The night sky covered Toolig University, falling over its beautiful trees and elaborate buildings like a veil. Classes had ended hours ago. The professors, content with their instruction, retired to drink and dream of sugarplums and tenure tracks, while the janitorial staff picked up on the hours that the privileged leave off. The students, the life force of the institution and the sole hope of the generation to come, shunned sleep for something far greater, and left their dorm rooms with their debauchery in hand.

Laughter split the air of the college campus, as many streamed into the local frat house. Music made by people their age blasted from the large stereo in the corner. The students jumped up and down, and shouted excitedly about the deaths of those who didn't look like them. The robberies and the gunshots in the drug houses during the police raids in the projects that they had never seen. The multiple kegs in the corner begged to be feasted upon, and the smoke in the air brought laughter to those who had never even touched the small white baton. Hormones leapt around the living room as young men and women threw their cares to the wind. Lines of white powder were agitated from their beautiful symmetry, sniffed into the bloodstreams of those longing to escape a life that many would die for, and though sex became inevitable, many would have no memories to show for it in the morning, just a hangover and sore genitalia.

No one cared that Jamal Jenkins had escaped custody. The notices had been placed around the school campus, and the security had been put on high alert, but for the students it was just a punch line to a sordid joke. He didn't belong there in the first place.

Nathan vaguely remembered the campus as he and the former student walked through the quad with hate on their faces. He was there a few days ago, but it was a different world then. Now, the voice in his head scratched and clawed, and it was only a matter of time before he got out. He tried to hide the burning in his midsection as he followed Jamal across the field.

The security guards took note of the two men, but many had been reprimanded for hassling the handful of black students that lived on campus. All black people looked alike, and working security for the college was a great gig, so they stood down and waited.

Jim stood at the front of the frat house, overseeing the party with the rest of the starting players from the football team. The army swayed back and forth as the narcotics and alcohol began to take effect, and randomly yelled obscenities into the air. Three young women, with long blonde hair and mini-skirts, stood at the front with them. Two of them would become the perfect ending to the night's festivities. The last one, Stacey Rousch, hung protected on Jim's arm as he waved his hand back and forth to the music.

A group of students from the math fraternity, too unpopular to make their way through into the core of the crowd, watched as the frat house door flew open and Jamal Jenkins walked in. Largely sober, they were the only ones who recognized him, and scrambled to get out of his way as he and Nathan began making their way to the front. Between the deafening music, the free flowing alcohol, and the effects of everyone's drug of choice, Jamal and Nathan became invisible as they swam through the crowd. It was not until they got to the front that Stacey Rousch's mouth fell open, and she dropped Jim's arm as her hands began to shake.

"Oh my God…"

Jim followed Stacey's gaze to the two black men that stood in front of him. His vision was hazy, and he struggled to recognize them as he reached over and cut the music off. The boos of the crowd tried to drown out his words as he pointed to Jamal and Nathan.

"The hell is this? An NAACP rally?"

Jamal looked straight at Stacey. His gaze pierced her as he stood frozen. "You…you were going to let me go to prison?"

Jim recognized the voice, and started to shake the fuzziness out of his brain. "Jamal?"

Jamal didn't answer. His eyes were stuck on Stacey. "You were going to let me go to prison?"

Jim smiled as Stacey stepped behind him, shielding herself. "Lighten up, man! You would've only been there a few years! I figured you could say hi to some of your homies!"

Nathan screamed out as the fire in his gut began to overtake him. Jim looked over at him and narrowed his eyes in recognition.

"I remember you…you're the one with the crackhead son!"

Assured of his discovery, the jock laughed out loud as he looked over at his friends. "Dude, this is rich! We got the rapist and the world's number one dad in the same room!"

Jamal stepped forward into Jim's face. Jim grinned, unafraid, as he is confronted.

"You know I didn't rape her!"

"That's not what the court said, homie!"

Jamal looked back up at Stacey as she peeked from around her new boyfriend. His eyes lightened as his face turned confused. "How…how could you do this to me?"

All of the football players follow Jim's lead, and burst out with laughter. Jim looked down at Jamal with smugness on his lips. "You just don't get it, do you? You never did. If you'd stayed in your place, this never would've happened."

Pain replaced Jamal's anger as the boos from the crowd continued to grow louder. "I loved you, Stacey."

Seeing his anger dissolve, Stacey stepped out from behind Jim. "Jamal, I'm sorry this happened. I really am."

"You were going to send me to prison, Stacey!"

"I didn't have a choice! The pregnancy and my dad…don't you know who I am, Jamal? I'm Stacey Rousch! I can't have a black baby!"

Jamal was forced back into the booing crowd by the words, and Jim came forward and faced him again. "Tupac said it best, homeboy. It's a white man's world. Now take Uncle Tom here and get the hell out. I feel a hate crime coming on."

Disturbed and confused, Jamal looked over at Nathan, but Nathan was gone. In his place was a dark figure with jet-black stone eyes and a growl in his windpipe.

Concern still written on his face, Jamal reached past the smiling football player and turned the stereo back on. The crowd cheered as the bassline made the walls shake, and as the party resumed he stepped back and stood beside the stranger.

His eyes searched the ground as he uttered. "Kill them. Kill them all."

Jim and Stacey noticed the dark, glowing eyes for the first time as the stranger approached them, and Jamal could see traces of fear in their keg reflection. The stranger stopped directly in front of Jim.

The quarterback could feel his breath as the dark figure leaned forward and spoke through gritted teeth. "Reckon you'se mind me, a', Massa Talbert…"

With one swipe of his hand, Jamal's companion had Jim up and off of the ground with his throat clenched between his fingers. Jim's blood began to drain from his face as he choked, and as his teammates ran over to help, the vigilante dispensed with them one by one.

The music shook the walls as the party turned to frenzy. Stacey's screams were inaudible.

The dark eyes turned to Jamal and glared brightly. "Get out 'chea!"

Jamal began running, shoving people out of the way as he burst through the crowd. People shouted profanities at him as their beers spilt and joints dropped, but Jamal couldn't hear them as he exploded out of the back of the crowd and out through the door.

Jim dangled and kicked for the ground, at the mercy of the hand that had gripped his neck, as the stranger found a door in the kitchen and walked down the stairs and into the basement. Jim was gagging, but he wouldn't suffocate. The stranger didn't want him to. He allowed him to breathe enough air to stay conscious as he observed the columns that held the ceiling up.

Upstairs, the party reached a fever pitch. Stacey Rousch bent down, tending to the injured players and uselessly screamed for help as the rest of the crowd leapt to and fro, shouted music and lost themselves in their stupors.

The basement was eerily quiet. Echoes of the madness upstairs fluttered down the steps and through the walls and ceiling, but the house had withstood that type of trauma before. The Greek symbols on the front door and awning gave it a stature that was not easily shaken. But those who walked by, doing late-night studying or escaping with significant others, insisted that, whether from the music that beat on it from the inside, or from the man downstairs in its belly, the house began to tremble.

The stranger in the basement took a long look at Jim as he held him high in the air, and then swung his body around three hundred and sixty degrees and smashed him into the closest column.

The crowd upstairs would barely feel the dip in the floorboards. A few dance couples lost their balance, and laughed sloppily about whether or not it had been an earthquake, as the dark figure took Jim's body over to the next column. The young man's feet still dangled, but there was no more kicking. The stranger still felt him trying to breathe through his fingertips.

Swinging him full circle again, he destroyed the second column.

The stranger heard the startled cries through the crack that appeared in the basement ceiling. He held Jim's unmoving mass up high as the slit grew into a gaping hole above, spreading wider and wider, and then watched as the ceiling, in a large, thunderous mass, crashed down around him.

The music had stopped sometime during the fall. A few students stared in shock down into the chasm that used to be the living room, but most lay broken at the stranger's feet, and cried out for help. He felt their blood in the air and closed his eyes as he inhaled, taking in his fill.

Jim was dead, and his body was dropped in a heap to the floor as the dark figure brushed the debris off of his clothes. He looked up, observing the canyon that he was now in, and nodded his head in approval.

But he wasn't satisfied.

Leaping from where he was to a remnant of the floor above him, the stranger walked outside as the spectators ran away screaming. His eyes burned like hot coals in the darkness, and Jamal stared in disbelief as his companion made his way over to the east wall of the house, and placed his hands on it.

The stranger screamed and the earth shook as he lowered his shoulder and collided over and over with the wall of the house.

BOOM! BOOM! BOOM!

Every connection sounded like dynamite exploding. The dark figure began working his way long ways down the side of the dwelling, throwing himself into the mortar and concrete with the ferocity of a battering ram.

Finally, the house could take no more, and the east wall began to cave. The Greek letters rocked back and forth as one of the sides began to give way, and when the wall could hold no longer it collapsed inward; the roof and everything under it came crashing into a hole in the ground that was once the basement.

Dust and debris filled the air of the immediate area, making it impossible to see, but Jamal made out the shining eyes and silhouette that came out of the destruction and marched toward him. He stood unafraid as the vigilante stopped in front of him, and watched the cold calculation as it began to form in his stare.

"We gotta go."

Jamal turned, but heard the stranger's voice before he could get a good stride going.

"Naw."

Stopping, the former student stared in disbelief. "What is it?"

The stranger stepped closer to Jamal. His eyes pierced the young man somewhere deeper than the soul, and a drip of the memories that afflicted the stranger fell into Jamal's psyche. Recollections of death and torture, lynchings and brandings begin to bounce around the young brain, and Jamal vomited as the stranger pulled away.

"I ain't done yet..."

Dropping to his knees, Jamal watched as the stranger disappeared toward the nearest dormitory. He didn't even feel the gun barrel at the head.

"Freeze!"

Chance shoved Jamal to the ground as he grabbed both of his wrists, but Jamal was still reeling. He didn't fight the detective at all, just cried out from the ground.

"I...I didn't know! I didn't know..."

Chance spun Jamal around to face him, and tried to slap him out of his delirium, but it was pointless. The former student had collapsed into tears on the grass.

"He's up there!"

Xavier ran up from behind his partner, pointed forward, and ran ahead while Chance shouted orders for the tactical team to set up.

The stranger walked through the doors of the third floor of the dormitory, anticipating the massacre. The frat house was beautiful, but it was too quick, and his lust for enemy blood grew stronger. Here he could take his time. Here he could enjoy every inch of the kill, every pained groan and dying cry. Then, maybe, he would be satisfied.

He turned back around and tried to contain his restlessness.

His plan was to stand at the doorway, destroying his enemies as they tried to escape, but he reconsidered now. He thought about the intimacy of going into room after room, one by one, spending hours until he was fulfilled. The thought itself made his heart race.

He walked down the hallway with his hands out, tracing the lines on the wall, and tried to decide how best to fulfill his need, when he saw someone else come through the door on the far end of the hall. Excitement fell over him, as it seemed his decision had made itself, but disappeared as the image in front of him sharpened and cleared, and the man's voice boomed through the hallway.

"I KNOW WHO YOU ARE!"

The stranger looked up at Xavier, and his hands began to shake as he sneered.

"You..."

The shining eyes of the man in front of him gave Xavier pause, but it was his fire and fury that made the Special Forces operative gasp. He felt a rage that was getting stronger as he approached the university, even began to feel it in his bones as they parked, but now, face to face, it was nearly unbearable. It echoed off of the walls and filled every part of the space, until Xavier found himself doubled over, grimacing, struggling to breathe.

After a while, the stranger was standing over him, but he couldn't bring himself to raise his head. The vigilante leaned down beside Xavier's distressed frame, and whispered acid in his ears. "You'se cain't save 'em..."

The words penetrated Xavier where they weren't intended. Somewhere in a crevice of his mind, he believed the stranger was talking about his family.

He lunged into the dark figure, rammed his body against the wall, and then turned toward the small scenic window overlooking the quad and pushed forward with every ounce of strength he had.

Chance was outside on the edge of the square field, giving orders to the tactical team and scolding himself for letting Xavier go in alone, when the two men detonated out of a third floor window and came crashing into the middle of the field. Chance immediately saw the dark, glowing eyes that his witnesses described as the figure jumped up and kicked Xavier into a tree that stood a few feet away.

Chance's mouth dropped open and he was convinced that his friend just died. But Xavier rolled over to his hands and knees. In obvious pain, he struggled to stand, and as he swayed on his feet he shrieked like a madman.

"SHOOT HIM! SHOOT HIM NOW!"

Jamal broke his delirium to fill the air with his own scream, as the circle of tactical officers all discharged their semi-automatic rifles at the same time. The ones closest to the killer took no chances, and fired shotgun rounds until they ran out, while Chance struggled to keep Jamal from running into the gunfire.

When it was done, a cloud of dust lay in the middle of the field. Chance ran into it, weapon drawn, and fully expected to see pieces of what used to be a serial killer. Instead a man, fully intact but slightly bleeding, lay semi-conscious on a mound of dirt.

Chance aimed his pistol at the stranger's forehead and fired one last round, and the glowing eyes closed as his head hit the soft dirt.

"This is a goddamn catastrophe!"

Commander Nash was on the phone with Chance, who rode nervously in the back of an armored van with Xavier and three heavily armed SWAT team members. Nathan Freeman lay unconscious on a gurney. He hadn't moved in the last two hours, since Chance's bullet had struck his skull, but everyone in the vehicle had seen the remains of the frat house. They kept their weapons trained on him just the same.

"The sheriff of that college town you all just left is on the other line chewing me a new one! He says I should have let him know where that madman was as soon as I found out!"

"It was a lead, sir. It wasn't concrete. You made the right call."

"Yeah? Those kids are all dead. A hundred thirty-four of 'em, all confirmed. Damn sure doesn't feel like the right call to me."

Chance paused, recognizing the regret in his superior's tone. He wanted to do more to assuage it, but every time Nathan's body moved from a shift or sway on the road, his palms began to sweat.

"Sir...what do you want us to do?"

The commander took a long, hard sigh.

"Okay, look...there's a super max prison about a hundred miles from your location. Put it in the GPS. They've been notified of your arrival, and are prepping to take this guy off your hands. They assure me they can contain him, so I'm gonna take their word for it."

"Sir, have you told them...?"

"I told them everything I could. They said they have a room that could withstand a bomb blast from inside and still keep intact. Right now that's our best bet."

"Yes, sir."

"Call me after you make the drop-off, and bring your friend back here. He needs to be debriefed."

"Yes, sir."

Chance ended his phone call and opened the divider, revealing the two men in the front of the van. "You know where the closest prison is?"

"You talking about Axelake? That's another two hours out!"

"We got orders to drop him there."

"And if he wakes up before then?"

Chance glanced at Nathan's limp body, and then back to the driver. "Just put on your sirens and gun it. The sooner we can drop him the better."

Ninety minutes later, the armored van pulled into the entrance to the prison, and followed an escort through the gates and down to the solitary confinement units. A prison official, dressed in full riot gear, opened the back of the van when it stopped.

He looked down at Nathan, and then up at the passengers and laughed out loud.

"They had us thinking this guy was going to be some kind of 'roided-out madman! Made us put all this crap on for nothing! Look at this guy! He's harmless! Looks like a college professor or something! Hey, Davis, come check this out!"

Another prison official came from the front of the van and looked inside.

"Davis, you believe this?"

Davis glanced inside the back of the van. "Wait...this is the psychopath?"

"In the flesh."

"Really? They're calling in the National Guard for a middle-aged black guy? He looks like a tax attorney."

"Look!" Chance jumped out of the car and stepped up to the head guard. "I don't care what he looks like. You put him under the goddamn prison, and you keep him there until you hear otherwise."

The guard looked at Nathan again, and then back at Chance.

"Alright, you got it. Come on, guys, chain him up and let's get him in."

Xavier stayed inside the van while the rest of the officers climbed out after Chance. Three additional prison guards came from around the other side, and they began putting Nathan's body in shackles that connected his ankles, wrists, and neck. When they finished, the head guard turned back to Chance.

"Don't worry. This guy's not going anywhere."

The guards sat Nathan's body in a wheelchair and began pushing him toward the door, and Chance and the rest of the officers followed. Xavier sat in the van, pondering. He'd been stuck in his own thoughts since they'd left Toolig. Earlier, as Chance brought him up to speed, he told Xavier that it had taken one bullet to the head to stop the precinct attack. But Xavier watched just a few hours ago as the tactical team fired a small armory of weapons at his adversary, and it still took for Chance to fire a round at point blank range just to put him to sleep.

He climbed out of the van and looked up at the dark sky as realization settled on his face, and dread in his bones.

"He's getting stronger..."

That's when the first light bulb went out.

There were a total of ten men escorting the inanimate Nathan to the door, and all of them paused as the light bulb closest to the door, and directly above their heads, went out. Fear passed through the group as they all stood at the ready and the officers drew their weapons. After a few seconds of silence, sighs of relief and nervous laughter began to emerge, as each man began to rue the eerie coincidence.

But then the second light bulb broke, and the third, and by the time the men figured out that the bulbs were being shot out, they were standing in total darkness. Xavier tried to run forward, but his eyes hadn't adjusted yet. In the seconds that he was totally blind, he called out to Chance, but all he heard were swift, clean movements, shocked cries, and pained groans as the men he was with fell to the ground.

When his eyes finally adjusted, remnants of random light bulbs began to flicker on and off. Xavier could see flashes of ten men. Each tried unsuccessfully to find their way back to their feet.

Nathan Freeman's chair was empty.

Xavier stayed where he was, with his pistol drawn and his legs crouched and ready, but he quickly became confused. The distraction, the rapid attacks in the dark, the ability to remain unseen, they were all familiar to him.

If he were to have planned an ambush, this was exactly the way he would have done it. And there was only one other man he knew who could've pulled it off.

"Hello, Xavier."

It's not the fact that the voice came from behind him, but the African accent laced within the words that made Xavier drop his gun. He turned around with his mouth open and a tear in his eye.

"Diop?"

The African nodded his head. His pride in his student showed in his gaze as he stood tall, with the shackled and unmoving Nathan thrown over his shoulder.

"I beg your forgiveness, Xavier, but I must speak with your brother. And I must speak with him now."

The thought of stopping his teacher never crossed his mind as Xavier watched Diop's back disappear into the shadows.

The abandoned barn was the only thing left of a dream. It sat on ten acres of bare land that an overzealous young farmer purchased before his common sense had fully developed. The dirt underneath it was sandy and light-colored. It blew around with the breeze and stung the kids' eyes when they went out to play, and the landscape surrounding the lone structure had enough hills and valleys to hike over. It didn't take much of a wake-up call for the young agriculturalist to cut his losses.

The barn stood solitary, statuesque in its loneliness, for years, until a man in chains from head to toe was brought through the rusty, rotted doors, and sealed its fate.

Nathan was still unconscious when Diop began working. He lay his friend gently on the ground before he reached into his sack, and carefully pulled out the objects he had brought with him; shells, minerals, candles, water from the river that flowed through his village, and two small vials: one with a dark, syrupy liquid, and the other containing the blood of each of the elders from Telemut.

Then Diop went to work, setting candles in specific places in the barn, based on the angle of the sun, and setting the different rocks, minerals, and shells around Nathan's unconscious body, covered by the dirt from both the farm and the village. Finally, he took the small vial of blood and dripped it over Nathan's body as he began to chant.

Finally, as Nathan was beginning to stir awake, Diop somberly took his head and poured the dark liquid down his throat.

Nathan could feel things shifting in his body as he pulled his eyelids apart. It took a while for him to blink the blurriness out of his eyes, as he tried to sort out where he was. He had memories of a college campus, of following Jamal into some sort of party, but the recollections stopped there. His connection with the voice in his head picked up where his memories leave off, however, and he began to sing as he lay on his side.

"O whilst the spring and rain of day

And midst the morning dew

Fall fresh among her laudy frame

We hail to Toolig U!"

The alma mater echoed inside the barn house walls as Nathan worked his way up to a sitting position. He continued singing until he noticed the man sitting in front of him, leaning forward, with his elbows on his knees. Even in his stupor, he could not hide his amazement.

"Diop?"

"Hello, my old friend."

The shackled man stared at his friend as his lips curled into a grin. "Diop, I got blood on me."

Nodding his head and wringing his hands, Diop looked at the ground. When he looked back up, his sadness was evident. "What have you done, Nathan?"

"No, no Diop, no....no, no, no, no, no, no...it's not me, Diop..."

"But it's inside of you."

Nathan nodded his head vigorously, like a child agreeing with a statement. "Yep, it's inside me. And it's beautiful! It's even better than we imagined it! It's perfect!"

"You're killing people, Nathan!"

The African jumped up from his seat, with mixed emotions running across his face, as Nathan began to feel a tingle in his chest. He coughed violently, then looked back up at his friend as he talked with a strained voice.

"You...you don't get it. They starve every day, Diop. They like pigs! They get fed, and yet they starve every day, and every day we put the plate back in the oven!"

Nathan used his pointer finger and repeatedly tapped on his forehead. "You think they don't know that, Diop! Huh? You think they happy with that?"

Diop stared at Nathan, confused. "You talk crazy, my friend. The *doole* has ruined your mind."

"No, it's freed my mind! Can't you see? All these years...all these years we've been afraid of what'll happen if we freeze it! But it's got to be frozen, Diop! If it's not, we're just the help! We're just the help!" Nathan climbed from the sitting position he was in, up to his knees, so that he could look at Diop straight. "All he's doing is serving it frozen. Serving it like it was meant to be. Otherwise, we're just the help. Don't you understand? Don't you..."

Nathan collapsed back to the floor, racked with another coughing fit. He convulsed so hard that his chains began to break. When the episode was over, he could feel his chest start to close. Struggling to breathe, he reached out for Diop's help, but could not find his hand.

"Diop, where are you?"

"I'm right here."

The accented voice came from directly in front of him, but his hand still went un-held. The realization hit him as he wheezed on the ground.

"What…what did you do?"

Diop covered his mouth, grateful that Nathan could not see the grief that he tried so desperately to hide.

"This is not what the *doole* was meant for, Nathan. I spent my life preparing, training to receive it, to control it, and to bring my people back to their former glory. To restore honor to our land, and take back what was stolen from us. Even when I was sure I would never taste it, I still came here to the States after you left, and traced the bloodline as best I could. I found your brother…"

"I…don't…have…a brother…"

"Yes, you do. Your father had another child, after you had already become a man. His name is Xavier. He is a warrior. I found him, and I trained him, just as I had been trained. But he did not receive the *doole*, you did."

Diop paused, then walked in front of Nathan and stood tall, prepared to deliver official news. Nathan continued to try and push himself up from the floor.

"The elders have decided. The *doole* has been lost. If it cannot be controlled, then it must be destroyed."

Nathan finally worked his way back up to his hands and knees. He found Diop bent down, looking him in the face.

"You may feel like you are dying, but you are not. I gave you a dose large enough to kill fifty men, and yet you still breathe. You have its strength, even when it is dormant. But I have more. And what must be done, must be done."

"Diop…"

He heard Nathan's lungs as they struggled to suck in breath, and Diop looked at his company with soft eyes.

"I'm sorry, my friend. Today, you must die."

Axelake Prison looked drastically different in the daytime. The menacing shadows and dark walls that made it look like a movie advertisement were gone now. Instead, the brownstone building looked more like a business. It sat on multiple acres of well-groomed land, with immaculate lawns and flowerbeds that could be photographed and placed on greeting cards. Even the sign at the entrance of the building had the feel of a corporate logo, with the limestone slab screaming 'reputable establishment' to all who entered the mile-high gates and barbed wire perimeter.

The prison guards had grown accustomed, and the cold air made their injuries flare up as they waited for the Commander and the Governor. The tactical officers were too busy trying figure out how they were attacked, and Chance had been on the phone with multiple officials since he'd regained consciousness, trying to convince them that there was nothing anyone could've done. Only Xavier recognized the beauty of the landscape, and the irony therein.

The men heard the helicopter as it approached, and tossed worried glances back and forth as it landed and the Commander and Governor made their way down to meet them.

"Explain to me again how the hell you lost this man?" The Governor was tall and dapper looking, with strands of gray and white hair decorating the top of his head. He was trying to hide his trepidation as he spoke.

"Governor, like I explained over the phone, we were ambushed, sir. It must have been five or six guys, definitely highly trained. We never even knew what hit us. We're lucky to be alive, sir."

The Governor looked at the Commander, and then strung a line of curse words together and launched them into the air.

"This is a goddamn nightmare! How am I supposed to go public with this? Most people still think we're dealing with a group of psychos! I'm supposed to hit the air and tell them that not only is it just one man, but that he escaped custody, aided by a group of highly trained professional killers, and is now on the loose? Can you say civil unrest? This guy is about to start a race war!"

"Governor, we could have started a search hours ago. We were given orders to wait here..."

"You damn right I told you to wait! You take to the woods with flashlights and bloodhounds and the media is going to know you lost him!" The Governor turned to Commander Nash once again, this time with desperation on his face. "Nash...Nash, please tell me you've got some kind of plan. This whole thing started in your jurisdiction."

"Governor, my suggestion is that we launch an inter-departmental search effort. We call everybody, FBI, National Guard, Homeland Security. I mean, we pull out all the stops, sir. We start from here and span out as far as we need to until we find this guy."

"Or until he mass murders another group of people, right?"

Commander Nash started to speak again, but decided against it. He closed his mouth as he awaited the Governor's orders.

"You're not going to find him, sir."

Both leaders looked over at Xavier, who stood at the end of the line.

"What did you say?"

The Governor, already at his threshold for stress, had every intention of overreacting, but the Commander stopped him.

"Governor, this is Xavier Turner. He's working as a liaison with us on this case. I checked him out myself. Ex-special forces, ex-CIA. Governor, he's the real deal."

The Governor paused to look Xavier over. "You said we're not going to find him? You're talking like it was one man."

"It was, sir."

"Your colleagues here just told me it was five or six."

"It was one, sir. I saw him."

Everyone froze and stared in shock at Xavier and his new information. It's not until Chance broke the line and hustled over to his friend that everyone snapped out of their trances. "Are you trying to make me look like an idiot? I've been on the phone all morning telling people we were attacked by some sort of commando team!"

"Chance, please believe me, it's better if they think that. If I had told you it was one man, we would've tried to go after him. I promise you, you all would not have come back."

"And you would've?"

"Yes."

"Why? What's so special about you?"

Xavier rubbed his brow as he tried to sort the pieces out in his head. Finally, he turned to the Governor. "His name is Diop, sir. He trained Special Forces operatives for the military. And he trained me."

"Special Forces? What does he have to do with this?"

"I believe I know the answer to that, sir, but I need to be sure."

"Well, tell me what you know!"

"I...I can't, sir. Not until I'm sure."

"I don't have time for this! Arrest him!" The Governor looked at Chance, who looked back, perplexed. "I said, arrest him!"

"Wh...why?"

"The man has admitted that he knows your attacker personally! For all we know he was a part of the attack! Hell, for all we know, he attacked you!"

Commander Nash looked at Xavier before he addressed the Governor. "Sir...with all due respect...this man saved God knows how many college kids last night by taking the suspect down. And if he's right about the guy who attacked them, then we're not equipped to track him, much less subdue him. He's our best chance right now."

The Governor traded hard glances between Commander Nash, Xavier, and Chance. His eyes came to rest on Xavier. "Can you find him?"

"I don't know, sir."

"I don't want to hear 'I don't know!' I want this Nathan Freeman back in custody before I have to go public! Now, can you find him?"

Xavier stared back at the Governor long and hard, before glancing at his friend. He saw the concern on Chance's face, and the reality that he was in over his head began to show on his friend's face.

If he was ordered, Chance would go after Diop without him. And if he did, he would die. Xavier shivered at the thought of losing someone else he loved, then broke his gaze with Chance and looked back at the Governor. "Yes, sir. I can find him."

"Good. You've got until nightfall."

Nathan jumped awake from his third time of losing consciousness. He was suffocating, but the voice in his head wouldn't let him die. It screamed him back to life, knowing its existence depended on the host, and with each gurgling inhalation Diop's trepidation grew more severe.

The African knew all too well that only one of them would leave that room alive.

Desperate, Diop jumped on top of Nathan's writhing body and reigned down blows to his chest and face, striking him with reckless abandon. Weakened by the ritual and the poison, Nathan's face contorted like soft clay.

"Stop fighting it, Nathan! It has to be destroyed! It must be destroyed!"

Finally, Nathan's body could take no more. In a last burst of strength, he threw Diop off of him, but as he climbed back to his knees his body froze, paralyzed by the onslaught, and his heart stopped.

Nathan felt the fire burst forth in his stomach as the darkness closed in. He shook his head as if to deny the inevitable, and his mouth dropped open, looking for air that was no longer available. His eyes went wide as his chest tried to contract, but found nothing to inhale.

"DIE!"

Nathan's head dropped, and he was still.

Diop sat with his face frozen in shock. As the room grew quiet and the air became still, he felt his strength dissolve in the body of a dead friend. He looked away from Nathan's still frame, and consoled himself with the knowledge that the elders would be proud. They had sent him to accomplish a goal, and he had accomplished it.

He began to stand up, but found himself weighed heavily by his grief and exhaustion. So he continued to sit still, mourning, and tried to gather the courage to say goodbye to his friend one last time.

When he was ready, he looked up slowly, prepared to apologize to the corpse that he created. And his heart stopped in terror as two pitch-black, glowing eyes stared back at him.

Diop stumbled backward, mouth agape, as the stranger stood deliberately and broke free of the remaining chains. The African's life began to flash through his mind, as he quickly came to terms with his impending death, and closed his eyes, prepared for his final blow.

But it never came. And when he opened his eyes again, he saw the dark figure march toward the door of the barn.

"Wait…wait!"

Diop called out to the stranger, but he didn't stop. His mission was clear, and showed through his infinite eyes. Diop knew he was going to satisfy his lust once again.

"WAIT!"

The stranger neared the door. Diop could feel the power in the ground as his footsteps pulsed through the dirt and cold floor. He was almost gone.

"TOBY!"

The air iced over as Toby stopped, then turned around to face the African.

"You…" Diop walked slowly over to Toby, easily drawn by the dark light shining through his eyes. To him, the change was spectacular. He could see the power in his shoulders, the thunder in his fists. And his eyes were just like the elders used to describe. They were just like he imagined when he was a boy.

Diop came face-to-face with him, no longer caring about living or dying, just experiencing the presence. "You are incredible."

Toby turned to leave again, but Diop jumped in front of the door and, blocked it with his body. "You…you represent the power of our people! You represent our greatness! I was mistaken…the elders were mistaken. They haven't seen you! They haven't felt your power in their midst! You can return us to glory!"

Toby's eyes burned as the African continued to speak.

"Return with me! Come back and take your place! You have the memories and souls of our kings running through you! Our princes! Our greatest warriors! Come and be our savior!"

Toby stepped forward, and Diop couldn't hide his fear as the dark eyes came close enough for him to touch. The African's eyes fell to the ground as Toby roared softly in his ear.

"I'se got yo' kings inside me, n' all dem folk you was talkin'. I'se got 'em, but I cain't hear 'em. Alls I hears da crack of da whip, da cries of da women n' babes. Screamin' from de plantation fields all's I be hearin."

Grabbing Diop by the shoulder, Toby tossed him to the side, and sent his would-be killer crashing upside down into the flimsy wall. The barn rumbled as the force of the collision was too much for it to bear.

"Got's me a' debt. I plans ta pay in full."

Diop kicked out through the hole his flying body created, and Xavier, who approached the barn with the rest of the tactical team, saw his teacher sprint and dive into the field just as the barn came crashing to the ground. He ran up to help the injured Diop, who was only concerned with finding Toby, but by the time Xavier helped him to his feet, the slave had disappeared into the night.

Nathan's body lay reclined in a chair in the middle of a living room. His mouth was slightly open, and his head was tilted peacefully, as if he himself wondered when he would awaken. The news reporter on the television screen tried to rouse him with the urgency in his tone, but Nathan couldn't hear him. It would have taken a bystander some time to notice that his chest was absent of its usual ebbs and flows, and the rising and falling tide of his breath had grown still.

He lay dead on a stranger's lounge chair, his skin pale and fingertips blue from the oxygen that no longer pumped its way through his blood. His bones and joints had begun to stiffen as rigor mortis welcomed itself into his body, attempting to permanently set his fingers in the awkward position in which they lay. He was alone and did not know it. The synapses stopped firing in his brain as soon as Toby was finished, and the stillness of the room made it ripe for violin music and a somber interlude.

The distinguished corpse lay there, comfortable in its mortality, and prepared to stay forever. Its job was not done, though, and the rage inside of him poured the color back into his skin and beat his chest until his heart leaped in his ribcage.

With a deep gasp and a cry of horror, Nathan's eyes shot open, and he fell forward out of the chair, clutching at his chest and coughing life back into his lungs.

It took several minutes for his body to perform properly, and his eyesight and mobility were the most stubborn in their repair. Eventually, after he shakily made it to his feet and got his vision down to double, he began to sort out the things around him as best he could.

He knew he was in a foreign place before his vision cleared, but it took him a minute before he realized he was in the living room of a one-story house. The couch, and the recliner that had recently housed his corpse, were old and worn, with unexplained stains that made him wish he'd died on the floor instead. Crushed beer cans and potato chip bags were strewn around the room along with dirty clothes, and recently used drug paraphernalia decorated the tabletops.

Still not recognizing anything, Nathan turned and saw the kitchen, where the refrigerator door was left open, revealing more beer and a half-eaten plate of food. He counted six ashtrays in total, all of which needed to be emptied, two full trash bags that had been knocked over and spilled before they were taken out, and one huge confederate flag hanging from the wall.

Despite the trashiness of the space, Nathan noticed that everything, from the furniture to the tables to the refrigerator, all seemed to be in the same pattern. His vision was still a bit blurred as he looked around. The trashcans, the windows, even the sink had the same brick red, splotchy design, like someone had taken a can of Sherwin Williams and begun throwing it all around the room.

It wasn't until his vision cleared up completely that he realized the liquid wasn't paint, and the absence of other people began to make sense.

Nathan began looking around again, this time for clues of what had happened, but he was disturbed by the incessant voice coming from the television screen. The set had been on since before he was revived, but he had not noticed it. Now, annoyed at the distraction, he marched over to it and raised his foot, prepared to turn it off permanently, before the lady on the screen stopped him cold.

Her face was worn. Her coffee brown skin had sunken in, wrapping around the contours of her skeleton, and the strands of stringy white hair tried to rest atop her head. She shook slightly as she sat, and rung her hands as she tried to ignore the soreness in her knuckles.

Nathan was struck hard by the woman, and blinked as he stared at her image. He blinked again, and the room begun to spin around him, the furniture tables turning into blurs in front his eyes. Before he knew what was happening, the old lady, along with the house and the television, were gone. And he was looking at an old woman, similar to the one he'd just seen on the television, on her knees, hunched over a body. Nathan spun around, confused, as the plantation land around him burned, and the night sky was bombarded with flames and crying. Terrified, he ran up to the elder, whose tired frame rocked back and forth as she wailed over the man to whom she gave birth, grabbing him so tightly that she could feel the meat under his skin where the whip had torn through. The son's eyes fluttered before they rolled back in his head, and his last breath paralleled his mother's scream.

Nathan fell to the ground with his hands grabbing the back of his head and his eyes shut tight, mortified to look up. The sudden change of sound forced his hand, though, and when he opened his eyes again he was back in the living room, with the television still blaring in front of him. Heart racing, he jumped up to find that the plantation and wailing mother were gone, and the fire that surrounded him had disappeared. Other than the television, everything else was silent. Only his sweat and pulse were proof of what he'd seen.

He looked back at the television, where the image of the old woman had been frozen in place. Disoriented, he allowed himself to fall back to the floor as he listened to the news report.

"...and we are hearing that the situation is growing worse. Once again, a protest has started here in the downtown area after the accosting and subsequent hospitalization of Ms. Hattie Mae Jenkins, the grandmother of Jamal Jenkins, who is one of the suspects in custody in connection with the mass murders. Ms. Jenkins was let go from her job as a domestic worker after an interview this morning, and after leaving the house where she worked, was confronted by a group of unknown persons. The details are unclear but we do know that sometime during the confrontation Ms. Jenkins fell down a small flight of stairs and was hospitalized immediately after. The African-American community where she lives was outraged, and began protesting in the downtown area, and we are now hearing that a counter-protest of white residents is taking place as well..."

Nathan stared at the television screen, engulfed in the images that ran across.

"I'm...I'm hearing that we've just now received a copy of the interview with Ms. Hattie Jenkins. The footage is unedited, but our producers have decided to air it for the public to see. Ladies and gentlemen, here it is..."

Hattie Mae Jenkins sat in front of the camera wearing a housedress and a dingy yellow apron. The house behind her was enormous, and immaculately clean, with tables and furniture that had wealth stitched into their fabric, and it was clear that Hattie only belonged there in one capacity. She continued to wring her hands as the cameramen made the finishing touches to their equipment, and a thirty-something vibrant white woman ran up and whispered in her ear. She didn't realize Hattie's microphone had already been turned on.

"Hattie, I'm so proud of you. We can't always control what our children do, you know? I'm so sorry, Hattie. I know how hard this must be for you. Forget what we said earlier, okay? You're welcome in this house for as long as you live!"

The interviewer gestured to the lady of the house, who quickly ran off screen as the cameraman counted down from five from behind the camera. When he got to one, he pointed to the interviewer, who raised her head and spoke strongly into the microphone.

"I am here with Hattie Mae Jenkins, grandmother of Jamal Jenkins, who has been taken into custody in connection with the mass murders of the last three days. Ms. Jenkins, can you tell me, did you have any idea that your grandson was capable of these kinds of atrocities?"

The old woman looked forward, not into the camera, but somewhere beyond it. She rung her hands and did not speak.

"Ms. Jenkins, can you think of anything that would've made your grandson, the college student, snap the way he did? To be convicted of rape, and then being broken out of custody to participate in these horrific crimes? Do you have any idea what happened to him?"

Again, the old woman sat quiet. Her brow furrowed as she began to think, but no words escaped from her lips.

"Ms. Jenkins, your grandson has been part of a massive hate crime, maybe the largest in history. White people are being targeted due to their race. They're afraid to come out of their homes until this thing is over. Considering how old you are, and what you must have lived through, how does that make you feel?"

The old woman turned to the interviewer curiously, and then turned her eyes to the floor.

"Ms. Jenkins, I…"

"*I be seventy-three years old this year. You know that?*" Hattie Jenkins shook her head painfully. "*You know, I grows up in the South. Mis'sippi. Seen my uncle hung by da Klan when I was nothin' but six years. He was runnin' round wid a white woman. They did things to him befo' he died that give me nightmares to dis day. Scared me so...I wouldn't leaves my house. Den I grows a lil older, and they tells me things is changin'. Get out da South. Go North, where black folks don't gotta be scared no mo'. Where blacks folks got a chance. So I moves North, and says I'ma raise me a family. And I gets me a husban', and we gets two beautiful chirren, and the world be perfect.*"

Hattie Jenkins smiled, reminiscing of the past, but her happiness faded as she looked back at the floor.

"*Den my husban' decide it ain't right dat black folks cain't vote. He decide and go out marchin', and I gets scared again. I gets scared, cause I know what white folks like when dey mad. And he go out and get hit 'cross the head. Knocked the sense right outta him. It never come back neither.*"

The interviewer tried to find places to interject and direct the conversation, but Hattie was in her own world. The woman turned to the cameraman, who shrugged, and signaled to let her finish.

"*So den it's just me and my kids, and we holdin'. We yet holdin' on. And I rings dey neck they ever talk 'bout marchin' or protestin'. I makes 'em swear to stay outta white folks business, and dey do. They graduate from dey high schools and get jobs, and we doin' aight. For a long time, we doin' aight. Then...all of a sudden, dey ain't aight no more. My kids and Lula kids and Joe's kids too, they all start actin' strange. People tells us it's some new drug, but none our kids do no drugs. We all got good kids. But I starts growin' scared, cause like I been tellin' Lula fo' years, we been gettin' into white folks business too much! King been marchin', and dem Muslims been saying all kinds of stuff, and then young boys wid the funny black hats been talkin' crazy* to the police. We gettin' into white folks' business, and I seen what white folks like when dey get mad."

The interviewer eyes started to go wide. *"Alright, Ms. Jenkins, thank you…"*

"I lives in my 'partment building for near to thirty years. Seem like overnight it go from bein' decent to bein' a rundown piece a' junk. People droolin' in the hallways and thugs runnin' in and out. An' dey keeps tellin' me an' Lula that it's dis new drug, but drugs ain't new! Den the President gets on the television talkin' bout it, and I gets scared. I gets scared 'cause I knowd it's da white folks. We done got in dey business too much."

Hattie rung her hands again as a tear crept down her face.

"By the time Jamal an' his brother get old 'nough to ask for they mama, she ain't no good for 'em no more. I decides to raise 'em up myself. But I be scared every day that pass by, an' I cain't shake it. They throw Jamal's brother in the jail for sellin' black folks' drugs. Say if he was sellin' white folks drugs, wouldn'ta been so bad. An that's when I decides I gotta do everything in my power to saves Jamal. He the only one I gots left. Seems like the only way a' keepin' 'em safe is to keep him 'round white folks, so dats what I does. I takes every penny I got an' send 'im to the white folks school. And when he graduate high school, and gets into the University, I says I finally did it!"

Hattie wiped the tear from her eye as she set her face hard.

"They calls me on a Sunday mornin' an' tells me my boy done raped a white girl. I knowd he ain't rape nobody, but dey say he did, an' dats all that matter. And I thinks to myself how things done come full circle. And I knows now why my husban' went out marchin' dat day."

For the first time, Hattie Jenkins looked up at the camera, and her eyes made Nathan gasp. With her face still solid, she sat back in her chair and crossed her fingers on her lap.

"White folks been scared for three days. I been scared all my life.

Don't know who Jamal been runnin' wid, an' I don' wish death on nobody. Who live an' die is a decision for the good Lord, and Him only. But if you askin' me to feel sorry…well, that's somethin' I jus' cain't do right now."

Hattie Jenkins turned her resolute face to the flabbergasted reporter.

"I done said all I got to say."

The interview footage cut off, and revealed the male news reporter with the growing crowd of protesters in his background. He yelled into the microphone as the commotion behind him grew.

"There you have it, the interview of Hattie Jenkins that sparked an already flammable atmosphere here in the city this morning. As you can see here behind me, law enforcement is out in full force, hoping to contain anything that ensues, but it seems like its just a matter of time before…"

Nathan didn't stay long enough to hear the rest of the news report. The urging of Toby had grown too strong to resist, and he ran outside frantic, prepared to sprint all the way back into the city. Stopping on the front step, he realized he didn't know where he was, and looked around to get a sense of direction. Seeing the pickup truck parked on the lawn outside, Nathan ran back inside the house and started rummaging violently through the cabinets and drawers, angrily throwing things to the side, until he spotted a ring of keys sitting on the countertop beside a half-eaten sandwich. Snatching them up, he found the one with the car insignia on it, ran full force back outside, and nearly broke the door off of the pickup as he yanked it open and jumped in.

Dead grass and dirt flew everywhere as Nathan floored the gas pedal, and the heavy vehicle went speeding off toward the metropolis.

"Nathan called it *The Seven Days*."

Diop stood with his hands cuffed in front of him. His ankle was broken, but he stood tall despite his injury, surrounded by the men who had captured him. Chance, Commander Nash, and the tactical team stared, nervously enthralled in his words, as he revealed to them exactly what they were up against.

Xavier sat a few steps behind. He was facing the side, but listened more intently than anyone else.

"The royal bloodline began in my village, with my ancestors in West Africa, centuries ago. It came here with the slaves."

"So what is it exactly?" Chance spoke up confidently, but still glanced at the handcuffs to make sure they were in place. "And why is Nathan Freeman killing all of these people?"

"It's not Nathan Freeman."

"Then who the hell is it?" Commander Nash's lack of sleep showed in his voice.

"Nathan Freeman is now two people. He is himself, and he is Toby."

"Who the hell is Toby?"

"Toby is a slave."

One of the tactical officers cocked his head to the side. "A slave? Like Kunta Kinte, 'give us freedom' kind of slave?"

"Yes."

The man looked around at his companions. "I don't know about everybody else, but you lost me with that one."

Diop turned to the doubtful officer. "Do you believe that a spirit can be troubled, even after death?"

"Yeah, I guess so."

"For those of our bloodline, if our spirit is troubled to the point of rage at the time of our death, then our spirits do not rest. They lie in wait for the next of the chosen. The next recipient of the *doole*. Nathan's theory was that because the bloodline had been brought here with the slaves, the number of spirits fueling the *doole* has increased exponentially. When the Seven Days returned, its power would be immeasurable. We never dreamed it would come for him."

Chance put his forehead in his palm as he tried to rub out the tension. "That's what his book was about, right?"

"Yes. His book was based on our research."

"So who is Toby?"

"The *doole* always takes the form of its former recipient. Toby was the last one. Nathan and I traced his records as best we could. He was a slave on the Talbert plantation in Virginia."

"So, what? He has Nathan Freeman possessed or something?"

"Yes…if you want to say it that way."

"And when Nathan is possessed, he…I mean Toby…starts killing people?"

"No. Not all people."

The officers looked around at each other. Commander Nash broke the silence. "So how do we stop him?"

"You can't stop him. I thought I could do it with the ritual, that's why I took him from you. But I was wrong. He's too strong for it."

"So you're telling me there's no way to stop him from murdering people?"

"I'm telling you that you can't stop him. None of us can, except him."

There was a pause, and Xavier looked over to see Diop staring at him. Each of the men surrounding him followed suit.

"What the hell?"

"I followed you to that University. I saw what happened. You forced him through that wall and out that window. And you should've died on impact from hitting that tree."

"What are you saying?"

"Think about it, Xavier. There would've been a time of extreme physical or emotional pain, something that nearly drove you to the brink of insanity. And you would've felt him trying to take you. It would've started in your midsection, and then worked its way through your body, probably the worst pain you've ever felt in your life. Think hard..."

Xavier didn't have to think. He knew what Diop was talking about before he finished, but it took his friend to mouth the words.

"The funeral..."

"He chose you, Xavier." Diop walked forward to his student, who continued to look away. "He chose you, and you were too strong for him. You wouldn't let him take you. But there's a piece of him still left inside, and as he grows stronger, you grow stronger."

Xavier turned to face Diop. "Are you saying I can kill him?"

"No. What you have is just a piece. It is not the whole. But you are our only hope at slowing him down, until he destroys himself."

"What do you mean, destroys himself?"

Commander Nash's ears pricked up at hearing a bright side.

"Rage is too volatile an emotion to ever hope to control for long. Nathan called this the Seven Days, because for each case that we discovered, on the seventh day, the *doole* destroyed itself."

"I don't understand...".

"Each day, Nathan will become less of himself, and more of Toby. And each day, Toby will be filled with more and more rage. Until finally, on the seventh day, Nathan will be no more, and Toby's rage will consume him. Each time that we found, the method was different, but the ending is the same. By the end of the seventh day, the *doole* is dead."

"And how many people would be dead by then?"

Diop looked over at the Commander and shook his head somberly. "With the amount of power he has, there is no way to tell. It would be historic."

Commander Nash didn't have time to take the information in. His cell phone rang on his hip in the middle of his reaction, and he composed himself as he picked it up. "This is Nash!"

The Commander's face grew increasingly concerned as he listened to the yelling on the other end. He didn't notice Diop's eyes close as he overheard the conversation, and began to meditate.

"Yes, sir. I'll leave right now." Nash hung up his cell phone and looked at the men. "I have to take the chopper back to the city. They're afraid it's going to be a riot. Hattie Jenkins got attacked this morning, and..."

Recognition flashed across Chance's face. "Hattie Jenkins? Jamal Jenkins' guardian?"

"His grandmother, yeah. Apparently she spoke her peace on an interview this morning, and some people didn't like it. You all stay here and do all you can to find this guy. I'll have local send you over some more SWAT, and as soon as things get under control, I'll take the chopper back out here."

"Commander!" The leader swung around to face Diop. The rest of the men stared intently as Diop looked at the Commander with alarm on his face. "Toby is headed back to the city."

Xavier and Chance both jumped forward.

"What? How?"

"How do you know?"

"The same way I knew he would be at the University, and the same way I found you all at the prison. I am a direct descendant of the royal bloodline. I have felt the *doole* since it emerged."

"So you know where it is?"

"I know it is going back to the city."

"Do you know why?"

"No...but it has something to do with Jamal Jenkins."

"What does Jamal Jenkins have to do with anything?"

"He is of the bloodline."

Commander Nash threw up his hands in exasperation. "Jesus Christ! Is every black person of the goddamn bloodline?"

"The royal bloodline was brought here with one of the first waves of African slaves, Commander. It's been passed unknowingly for countless generations. You would be shocked to learn how many people in this country have the blood of the kings in their veins."

"So what? Jamal Jenkins is gonna get possessed and turn into a psychopath, too?"

"No. It's not just the bloodline...you have to be chosen to receive the *doole*. Toby was the last, and he died sometime during the seventeenth century."

"So, again, what does Jamal Jenkins have to do with this?"

"There's something about the lineage of the Jenkins family that is drawing Toby to it. He's connected to them. I do not know why or how, but his connection with Jamal has inspired his actions thus far. Now, with the grandmother hurt, he is being compelled. That much I can feel. I guarantee you, he is returning to the city."

Commander Nash looked at Diop, and the African read his thoughts before he could speak.

"You will need my help!" Diop interjected, and Nash turned around to face him.

"Look, I admit you know more about this than all of us combined, and your expertise is proving to be valuable. But you helped a prisoner escape custody and attacked a group of police officers! I can't let that slide."

"You are making a mistake."

Nash looked from Diop, to Chance, and finally to Xavier. "Maybe I am…"

There was an orchestra of car horns that seemed to blow in tempo, keeping time with one another. The rhythm sped and slowed, grew louder and softer, and filled the air of the Interstate 24 with its own musical composition, while Nathan accented each note with the bass rumblings of a pickup truck.

Nathan had been dead. Killed by his friend, who was attempting to kill the fury inside of him. But it didn't work. And now he sat, alive, resurrected by the rage of the slaves. And their memories, their experiences from the past began to flash in his mind like film clips. Like twisted trailers to a feature that he prayed he would never have to see. He had only had two thus far, the first after he was revived, and the second while he drove. By the time he'd returned from seeing the castrated field hand with his genitalia in his mouth, the pickup truck had slammed into a tree, leaving a dented SUV in its wake. But he had to get where he was going, and after restarting the truck, he continued to speed the smoking, rattling monstrosity toward his destination.

It wasn't the visions themselves, but combined with the antici-pation, that began to make Nathan twitch and stutter.

Time was a sense that Nathan had lost, and he didn't know if he'd been driving for three minutes or three hours when he passed the bright, beautiful sign on the side of the Interstate that welcomed him back home. Even in his fragility, he could recognize the familiar landmarks, and smiled at them as if he'd been gone for years. The pickup truck kicked and bucked under him in protest, but Nathan drove it forward, looking down the streets as he passed them. Those that would have been bustling were almost completely empty, and the few people Nathan saw on the sidewalk all carried their fear with them as they rushed to wherever they were going.

Driving past Timber Lane, the afflicted man wanted to stop, but he couldn't. He wondered briefly if Sonya was still there as he continued past, ignoring the numerous police cars and yellow tape that had been placed around his residence. Driving forward and soaked in perspiration, he finally turned left on Main Street. He would be downtown soon, and the fire in his stomach let him know that there would be blood.

Groaning from the pain, he looked up to see his and Sonya's favorite diner approaching in the distance, and remembered the day that he had had the chocolate chip pancakes. It seemed like decades ago now, and...

Nathan's thoughts were brutally interrupted. His eyes rolled back in his head as he felt the steering wheel begin to turn in his hand, and then it was gone. The pickup truck, the city buildings, the landscape, it was all gone. Nathan blinked and he was in a field, surrounded by tobacco plants. He heard the group before he saw them, and spun around to find a congregation of wailing slaves in the distance. Inclined to help do whatever he could, he began running forward, but the closer he got to the wailing crowd, the heavier his legs felt. Finally he had to stop, and dragged his legs with him as he came close enough to touch the hard cotton fabric of the slaves' clothing. Their eyes were all to their immediate front as they cried out, and Nathan hesitantly put his eyes on their object of mourning.

Directly in front of them was a woman, who would've been tall and statuesque under any other circumstances. Her feet kicked for the ground as the noose around her neck held her up, and her arms swung out in front of her, fighting for a hope that was not there. Her eyes were wide as she reached for her sister, who was in the front of the wailing crowd, reaching back at her sibling from her knees and screaming loud enough to burst hell open. As the woman on the tree felt her life inching away from her, she let her hand fall down to her enlarged belly.

"You takes' yo' baby an' bees free! You bees free!"

The sister screamed to her dying relative and unborn nephew as a white man in a pressed cotton shirt and brown pants walked forward from behind the tree. He looked at the sister on the noose, and then at the sister on the ground, as he pondered. Then, without warning, he took a large knife out of his back pocket, shoved it into the hanging woman's belly, and ran it down to her crotch.

Nathan was still screaming when his vision ended. The image of the baby burned in his head as he hit the gas on the pickup truck. It hit the curb while turning sharply and going full speed, and flipped over in mid-air as it smashed through the sidewall of the diner and came to rest at his and Sonya's favorite table.

The diner was only half full, but the pandemonium was immediate. Nathan could barely make out the images of people who ran for their lives. When they were gone, and everything was quiet, he pulled himself out from under the mangled dashboard of the truck, and crawled out from the upside down wreckage. Making his way to his feet, he used the booth to steady himself as he walked around to the seat, and let himself fall into it as he collapsed into tears.

He didn't see the person walking up to him from the hole in the wall.

"Yo, you aight, man?"

Nathan jumped up from his seat with his fist drawn back, ready to attack. The young man in front of him raised his arms in surrender.

"Yo, chill! Chill! I was just checkin' to make sure you was aight!"

The young man looked vaguely familiar, but Nathan's mind was in no position to go strolling through its memory index. He wore a pair of tan boots, blue jeans that hung from his waist, showing his boxers underneath, and a dark black hoodie. Slowly, he pulled off his hood and revealed a headful of dreadlocks and a boyish face.

"It's you. I knew it was you. I saw you drivin' down Main Street. I thought it was you an' followed you. I seen you crash and everything."

Nathan began to lower his fist.

"You don't remember me, do you?"

There was a pause as Nathan stared at the man in front of him.

"Couple months ago, you came up to me n' my niggas talkin' bout some book. We was out front here, where we always be before we hit the block. We laughed you out, but ain't nobody talk to me 'bout no book since I was in high school. Guess that made me remember you."

The recollection came back to Nathan slowly.

"Few days ago, they starts puttin' yo picture on the news, talkin' bout you involved with all the killings goin' on. I remembered yo' face, and I remembered what you said, and I went an' found yo' book in da library. Read da whole thing."

Nathan rested his arms on the table as his stomach began to burn again.

"That's what this is, ain't it? It ain't no thugs an' gangstas like they keep sayin'…it's Da Seven Days…"

Nathan didn't answer, but he didn't have to. The urbanite sat down in the seat across from him. "You gon' kill me?"

"No."

"Aight…well, I'm Jay."

Nathan nodded as the perspiration dripped from his face.

"Look, I'll help you if I can. I ain't killin' nobody but…Ms. Jenkins live in my building. She ain't never do nothin' to nobody. All she did was tell da truth."

"Is…is she hurt?"

"Nobody know. All they keep sayin' is that she still in the hospital. They won't even let nobody on her floor."

"And downtown?"

"All the black folks ain't goin' nowhere till they hear she aight, and all the white folks pissed at what she said in the first place. Police and the guard there, but they can't control 'em all. It's 'bout to be a war, man."

Nathan stood up and tried to shake the voices out of his head. "You have to take me down there."

"Downtown? Hell naw! I told you, yo' face been all over da news! You ain't gettin' to the end of the block without gettin' arrested! What you gotta do is find a spot an' lay low for like two, three weeks! Let stuff die down some. But you damn sure can't go downtown!"

Nathan arms flew out and grabbed Jay's hoodie. He lifted him straight up, holding him at a full arms length as he scowled. "I have…to go…downtown…now!"

"Aight! Aight, man! Aight!" Jay conceded as Nathan placed him back on the ground. "All the streets is blocked off around the protests. Only way down there now is the train!"

Nathan nodded to Jay, and began to make his way out of the restaurant.

"Hey! Hey, hold up!" Jay ran up behind Nathan and pulled off his hoodie. "At least take this. Put the hood on. It'll cover yo' face some."

Nathan looked down at the fabric, then slipped the hoodie on and pulled the hood over his head.

"I'm goin' with you, cuz. White folks been crazy since this whole thing started. Might be safer with you than by myself."

Nathan looked at his new companion, and began walking toward the subway station. Jay followed closely behind.

The Subway Transit System opened in the late seventies, with one underground rail line, the red line, going from one end of the city to the other, and straight through the heart, like a well-placed arrow. Excited citizens would go out of their way to ride, paying the cheap fare and speaking to each other about how technology had changed the world. The wealthy would beg the pardon of the poor while sliding out of rows to get to the exit doors, and corporate heads and construction workers would strike up conversations about the state of the economy and the complexities of fatherhood. The subway cars were equalizers, and a five-minute trip would tug on the humility of the successful, and make the downtrodden feel like they could take on the world.

Now, the STS housed five different rail routes, which all snaked through the underbelly of the metropolis, circulating people like a life-giving plasma. The gray and brown lines stations became home to creative graffiti and tag signs, attempts from the riders to show the world that they existed. Condom wrappers and sunflower seeds marked the walkways to the train platform, and youthful rebellion caused transit security to call the police for backup once the sun went down. Every so often, a passenger from one of these rails would find a promising place of employment, and travel just long enough to notice the desperation around them, before they got off and transferred to the silver or yellow lines. It was here that they encountered a new world, one with freshly cut flowers and manicured lawns, and handbags that could keep them from being evicted. Business suits and ties replaced the jeans and basketball shoes, and talks of stock market prices fluttered through the air.

The two worlds collided in the middle, in the stations housed within the downtown area, where dismal public schools could be found steps away from Fortune 500 satellite offices. Where the rich and the poor shared space, but never touched, for fear of swapping realities.

The last line on the transit system was a special one. It has been petitioned for by those living outside the city who grew tired of taking their luxury cars through two-hour traffic jams. Money passed both on top and underneath the table, and construction started on a line that would come to be both named and nick-named the same thing. Completed in record time, and with very limited stops, it ran in a straight line from downtown to Ravencrest, a township forty-five minutes outside the city, but third from the top on the census' list of wealthiest in the country.

A gray line station was the closest to the diner, and Nathan and Jay walked inside and dove headfirst into the madness. With the streets blocked off, and the tension in the air, people crammed into the station like mice, climbing over one another, sadistic in their fear of what was coming. Nathan was easily lost, pulled under the tide of everyone's frenzy, and Jay gripped his arm to guide him to safety.

"Keep the hood on, man! Keep the hood on!"

The national guardsmen lined the train platform, machine guns in hand, attempting to keep the peace as people pushed and shoved around them. Jay ducked away from the guards, pulling Nathan with him, and found a dark corner at the edge of the station.

"We can't be here, man! They got army dudes on the train platform!"

The burning in Nathan's stomach was growing severe, and he could only utter in between his breaths. "Downtown...!"

Jay looked at the agonized man and sighed. "Aight, look, we'll take this next train for two stops and transfer! The Ravencrest train gonna stop on both sides of the square before it go out the city! The protest is on the North side! We'll get off there!"

The gray line train pulled into the station and Jay yanked Nathan through the mob, getting through the doors just as they were closing. His groans became audible, and the people packed around him looked questioningly at Jay as his companion cried out in pain.

When they got to their transfer point, Jay pulled Nathan off the train and rushed him upstairs, where a Ravencrest train was pulling into the station. The guardsmen on the platform yelled out to the mob of people as the railcars screeched to a halt behind them.

"This train is for Ravencrest passengers only! Ravencrest passengers only! If you are going downtown, take the silver or brown lines! This train is not for downtown passengers! This train is for Ravencrest passengers only!"

Anger immediately erupted from passengers who planned to ride the arriving train, and quickly spread throughout the entire station. Jay gripped Nathan as he approached one of the train doors, but the look on the guard's face let him know he wouldn't get in. Quickly, he retreated, then pulled his new partner further down the platform, looking for an opening. The crowd grew tumultuous as he approached the last railcar, and the guardsman stepped away from his post to stop an altercation that was brewing between two men. Jay pulled Nathan through the doors and into the final seat on the train.

Nathan never looked up, but he knew who he was surrounded by. He slammed his fist on the seat as he felt the rage begin to take over.

"Hey, what the hell are you doing here?" A stocky white man in his thirties, in a silk designer suit and shoes, stood up and pointed menacingly at Jay and Nathan. "You heard the guards! This train is for Ravencrest passengers only!"

"Yo, chill, man; we don't want no trouble…"

"I've taken this train every day for three years, and I've never seen you! Why the hell are you on this train?"

"Look, my man right here, he just—"

"He what? Huh? What's he got under the hoodie? You one of those thugs? You here to kill us?"

"Naw, man, look, we just tryin' to…"

"I don't give a damn what you're trying to do!"

The man opened his briefcase and pulled out a small pistol, and the sea of white faces behind him gasped in horror.

"Chuck, what are you doing?" a woman's voice cried out.

"I got a wife and three kids, and I'll be damned if I'm going down without a fight!"

Jay shot his hands up in the air, as a petite young woman in a Burberry coat stood up.

"Chuck, please! I know you're scared, we're all scared! Just put the gun down, okay? They'll get off at the next stop—"

Jay nodded his head in agreement. "All we tryin' to do is get downtown, aight? That's it! That's all! Next stop and we outta here, I swear!"

Chuck narrowed his gaze and lowered his gun. "Downtown… to the protests?"

"Yeah, that's it, man! I swear! We just tryin' to get to the protests!"

Looking around at the people behind him, Chuck finally looked back at Jay with disgust. "Goddamn black people…"

"Chuck!"

"No! No, I'm sorry, Lisa, but somebody has to say it! Somebody has to say it, and I guess today it's going to be me!" The irate man turned back and glared at Jay. "You are the most ungrateful bastards I've ever seen in my life! Every goddamn quarter I go through the job applications and pick out a black person to hire! Every one! And you know what? Most of the time, I know exactly what I'm going to get! You get to work late, you take lunch breaks twice as long as everybody else, and you're half as productive! Hell, most of the time I'm hiring a black person to replace another black person I had to fire! But I keep doing it! You know why? Because I've read the reports! I know that your father is probably in jail, and your mother is probably on welfare or crack, and I want to try and do my civic duty!"

Jay looked over at Nathan. His head was still down, but his groaning had stopped. "Yo, you might wanna sit this one out, dogg."

"Listen to you! You can't even speak any decent goddamn English! But it's my fault, right? I'm white, I went to college, I have a degree, and I started a successful company, so it's my fault you can't read or write or talk straight or put a decent goddamn sentence together! All you people do is blame whites for your crap! We've thrown you lifeline after lifeline! Opportunity after opportunity! Affirmative action! Minority scholarships! Welfare! I pay my hard-earned money for most of you to sit around and smoke weed all damn day! What the hell else do you want? You should be on your knees, thanking us! But instead, some group of crackhead thugs want to start killing people simply because they're white, and here you are cheering them on!

"After all we've done for you! You ungrateful bastards! One old, crazy black lady gets on television, and all of a sudden they're heroes! All of a sudden murder is justified! You're fighting back against oppression, so it's okay! To hell with all of you! You want to stay in the ghetto and shoot each other every night, that's fine by me! You want to beat other black women and leave your kids and smoke crack and go to jail, then do it! Do whatever you want! But you leave us the hell out of it! "

The lights began to flicker in the subway car as Toby picked his head up, but no one noticed his glowing eyes. Everyone looked at Chuck, who had raised his gun again and taken a step closer to Jay. His voice trembled with anger as he spoke.

"You come near me, my wife, or my kids, and I swear I'll blow your head off…"

The train rounded a corner in the tunnel and Chuck, whose anger had already made him unsteady, fell to the side and hit one of the standing rails as the lights flickered off. The pistol fired in the darkness, and when the lights came back up, Jay was on the ground still, and Toby stood in the middle of the aisle, his dark eyes shining impossibly bright from under the dark hoodie.

Toby screamed, and the fury inside of him made the subway cars shake.

The passengers that waited at the North Square subway station had already been segregated. In anticipation of the Ravencrest train's arrival, the National Guard had split them up into two groups. One stayed in a straight line going down the edge of the train platform, to ensure safety for those entering the train. The second group asked for all Ravencrest passengers to step forward, and positioned themselves in between the privileged passengers and the remaining ones, forming an armed, human shield.

Outraged, the remaining passengers began pushing back against the guardsmen, throwing profanities and soda bottles, and demanding to be let through, before the guardsmen let off warning shots that echoed off of the thick walls.

It was the private closest to the subway tunnel that first noticed something wasn't right. He could hear the train approaching, but the sound was disorganized, chaotic even. He tried to tune out the sound of furious passengers as the rolling grew louder, and braced despite himself as the symphonized crashing and screeching all began to crescendo, shaking the tunnel it was enclosed in.

The guardsman turned his head, and four speeding tombs of seared iron and shredded flesh exploded out of the tunnel, tumbling across the tracks, and burning like they'd just been kicked out of hell. The guardsmen dove forward instinctively, colliding with the very people they were trying to protect. Three Ravencrest passengers were so eager to escape the chaos of the city that they had stood alongside the armed military personnel on the platform, where they felt the safest. When all was said and done, they stood alone to face their fate, and were devoured by the wreckage before it came to a stop.

What was once an angry mob in the subway station was now a sea of shock and quiet, as spectators saw bodies hanging out of the flaming train debris like Christmas tree ornaments. The silence was deep and penetrating, and it lasted as long as it could, before the shouts of the paramedics forced their way through the quiet, and the tears of black and white onlookers mixed together on the ground.

"ZF646, you are cleared for landing."

The Gulfstream G650 aircraft banked right, preparing to touch down at the airport, where a town car awaited both of its passengers. The aroma of a gourmet meal wafted about the cabin, and a filet mignon, cooked to perfection and surrounded by a floral arrangement of vegetables, sat untouched on a plate beside a modestly poured glass of sixty-year-old scotch. The man who sat in front of it did not know that he was hungry. His sadness had slowly dissipated his appetite, and he had barely taken a bite in the last two days. He sat with the lights dimmed in the cabin. His right hand covered his mouth in disturbed contemplation, and his left held a wallet-sized photo of a college-aged daughter with her eyes beaming. Her long, blonde hair fell softly across her shoulders and down her back as she showed off her new Toolig University sweatshirt. He looked down at the photo once again, torturing himself as he remembered how much she had her mother's eyes, and he shed another tear that found its way down his unshaven cheek and into his gray moustache and beard.

"Mr. Rousch? Mr. Rousch, we've landed, sir." The billionaire's personal assistant walked softly from the front of the plane. "The car is outside waiting."

Don Rousch wiped his cheek as he nodded, and slowly worked

his way up from his chair. His muscles seem to have aged years in the last forty-eight hours, and he limped slightly as he made his way to the door. His assistant emerged again as he was about to step out.

"Mr. Rousch, I'm sorry, sir, I have a representative from Blackthorn on the line for you."

Rousch paused, his designer suit lying unkempt on his withering frame, before he turned with his hand out and faced his companion. "Why don't you go wait in the car, Brenda? I'll be right there."

"Alright, sir."

Brenda handed Rousch the cell phone before she trotted down the steps and strolled to the black car. The driver opened the door as she approached, and once she is safely inside, Rousch stepped back into the plane and sat in the nearest seat.

"This is Rousch."

The rough voice on the other end of the phone almost made the billionaire reconsider, but the picture in his hand overruled.

"Rousch, this is Gray. I have a team prepped and ready. If you want to reconsider this op, I would advise you do it now. Otherwise, we're a go."

The billionaire stared forward, allowing his vision to blur into the mahogany lining of the flight deck door.

"Rousch?"

"We're a go. You just make sure your men are ready."

"I assure you, that won't be a problem."

"Good. Then I'll see you downtown."

On the fourth floor of St. Mercy's, Hattie Mae Jenkins lay asleep on her hospital bed, oblivious to the nurses and orderlies that passed by her room, trying to get a peek at the old woman who'd been on the news for the last day. Soap operas played in the background as she began to rouse, and the ache of her stiff neck helped to draw her out of her slumber. She looked around the room as she allowed her vision to clear, but the soft smell of muscle ointment gave her the answer to her question before she could ask. She turned to her left and saw Lula sitting in the guest chair, half-asleep, with her head falling off to the side and jerking back up as she tried to stay awake.

"Still here, huh?"

Lula opened her eyes and slowly shook the sleep off of her before she responded. "Cain't leave you by yoself. You wouldn't knows what to do without me."

Hattie started to push herself up in the bed, and was reminded of the brace she had on her wrist. Annoyed, she lay back down. "How longs they plannin' on keepin' me?"

"Doctor says he lettin' you out here today. Aint nothin' else wrong but that sprain you got."

Hattie nodded, satisfied at the news. "Good. Nothin' like bein' in yo' own home. Ain't never been too fond a' hospitals no way."

Lula hummed her agreement, then glanced out the door, where three nurses were whispering back and forth to one another. When they saw Lula looking back at them, they quickly dispersed, and the old friend turned to her partner with new concern.

"Hattie, you ain't seen the news since you been here, have you?"

Hattie looked curiously back at her friend before the dread began to creep on her face. "Jamal…?"

"No…no they still got 'im at that prison, last I heard."

Relieved, Hattie exhaled, shaking her head. "Naw, I ain't seen no news. All the tests they done run on me, it's a wonder I got to see my stories."

Lula used her cane to stand up, and made her way over to Hattie's bedside. "Hattie, you been on the news."

"Cause a' what I said to them reporters?"

"Yeah. They been playin' it since yesterday."

Hattie looked at the concern on her friend's face, then pushed herself up despite the pain in her wrist.

"Well, I ain't takin' it back! I say what I had to say! If white folks is mad, then they jus' be mad!"

"It's more 'n that, Hattie. Black folks heard you got attacked and got to marchin' downtown, and then white folks got mad an' started marchin' back! They say its jus' a whole bunch a' folks downtown jus' yellin' and screamin' at each other..."

"Shut yo' mouth, Lula!"

"I'm serious! They say it's gon' be a riot 'fore it's all over with."

Hattie grabbed the remote on the side of her bed and flipped the television off, then let her eyes wander the room as she contemplated. "When they lettin' me outta here?"

"Doctor say he be back in a couple minutes with yo' papers, then you free to go."

Hattie looked at her friend with a confidence that Lula had never seen. "We goin' down there, Lula."

"Goin' down where?"

"To where they marchin' at!"

Lula shook her head. "Naw, Hattie, we can't go down there."

"Why not?"

Lula took a deep breath. "Hattie, look, I knows you been upset 'bout what's been happenin' with Jamal..."

"They lied on my boy!"

"But this is serious, Hattie! White folks is dyin'!"

"An' black folks been dyin'!" Hattie felt herself start to get upset, and calmed before she continued. "Lula, I say what I say to them reporters for me, not for nobody else. But people wouldn't be mad at me gettin' knocked down them steps if they thought I was lyin'. This the first time since I send Jamal off to school that I'm feelin' like maybe I done somethin' right. You ain't got to go, Lula, but I owes it to 'em. I got to go."

Lula looked hard at her friend, then sighed and walked back over to the guest chair. Slowly, she lowered herself onto the cushion, and when she was comfortable enough, she lifted up her cane and laid it in her lap.

"Well…guess I can't let you go by yo'self. You wouldn't knows what to do without me…"

Police tape flooded the subway station like party streamers as Xavier, Chance, Diop, and Commander Nash were ushered in. They were informed of the train wreck yesterday, minutes after the carnage had occurred, but an ensuing explosion from a ruptured gas main had rendered the scene so hazardous that only essential personnel were allowed into the station overnight. It was cleared for investigators an hour ago, and Commander Nash made a call directly to the fire chief, making sure they were the first on the scene.

With the exception of his hat, the chief was dressed in his full uniform as he pointed to the twisted metal and plastic. "There's no doubt about it, Commander. Something destroyed this baby from the inside out. Damndest thing I've ever seen."

Diop stepped forward and looked at Nash, who nodded his head in understanding as the African turned to the fire chief. "Did you all find any bodies inside the train?"

"Hell, that's all we've found is bodies! Train was full of people trying to get out of the city. Damn shame, I'm telling you."

"Have you found anyone that matches the description of Nathan Freeman?"

"The guy involved with all the murders? No…he was black, right? Yeah, he was black. This train was going straight to Ravencrest. Everyone on there was white."

"You're sure?"

"I'll have my guys give you the final list of deceased, but yeah, I'm pretty sure."

Chance shook his head at the wreckage. "Have you all started notifying families?"

"Can't yet. We haven't been able to get all the bodies out. The fire from the explosion was so strong it damn near welded the train to the tunnel. Hell, there's still a fire burning underneath this mess that we haven't been able to reach. We're going to be here for a few hours trying to get the thing loose."

"You let me know when you start, okay?" Commander Nash spoke somberly. "I'd like to pay some of the families a visit."

The chief looked at the Commander, trying to hold back his words. "Nash, they're not gonna want to hear from you until you catch these thugs running around here killing people! I told my guys to keep their mouths shut, but words already starting to get out that all these victims were white. People already saying it's the same murderers from the police station and Toolig, and for all I know they're right."

Nash placed his hand on the fire chief's shoulder. "Let me handle that, okay? Trust me, we're going to catch whoever is behind this."

"Make it quick, huh? My kids are scared to walk to school…"

The four men began to make their way back out of the station as the fire chief shouted orders to his men in the tunnel. As soon as they were far enough away, Nash stepped in front of Diop.

"Do you know where he is?"

"No."

"What do you mean, you don't know? You knew he was coming to the city, but you don't know where he is?"

"He's here, in this area, but I do not know where."

"Great."

The Commander began walking away, but Diop paused where he was, his brow ruffled in contemplation. "This does not make sense."

Xavier focused on his teacher as he pondered. "What is it, Diop?"

"This wreckage was caused by Toby, but it was not his goal. He did not come here for this. He came back because of what happened to the woman. He came back because of the protest."

Chance shrugged his shoulders in confusion. "So what was this, some kind of collateral damage?"

"Yes. Something distracted him, but his goal is still the same. He's not leaving…"

Xavier looked up at Diop with concern in his eyes. "…because he's not finished yet…"

Commander Nash looked at the two men as the heaviness of their realization fell on him. "Aw Christ Almighty! Okay…the National Guard is already set up. We'll coordinate with them and use their equipment to help find Freeman. Diop!" Diop turned to face Nash, noticing the fear in his eyes as his voice softened. "If…if he comes to this protest, it'll be a massacre. How sure are you, Diop? How sure are you that he'll show?"

Diop sighed as he looked back at the Commander. "He will come, Commander. He will come, and people will die."

The four men rushed up the stairs of the train station, with urgency etched across each one of their faces. They left the train wreckage in their background as they sprinted, with the snarling metal and debris snaking its way around the random fires that still burned. There were still dead bodies lying in wait, contorted around the seats they had once sat in, inanimate in their deaths. Only one remained alive. Weakened by the force of the collision he had caused, and trapped underneath the full force and weight of the devastation, he lay engulfed in the flames that continued to burn under the wreckage. His eyes were the only things burning brighter than the inferno around him, and a slow rumble swelled inside of him as he waited to regain his strength.

Sergeant Morris was scared, but he was trained not to show it.

Masses of enraged people threw themselves against the concrete barriers as he shouted orders to his soldiers to stay in formation and hold the line. His two squads had been stationed at the epicenter of the protest for the last thirty-six hours, and while his privates had shift changes, Morris had been in command the entire time. The most he had taken was fifteen minutes to guzzle a Red Bull and splash water on his face before he dove back out into the chaos.

And the chaos seemed to be growing.

The population of the protest grew with emerging rumors of another attack right under their feet, in the North Square subway station. Morris hadn't heard it verified, but the people stampeding in from both sides let him know that something had happened. He climbed on top of one of the jeeps to get a better view of the volatile crowds, and his hands started to shake. A legion of white people stood to one side, hollering for justice for those murdered, while scores of black people shouted back from the other side, yelling about the attack on Hattie Mae Jenkins, and the truth she had raised. As the hollering and shouting turned to screaming and cursing, and objects began to fly from one side into the other, the sergeant realized dreadfully that there was only one way this episode would end.

He and his two squads were stuck in the middle of a blast radius, with only the concrete barriers in front of the black crowd and the white crowd to protect them from the detonations of both. As he climbed down from off of the jeep, he feared that that wouldn't be enough.

Sergeant Morris' concern was interrupted by a man who ran up and leapt over the barrier. Immediately, Morris pulled his sidearm and aimed it at the man's chest. "You! Freeze! Stop right there!"

The man stopped where he was and threw his hands up in the air. "Whoa! Whoa, hold on a second, okay? Look, my hands are up! I'm wearing a badge around my neck! You can come and check it out!"

Morris looked at the man suspiciously before he approached. He kept his pistol trained with one hand as he grabbed the badge with the other.

"My name is Commander Nash. I'm with the police department here. Are you Sergeant Morris?"

Satisfied with the badge, Morris put his pistol back in its holster. "Yeah."

"Great. We need your help."

"We've got our hands pretty full here, Commander."

"I know. I wish I could bring you better news."

Commander Nash signaled for Chance, Diop, and Xavier to come over the barrier as well. "The three of them are with me.

We have reason to believe that the man behind the recent murders will be showing up here today."

"You mean that gang that's been killing everybody? How are you planning to sort out a gang in this crowd?"

"It's not a gang, Sergeant. It's one man."

Morris looked at Nash, then at the three men behind him. "Yeah, right."

"Look, you can believe what you want some other time. Right now, I'm telling you that this guy is coming here. And if we don't do something, a lot of people are going to die."

Morris looked at the four men again. The seriousness in their faces made his decision for him. "What do you want me to do?"

"You have resources and manpower that we don't. We need to have a team keeping an eye out at all times, and a plan of action if someone spots him."

"I've got a couple sharpshooters…"

"No, sharpshooters won't help. This guy is more dangerous than you can imagine. Our best chance is to hit him hard, with everything, and hope for the best."

"Everything? What do you mean, everything? There are people all around here."

"Let's cross that bridge when we get to it. How about manpower? Can you spare some guys?"

"I've got my guys on three-hour rotations. The last shift ended a half-hour ago. Talk to the guys over there in the trucks, and see if you can work something out."

"Thank you, Sergeant. This is…"

Commander Nash stopped talking as he began to notice the sea of white faces parting down the middle. He tapped Xavier, expecting the worst, and braced for the war that he thought was coming. Once the break in the line worked its way up to the front, Nash relaxed. A caravan of three Hummers made its way through the crowd and stopped directly behind the barriers. The Commander glanced over at Sergeant Morris.

"This your backup?"

Morris didn't return the glance. Instead, he stared confounded at the military vehicles as their engines shut off and doors started to open. "No, this isn't us."

Fourteen men, all dressed in army fatigues and masks, and armed with full tactical weaponry, filed out from the Hummers. Twelve of them began dispersing into the crowd. The national guardsman looked at Morris confused as the armed men burst past them and over the barriers, disappearing quickly.

Morris looked at Nash with his eyes narrowed. "Did you do this?"

"If I had these guys, why would I come to you?"

"Then what the hell is going on?"

The passenger side door of the first Hummer opened, and an unkempt, gray-haired billionaire, left weak from his days of mourning, stepped out of the seat and approached Morris sternly. "You in charge here?"

Morris looked at the man in disbelief. "What the hell are you doing here?"

"Are you in charge here?"

"I'm in command, yes."

"Do you know who I am?"

"You're Don Rousch! I know who you are! Now what the hell are you doing here?"

"I've got business with these people."

"No, sir, you don't! It's my job to keep the peace here, and that's been hard enough! I'm trying to stop a riot, and you're going to start one!"

"Then so be it."

Morris put his hand on his sidearm, prepared to force Rousch back into his vehicle, but two men armed with AK-47s stepped to either side of the billionaire and gripped their guns.

Rousch watched as Morris let go of his pistol, and then reached for the intercom inside the Hummer. The amplifier on the roof propelled his voice over the crowd, and he looked past Sergeant Morris to the crowd of black people in front of him. Flashes of a closed casket echoed through his mind as he talked.

"I want you to hear me very clearly." Rousch spoke calmly to the crowd, with the sadness bringing his normal, commanding timber down to an even pitch. "I want you to hear me very clearly. I want you to understand very clearly what is happening right now. There is a group of very highly trained military personnel positioned around this area. They are very good at what they do. I only hire the best, and they are the best."

Rousch paused as the crowd on the other side of the concrete began to quiet. He let his words soak in before he continued. "A few days ago, my daughter was murdered at Toolig University. One of you in this crowd knows who did it. I am sure of it, and I am prepared to offer a substantial reward to anyone who can tell me definitively who killed my daughter."

A chorus of profanity erupted from the crowd of protestors, and the response let Rousch know that his offer would not be accepted. "Let me make myself clear! I am not leaving here until I know who murdered my daughter. The National Guard can play games with you people all day, but I will not."

Morris jumped up and faced Rousch. "Jesus Christ! What are you planning on doing?"

"Whatever I have to."

Dumbfounded, Commander Nash turned to Xavier, whose eyes darted around the crowd. "Xavier, do you know what the hell is going on?"

"Those are mercenaries." He spoke as he continued to scan the perimeter. "Military for hire. They each took a vantage point around the crowd."

"What does that mean?"

"It means that, unless they get what they want, they're going to start shooting. Only reason you would need to hide your identity is if you were planning on taking out civilians."

Sergeant Morris spun around. "They're gonna start shooting? Shooting who?"

"Ask him." Xavier pointed to Don Rousch, who stood with the intercom in his hand, facing the crowd.

"I'm not going to ask you people again! I want the person or people who killed my daughter! And I want them now!"

"Rousch, you can't do this!"

"I can do what I damn well please!" Don Rousch took a smaller walkie-talkie out of his pocket. "Gray...open..."

"I KILLED YOUR DAUGHTER!"

Rousch froze as the sea of black people began to part, and Commander Nash again braced himself for the impact of Toby's wrath. Instead, Hattie Mae Jenkins emerged from the crowd, followed by Lula, who followed faithfully behind her.

Hattie signaled for Lula to stop as she walked up to the barrier and glared hatefully at Don Rousch, who made his way up to the barrier on his side as well.

"You're that lady from the interview...the grandmother! All this is happening because of your bastard of a grandson!"

"Mr. Rousch, my grandbaby ain't nobody's bastard..."

"The hell he isn't!"

"...and I tell you one thing, I ain't kill your little girl, but I swears fo' God I wish I had!"

Rousch ground his teeth as he considered giving the team the command to shoot the old lady in front of him.

"She was gonna send my baby to jail for nothin'! Nothin'!"

"He raped my daughter!"

"You knows damn well he ain't rape your daughter! He told me everything 'bout how that girl was pregnant and goin' all kinds of crazy 'bout it! She wasn't raped no more than you was!"

"So what? So what if he didn't rape Stacey? You people just don't get it! That was my daughter! Not some trash off of the street! Not some drunk trailer park redneck! My daughter! He took my little girl's innocence! He deserved to pay!"

"Mr. Rousch, that girl innocence was gone long befo' she met Jamal and you knows it!"

"No, it wasn't! She was just fine before she met your boy! Just fine!"

Hattie lowered her eyes. "Ahh…now I gets it…she sleep 'round with as many white boys as she like, but she lay with my boy and her innocence gone…"

"You…people…don't…get it!"

"I gets it just fine, Mr. Rousch. You can mix at the bottom, jus' not at the top."

"I don't make the goddamn rules, lady!"

"But you was gonna send Jamal to prison 'cause of them rules, wasn't you?"

"I don't have time for this! You want to help these people? Get your grandson to tell me who murdered my daughter!"

"You know, I talked to my grandson since he been in that prison, Mr. Rousch. Maybe I knows who killed yo' little girl, maybe I don't. But I die befo' I tells you anything, sir. I goes straight to my grave befo' I says a word."

"That can be arranged, Ms. Jenkins…"

Commander Nash stared in awe at Hattie and Rousch going head to head, while Diop looked out at the unruly crowd. Unnerved at the potential massacre, he turned to his student, whose eyes still moved around the perimeters of the protest and the adjacent buildings.

"Xavier…"

"I've got six of them. Maybe seven if the last hasn't changed position. But there are twelve of them, Diop. I don't have them all."

"You can find them."

"You'll have to help me."

"You don't need my help."

Xavier spun around. "There are twelve shooters, Diop. All spread out, all with different angles. Even on a good day, that's nearly impossible. I need your help."

"Trust yourself, Xavier. This is the fifth day. You're stronger than you know."

Xavier stared down at Diop. "I don't…"

"When that man gets ready, he's going to give the command, and many of these people will die. You must leave now."

Nodding, Xavier looked around before snatching a pair of binoculars off of the closest guardsman. "Give me an eyeball, and see if you can find the last five."

Diop nodded back, and Xavier leapt over the barrier and into the yelling crowd.

"Alright, guys, it's coming loose!"

The workers in the subway tunnel had finally begun to make progress on the wrecked train, and the men on the hydraulic lifts with their blowtorches shouted their achievements down to the remaining workers. Underneath it all, Toby's body began to shake. He could feel the pressure building on the surface above, but still could not get himself free. Instead, he began to boil, and concentrated his rage as his eyes became suns in his head, burning whatever was not already burnt around him. He could feel the explosion within him building, and gripped the metal that tried to crush him as the workers above disconnected the molten steel with the stone of the subway tunnel.

Toby gnashed his teeth as he felt the weight on top of him finally begin to shift. If he could hold on for a few more moments, he would be free, and the havoc would be glorious.

The first shooter was on the third floor of the building directly to his right, and Xavier ran through the doors and bounded up the stairs into the conference room, ignoring his increased speed. The M240 machine gun sat perched in the windowsill, overlooking the mob, while the masked soldier stood behind it, waiting for his command from Rousch. He heard Xavier's footsteps and immediately spun around with his silenced pistol drawn, firing shots as the intruder dove behind the large mahogany table. Creeping along the floor, Xavier popped up close enough to grab the shooter's hand and forced the gun to ground. The masked man threw a punch that Xavier blocked, and twisting his wrist with his right hand, he used his left to break the soldier's arm before bringing his leg around and kicking his knee, breaking that as well. The mercenary only had a second to cry out in pain before Xavier grabbed the back of his head and slammed his forehead into the wall. As his adversary fell unconscious, Xavier scooped up his pistol and, with a running start, jumped out of the third-story window. He landed, breaking his fall with a roll, and to the amazement of the onlookers, used a wall in an alley to jump off of and grabbed a fire escape that lay parallel to the building. He climbed the rungs with his feet still dangling, and kicked his way into the second building, where the next two shooters were perched on the roof.

"You leave these people 'lone!" Hattie Jenkins chest began to hurt, but she ignored it as she threw her voice across the barrier. "You hear me! You leave these people 'lone!"

Don Rousch slammed his fist down on the concrete slab in front of him. "To hell with you! These people killed my daughter!"

"No, you killed yo' daughter, Mr. Rousch! You killed yo' daughter! The second you tell her to say that my boy raped her, she was already dead! You ain't know it, and I ain't know it, but she was already dead!"

"You shut up!"

"You leave these people 'lone, Mr. Rousch! They don't know you! Me and you 'round the same age! Come from the same time! They don't know a world where white folks kill you jus' 'cause how you look! They don't know you, Mr. Rousch, but I do! I do! You got's a problem with me, then you comes to me! But you leave these people 'lone!"

"To hell with you! To hell with all of you! All of you killed my Stacey! All of you!"

"Mr. Rousch...!"

"No, you shut up! You shut the hell up! All of you did it! All you people, I hate all of you! Each and every one of you! Every goddamn day I go and not have to lay my eyes on one you is a great day! You hear me!"

"You leave these people 'lone!"

"You're a pollution is what you are! A pollution on this goddamn country! Even the founding fathers knew it! They knew you were animals! They knew if you weren't slaves, then you'd be a goddamn menace! And now look! You got good kids walking around with their pants off their butts, trying to be like you! Goddamn rap music and drugs and guns…everything you people touch goes straight to hell! And now you killed my daughter! You killed my Stacey!"

"These people ain't do nothin' to you, Mr. Rousch! You leave em' 'lone!"

Mr. Rousch stopped yelling, but Hattie could hear him clearly, as if someone hit mute on the world and only left sound for the two of them.

"You people are a plague. A goddamn infestation. It's about time somebody exterminated you."

"Diop, I need the last one! Diop! Diop, where's the last one?" Xavier shouted into the radio, but Diop's horrified eyes were stuck on Don Rousch. He raised the communicator to his lips without moving his gaze.

"Xavier…it's too late…"

Don Rousch stared at Hattie as he raised the radio from the Hummer to his lips. "Open fire."

The gunshots sounded like small bombs as they flew from the window of an apartment building, and screams from the mass of black people began to echo through the air as they began to trample each other, scrambling to escape the bullets. Hattie Jenkins stood horrified, cringing at the gunfire as it emerged in spurts, and staring at Don Rousch, who stared back at her, stiff and stone-faced.

"What the hell is that?"

The crane had been set, and had just latched onto the train wreckage when the screaming started. The crew was too far down to hear the chaos taking place up on the surface, but the uttered screams coming from underneath the wreckage were enough to make them stop.

"Is there someone under there?"

"That don't sound like nothing human to me."

Toby sounded as if he were dying. Each bullet fired above pierced a piece of him, and his agony began to make the tunnel shake. His strength was regained, but it was too late. The massacre had started, and his rage could no longer be contained.

He could wait no longer.

"Get that thing out the way!"

The crane moved the train wreckage just as Toby's screaming stopped, and his eyes faded away, leaving Nathan Freeman's black pupils in their place.

"Hattie, Hattie, we gots to go! They shootin' now! We gots to go!" Lula moved as fast as she could up to her friend, who continued to stare at Don Rousch as if he were the devil himself. She pulled and tugged, trying to get Hattie to move, and finally her strength betrayed her and she fell back. "Hattie! Hattie, I ain't leavin' without you! Come on! We gots to go!"

Hattie heard her friend behind her, and fought to make herself move. She pursed her lips at Rousch, and turned around just in time to see the bullet explode out of her friend's stomach.

"LULA!" Hattie ran over to her friend as she fell onto her back. She could see the light fade from her eyes as she bent down and grabbed her up in her arms. "Awww God no...no, please no..."

Hattie rocked back and forth, cradling her friend in her arms, as the deep echoes of gunfire and screams of panic painted her background. Rocking her longtime confidante like a baby, she leaned over her and, with a hoarse and agonized voice, began to sing.

"O freedom...

O freedom...

O freedom...over...

AHHHHHHHHHH!!!"

Trayvon Adams pulled himself up from being trampled on the sidewalk. Fighting his way back to his feet, he looked around frantic for his friends as the gunfire engulfed the air around him.

"Tray! Tray!"

He could barely hear the shouts of his friends as he threw his head around and fought to stay on his feet. Finally, he saw them a few feet away, and began to run toward them.

"Tray! Come on, man! Come on!"

The seventeen-year-old began to sprint, but stopped suddenly, bending over at the waist and clutching at his stomach.

"Tray, what the hell, man! We gotta go, homie! We gotta...!"

His friend's voice got caught in his throat as Trayvon looked up. His fitted cap and hoodie were still in place, but there were two dark, obsidian eyes glowing out from beneath his eyelids.

Growling deeply, the teenager's body yanked around and lunged toward the concrete barriers.

Lawanda Perry screamed as she tried to keep hold of her children. The force of the stampede overtook her, and she screamed again as she felt her son's hand escape from her grasp.

"DJ? DJ?" She yelled insanely until she saw her fifteen-year-old son with his five-year-old sister in his arms.

"Mom!"

"DJ, go! Get out of here! Go now!"

"Mom, what about…"

"Go now!"

She felt the burning in her stomach as she watched her children escape to safety, and once they rounded the corner the rolling in her throat began. The pitch-black eyes matched the color of her braids as she leapt straight up toward the window with the firing machine gun.

Don Rousch refused to let himself show any remorse. He stared at the ensuing onslaught with retribution on his face, while the crowd of white people behind him looked on in terror with their mouths covered, watching people they didn't know die.

It was the ceasing of the gunfire that got his attention, and he lifted the Hummer's radio up to his mouth as the silence grew. "Gray, what's going on? Gray?"

Out of nowhere, two blurs came exploding through the concrete in front of him and rushed past him on either side. And the screaming that was once in front of him was now behind him. Confused, he started to turn around, but the old woman was quick. She came through the new path in the barriers and grabbed his neck, lifting him off of the ground as her black eyes burned and Toby's voice bellowed low and deep from her throat.

"An befo' I'se be a slave…"

The torture behind him was deafening, and even as he suffocated he knew that the people behind him were dying.

"I'se be buried in my graves…"

The man's voice coming out of Hattie's mouth was all he could hear now, and as he grabbed the calloused hand wrapped around his throat, his eyes found the dark stone orbs that now replaced Hattie's.

"An gone home ta my Lord…"

The old lady clenched her fist closed, and the portion of his throat that she gripped crushed in her grasp as the rest of Rousch's body fell to the ground.

"An bees free…"

"Is that…that's him! That's the Freeman guy! The guy they want for the murders!"

The three police officers assigned to the subway wreckage drew their guns as Nathan Freeman walked out from under the destruction and climbed shakily onto the platform.

"Freeze! Freeze goddammit! Hold it right there!"

"Don't shoot! Please, don't shoot!" Nathan held his hands up in the air and laced them behind his head. "Look, I've got my hands up! I'm unarmed! Please, don't shoot!"

The officers looked at each other confused.

"Was he under the train? There's no way he was under the train! He would've been crushed! No one could've survived that!"

"I think I was…"

"Shut up and put your hands in the air! Don't move!"

"Okay! Okay, look!" Nathan turned around and got down on his knees, then lay down flat on the ground. "Look! Look, I'm on the ground! I'm on the ground, okay! Just please, don't shoot!"

The two officers looked at each other once again.

"Cuff 'em."

"No, you cuff him."

Rolling his eyes, the third officer walked up and placed the handcuffs on Nathan's wrists before standing him up. "You're going to jail for a long time, Mr. Freeman."

"Look, I just need to speak to my wife! Let me speak to my wife, okay? Sonya, her name is Sonya. I just need to speak to my wife."

"Your marriage is going to be the least of your troubles where you're going."

"Just…tell her I didn't mean it! Tell her I forgive her, and that it wasn't me! It wasn't me, it was somebody else! Can you tell her that?"

"They'll give you a phone call at the precinct, Mr. Freeman. You can tell her yourself."

When it was all over, there was nothing but bodies.

Diop stood still with his eyes wide. He was fearful of moving as he watched Hattie, Trayvon, and Lawanda heaving, their shoulders rising and then falling like rockslides. Their eyes burned brightly as they stand in the middle of a sea of dismembered Caucasians.

Chance ran through the smashed opening in the barrier, checked for life in bodies on both sides. He felt his sanity begin to slip as he encountered corpse after corpse of men, women, and children, their pale white and brown skin matching the coldness of the sidewalk.

Commander Nash stood in the middle, where the National Guard used to be, with his hands behind his head, muttering words that only he could understand. Sergeant Morris took stock of his dead soldiers, and Nash broke his muttering long enough to stand beside the commanding officer as they both stared forward at the blood-covered trio.

Hattie Jenkins' head turned toward the two leaders, and they each took a step back as her obsidian eyes burned. "You'se let 'em be…"

The two men froze, and their terror brought forth their obedience. Hattie's head turned back around, looking at the glowing eyes of Trayvon and Lawanda, and her fists began to clench tightly. "I'se cain't hold em…dey too far gone…"

And their eyes flickered, and then burnt out, leaving the confused faces of the three hosts. Only Hattie had a semblance of an idea of what had happened. She looked over at Nash and Morris, who had no intention of being disobedient, and then looked earnestly at the young man and woman in front of her. "We gots to go…"

Utterly confused, Trayvon looked at her, shaking his head, and then down at the ground. "Yo…how'd I get blood on my Nikes?"

The two officers escorted Nathan up the stairs and out of the train station as they talked excitedly back and forth. Each of them grabbed one of Nathan's handcuffed arms. The third walked in front.

"You know we're probably gonna get promoted for this, right?"

"Hell, we'll get medals and everything! The guys who brought in Nathan Freeman!"

The officer in front began to comment on their stupidity, but as they emerged from the station the scene in front of him shut his mouth. The ground was covered with dead bodies. "What the hell?"

Quickly, he turned around to face Nathan, whose face was drawn tight in discomfort. "Did you do this?"

"I was…with you. How could I?"

"Then what the hell happened? And what the hell is wrong with you?"

"My stomach."

"Well, you better—"

Nathan's head shot up and the glowing orbs in his eyes blinded the officer in front of him. Crying out, he snapped out of the handcuffs, knocked the officers on either side of him to the ground, and then leapt straight up and disappeared into the sky.

Day Six

"Lula…"

Hattie Mae Jenkins leaned over her bathroom sink, trying to contain her tears. She remembered watching her best friend fall, screaming as she saw her ally collapsing heavily onto the sidewalk. She remembered bending over her longtime comrade, singing the only words that would come to mind, trying to serenade her best friend's soul into a heaven built especially for the both them. She remembered that, but everything else was a haze. Everything else was red flashes and dying cries, blood-stained street signs and bus stop advertisements, and a dead Don Rousch lying at her feet when she finally came back to reality.

There was a part of the old lady that was confused about what had happened, and there was another part of her that understood it all. It was the part of her that still remembered sitting on her grandmother's lap as she told old plantation stories, tales from the cotton fields conveyed with so much fervor that Hattie would nearly stop breathing when she reached the peak of the action. It was the part of her that realized her grandson wasn't crazy when he told her about a man with glowing black eyes during their last phone call. So when Diop, Chance, Xavier, and Commander Nash tracked her down to her apartment at 21st and Grove, and came to the door with a story that sounded too fantastical to even consider, she invited them in and made them coffee.

"I gots the other two here with me." Hattie spoke in passing while going back to get the sugar. She noticed Diop staring at her on the way back.

"The other two who received the *doole*? Where are they?"

"They in the back room sleep. Been sleepin' since I bring 'em back here. Whatever happen musta took a lot out of 'em."

Commander Nash was instantly uneasy about being in the same apartment with a trio that he had witnessed commit a mass murder, but he yielded his instincts to the fact that there were things going on that he couldn't possibly understand.

It was Diop who insisted that they go against the orders from the police chief and seek the old woman out, instead of helping to mobilize a small army in front of the crumbling apartment building. Witnesses had already said they'd seen her and two others come into the dilapidated complex not long after the slaughters. They fit the description from the few people who had come from downtown alive, and the Governor was pulling out all the stops to make sure this twisted saga ended today.

"Nash! Nash, what the hell are you doing!" The police chief's high-pitched voice rang through the walkie-talkie as the commander walked with Diop, Chance, and Xavier up to the fourth floor. "I'm under strict orders from the Governor, Nash! You get back out here! That's an order!"

Chance looked at the Commander as he raised his radio.

"Chief, I'm sorry...I have to check this out. There's some things going on that...look, I just have to check it out, chief. You have to trust me."

"Who I trust doesn't matter, Nash! The Governor has flipped! He's talking about bringing that whole goddamn building down!"

All four men paused, looking back and forth at each other with new worry drawn in their faces.

"Chief, there's people all over this building!"

"You think I don't know that? Drug dealers been running that building for years! You've probably got addicts lining the floors!"

"Yes, there are. But addicts or not, I've seen enough people die this week..."

"It's out of my hands. Get your people and get the hell out of there now."

Commander Nash looked at Diop, who shook his head emphatically.

"I can't do that. Look, we play this the wrong way, and a lot more people are going to die before it's all over with. You've got to buy me some time."

The police chief stalled, and Nash continued before he could be denied again.

"I've been on this since the beginning, Chief! Since the attack on the precinct! I've been following this thing for almost a week, and I'm telling you, you take this building down, and more people are going to die! You have to buy me some time!"

The chief looked around angrily at the police officers surrounding him, and then moved away from them before he responded. "Nash...look, I'll do what I can, okay? But we've got explosive charges on the way, and they've already got pros waiting to set them at the base of the building when they get here. Public opinion is all that matters at this point, Nash...you know that. Rousch ordered the Blackthorn guy to shoot into the crowd at the protest, and they're both dead. But the people who murdered the counter-protesters are still at large. And they're the same ones who murdered everybody else this week. People are scared, Nash. They're scared as hell. They'll forgive the death of a few crackheads if they can sleep better at night. You know that. You know how this is going to end."

"Yeah."

"I'll do what I can, but when I call and tell you to get out, you haul tail out of there. They'll forgive the death of a police commander, too."

Now, as he sat in Hattie Jenkins' apartment, Nash wondered how it would feel to be inside a building as it exploded. "Ms. Jenkins, I'm confused. You said the other two attackers have been asleep since they got here. They're both much younger than you, ma'am. How is it that you have the energy to talk to us, and they don't?

Hattie sipped her coffee as she listened to the commander's question.

"Don't knows exactly. Alls I knows that whatever gets into us couldn't stay. Least that's what he say."

Diop turned his head slowly. "That's what who says?"

"Young man started all this."

"You mean Nathan? You talked to Nathan Freeman?"

"Naw, I ain't heard of no Nathan Freeman. Man I talked to's name was Toby."

The four men looked wide-eyed at each other before Diop jumped up from his seat and ran over to Hattie, gently but excitedly bending down beside her chair.

"You talked to Toby?"

"Yes, sir."

"When?"

"Last night I believe."

"Do you know where is he now?"

"If he ain't move since I left him, then he upstairs."

Commander Nash and Chance leapt up at the same time.

Frantically, the two men bounced around each other, ecstatic and terrified, as they processed what they'd just heard.

Diop sat at the old lady's side with his head in his palms, calmly trying to do the same thing. When he could hide his thoughts no longer, he raised his head slowly and looked at his student, who sat shocked on the plastic-covered couch, and then at the two police officers.

"Gentlemen!"

Nash and Chance stopped and look at Diop.

"Please sit down."

Both men hesitantly took a seat as the African walked back over to the couch as well.

"If he is indeed here, then he is here for a reason, and no one is better suited to find that reason than Xavier." Diop nodded at his student, who looked back dumbfounded. "Trust yourself, Xavier. Trust that you will know what to do."

Xavier sighed as he nodded back at the African. He turned his head to Hattie amidst the silence. "How...how did this happen? How did he get here?"

"He come here last night, lookin' like somethin' was eatin' at him from the inside out. Like he was tryin' to keep himself from explodin' right in front a' me."

"Toby came here?"

"Yes, sir. Crashed all the way up the steps. Thought it be a stampede outside my door at first."

"Didn't he frighten you? Didn't you see his eyes? You had to have known he wasn't ordinary..."

"I knowd who he was. Can't tell you how I knowd, but I did. I brought him inside and he start talkin' like my granddaddy used to talk. Talkin' like they used to talk out in them fields. And I knowd what he was then. He ain't even have to tell me. I thanks him for helpin' my boy, and I takes him upstairs to the empty unit, where nobody'll bother 'im."

"Did he say anything about what happened yesterday?"

"He just said that we was too far away. He said he come to us, but he couldn't stay, or we'd have died."

"What does that mean?"

"I ain't know when he said it, but I been thinkin' 'bout it, though."

"I believe I know what it means." Diop moved up and sat on the edge of the couch with his hands grasping each other. "It means that this is my fault."

Everyone turned and looked at the African, who in turn looked back at no one.

"Diop, what are you talking about?"

Diop raised his eyes to meet Xavier's. "The ritual."

"I don't understand."

"The ritual was meant to destroy the *doole* by setting free the spirits that it held captive. It was meant to give Toby, and the spirits that brought him here, a door to escape and rest peacefully in the afterlife."

Chance looked questioningly at Diop. "So what went wrong?"

"It had never been done before. The elders and I assumed that the spirits, that Toby, would have their eternal rest if given the chance. But we were wrong. Toby has the door, but he will not leave. He does not want peace. He wants war."

The African ran his hand across his mouth. "I fear my ceremony has had its consequences. There has been no evidence, not even in the village stories, about the *doole* being cast into others. Yet I watched it happen with my own eyes. The only explanation that I have is the ritual."

Commander Nash leapt up to his feet again. "So you're saying he can send the black eyes into anybody he wants?"

"It is likely just people of the bloodline. We know that Ms. Jenkins is one. It is likely that the other two are both descendants as well."

"So how do we stop him?"

The men fell quiet, looking dreadfully at one another as they realized they all knew the answer to the question. Nash considered calling down to the police chief to share the new information, but quickly decided that he'd be better off labeling himself insane. Chance paced the room as Diop continued to sit quietly, internalizing the gravity of the mistake that he made.

Xavier broke the silence once again as he stood up slowly and faced Hattie Jenkins. "I have to talk to him."

Chance waved his hand back and forth, dismissing the thought. "No. Hell no. One, we don't know if that's really him up there. Ms. Jenkins here could have taken a bump on the head. Two, he already tried to kill you once. I wouldn't push your luck with this guy, X."

"If he wanted us dead, we'd be dead by now, Chance. He had to have known we were coming here…" Xavier stopped in mid-statement, hesitating to complete his thought. He threw caution to the wind as he turned back to Diop. "I feel like he's waiting for me."

"You are the only one who would know."

Xavier turned back to Hattie. "Ma'am, can you take me to him?"

Hattie took one last sip of her coffee and pushed herself up to her feet. "Come on…"

Xavier's knees weakened as he climbed the steps. By the time he reached the top, he found himself on the floor, hyperventilating from recollections of a past life.

Twenty-First and Grove. The familiarity of the building had

started striking him when he'd first arrived, and he could feel something knocking at his consciousness as he entered the run-down building. It hadn't settled on him then, hadn't quite forced its way through to the front of his brain, and so he was able to function. Now, bent over at the top of the fourth floor staircase, the memories came rushing back, drowning him in their under-current. Memories his mind had forced itself to forget in order to track a mass murderer. Memories of a wife and son and daughter, of a family destroyed by a drug addict's bullets.

Xavier collapsed into the corner at the top of the staircase and shook violently, afraid to move any further.

"You alright, baby? You looks like somebody done broke you..." Hattie Jenkins took a moment, and then bent over the crippled father. "You been here before, ain't you?"

Xavier nodded his head slowly.

"Ain't nothin' but pain n' sufferin' trapped up here. If you been here befo', it wasn't for nothin' good."

Xavier listened to the old woman sigh slowly as he tried to stop shaking.

"I'm goin' on back downstairs now. Whatever you sufferin', ain't my place to see. He in room 409, down the hall there."

Xavier's neck became stiff as he watched Hattie walk away, and some minutes passed before he made his way back up to his feet. He wondered to himself how he could've forgotten them; how he could have forgotten his plan. He wondered if his would-be tomb was still the way he left it, with toys and trinkets belonging to XJ and Felicia, and love tokens from Theresa, piled high enough on the bed to cushion the fall of his dead body. It had been almost a week since the day he was supposed to die, but it felt like an eternity. It felt like he'd inadvertently started another life, and had become so enthralled in it that he'd forgotten about his first one. Now that the pain had returned from his subconscious, it rendered him almost invalid as he pulled himself up to the door marked 409 and pushed it open.

It was still the way he remembered it. Nothing had changed, except the absence of the young corpse that he'd left on the floor at the conclusion of his first visit. In its place was another man who sat on his knees in the middle of the living room, muttering to himself faster than Xavier could translate, and striking himself periodically. He rocked back and forth, trying to shake the multiple voices out of his head, as Xavier approached.

There was darkness in the room where there should have been light, and the abnormal shadows cast on the wall tried to make Xavier's blood run cold, but they proved no match for the echoes of his son's laughter in his head.

"Toby?"

The man on his knees shook his head vigorously, and Xavier cocked his head to the side.

"Nathan?"

Nathan spun around on his knees, and his face made Xavier jump back. His eyes were such a dark red that his pupils were barely distinguishable, and his blood pulsed so hard that his skin rose and fell with every heartbeat.

"Shhhhhhhh!!!" Nathan pointed to his head, and then struck his forehead multiple times with his palm. "They can hear you…"

"Are you Nathan Freeman?"

"I am…the invisible man…who is not seen…because they choose not to…but they have to now…they have to now!"

Nathan laughed hysterically as he fell over onto the ground.

"I know you're Nathan Freeman."

"How do you know…what you know…when you think you know…what you don't know?"

"I know that you're Nathan Freeman. Your father was Thomas Freeman, same as mine. We're brothers."

Nathan continued lying on the ground, but he stopped laughing as Xavier's voice lowered.

"I've been looking for you."

"And what...did you find?"

"I don't know. What are you, Nathan?"

Nathan rolled over to his knees, but kept his forehead on the ground. "Strange...fruit. I taste like strange fruit. Ain't I bitter! Lord Jesus... God Almighty...I'm bitter as hell!"

He fell into laughter again as Xavier looked at him confused.

"Nathan, do you know who you are? You're Nathan Freeman. You have a wife...you had a son..."

Nathan swung his head around and began a kindergarten tune. "I...had a boy...who killed a boy...who killed a girl...who killed a woman...who killed himself...and died happily...ever after..."

The words struck Xavier hard. He used his hand to cover his face, and then mouth, before he looked back at the man on the ground. "He didn't kill himself, Nathan."

"Didn't you...hear the end? He killed himself...and died..."

"I killed him, Nathan."

Nathan sat up from the floor quickly. "I had a boy, who killed a boy, who killed a girl, who killed a woman, who killed himself and died happily ever after!"

"I'm Xavier Turner. Your son killed my family. I cut his throat right here in this room. He didn't kill himself. I killed him, Nathan."

Nathan tried to make his way to his feet, but the frenzy inside of him brought him screaming back down to his knees. His bloodshot eyes darted back and forth in his head as he spoke slowly.

"I had a boy. I had a boy...who killed his cousins...who killed his aunt...who died by his uncle...and everyone...everyone died..."

The room lay silent as the pain bounced between both men.

"I...I just thought you should know."

Nathan roared as he lunged forward and grabbed Xavier, but the eyes, the glowing black stones, had already come by the time he had him off of the ground.

"You..."

Toby leaned in close, then dropped Xavier as he collapsed back onto the ground. He shook like Nathan shook, and gritted his teeth as he fell back onto his knees. For the first time, Xavier saw pain in the glowing orbs, and he stared at the agonized figure in front of him.

"T...Toby?"

"GETS OUT 'CHEA!"

The rumble above made Chance wonder if his friend was still alive.

"Toby...do you know who I am?"

"I say...get on...from 'ere!"

"I'm not leaving."

"You'se stay...and you'se dead..."

"Fine, but I'm not leaving."

Toby shook his head. "You'se can't save 'em..."

Xavier jumped forward. "And you can't kill them all! You can't just go around killing innocent people!"

"AIN'T NO WHITE FOLKS INNOCENT!"

Glasses and plates fell off of the kitchen counter in Hattie Jenkins' apartment as the building shook from top to bottom. The police outside scrambled back from the perimeter as the chief, convinced of Commander Nash's words, continued trying to talk the Governor down from his plan.

In apartment 409, Xavier stared as Toby crouched on the floor in front of him, grimacing. "What's happening to you?"

"Slaves...want dey blood..."

"So why aren't you out killing..."

Xavier stopped short. His eyes narrowed as realization crept on his face, and he discovered for himself what Toby was up to. "Tomorrow...tomorrow's the last day..."

Toby grunted in protest as the pieces came together in the mind of his nemesis.

"My God...the ritual..."

From the ground, the slave looked up at Xavier, scowling through his affliction. "Youse...so quick...savin' yo' massas..."

"Look, Toby, you can't do this! This is a different world! There aren't any slaves here! There aren't any masters here! Just regular people!"

"Massas... an' slaves...be all over dis 'ere world...youse cain't see 'em."

"Toby!"

"I sees 'em...jus' fine!"

"I can't let you do this..."

"I gots me...a debt..."

Xavier turned to run from the room, frantic about telling Diop the new information he had, when Toby's voice came booming from behind him.

"XAVIER!"

Xavier froze at hearing his name. He stood with his back to Toby as he listened to the strained voice.

"I comes...for you'se first. Whens yo' woman an' chillen...lie gone in yo' eyes...I comes for you...but you runs from Toby."

"I had to."

"African...done bring you up."

"He trained me. Taught me to control it."

Toby looked back down at the floor, fighting to control himself. "He done good..."

Xavier turned and walked back into the room, and he gasped as Toby's memories became his. The connection between them began to manifest as the shadows shifted about the room, and Xavier could see Toby's wife and daughters playing with dolls that their father had handmade for them. He could feel the love that the slave once had in his heart, and cried out as it was taken away by the lash of the slave master's whip. Weakened, Xavier collapsed to the ground as he finally got a taste of the rage that now fueled his companion.

"Youse...so quick...savin' your massas."

Xavier forced himself to climb back to his knees, and before he could get a hold of himself, he began weeping. "Toby, look, you can still go. Diop's ritual...you can still go. Leave this body and... and rest. I mean...how many years? Centuries...have you...?"

"What you'se seen...be nothin'. Be no rest. Ain't...no ways tired."

"You're talking about killing thousands of people."

"Gots me a debt."

"Stop saying that! You don't have to pay back anything!"

"Spirits done showed you!"

"I saw the past! The past, Toby! Let it go!"

Toby's strength filtered through his pain as he looked up at Xavier. "Time don' change nothin'. Dey trick you'se to believin' it done change, but it ain't. Ain't nothin' change...an' I'se still gots me a debt."

Xavier wiped his eyes dry and stood up. He was tall and resolute, and spoke definitively. "I will find a way to stop you."

"Den...tomorrow...one a'us be findin' dat rest you talkin' 'bout."

"I guess so."

Toby's tortured eyes look up at Xavier. He nodded through his shaking, and Xavier nodded back. They stared at each other, searching one another's soul, and then Xavier turned to leave.

When he got back down to Hattie's apartment, Trayvon and Lawanda had woken, and sat in the corner visibly shaken as Commander Nash tried to question them.

Diop jumped up when Xavier walked into the room. "I began to fear the worst."

"You're fears are right. We've got a problem."

A half-hour later, everyone in the apartment sat silent. Diop's face was strained as he looked at Xavier with disbelief. "It is not possible."

"It wouldn't be on any other day, Diop. Think about it. You said it yourself, on the seventh day, the *doole* always dies, right? It can't contain the rage, and it consumes itself. But what if didn't have to contain all the rage?"

Chance looked at Xavier. "You mean, send it into other people, like he did yesterday?"

"Yeah. Toby knows he can do that now. Yesterday, I believe he did it on accident. That's why the cops that had Nathan in custody said that he seemed like a normal guy. He'd left Nathan completely. But he couldn't stay in anyone else for too long without them dying, like he told Ms. Jenkins. So he had to go back."

"I still don't understand why he's sitting upstairs torturing himself."

"He will never be stronger than he will be tomorrow. Normally, that power would cause him to consume himself. It would cause his own death. But he doesn't have to contain it within himself anymore."

Commander Nash paced the floor. "How many people do you think he can get to?"

Diop's disturbed face looked at the Commander. Xavier spoke even though Nash had his answer.

"That's why he's sitting upstairs, forcing himself to withstand his urge. He wants all the power he can have for tomorrow. All of the power of the sixth day, and the seventh…"

"How can we stop him? What can we do?"

Xavier shook his head. "There's nothing we can do. He's too powerful now. You go upstairs and try and kill him, you'll only piss him off. He can barely hold himself together as it is. You unleash him now, and you're still looking at a bloodbath, just a longer one."

"So we stand by while he murders hundreds of thousands of people in the morning? Is that it?"

"There is only one option." Diop stood, grasping his hands. "It is not guaranteed, but it is our only hope."

"What is it?"

"I will tell you, but first we must leave."

Diop began to make his way out, and the other men followed suit. Xavier was last, and stopped in the doorway of Hattie's apartment before he exited. He looked curiously at the old lady as he spoke.

"Ms. Jenkins, did Toby ever tell you why he came here? Why he came to you?"

Hattie glanced over at Xavier. He could see the hesitation on her face as she tried to decide how to answer, and finally tried to ignore the question.

"Yo' friends leavin', son."

"He did, didn't he?"

"Maybe he say, but ain't no business of—"

Diop and Chance began to return to the apartment, but Xavier motioned them away before he shut the door.

"Ms. Jenkins, Toby tried to take me before he took Nathan. I'm Nathan's brother. So I'm connected with this whole thing, just like you are. I need to know…why did he come here?"

Hattie looked at Xavier longingly, then made her way back to the couch. "All while I was a young girl, I hears stories about 'em."

"What? What stories?"

"'Bout a granddaddy a' mine wid the devil in his eyes. They say he kill so many white folks that the rest jus' pack on up and leave town."

"What did he say, Ms. Jenkins?"

"He say he and his wife and chillen was on the Talbert plantation 'fore he got himself killed. Say on the day he die, his wife and daughters try and escape, but gots caught in the next state over. Master Jenkins kept 'im 'stead of returnin' them to Talbert…"

"Master Jenkins? Is that where your family…?"

"…gets our name, yes."

"So…you descend from both he and his wife. That's why he was drawn to Jamal from the beginning…that's why he came to you…"

Hattie nodded her head proudly. "I always knowd we had strength in our blood. 'S why I never took my husban' last name. Always knowd my peoples was somethin' special."

"Do you have any other family in the area, Ms. Jenkins?"

"No, all my folks is gone 'cept me an' Jamal. Jamal's mama died some years back. Had a brother went over ta D.C. years ago, lookin' for work. He passed on now but me an' his wife talks almost every week. She busy wid her daughter-in-law an' grandbaby. Las' I heard she say he was tryin' to be some kinda rapper or some nonsense…whatever keeps 'im outs the street, I guess."

Hattie reached onto the coffee table and pulled a wallet-sized photo from out of her Bible. "His name Moses. Moses Jenkins. Here, you can have this picture. Gots me a few more upstairs."

"Thank you, Ms. Jenkins."

"Thank you, baby."

Day Seven

MORNING

Lawanda awoke first, rousing herself slowly from off the plastic-covered furniture that she found herself slumbering on. There was a brief moment of panic as her eyes opened, and she realized that the room she was in did not belong to her, before the memories of the past forty-eight hours began to take hold. She shuddered as she recollected getting off of work early and picking her children up from school to take them to the protest, only to get there and have them almost be killed. She jumped as she recalled the baritone gun blasts and random bodies falling limp in the street, dead with their eyes open, as she screamed for her two children to run as fast as they could. And then there was nothing. After that, there were no memories, just feelings. Just streaks of euphoria. Like an addict, she had no memory of what happened after the hit, but the sensation had been more than enough to chase, if she knew where it had come from. She came back to herself standing in a pool of dead white people, and the flashes of the corpses made her gag as she walked into the kitchen. Gripping the edge of the sink, she poured herself a glass of water and gulped it down, hoping it would help to settle her stomach.

Once she had regained her composure, she picked up her cell

phone and dialed the number of the last incoming call. An alert voice picked up on the other end.

"Wanda!"

"Hey, girl."

"Where the hell are you, Wanda? Everybody's askin' about you!"

"I can't tell you right now. How are the kids?"

"They're still shaken up from the riot, but they're okay. DJ been real quiet, and Princess won't stop crying unless somebody's holdin' her. They been sleepin' late, too. You want me to wake 'em?"

Lawanda rubbed her forehead, wishing she could be with her children. "No, just tell them that I'm fine and that Mommy will be home soon. Did you get the money?"

"Money ain't an issue, Wanda. I don't have no problems caring for my niece and nephew, you know that. I'm worried about you. What happened?"

"I can't talk about it right now."

"You scared me half to death! They showed all those people dead downtown, and I almost had a breakdown right there in the salon! And now you telling me you can't tell me anything!"

"Look, Tee, when I can tell you, I will. For now, though, I need you to take the kids out of school and keep 'em at home."

"You ain't heard the news, have you? Police say everybody gotta stay in until they say it's okay. Nobody's leaving their houses."

"Okay, good. You and the kids just keep inside, okay? Stay inside, lock the doors, and wait for all this to end."

"Wait for all what to end? You scarin' me, Wanda…"

"Tee, just please do what I'm tellin' you to do. If they right, then it'll all be over after today anyways."

Lawanda could sense the fear in her sister's voice as she ended the conversation. She regretted having to scare her, but the fear was for her own good. If she was scared, then she'd do what Lawanda asked.

Still in the kitchen, Lawanda decided to make a pot of coffee. She probably wouldn't drink any, but it was the least she could do for Ms. Jenkins after all she'd done for her and Trayvon. They may have been away from their families, but they hadn't gone without a home-cooked meal since the old lady had brought them to the building and begun washing the blood off their clothes.

The mid-morning sun teased through the blinds as Lawanda scooped the coffee grounds into the coffee maker and filled the back of the machine with water. The little spots of sunlight danced through the blinds as she finished pouring the water, and she lifted up the blinds before replacing the coffee pot.

Her sharp breath came paired with the sound of breaking glass. She didn't realize she'd dropped the coffee pot as she started yelling for Ms. Jenkins.

Trayvon came in first, leaping up from his spot on the other couch. Scared and confused, it took him a moment to realize that it was Lawanda hollering, and he bounded into the kitchen to see what the commotion was all about.

By the time Hattie made her way in, carefully stepping around the broken glass, both Lawanda and Trayvon were staring out the window with their mouths gaping. Outside, immediately in front of the apartment building, was an entire squadron of heavily armed Marines, and six M1A1 tanks with cannons trained directly at the rundown complex.

"Ms. Hattie?" Trayvon spoke timidly while observing the war-zone outside. "They here for us?"

"I 'spects so."

Lawanda whimpered as she imagined her daughter's laughter fading away. "What are we gonna do?"

"We ain't doin' nothin', sweetheart. What happen today ain't up to us."

"So we're gonna sit here while they kill us?"

Hattie lowered her head and narrowed her eyes. "Ain't nobody killin' us today, baby. That boy upstairs knows what he doin'. You feel 'im coming on again, you jus' don't fight him none."

Hattie looked at her two houseguests, then back outside the window. "If he need us, we be ready."

Commander Nash flashed his badge and burst through the perimeter with Marines set up all the way back to Nineteenth Street. He felt his anger grow as he ran the next two blocks, and passed soldiers decorated in camouflage and tanks that sent shivers through the ground beneath him. He was able to piece together at least part of the story from the bits and pieces of talk he overheard as he passed: emergency deployment, hostile civilians, mass murderers, neutralization. Contain or destroy the threat. His heavy breathing was more from infuriation than fear as he reached the front lines, and the Police Chief, the Governor, and an unknown soldier stood in a power huddle as they called out plays and figured out their next moves.

"What the hell is this?"

Nash's voice broke up the pow-wow and got the attention of the three men, who each carried different emotions as they saw him approaching. The one that caught Nash's immediate attention was the unknown soldier, whose face tensed slightly as he placed his hand on the butt of his sidearm.

"Commander, it's nice to see you."

The Governor was unimpressed by Nash's entrance, and spoke sarcastically as the Commander walked up to him directly. "I told you to evacuate the city! Evacuate!"

"What the hell is going on here?"

"You gave me your assessment of the situation, Commander, and it was taken into advisement."

"Advisement? None of you even knows what you're up against here!"

"And that's exactly why I called in a few favors with some old Marine buddies. Nash, this is Second Lieutenant George Rogers. He'll be our tank commander."

Lieutenant Rogers nodded at Nash as he removed his hand from his pistol grip. Nash looked at him, and then back at the Governor.

"This isn't Afghanistan, Governor!"

"Really? Because when I saw those aerial shots of the dead bodies downtown from two days ago, it sure as hell looked like the Middle East to me!"

At wit's end, Nash looked over at his boss. "Chief!"

"This is totally and absolutely out of my hands, Commander. I'm here to assist these men in any way that I can. If you want to help, I suggest you volunteer your services as well."

"You came to us last night, did you not?"

The Governor was unmoved by the fury in Nash's face.

"You came to us, and you told us that the threat was…I believe your words were 'severely more substantial than you originally thought', right?"

"…in order to urge you, in the strongest possible terms, to evacuate the city!"

"Well, this…this is our citizens taking a stand! This is us saying that we won't be run out of town by thugs and hoodlums! Nobody wants to leave their homes, Commander! They just want these people gone! The charges are set at all four corners of this god-awful place! It would have come down last night, if you hadn't talked my police chief into stalling me. But it's coming down today. And if, by chance, anything survives that, then the tanks will finish the job."

"Sir, if I may?" Rogers looked to the Governor for permission to continue speaking. Once he got it, he turned back to Nash. "The Marine Corps recognizes how delicate a situation this is, sir."

"Do you now?"

"Yes, sir. Even though this was an emergency deployment, we handpicked every soldier out here."

"Handpicked?" Nash looked around at all the armed military men that surrounded him. "They're all white!"

"We didn't want any conflict of interests, sir."

Nash threw up his hands. "You're going to get these people killed!"

"Our goal is to have as little civilian casualties as possible, sir."

"I'm not talking about the civilians, you idiot! I'm talking about your soldiers!"

"Sir, my battalion is well-trained to face any enemy attack."

"You're not trained for this, Lieutenant. Believe me."

"See? You see?" The Governor pointed accusingly at Commander Nash. "It's you talking like that is what got me ordering the tanks in the first place. Everybody else thinks I'm crazy, you know that? These guys are some sick bastards; I'll give you that. But I'm willing to bet, at the end of the day, they're just your average pants-sagging, crack-smoking criminals who decided to get their rocks off by killing white people. Maybe they took a hit of something stronger than usual and what little bit of brain they had left snapped, I don't know. You came in running your mouth last night like Freeman and the rest of them were some kind of super villains, and damned if I didn't fall for it. But frankly, at this point, I'm a bit concerned that we've brought a gun to a knife fight."

The police chief glanced over to the Governor with this brow wrinkled. "Governor, did you get a chance to look at that footage I sent you?"

"No. Been too busy putting out all the fires that started because of this thing. I've even got the President up my behind now!"

"With all due respect, sir…" Rogers turned to the Governor. "I have. I watched all of it alongside the general before he deployed us. Our tanks are equipped with multiple weapons. If we can get the job done using just the machine guns and fifty cals, then we'll call it a good day. But we're Marines, sir. We will get the job done. We were called here to neutralize a threat, and we're not leaving until we do."

The Governor nodded his head, and then slapped Rogers on the back proudly before he turned back to Nash. "Guess that settles it, Commander. I'm blowing the charges in one hour."

"Can I at least evacuate the apartment building?"

"No. At this point, we don't know how many perps we're dealing with. I can't guarantee the public that all of them were all destroyed if I gave one or two a chance to get away beforehand, now can I?"

"So you're just going to kill everyone in there?"

"I'm sure the Chief has already told you this, Commander, but let me reiterate. Public opinion has spoken. Most of the people in this building are already dead. They just don't know it yet."

"I can't do this."

Xavier sat with his hands trembling as he looked back and forth from Diop to Chance. He wanted to close his eyes, to pretend like he couldn't see what he knew was there, but the carpeted floor and light-colored walls that surrounded him were too familiar to ignore.

"Diop, I can't do this. I can't be here."

"This is no time for doubt, Xavier. This is why I trained you. Only you. You must try and focus."

"What if I can't do it? What if I can't control it?"

"You must, Xavier. It is the only way."

The television was on, and footage of military tanks challenging an apartment in the ghetto were projected out into the living room space. Xavier didn't see the images. The stain on the carpet where Felicia spilled her grape juice had taken all of his attention, and he relived seeing her remorseful face and tearful eyes as Theresa scolded her for taking it out of the kitchen.

"It's alright..." he spoke aloud despite himself, "...she didn't mean it."

Chance sat on the couch with his body tense, trying to stay quiet. He had a hard time watching his friend suffer, and an even harder time watching images on the television when he felt he should be on the scene. Frustrated, he jumped off of the couch.

"Diop, come on, man! We need to get out there!"

"No. We need to be here."

"We can't just let them die, Diop!"

"The only one who can save them now is Xavier."

Diop looked back at his student, whose face was beginning to turn pale. "I know this is hard, but you must connect with your pain. It is the only way this will work."

The African took a small vial out of his pocket. The red liquid that was in it before was all but gone. There were three drops left, and Diop held the tiny container upside down until all three dripped onto his fingertip. He looked intently at the blood, and then reached forward and pressed it onto Xavier's forehead. Once the blood had stuck, he took his thumbs and separated it, rubbing firmly on Xavier's forehead in small, circular motions, as he chanted.

"*Bayi lén niou dounde louniou yélool…bayi lén niou dounde louniou yélool…* "

Xavier felt something, but he didn't quite know what it was. He tried to focus on it, but the laughter of his wife echoing through the air snatched his attention away. He tried to yank his head away from Diop's grasp, but his teacher's hold was firm, and the chants continued as Chance walked up to the television.

"Diop! Diop, look, the tanks are moving!"

The African turned his head as the tanks on the television screen began to change formation, giving each a clear firing angle of the complex.

"They're going to blow the building! Jesus Christ, Diop, please! We gotta go! We gotta do something!"

Diop pulled Xavier's head up, so that their eyes met. "It is time. You are the only one who can stop what is coming."

Xavier tried to look away, but Diop held his head in place once again, and tried to shake the uncertainty out of his eyes. "You will not fail, Xavier."

"How do you know?"

"Because I know you will do what you must."

AFTERNOON

It was time. Toby could feel it. If he could make it to the roof, then his enemies would know his pain. If he could make it…

Inch by inch he rose from off of the ground, and stood with the pain of generations of slaves weighing down his every movement. He wanted to scream, but he could not. Even the slightest release of power could cause him to break, unleashing himself upon himself, and though he would destroy anything he contacted, he would also perish; imploding from the inside out. No. He was determined to grab the reigns of his fury, leading it to where he wanted it to go. He would give his adversaries the reckoning that they deserved.

Though the lights were still on, the hallway went dark as Toby stepped out of the apartment. He braced himself against the wall, leaning heavily, and stumbled as the spirits nicked him, one by one, like an army of bees. The darkness around him was alive as he moved, and people on the floors both above and below him began to hear the voices. The screams of those who were stuck in the state of their deaths; hung from trees, burned alive, and raped until their lives spilled out of their legs. Even the addicts grew terrified of the screaming and wailing, and began praying to a God that they had long since forgotten.

Toby could not hear their prayers. He stopped at the end of the hallway, agonized and exhausted, and felt his muscles tighten until they almost snapped.

He moaned, but he didn't scream, and for just a second, Toby considered Xavier's proposition. He considered resting, and directing the other spirits to rest, to find peace after the many years of anguish. But as he reached the final staircase, the one that led to the roof, to the outside, he realized he had come too far for that now. The shrieks of the ancestors that deafened him as he fell up the steps reminded him of his calling. Peace was much too easy to attain. Vengeance was not. They had waited for decades upon decades. Centuries upon centuries. They would have their vengeance.

Keeping his screams locked inside his chest, Toby burst through the door at the top of the stairs and fell onto the flat, concrete surface of the roof. The sky darkened as he crawled slowly, pains-takingly, to the edge, where he could look over and see the Marines and tanks that lined up for him.

"Is there a storm coming?"

"Who the hell is that on the roof?"

"Christ, that's Freeman! That's Nathan Freeman!"

"Give me the goddamn detonator! This ends today!"

"Governor, you..."

"Give me the detonator!"

Again, slowly, Toby began to stand, inch by inch, until he was upright. Until his silhouette blocked out the brightness of the afternoon sun, and the blackness around him began to form into the images of contorted faces. Soaked in sweat, Toby stood shaking, with his hands clenched, his elbows in, and his eyes closed.

"Sir, they won't detonate all at once, sir! You have to press it four times, one for each explosive!"

The Governor stared up at Toby, who already looked half-dead, and raised the remote detonator above his head. "You burn in hell, you black bastard!"

Toby inhaled, breathing in impossibly deep, and the blackness surrounding him was sucked into his nose and mouth and eyes and ears, rushing into him like a wind. The air stirred as the blackness was drawn in to Toby's body, and the Marines below could feel a breeze become a cyclone as they fought to keep themselves steady and on the ground.

And then it stopped, and the blackness was gone, and every-thing was deadly silent.

And Toby's eyes shot open, and he screamed.

The blackness detonated out of him like a shockwave, pushing even the tanks back as it went forth into the atmosphere. The onslaught made each of the soldier's bones chill where they stood, and they immediately began to feel the death that was on its way.

Toby fell to his knees, breathing like his chest had collapsed. And then he smiled.

Jamal Jenkins sat in his cell in the solitary confinement section of Axelake Prison. He'd been told that he'd be kept here indefinitely, or until Nathan Freeman was found and he and the rest of the thugs were brought to justice, and things went back to normal in his hometown.

"Things are never going back to normal." He laughed at his court-appointed lawyer through the same small, square hole that managed to feed him three times a day. "I guess I'll be in here for a while, huh?"

When the thin, wiry man left, Jamal stood up from the floor and walked the step-and-a-half over to his cot. There he sat still, with only the memories of his time with Nathan Freeman to entertain him. Every so often, he'd change the channel in his head, and end up streaming together recollections of himself and his grandmother, but that program never had a happy ending. The final scene was always him sitting behind the bars of a jail, watching Hattie Jenkins cry out to the police officers to set her baby free. That program was painful to watch, and when he felt the tears start to come, he would blink and turn the channel back to Nathan Freeman and his deep, dark eyes. Then he would feel better.

There had been surprisingly little commotion since Jamal arrived at Axelake, a feat the warden had attributed to his security system and personnel. Chaos ensued in the city, but the young man sat peacefully in his confinement, and made no noise and no trouble. So, as a reward for his good behavior, and as a deterrent for any bad ones, the warden approved thirty minutes of solitary rec time, and Jamal was taken out in the prison yard to feel the sun on his skin.

He was too busy enjoying the fresh air to notice the five white men who shoved a handful of cash in the hand of the guard, and entered the yard behind him.

"Hey, boy."

Jamal turned around to see a huge man with an almost bald head and a swastika tattoo on his chest. Frightened, Jamal began to back up.

"They said I would be out here alone. What do you want?"

"Hell, what you think we want?" The large man pulled an ice-pick out from under his waistline. "You think you can rape a white woman, and then kill a bunch of white people, and not have to pay for it, boy? Hell, I'd take another life sentence for killin' you any day."

Jamal's eyes started to go wide but he remembered Nathan Freeman, and forced himself to stand up straight. "I didn't kill anybody."

"The hell you ain't, nigger. It's high time somebody taught you a lesson."

The large man signaled to the men behind him, who all rushed forward. The first punch sent Jamal flying to the ground, and the kicks that followed seemed to make every inch of him swell. By the time the four men stood him back up, one of his eyes was almost swollen shut, and his right cheek looked like it was storing food. The large man stood in front of him with the icepick ready.

"This is for the nation! White power!"

"White power!" the rest of the men shouted back in response as Jamal began to scream wildly.

"Damn, Ray, you sure stuck him good, huh?"

"Naw, I ain't stuck him yet! Hell's goin' on?"

Jamal's screams began to bounce off the prison equipment as the four Aryans held him up and looked at one another, confused. Only Ray, who was standing directly in front of Jamal, could see his eyes go black as night.

"What the…?"

Jamal snatched his arms out of the grasp of the four men, yanked Ray's icepick out of his hand, and shoved it into his left and right eye sockets.

Blood began to drip onto Ray's swastika as he shrieked in pain, and Jamal spun around to face the four men behind him. They stared frozen at the young man with the burning eyes, and he smiled at the man on the far right before he shoved the icepick in through one of his ears, and pulled it out through the other. The last three attempted to run for the door, but Jamal pounced on them one by one, leaving their blood on the weight equipment and basketball court, and then smashed through the door just as the guard began to call a code red, and beat on the heavy metal mass until there was no movement underneath.

Slowly, Jamal strolled back into the prison yard, and leapt clear over the tall, barbed wire gate. He wasted no time as he landed on the other side, and began sprinting toward the city with the echoes of a prison-wide alarm sounding behind him.

Fifty miles east of Hattie Jenkins' apartment building, in the next city over, Brandon Lincoln sat nervously in the small, corner office of his corporate law firm as he pored over the details of his new case. A picture of him and his younger sister, taken in front of her freshman dorm room, sat beside his desktop, accompanied by a larger picture of his entire family, spanning from his blind grandfather with the rickety cane to his newly born nephew, wrapped in a blanket and held over his eldest brother's shoulder. His designer suit stood out amongst the jeans and work clothes, but he still had his father's smile.

"Yo, B!" Tim came rushing in the door with a mischievous grin on his face. "You go out with Adrianna yet?"

Brandon sighed as he tried to ignore his fellow lawyer. "I told you, I don't date coworkers."

"And I told you, she likes black guys! It's an easy lay for you, bro!"

"I'm not interested, man."

"Like hell you're not! Everybody in here would screw Adrianna, except she likes black dick! I'm just a white guy with a tiny one, what can I do? Come on, man, you gotta screw her for me! You gotta screw her for all of us!"

Charlie came creeping into the door after Tim. "Christ, Tim, you want the whole floor to hear you?"

"Charlie, Charlie, come on, bro! Please tell Brandon he has to screw Adrianna!"

Brandon looked up from his brief, trying to control his anger. "Tim, would you let it go, please? Jesus…"

"Alright, fine! Fine! But you know you want to!"

Tim looked at Charlie. "How are your witnesses coming?"

"They're pretty solid. I think we're good to go."

"Guys!" Charlie and Tim looked at Brandon, who glanced up at them annoyed. "I'm trying to review this case. Can you guys come back later?"

"Hey, Charlie, what are you bringing to the company picnic?"

"Umm…I don't know…maybe a pasta salad or something…"

"Brandon says he's bringing fried chicken and watermelon!"

Brandon slammed his hand down on his desk. "I never said I was bringing fried chicken and watermelon."

"Awww, come on, bro! Who the hell else is gonna bring it?"

Charlie shrugged his shoulders in the doorway. "Fried chicken and watermelon sound good to me."

"See! Everyone wants you to bring it! It's not a party without the fried chicken and watermelon! Oh, and Kool-Aid! Gotta bring the Kool-Aid!"

Brandon's face began to grimace as the rumbling in his stomach turned to a fiery pain.

"Yo, Charlie, check this out…what do you call a bunch of black kids running down a hill?"

Charlie looked uncomfortably from Tim to Brandon.

"Oh, don't worry about Brandon, he's cool. So…what do you call a bunch of black kids running down a hill?"

Brandon cried out in pain as he pushed the table away from him and fell over onto the ground behind his desk.

"Whoa, Brandon? You okay? You okay, man?" Charlie ran over to Brandon, who was writhing on the ground. He bent down just in time to see the dark, charcoal eyes shining in his head. "Brandon, what…?"

Brandon reached up from the floor, grabbed Charlie's tie, and yanked him down, slamming him into the floor beside of him. He stood up deliberately, and Tim stared with his eyes wide with horror as he reached back down to the floor, grabbed the back of Charlie's shirt, and hurled him effortlessly through the windowpane and into the ninth-story air outside. He stared back at Tim, growling, as Charlie's scream grew more and more distant. When the thud of his body crashing into the taxicab below came through the broken window alongside the cold air, Brandon leapt forward at Tim, who ran hollering out of the office.

Everyone on the floor had heard Tim's boisterous comments, and sat in their offices feeling their particular ways. Now, with the commotion and screaming, they stepped out into the hallway, frightened at the sounds they'd heard. Tim sprinted, with his eyes darting back and forth, straight down the hall and around the corner, shrieking incoherently as he passed everyone, and ran headlong into the elevator doors before he picked himself back up and started banging on the down button.

No one had the chance to ask what was wrong before Brandon came blowing out of his office, his devastating force breaking through the narrow doorway of his working space. He tore down the hallway screeching, with his arms fully extended, grabbing coworkers before they could react and bulldozing them through the walls as he rounded the corner to see Tim rapidly smashing his palm against the elevator button. He cried out again as he tore forward with his arms out, dropping the heap of bodies he had wrapped around his arms in front of a petrified Tim as he grabbed him around the throat.

The elevator was still five floors up, and Brandon smashed down metal doors with his free hand and dropped a high-pitched, screaming Tim down the dark, unforgiving shaft. He then jumped down himself, landing massively on Tim's already unmoving body, and leapt up to the first floor elevator doors, prying them open. The attorneys and corporate representatives would only see two obscure, glowing orbs before a force would thunder past them, knocking them all to the ground as it shattered through the glass doors and rapidly made its way to the neighboring city.

Fifty miles south of the screaming slave was a large city still trying to hold on to its country roots. Pecola Brown sat in the auditorium of one of its three high schools, and she sang to herself as she read her book. She was only in the fourth grade, but her science fair project had won her a special commendation, and she'd been asked to attend this assembly, along with the other elementary and middle school recipients, while the high-schoolers were all away on an all-school field trip. She sat in her school uniform, with the colors faded from overwashing, and her socks folded down so that the hole didn't show. Her hair fell into five, large, neatly woven plaits that lay on her head. She looked up from her story long enough to notice that she was the only black girl in the room, and then shrugged and looked back down to continue her adventure.

Three sixth grade girls from the local primary school approached Pecola, recognizing that she was from the other side of town. They were all from the same class and hung from similar rungs on the social ladder, and their flowing heads of blonde and brunette hair swayed as they drew closer, filling the air with sweet shampoo fragrances and mesmerizing the preteen boys that stared, imagining doing things that they didn't yet understand.

"Hey, what school are you from?"

Lizzie, the blonde, sparked the conversation, and Pecola looked up innocently from her book. "Malcolm X."

Lizzie scrunched up her face. "That school is in the ghetto. My mom says only poor kids go there."

Pecola didn't understand, but the tone of the girl's voice was enough to make her want to end the conversation. She looked back down at her book.

"Can I touch your hair?"

Pecola looked up again, confused. "Huh?"

"Can I touch your hair?"

"Ummm…okay."

Lizzie reached down and touched Pecola's plait with her thumb and forefinger. She yanked it back instantly, and began rubbing her hand on her jeans. "Your hair feels weird."

"No, it doesn't."

"Yes, it does. It feels like the thing my mom uses to clean her pots when the grease gets stuck."

Lizzie's two friends laughed from behind her. "Ewww!"

Lizzie laughed along with them, and then turned her attention back to Pecola. "Why do you wear it like that? It's ugly like that."

Pecola's eyes began to water.

"It is not ugly! My mommy did it for me this morning! Go away!"

"It is ugly. Why do you wear it like that?"

"I said, go away!"

"I see black people on TV all the time, and their hair doesn't look like that. It's always really straight and pretty. So why does yours look like that?"

Pecola started to answer, but the sensation in her midsection stopped her.

"I know! I'll give you a makeover! My mom always says I should find a black kid to hang out with, so it might as well be you!"

"My stomach hurts…"

"I know a black girl whose hair is always straight and shiny. I'll invite her over to do yours! And we can paint your fingernails, and put on perfume, and I'll even sneak out a pair of my mom's contacts for you! Oh my god, how cute would you look with blue eyes! You'd be the cutest black girl in the world!"

Pecola cried out as the three girls jumped back, and her eyes became opaque and brilliant in her head as she snatched them away. They died without knowing what had happened, and their bodies lay limp across the auditorium seats as Pecola disappeared out through the window.

Trayvon, Lawanda, and Hattie all knew what was coming before it actually came. They looked wildly at one another, eyes going back and forth between the three of them as the swirling feeling in their stomachs turned to an ache, and then to a burn. When the time finally was upon them, their eyes exploded simultaneously with the first charge set at the south corner of the building, and they wasted no time blasting through the walls and grabbing as many people as they could. Moving impossibly fast, and ignoring the falling debris, they each went back and forth into the collapsing building, getting people to safety before darting back, and getting the last of the hazy-eyed addicts out of the hallway before the 21st and Grove apartment complex crumpled in and collapsed on itself.

The cloud of dust and sediment hung low in the air, and blindness struck everyone within a block of the collapse. Lieutenant Rogers ordered his men in the tanks to use thermal imaging to determine if any threats still stood, and the report he received back prompted him to order the locking and loading of each of the six cannons on top of his tanks.

"Sir, we got four hostiles, but we can't see 'em worth a damn! They got some kind of light coming out of their heads, sir! It's blinding us through the thermal lenses!"

"Can you tell if they're armed or moving?"

"No, sir! Best I could make out was that it was four of 'em, and I had to pull my eyes away, sir! I still can't see much of anything right now!"

When the dust settled, all guns are pointed at a crouched Toby, who knelt atop the fallen building, still trying to gather the energy to stand. A few feet in front of him were Trayvon, Lawanda, and Hattie, whose eyes burned hatefully as they stood poised with fury in their throats, scowling and ready to attack.

Lieutenant Rogers recognized what was going on, and grabbed his communicator. "They're protecting him! They're protecting the one on top of the wreck!"

"What do we do, sir?"

"Hold fast! If they make the first move, blow 'em to hell!"

"Yes, sir!"

The standoff only lasted a few minutes, but each second seemed like an hour, and the tension in the air made trigger fingers jumpy. No one moved, though. With the exception of the growling from Toby's protectors, no one made a sound, anticipating the war that could start at any second. Single beads of sweat turned to soaked fatigues as Marines stood ready on foot alongside the tanks. Assault rifles trained on the four hostiles began trembling slightly as the shooters visualized their targets, and prepared to take them out.

Then the ground began to shake.

Rogers looked at the police chief and the Governor for an explanation, but their confusion was obvious as they fought to maintain their footing. Tank operators began opening their hatches, peeking out into the clear air as they tried to figure out what was going on. It was not an earthquake, the Marines deduced amongst themselves, but a rumbling. A slow, growing rumbling that made them unsure of where they stood.

From a distance, they looked like fallen stars. Thousands upon thousands of bright, glowing orbs that rushed toward them excitedly. It was the Lieutenant who could first tell the difference. They weren't fallen stars, he began to see, but eyes. The same burning eyes that sat in the heads of the hostiles in front of them. And it was not excitement that they rushed toward the soldiers with. It was rage. Pure, unbridled, maniacal, soul-deep rage.

His fear echoed through his communicator. "Jesus...there must be thousands of them..."

An army of young and old, of men, women, and children, stampeded toward the tanks with identical bloodlusts resting in their mouths. They destroyed everything in their paths, crushing cars and downing trees, as they sprinted forward, eager to satisfy their lust for vengeance.

"Turn the cannons one hundred eighty degrees! Focus on the incoming hostiles!"

The cranking and stirring of metal sounded as the 120mm cannons shifted positions and turned to face the coming on-slaught. The army continued to sprint forward with reckless abandon, tasting the blood of their enemies in the air.

And then they stopped. Each of them stopped dead in their tracks.

Lieutenant had been so preoccupied with the coming attack, that he didn't notice Toby, who now stood erect. There were still remnants of pain in his visage, but it was outweighed by his pride as he looked past the Marines to the soldiers he had made. Again, he inhaled deeply, strengthened by the fury that crippled him, and closed his eyes. When he opened them again, they were set low and narrow, and the brightness slid out through the slits.

"Now, we's kill 'im all. KILL 'IM ALL!"

The sky turned black as Toby's army leapt into the air, blotting out the sun as they screamed, and murdered as they landed. Machine gunfire rang out into the sky, but it is of no use. The bullets did not stop the impending deaths, and the first ones to die lost their lives with their fingers on a trigger.

"Fire the cannons! Detonate! Detonate!"

The sound of the thunderous guns cracked the air in two as they fired into the descending black cloud. Toby cringed, feeling the agony of those who were hit as they descended from the sky and crashed to the concrete without moving.

"AHHHHHH!"

His war cry sent more fire into the eyes of the attackers as they landed on the tanks, pounding the metal encasings and bending the steel weapons. They hungered for the lives of the soldiers inside, and when they found they could not break through the armor, they smashed and stomped, ripped and tore, until one by one, they left the tanks inoperable.

There were screeching tires two blocks away, and a few seconds later Xavier shot in from behind and ran headlong into the ensuing melee, with Diop trailing and hollering after him. He tried to help the panicked Marines, but their distinction of friend and foe had already been determined, and he ended up receiving the curses and dodging the bullets of his allies.

"I'm trying to help you!"

The Marines looked at him, confused, as they realized that his eyes weren't luminescent, and he turned to find members from Toby's army preparing to attack him. He fended them off, one after the other, striking and kicking with pinpoint accuracy, and sent them flying and tumbling about the concrete. Inevitably, though, their sheer numbers began to overwhelm him, and after being hit repeatedly by a mass of possessed civilians, he stumbled to the ground and was pounced upon viciously.

By the time Diop reached him, Xavier lay beaten at the bottom of a small crater, struggling to move.

"You cannot defeat them, Xavier. Not like this."

"But...what if...it doesn't work?"

"Listen around you, Xavier."

Xavier struggled to hear beyond his own strained breaths, but when he did, all he heard was crying and screaming. Shouts of death rung in the air. It sounded like hell.

"There is no other way, Xavier."

Xavier set his face hard, then looked at Diop and nodded his head. Diop placed his thumbs back on his student's forehead, in the exact same spots where they were before, and used the rest of his fingers to grip Xavier's skull as he shouted up to the sky.

"RAY KO! RAY KO! RAY KO!"

The world began to spin swiftly around Xavier as he lay there in the crater, and in his fear he tried to fight his way to his feet. Diop held him down as best he could, using all of his strength to keep him contained as the concrete around Xavier faded into a blur and disappeared, and Xavier went limp as he felt himself snatched away.

It was dark outside, and there was nobody on the street. Xavier looked around, confused at the peace in the air, and though he couldn't quite remember, he felt distinctly like he was supposed to be somewhere else.

As he began walking, the scene in front of him became clearer, and Xavier realized that he was in his neighborhood, about a block up from his house. His confusion began to dissipate as he discovered how close he was to seeing his family. The last thing he remembered was driving to the store, preparing to get groceries in order to surprise Theresa when she got back home with the kids. He didn't remember how he had gotten from the car, on the road, to here, at the entrance to his development, but it seemed painfully unimportant as he walked briskly down the street. He was here for a reason, of that he was sure. He just didn't know what.

From a distance, he could see his home, with the porch and living room lights on. It invited his family in as Theresa's car brushed past him and pulled into their driveway further down. He could see his children jump out from the backseat, playing with each other as their mother grabbed her things from off the dashboard.

"XJ! Felicia! Daddy's right here!"

He could hear his own voice, but there was no echo. No reverberation off of the trees and rooftops, and before the strangeness could dawn on Xavier, he saw a man come out from the shadows. The young man, beaten by life, who walked as if there were needles in his shoes, began to approach his children.

The scene crippled Xavier as he recognized Clarence Freeman.

Everything after that happened in slow motion. Xavier hurled himself down the street, using all the power his legs could produce, but he knew he wouldn't make it in time, and his screaming still had no echo. He could see the glint of the streetlight off the metal that Clarence held in his hand, and he got to the edge of the driveway just in time to hear the gunshots ring out. Dropping to his knees, he wailed as his children's bodies' fell to the ground.

Xavier couldn't bring his muscles to move, so he fell forward, landing on his palms as his face dropped and contorted, and his insides turned to stone. It was only when the shadow passed over him that he realized that his children were not the only ones to die. Theresa ran up to her kids, grabbing them and shaking them where they lay, and Xavier fell to his stomach.

"THERESA! THERESA!"

Clarence ran over to his wife as he tried to pull the pocketbook off her arm, and Xavier already knew what was coming. He reached for his wife, clawed the air for her as Clarence pointed his gun, and suddenly she turned to him, her face ridden with anguish, and opened her mouth.

"XAVIER!"

And the bullet quieted her scream as the world spun again, fading the houses and the murders into a blur, and Xavier screamed as he was snatched back.

"AHHHHHHH!"

Xavier felt the match ignite in his stomach, and the fire in his blood, pumping through his veins, before he realized he was back in the crater where he was left to die. He clawed at his chest, trying to tear away whatever was burning around him. But the inferno was inside, and when he realized it, he screamed all the more.

"Control it, Xavier! You must control it!"

Xavier rolled over onto his stomach, clutching at the back of his head, trying to make the pain stop. His eyes rolled back in his skull as he slammed his fists into the ground and felt both the rage and the torture build alongside each other.

His screams caused the warriors with the glowing eyes to stop, and they each looked toward the crater as the cries emerge and bounced off of the sky.

"Control it, Xavier! Control it!"

Xavier began to shake, convulsed where he knelt, and wished for death to come and take the pain away. Collapsing, his body curled itself into a ball, and just before his heart stopped beating, his eyes tinted over, and the dark radiance burst out of them and up to the sky.

Pecola shook her head, her plaits swaying back and forth, as she wondered where she was and how she got there. The blood on her uniform began to scare her, and her crying got the attention of Brandon, who was nearby and just as confused. Tripping over the dead bodies that littered the ground, he stumbled over to her and picked her up, gently patting the back of her head as her tears stained his already ruined suit.

"I want my mommy…"

Jamal saw them both, and his eyes darted across the bloodied ground as he tried to figure out what happened. *It had to be Nathan*…he thought to himself as he raised his eyes, looking around. When he found the confused Toby, standing on a mountain of rubble, and his grandmother standing in front of him, he ran forward to embrace them both.

The Marines on the ground had been decimated. The few that were left trained their guns on the discombobulated civilians, knowing that all of their clips were empty. The confused mass of people looked around at each other as one of the privates, with an arm hanging limply by his side, grabbed a radio from off the ground.

"Lieutenant Rogers! Lieutenant Rogers, come in!"

There was some static before the sergeant responded from inside one of the tanks. "Who is this? What the hell is going on?"

"This is Private Yeats, sir! I think…I think the hostiles are standing down! I don't know what's happening, sir!"

"What do you see?"

"Their eyes are different. They ain't burning no more, sir! And they look confused, like they don't know what's going on!"

"Take them out, then!"

"That's a negative, sir! Ammo's all gone and it ain't but a handful of us out here still alive! It's too many of 'em, sir!"

"Then take out the ones you can!"

"Sir…we just got slaughtered out here, sir! Even if we had

ammo, there's too many of 'em! Sir…with all due respect, if for some blessed reason they decided they don't wanna kill us no more, I ain't gonna be one of the ones trying to provoke 'em again!"

The Lieutenant grabbed the machine gun he had tucked tightly by his side and opened the hatch to the tank. "Goddammit, I'll do it myself then!"

Toby saw Rogers come out of the tank, and prepared to slaughter him, but the crushing sounds coming out of the crater diverted both of their attention, and their eyes came to rest at the same place. Xavier climbed up out of the ground with two suns burning brightly in his head, and a madness on his face that made the Lieutenant climb back into his tank, shutting and locking the hatch as he shouted to the gunner to prepare the cannon. Xavier looked dead at Toby as he walked forward and his hands shook with the fury inside of him.

Toby began walking down from the wreckage, staring hatefully as he approached Xavier, and the masses of black people stared forward in fear as they watched two titans get ready to clash.

"How you done dis?"

Toby sneered out his question, but Xavier couldn't answer. He had to keep his mouth clenched shut, and his jaw locked tight, for he could feel the rampage inside of him, fighting to come out. His sweat poured as the veins of his body protruded out from his skin, and his hands continued to shake as his body twitched. His eyes burned as he snarled with primal instinct, trying to resist the acrimony in his blood.

Rogers saw both men through the periscope in his hatch. "Yeats, you still there?"

"Yes, sir!"

"You seeing this?"

"Yes, sir!"

"The hostiles out there…how are they reacting?"

"I don't think they're hostiles anymore, sir! They look just as scared as we are!"

Lieutenant Rogers thought hard as he looked over at his gunner, and then got back on his radio.

"I need updates from all tank commanders, asap!"

"This is Baylor, sir! Our tanks have been beat to hell, but the cannon is still operational!"

"Anyone else? Does anyone else have an operational tank?"

A chorus of "no sirs" came back through the radio.

"Baylor, you're up front with me, right?"

"Yes, sir!"

"Okay, here's the deal! We're down to two hostiles, and they're right in front of us! We're taking the shot! Are you ready to fire?"

"Yes, sir!"

"Take aim at the one on the left! I'll take the one on the right! We're gonna take these bastards out once and for all!"

"Yes, sir!"

Xavier stopped moving as he heard the turrets crank, and saw the cannons on top of two tanks point at him and Toby.

Toby looked at him and smiled. "You'se thinkin' dey ain't gon' kills you? Deys knowd you be a good nigga? You'se see now."

He set his face hard as Xavier opened his mouth to speak to the soldiers in the tank.

"BOOM! BOOM!"

The blasts ripped the concrete up from the ground and sent the remains of the apartment complex flying into buildings almost a half-mile away. The dust cloud that formed blinded everyone once again, and Rogers got on his radio eagerly.

"Everybody switch to thermal! Baylor, do you have any sight of them? Any sight of the hostiles?"

"Negative, sir!"

"Are you sure?"

"Yes, sir! I don't see anything, sir!"

Rogers dropped the communicator and let his shoulder fall against the computer equipment.

"Jesus...we did it. We..."

"Look out, sir!"

Xavier came running, piercing through the dust cloud, and smashed headfirst into the tank. Lieutenant Rogers fell over sideways from the impact as Xavier climbed the huge machine and ripped the hatch door off. Rogers froze as he came face-to-face with Xavier's incinerating pupils, and yelped despite himself as Xavier yanked him out of the armored vehicle and leapt back down to the crumbled concrete with him in hand.

Growling, Xavier threw him to the ground, where he landed facefirst, and prepared to force his foot through the Lieutenant's skull.

"Dats it!"

Xavier froze with his foot raised, as Toby appeared, standing directly beside him.

"You'se be whose you is! Give da spirits what dey 'serve!"

Xavier trembled, feeling the urges of the rage inside of him.

"Kill 'em dead! You'se kill 'em dead, jus' like dey do me!"

Crying out, Xavier slammed his foot down, making a deeper hole in the already broken concrete beside Lieutenant Rogers' head. The officer sighed with relief as Xavier looked at Toby, who was stood in front of him, reeling with fury.

"I'm...not...you..."

"TRAITOR!"

Toby's voice pounded the sky as he lunged into Xavier, forcing him back and into the ground. He pounded relentlessly on his adversary's face and chest, one fist after the other, as the ground underneath them both trembled from the blows. Finally, Xavier kicked him away, jumped up to his feet, and rammed his shoulder into Toby's midsection as he grabbed him around the waist and launched him into the air. The slave winced as his feet left the ground, and yelled out as Xavier slammed his body into the already shattered concrete. Both men climbed to their feet, screaming with ferocity, and launched themselves at one another again. The collision made the tanks shake, and each blow sounded like crushing boulders as they began attacking each other ruthlessly.

Lieutenant Rogers tripped and stumbled his way back to his tank, and with the help of some of the crew, made it back up to the hatch where the reinforced steel door used to be. He grimaced as he fell inside, leaving blood on the computer equipment, and picked up the radio.

"Baylor!"

"Jesus, sir, I thought you were dead!"

"No..."

"What do we do, sir?"

Rogers made his way gingerly to the periscope, where he saw Xavier hurl Toby into an open space right in front of the confused civilians. They screamed and tried to scatter, but there was too many of them in too tight a space, and they ended up going nowhere.

Xavier landed heavily on top of Toby and began punching with enough force to make the nearby windows shatter.

"Take aim..."

"Sir?"

"Take aim, Baylor."

"But, sir, the civilians are right behind them..."

"We are Marines, Baylor! We were sent here to do a job, and we're going to finish it! Now take aim!"

The turret pivoted around, aiming the cannon at the warring men and the masses behind them.

"Detonate!"

The blast came in slow motion for Toby, but in reality he moved too quick for anyone except Xavier to see. Taking the punch as it came, he grabbed Xavier's shoulders and shoved him back, then kicked him away. As Xavier began to stumble, Toby got to his feet in a crouch and pushed forward, throwing himself headlong into the explosive tank round.

The impact sent shock waves that knocked the crowd of black people to the ground, and the heat singed and burned those closest to the detonation. Xavier's eyes narrowed as he watched the dust begin to clear. He recalled the first tank round that hit him. That did not kill him, but did enough damage to cause him to struggle standing back up before he could retaliate against the armored vehicle. He sneered as he wondered if the Marines had finished his job for him.

Painstakingly, Toby began to inch himself off of the pulverized concrete. The blood that ran from his mouth screamed in Xavier's ears, and he fought the urge to turn away.

"Youse...think dey cares...'bout us?"

Toby staggered to his feet, struggling to keep his balance. When he finally got steady, he released a guttural cry that made the people behind him cringe, and then leapt onto the rooftop behind Xavier and sprinted, jumping from roof to roof until he disappeared into the skyline.

Xavier knew he must follow, but there was a delay, as the reality of what had just happened ignited the rage already burning inside of him. He bounded over to the tank that fired and slammed into it, rattling the equipment and the people inside. Then, as he climbed the vehicle, he smashed it repeatedly, until the soldiers inside were trapped and all but crushed.

Having witnessed the destruction of Baylor's tank, Lieutenant Rogers climbed out of his hatch to find Xavier waiting for him. Vehemently, he snatched the officer out of the tank and held him up by his neck, growling as his eyes began to burn the Lieutenant's retinas.

"If anything happens to them, it will be my pleasure to rip you apart…"

Xavier dropped Rogers back into the hatch of the tank, and then disappeared after his nemesis.

EVENING

The sun tried to peek its setting rays through the trees as Xavier ran through the brush. The wood scraped his skin as he blew past the heavy trunks, hearing the echo of Toby's blood through the whispering winds. He knew he was out here. He had followed that echo, that low, moaning wail, for almost a hundred miles, tracking it as it left remnants parallel to Interstate 24. His urgency propelled him past the vehicles on the road and the wind gusts left in his wake removed leaves from branches. There was still a frenzy trapped in his blood, an urge to feel death on his hands, and whether it was Toby or the white people in the small towns he was passing, someone would suffer his wrath.

As the trees got thicker and the sky turned from light pastels to midnight blue, Xavier began to slow. The deep moaning of Toby's blood was growing louder now, and turned into wails with pitches that swelled higher as he moved forward. He was close, Xavier knew, and the rumble in his throat began to grow once again as his fist clenched and his body grew taut. He crept through the woods, crouched as his eyes continued to glow, and eventually stepped into a large clearing. The trees had been removed many years ago, and many tried to grow back as Xavier stalked around them, and found himself at a large, dark, cabin.

He could see the burning of Toby's eyes before his body stepped out of the door, but it was the screaming that came from the ground that caused his legs to give way. Xavier collapsed to his knees as Toby limped slightly down the stairs, glaring at him and speaking in a strained voice.

"Dis 'ere used t'be a cabin wid free slaves. Be da last stop for run'ways, fore dey reach ta freedom cross da state line. Dey says run'ways come, an' dey hides 'em under da floorboards or in da cellar, den throws vinegar overs da whole place, so's to mask dey smell from da dogs. Dey says once you made it 'ere, you'se free already. Jus' gotta cross da line."

Toby walked over to the downed Xavier and slammed his foot into his adversary's head. The blow reverberated across the night sky as Xavier went down hard. Despite his ringing ears, he tried to get back up, but the screams from the dirt weakened his muscles, and he collapsed back down.

"Den one day, da massas from da bighouse up da road finds out dey freein' run'ways 'ere, an' he get white folks from two plantations, an' comes on down 'ere t'get 'em. 'Cept dese free folks 'ere, dey done made a pact. Dey ain't goin' back to bein' no slaves no mo', and dey ain't lettin' nobody else goes back neither! Dey kills off three white folks 'fore dey gets kilt dey selves…"

Xavier had forced his way up to his hands and knees, and Toby ran over and lifted him into the air. Yelling out, he yanked

Xavier's body down and slammed him back into the ground, cracking the hard earth underneath him.

"White folks, dey gotta teach a lesson to da slaves, an' da run'ways never knowd da free slaves be kilt, so massas get some a' da house slaves ta comes out 'ere and keeps light in da window, an' p'tend dat dey's free. An when da run'ways come, dey sends word straight up da bighouse, an' da overseers comes down wid da field slaves, and makes da field slaves watch, an' beats da run'ways dead, right wheres you lay. An' makes da field slaves bury 'em. Dey says dis 'ere ground ain't made a' nothin' but slaves dat thought dey was free."

Xavier fought to stand up, but fell repeatedly, feeling both the agony of his attack and the torture from the ground, and he shed blood of his own. Grunting and gritting his teeth, he finally made it up to his knees, and with one last cry, pushed himself up to his feet to face Toby directly.

"I kills you dead fo' I lets you stop me."

"And I'll kill you...before I let...you go on."

Both men, injured and enraged, flew at each other once again, and exchanged blows like gladiators. Xavier fought to get the advantage, kicking, punching, and dodging, while Toby, smashing, clawing, and pounding, fought to kill. The forest shook in the darkness, and the animals fled from the disharmony, as the two warriors collided again and again.

It was Xavier who threw Toby into the still cabin, demolishing it as his opponent crashed through the wood and tumbled out of the back.

Immediately, Xavier felt the forces from the ground pulling on him, tugging at his body as they screamed in his ears. He stumbled back as Toby came forward through the wooden debris.

"Dey ain't lettin' you win dis, Xavier! Dey can't!"

Toby leapt forward and grabbed Xavier by the neck, throwing him down to the ground. Kneeling behind him, the slave hooked his arm around Xavier's neck, choking him. Xavier arms flailed about as he began to feel the lack of air in his lungs. Then, by instinct, he shot his arms up and grabbed at Toby. Once he had a solid hold, he flipped Toby over his shoulder, and maneuvered around to get a tight hold on Toby's head. Once he had hit, he jerked his waist, torso, and arms together, and broke Toby's neck.

Toby's arms went limp as Xavier kept the hold on his skull, and without warning the forces from the ground attacked so severely that Xavier fell back down with Toby's head still in his grasp. He looked down in disbelief as Toby's arms raised back up, and his head jerked back straight again.

"Dey can't let you win, Xavier! Dis power come from dem! Spirits be in our blood!"

Crying out in agony, it was all Xavier could do to keep a hold on Toby's head. He lay writhing on his back as the slave fought insanely to get free. Screaming, Xavier scanned the ground through his blurred vision, and his eyes rested on something that had been spewed up from the ground during their battle. He couldn't tell what it is, but the metal reflected his burning in his eyes as he let go of Toby's head with one of his hands and reached for it.

The rusty shackle had been buried there for centuries, a remnant of a time long gone. It lay open, its dirt-caked edge still sharp where it was supposed to lock into the other side.

Frantic and desperate, Xavier snatched up the sharp piece of metal, and screaming like a madman, plunged it into Toby's neck.

The blood flowed slowly at first, hesitant to come out. Then all at once it gushed forward, drenching the ground around them as Toby rolled out of Xavier's grasp. He didn't make a sound as the blood left his body, and the ground cried out in mourning as

Toby rested on his hands and knees for as long as he could, and stared at Xavier as his eyes began to fade and flicker.

With his mind racing, Xavier struggled to remember the words Diop instructed him to say, and when they come to him he shouted them into the night sky.

"DA MAY YÉWI DJAAM YI!"

And his eyes flickered and faded as well.

At the final moment, with the blackness gone, Nathan Freeman stared into Xavier's eyes, and then fell down dead.

It was midnight when Xavier got back to the city. The seventh day was over.

The helicopter hovering above the destroyed cabin found a severely beaten Xavier Turner lying on the ground. He was taken to the nearest medical facility, where he remained in critical condition for the next seventy-two hours. The dead body beside him was identified as that of Nathan Freeman.

The official report stated that the city had fallen victim to a biological attack. A weaponized strain of the rabies virus, genetically altered by Middle Eastern scientists to affect African-Americans, was dispersed in the water system by a known terrorist cell. Nathan Freeman was the first to be exposed, and the virus had spread rapidly, until the CDC was able to develop a cure and distribute the airborne antivirus during the attack on the Marine troops at the 21st and Grove apartment complex. Statements from expert medical personnel ensured that the anti-virus had been a hundred percent effective, and that the weaponized virus was destroyed in a secure government facility. The threat to the public was officially over.

The unofficial report, which would remain top secret and eyes-only, contained statements from Diop, Chance, Commander Nash, and a recently released Xavier Turner. The Department of Defense developed a task force that would track all known individuals that were affected by the phenomenon, and develop a contingency plan for reoccurrence.

The Governor and Police Chief embarked on an extensive public relations campaign, advocating a return to normalcy. The only enemies, they repeated, were the terrorists who had planted this virus among the citizens. The President of the United States echoed their sentiments, and ensured the national public that those responsible would indeed be brought to justice.

Chance and Commander Nash returned to work, with strict orders to stick to the official story if questioned by the press or anyone else. They oversaw a memorial built to the officers that died in the Zone 3 precinct attack, and keep a steady hesitation whenever they had to arrest a black man, looking deeply into their eyes before daring to reach for any handcuffs.

Hattie Mae Jenkins passed away peacefully in her sleep, two days after her apartment building had been destroyed. Her grandson, Jamal, who had been exonerated for the crime of rape due to public admission by Don Rousch, was by her side during her final moments. Trayvon Adams served beside her grandson as one of her pallbearers, and Lawanda Perry brought heartfelt remarks at her funeral.

Brandon Lincoln was forced to resign from his position at the corporate law firm due to pressure from the partners. He received a hefty severance, and eventually moved into another city, where he would get his teacher's license and become Pecola Brown's sixth grade science instructor. They nodded at each other in recognition on his first day, and once a month she went to him during lunch for unneeded tutoring, and they tried to piece together what had happened to them. The DOD recorded these conversations from a bug in Brandon's briefcase, and they were reviewed by the directors personally.

Sonya Freeman's sanity returned to her as her voice healed, and the news of her husband's death struck her deeply. She was told that Nathan's body could not be made available for an open casket. It had been autopsied extensively, and tests were still being done. She held what was supposed to be a small, quiet memorial service, consisting of only a few people, and was shocked when she arrived to find all the former residents of the 21st and Grove apartment building already there, waiting to pay respects to the man who'd saved their lives.

"You really did have a beautiful family."

As Diop helped Xavier up the stairs and into his bedroom, he noted the pictures hanging on the walls in the hallway.

"I am truly sorry."

"Thank you, Diop."

Still tense with pain, Xavier leaned on his teacher until he reached his bedside, and collapsed on the toys, teddy bears, and trinkets that he had put there days ago. Diop grabbed the nearby gun, looked strangely at Xavier, and then handed it back to him.

"Is this yours?"

"Yeah."

Xavier ran his hand over the shiny metal once again.

"Sadness may sometimes feel like death, but it is possible to mourn without dying, Xavier."

Xavier looked at Diop, nodding his head in agreement, and then grimaced as he reached over and placed the gun in the drawer beside his bed.

"Sadness isn't the only thing I feel, Diop."

"What else do you feel?"

"Anger."

Diop stopped short as he looked at Xavier's eyes, and breathed a sigh of relief when his black and white iris and pupil looked back at him.

"I mean, the *doole* is gone, I know it. When I felt it, it was like I was trying to control myself every second. Every inch of me wanted to kill."

"And now?"

"Now…it's like there's something in my chest. Something that won't leave."

Diop walked over to the other side of the room, pulling up the blinds and letting the fresh morning sunlight in.

"No one has ever had the *doole* before and lived, so it is part of you now. There is a difference between control and contentment. You have control, but you will only be truly content when you are shedding blood."

"Will it come back for me?"

Diop walked back over to the side of the bed. "No. It will not come back for you. It has come for you already, and you were too strong. It will not come again."

"So it's over, right? This whole thing is over?"

Diop looked at his student with uncertainty. "Spirits do not die, Xavier."

"But I set them free! I said the words you told me to say! I set them free!"

"But you did not give them rest. This is what I had to learn as well about the *doole*. Revenge will be their only peace. They will not rest until their vengeance is served."

"So what now?"

"I do not know. It's been centuries since the last time the *doole* struck this world; maybe it will be centuries until it returns. Or maybe it will not be able to return, and the spirits will not rest for an eternity."

"Why wouldn't it be able to return?"

The African began pacing around the room. "I have thought about this. Nathan Freeman received the *doole*, but it came in the form of Toby. Nathan had not been a slave, so he could not connect with the slaves."

"I don't understand. I thought it came as Toby because Nathan couldn't control it?"

"But you could control it, right? You could control it, and you have never been a slave! They fought against you, because you did not know their pain. You would not let their fury loose. That is why they will not come for you again."

"Diop, you're losing me…"

"There are no more slaves, Xavier. How will the *doole* become flesh, if no flesh knows its pain? How will it return if there is no one left who knows the rage of the slaves?"

"I don't know…"

"It cannot return as Toby, it will not return as Nathan, and it will not return as you. Neither of you has ever been a slave. So it has no other vessels."

"So then it's over, right?"

The uncertain look crosses Diop's face again as he made his way toward the door. "I do not know. But you need to rest. I will return again if you need me."

"If I need you? Diop…wait!"

The African trotted down the steps and out of the front door, and the manicured lawns and trimmed rose bushes offered their salutations to him as he disappeared up the street.

"Damn, X…"

Moses Jenkins sat stunned as he looked back and forth from Xavier to Dr. James Bailey.

"That was a hell of a story…you can't really expect me to believe it, though, right?"

A slight smile tried to cross Moses' face, but Xavier's was deadly serious, and his smugness disappeared.

"I'm telling you the truth."

"X, come on, man. The dude got black light bulb eyes and started murkin' white people? Are you serious?"

"Why would I lie, Moses?"

"I don't know, but I swear you just gave me the plot to a Play-Station 3 game."

Slowly, Xavier turned to James.

"Nathan didn't send you his blood. Diop and I did. I remembered him talking about you when we were in Telemut, doing research. He said you were a promising medical student. I thought maybe you could help, but so much was going on, I forgot we'd sent it."

"Well, I've been studying it ever since. Black rabies, my ass! I knew there was something else going on!"

"Hold up! Hold up!"

Moses jumped up from his seat.

"Even if I did believe this craziness, which I don't, what the hell does it have to do with me?"

Xavier stood up to look Moses in the eye.

"When I was in the apartment with Toby, there was a point where I could see his life...before he died. I could see his wife, and his daughters, and I could see where they were. Moses...they were on the Talbert plantation. That's where Toby was a slave. The lady in the picture at your grandmother's house, beside Aunt Sarah, that's Elizabeth. That was Toby's mother."

Moses' mouth parted slightly as he shook his head.

"I don't get it, X."

"He had to take you back, Moses. He had to...because there are no more slaves. There was no one else who would understand...who could connect with his rage. So he took you back, to go through what he had to go through. So that you wouldn't fight him when he came."

"You said Toby was dead. You killed him yourself."

"Spirits never die. Diop tried to tell me that. I understand now."

"So what are you tryin' to say, man?"

Xavier looked away from Moses with regret painted on his face.

"I'm sorry."

"For what?"

Xavier spun around and kicked Moses in the stomach, sending him flying across the room. James jumped out of his seat as he watched the rapper crash into the table on the other side of the room.

"X, what the hell, man!"

Before Moses could recover, Xavier charged at him again, kicking him viciously while he was on the ground.

"Moses! X, what the hell is going on?"

SaTia, rushing downstairs after hearing the commotion, burst into the room to find her husband being crushed under Xavier's foot. James stared horrified as she jumped onto Xavier's back, beating him.

"Get off of him! Get off!"

Xavier grabbed SaTia from off his back and tossed her lightly across the room. She cried out as she hit the floor and tumbled against the chairs.

Xavier turned back around to find Moses on his feet. His eyes were clouding into a dark gray, and he released a low growl as he swung at Xavier, knocking him to the ground. Xavier popped up quickly, recovering from the blow, and Moses grabbed his shoulders and forced him back against the wall, breaking the window behind him and lifting him off of the ground by his neck. He stood there, scowling, as his eyes grew darker, and his veins began to emerge.

Suddenly, Xavier escaped from Moses' grasp. He dropped to the floor and spun around his back, grabbing and choking him from behind.

He looked straight at James as he cut off Moses' breathing. "Tell me when his eyes clear!"

Moses' arms flailed about as SaTia pushed herself up from the floor, and James shook his head vigorously.

"I don't want anything…!"

"TELL ME WHEN HIS EYES CLEAR!"

Focusing through his fright, James looked at Moses' eyes and watched them go from midnight blue to gray, and then back to white.

"Xavier, they're clear! They're clear!"

Xavier let Moses go, and the two men collapsed to the ground, out of breath. SaTia rushed over to Xavier and began beating him with her fists. He did nothing to retaliate.

"You sonofa…!"

"SaTia, stop! Stop!"

Moses pushed himself up from the floor and grabbed SaTia, bringing him back down to the floor with him.

"I'm sorry, Moses. I had to be sure."

SaTia began to shout out again, but Moses calmed her down before he turned back to his bodyguard.

"I felt it. I felt it coming. What the hell is it?"

Xavier pushed himself up so that his back sat against the wall, and caught his breath before he spoke. "You are of the bloodline. I knew with you, just like Diop knew with me."

"What does it mean?"

"It means you've been chosen by the *doole*. It means you will receive *The Seven Days*."

Moses lay on the floor, holding his wife, and looking bewildered at Xavier. James collapsed down to the floor as well, his legs weakened from the intensity of the moment, and the four of them breathed heavily as the cool afternoon air brought a chill to their skin.

About the Author

R. Kayeen Thomas is one of Washington, D.C.'s hottest writers. He is the author of *The Seven Days* as well as the NAACP Image Award-nominated *Antebellum*. Having lived in the nation's capital since the age of three, he self-published his first book, *Light: Stories of Urban Resurrection*, during his junior year at Carleton College in Northfield, MN. Upon coming home to D.C. to market his first work, Thomas sold 1,000 copies of his book in the Washington metropolitan area before returning to college to finish his undergraduate studies. Now, at age 27, he is an author, poet, playwright, hip-hop artist, journalist, and social justice advocate. He resides in Southeast, D.C. with his wife and daughter.

IF YOU ENJOYED "THE SEVEN DAYS,"
BE SURE TO CHECK OUT MOSES'S TRIALS IN

ANTEBELLUM

BY R. KAYEEN THOMAS
AVAILABLE FROM STREBOR BOOKS

7

It felt as if someone had stuck an adrenaline needle in my heart. My head jerked up so fast from being facedown in the dirt that it threw me onto my back. I scrambled around, using my hands and feet to propel me, for about ten seconds before I realized I didn't know who I was running from. There was no one around me. In fact, there didn't seem to be anyone in the area at all. Just a big open field with golden grass and no shade.

I patted my chest lightly, expecting to be able to feel shredded clothes and flesh, but there was nothing there. No gunshot wounds. No blood. Nothing. I didn't have a scratch on me. It was as if I had dreamed it all.

"What the hell is goin' on?" I stood up as I spoke aloud.

The field stretched as far as I could see. There was nothing else around but grass and a scorching hot sun.

"SaTia? Ray? Brian? Henry? Where y'all at?"

I spoke but no one responded.

I began walking in an unknown direction. The sun was beating down against my body. When it gets this hot, your grill starts to give you cottonmouth. I could feel sweat gathering in my Air Force Ones and dripping down my face underneath my shades. I tried to wipe it away from my eyes and scratched my cheek with my pinky ring. My confusion took the sting away.

How had I gotten here? The last thing I remembered was lying half-dead on a hospital bed. People don't get shot and then wake up in the middle of nowhere with the sun cooking their hair grease. I stopped and looked around again. Scanning all around me, again, all I could see were fields.

"Well, it's too hot to be heaven..." I said aloud. "And too peaceful to be hell. And I'm not Catholic, so this can't be purgatory. Where am I?"

I continued to walk through the field. After a while, I quit trying to wipe the sweat away from my face and dealt with the sting of it in my eyes. My white tee was completely soaked and I had puddles in my Nikes. It got harder to put one foot in front of the other, and my path through the field began to zig-zag like a piece of artwork done by a two-year-old.

Maybe this is hell... I began to think as I staggered from left to right. Before I could finish the thought, I was back on the ground again.

"SATIA!" I screamed out as I rolled around on the ground. "BRIAN, HENRY, RAY...WHAT'S GOING ON?"

I began reaching out for something—clawing at the ground as if it would somehow provide me with an answer to my question. When I stopped, I considered lying there and letting whatever was going to happen to me play itself out. Then I remembered... I'm Da Nigga. I don't lay down for nothing.

The thought itself wasn't strong enough to get me back up to my feet, so I began repeating it aloud.

"I'm...Da...Nigga," I coughed out as I got up to my knees. "I don't...lie down...for nothing."

As I swayed back and forth on my feet, I forced myself to begin thinking rationally.

I'll probably pass out in a few minutes, I thought. *I might as well get as far as I can get before I go down for good.*

I could barely lift my head, but I took a step, and then another, and then one more. By the time I got to nine or ten, I lifted my head, expecting to still see an eternity of fields. Instead I saw a road. It looked like one of the back country roads that people have on their farms—as if someone had cleared all the grass and plants out of the way, but forgot to put down any pavement. I didn't care, though. A road meant that someone would be coming by sooner or later. They'd recognize me and get me back to some type of civilization.

By the time I reached the road, I could vaguely see something approaching in the distance. My vision was blurred from all the sweat that had found its way into my eyes, so I wasn't surprised when the figure began to look more like a horse than a car.

"I'm trippin'," I said aloud as I began to wave down the car.

"Yo, yo, I need some help! Yo, stop the car, man! I need some help! I don't even know where the hell I am, dogg! You gotta help me!"

There was something wrong with the car's engine. As it pulled up, it sounded like some type of animal. Even with blurred vision, I could tell I had never seen any car like this before. And it stunk.

"Yo, what's wrong with your....never mind, man. You got any water?"

I took off my shades and wiped my eyes with the back of my

hands. Before I put the shades back on, I looked up. There were two horses in front of me, with two white guys on them that looked as if they were straight out of an old Western movie.

"Wow," I said, looking at the men, then at the horses, then back at them.

Before I could say another word, the first guy hit me in the mouth with a rifle butt. I fell to the ground, stunned.

"Where you come from, nigger?" The shorter of the two men jumped off of his horse and walked up to me. The taller one, the one who'd hit me with the gun, did the same.

My mind was going eighty miles per hour. So these country rednecks obviously knew me, or at least knew my stage name. Maybe they were hired by the P. Silenzas. Maybe they were the ones who'd somehow gotten me out of the hospital and over here to No Man's Land. Whatever the case, they had guns and I didn't. This wasn't the time to be acting gangsta.

"Aight, look, fellas," I said as I started to get back up. It took longer than usual, considering how weak I already was. By the time I got back to my feet, the right side of my mouth was dripping blood onto the dirt. "There's obviously been some kinda misunderstandin'. Ain't no need for the guns, though. Look, whatever the Silenzas is payin' y'all, I'll double it. You know I got more money than them niggas. Just take me to the nearest bank, let me pay y'all off, and we'll pretend like none of this ever happened, aight?"

I looked both of them in the eye, waiting for a response. What I got was another gun butt to my mouth. I felt a tooth come loose when I hit the ground.

"Yo, what's your problem, man? What's wrong with you?"

The shorter one slowly walked up to me, observed me for about three seconds, and then kicked me in the side of my head.

I couldn't have gotten back up if I'd tried. I could barely open my eyes. Pain radiated through my skull as I began to drift in and out of consciousness.

"Looks like we got ourselves an uppity nigger here, Mr. Talbert." The tall one who'd hit me with the gun spit as he spoke.

My vision was going from different shades of purple to pitch black. I listened as well as I could in between consciousness.

"Yes, we do. But he's strange, though. Look at all this stuff he's got on, Bradley. Looks like something out of a child's nightmare." He stopped and used his foot to turn me over, and I plopped onto my back like a ragdoll. Eventually, he shrugged his shoulders.

"Oh, well, a nigger's a nigger. Bradley, string him up on the horse and bring him back with us. I don't know where he came from, but he obviously hasn't been properly broken."

"Lemme have the honor, Mr. Talbert. I'll have him kissin' my toes by the time I'm done with 'im."

Mr. Talbert shook his head slightly.

"This fella right here is foreign, Bradley. You don't want bucks like this stirring up the rest. Might be best to hang him soon as we get back—set an example for the others. I'll decide by the time we arrive home."

Bradley nodded, bent down and picked me up like a sack of flour. I was still going in and out of consciousness as he tied me to the back of the horse. When he began riding, my body flopped around uncontrollably. It had suffered all it could take. I blacked out while looking at the behind of a horse.